Shadow Copy

Exit Darkness. (The Shadow Copy Series Book 1)

Michele Leathers
Ryan Leathers

EMAR Publishing

CHAPTER 1

Becca

The cold hard slab beneath me drained whatever precious warmth remained in my body. Fingers and toes began to sting. My hips and back ached. Operating tables, it seems, are made for utility, not for comfort. I had been lying there for an eternity, often left alone with my thoughts, unable to ignore the perilous reality of my circumstances. Pick one thing and focus on it, I told myself. But I didn't choose well, and instead only tormented my fears. Survival rates are a terrible thing to fixate on unless they are overwhelmingly favorable. My odds were only mildly favorable . . . far less than overwhelming.

What was I thinking? A bunch of statistics could never offer any meaningful comfort. There was a very real possibility that my name would soon be added to the list of recipients who didn't pull through. I tried to be brave. I wanted to live more than anything, but now that the moment of truth had arrived, I was more afraid than I had ever been.

A thick jungle of medical monitors and wires closed in and enveloped me. Gowned workers were maneuvering around the room, slipping in and out, adjusting various instruments. One of these was a small device attached to the back of my neck just below my hairline. A bundle of wires connected it to a large computer with multiple screens. I watched as the IV that had been inserted into my arm dripped over and over again from the bag to the tiny tube. Each drop was like a speck of sand falling from one side of an hourglass to the other. My time in this body was quickly running out.

I wished Dad could have stayed by my side the entire time to comfort me, but he was frequently called away by the other doctors and staff. He was the head of the medical program. I never realized just how important and demanding his position was until I saw him from that operating table.

I watched one of the male nurses wheel an empty bed into the room. He stuck his foot out and clicked the brakes into place, then reached across the bed, smoothing the wrinkles out of the sheet that draped over it. That was the spot where they would place my new body.

Patients weren't permitted to see their donor body in advance. Dad said that he couldn't bend the rules for me. I argued that if it were to become my body, then in a way it already belonged to me. I should at least be allowed a peek. He was unmoved by my logic.

A million questions swirled in my mind: Was the body skinny, fat or somewhere in between? Was it short or tall? Was the hair curly or straight? What about ethnicity? Was it different from my own? Of course, none of these questions would matter at all if my procedure were unsuccessful, but hope began to penetrate my fears as I gave myself permission to imagine life after cancer. The answers to my questions were as eagerly anticipated as a thousand Christmas mornings.

I motioned Dad over and pleaded my case with him again, practically begging him to let me see my donor body. He squeezed my hand and kissed me on the forehead. His thick, gray-speckled eyebrows tilted downward on the outer edges. I could see both resolve and sadness in his eyes. I decided that if he could have done this for me, he would have.

Curiosity had been a useful distraction from my earlier apprehensions. With the matter settled, my emotions swung like a pendulum and I once again felt their full weight. It didn't matter what the donor body looked like. I had no claim on it yet. I had to actually survive the procedure first. I shouldn't have let myself jump so far ahead. Fear and doubt poured into my little lifeboat of hope, threatening to sink it.

A nurse who had been hovering nearby approached. The squeak of her thick-soled shoes announced her arrival. "Becca, dear, how are you doing?" she asked.

I turned my head slightly to face her, but could only see her dark eyes peeking from between her mask and white cap. She was smiling, judging by the way her eyes were squinted. Her ID badge read Olivia. I had never met her before.

I looked up at her, desperate for reassurance . . . even from a stranger. "I told myself I was going to be brave . . . but it's hard." I wanted to say more, but I couldn't. I had to pause to regain my composure and fight back the tears that were welling up in the corners of my eyes.

She took my hand and held it, her warm skin penetrating through to my cold fingers. "It's going to be okay, Becca. I know this is scary, but everyone here is going to take very good care of you. Your father hand-picked the entire team for your procedure this evening. You're getting the very best. We have all done this many times before."

Something in her tone assured me that her confidence was genuine. She honestly believed that the procedure would be a success. But how could she be so sure? Didn't she know how serious this was? Of course she knew. She had to know. The fact was, there was no way to know if my procedure would work. Even if everything went perfectly, a portion of it would come down to chance. No one could know if the odds would be in my favor tonight.

I shifted my position trying to adjust my head on the pillow, without disconnecting the device on the back of my neck. As I moved, I inadvertently let out a sigh, that teetered dangerously close to the sound of a whimper.

"Is that thing bothering you?"

"It's just a little uncomfortable." Uncomfortable was a good way to describe it. It didn't exactly hurt, but it was a constant irritant, like trying to sleep with your hair in curlers or being poked all day by a rebellious tag in your shirt collar.

The wired device was called a Direct Neural Interface, DNI. Supposedly this little box could read minds. To Dad, it was a triumph of technology, but it seemed spooky to me that private thoughts and memories could be plucked out of my head and stored in a computer.

No matter how amazing the technology may have been, I knew that not everyone survived the procedure. Dad said that the risk was small, and at this point it was my best option. We both knew the truth. My time was up. This was the only option left.

"I'm not ready to die," I told Olivia. "I haven't even lived yet. I have a journal full of lists and dreams and promises to myself." There were so many things I hadn't done yet, so many firsts I hadn't experienced. "What if I don't ever get a chance to do any of those things?"

I felt like I was pleading for Olivia to do her best -- for her and the rest of the team to do everything possible to save me if things went wrong. I wanted her to know that I intended to live a life worthy of every effort and every sacrifice made on my behalf.

She patted my hand. I could tell she was smiling again, behind her mask. "Becca sweetheart, don't worry. You will be able to live your life and do everything you always wanted to do. You can keep dreaming all of those dreams."

She was telling me exactly what I wanted to hear, but I still couldn't let myself believe her. I was too afraid.

I tried to lift my head again without disturbing the DNI. As best I could, I took one last look at my body, then rested back down on the soft pillow. I closed my eyes, but even with them closed the lights above me had become too bright, causing me to turn my head to the side.

I realized that I was surrounded by white -- white lab coats, white computers and white walls. It was like I was already heading to that bright light people talk about when they have near death experiences. Maybe it was a sign of what was yet to come. Maybe I should just accept my fate -- that my time was up, and no one can cheat death. That bright light might soon be my path to whatever lies beyond this life.

I wasn't sure if I believed in life after death, but I was certain that death would come for me very soon, one way or another. Dad told me that I would technically die during the procedure, but that I shouldn't worry. I wouldn't feel any pain, and within moments, the transfer would be complete.

I guess he was right. I didn't see any bright lights when I died. I didn't see or feel anything.

CHAPTER 2

Darla

I didn't know Becca. I had never even seen her before the day of her procedure, but the two of us might easily have been mistaken as sisters. We were about the same height and build, with the same color hair and strikingly similar features. They say everyone has a twin. We weren't identical, but we looked amazingly similar for complete strangers.

Upon entering the procedure room that day, Becca's father, Dr. Tanner, took note of me. The light in his eyes and the smile on his face signaled immediate approval. "This must be Dana," he said.

Nurse Olivia corrected him, "Meet Darla. Darla Monroe."

He nodded, still smiling, then turned his attention to his daughter.

This was my first time in the procedure room, and since I wasn't part of the trained medical team, I had no idea exactly what was about to happen, so I made sure to pay close attention.

From what I observed, every step of Becca's procedure had been meticulously planned. The medical team followed a carefully laid out schedule with the utmost precision. As her procedure progressed, the team continued to maintain its calm focus. Even Dr. Tanner seemed at ease, which surprised me. I expected him to be a nervous wreck. After all, it was his daughter's life at stake. I decided he was trying to be brave . . . for Becca's sake.

I don't recall exactly when I realized that things were heading off course. It might have been when one of the team members knocked over a tray of medical equipment. The sound of the instruments clanging against the tile floor struck a chord with everyone in the room. Something clearly wasn't right. I heard one of the team members say, "I'm not getting a reading." Dr. Tanner looked over her shoulder, then bounced from one monitor to another, rattling instructions to his team. After several minutes he stood up and placed both hands on the top of his head in frustration. "Stop . . . everyone just stop. The body is no longer viable."

Just then, one of the monitors connected to Becca went from a rhythmic blip to a long steady tone. The screen changed from sharp spikes to a perfectly flat line. "We're losing her," someone shouted. Instantly, the entire medical team jumped to a new level of intensity -- voices chattered, movements quickened. Panic was building in Dr. Tanner's eyes.

The medical team tried to shock Becca's heart back to life . . . once . . . twice. . . . After the third unsuccessful attempt, Dr. Tanner turned and bolted out of the room. He slammed his hands against the doors so hard, they ricocheted off the walls, sending an echo through the air as loud as thunder.

Nurse Olivia was quickly losing her resolve. "Where is he going? We need him!" she said, her voice rising, almost to the level of a scream. The rest of the team kept working, as the sound of Becca's heart rate monitor remained flatlined, a constant ringing in my ears.

Even with Becca's father out of the room, they weren't giving up. Another doctor continued to administer shocks to Becca's heart. I wondered how much longer they would keep going. She had no pulse. She wasn't breathing. Minutes passed. There was still no sign of life. When would they finally accept that she was gone?

The double doors burst open, followed by the rattling of gurney wheels. Dr. Tanner raced back into the room pushing a new donor body in front of him. "Get over here!" he yelled to his team. "Let's try it again." He quickly positioned the gurney, flung the sheet off the new body, and everyone immediately went to work.

Dr. Brimley, a short white-haired man, plowed through the double doors moments later. "You can't use that one!" he demanded, veins bulging on his forehead. "Frank!" He ran over to Dr. Tanner. "Frank, I won't let you do this! You simply can't."

Dr. Tanner wheeled around. With sweat pouring down the sides of his red face, he reached out and grabbed Dr. Brimley by the collar. "Don't tell me . . . " Dr. Tanner's voice boomed. The entire team stopped and looked at the two men. Dr. Tanner collected himself and with cool firmness said what everyone in the room already knew. "This is my daughter. I'm going to save her!"

Dr. Brimley stood there, speechless, but Dr. Tanner didn't waste another second. He immediately started preparing the new body for a second attempt.

Everyone watched the procedure unfold before their eyes. Through all of the noise and commotion, it's a miracle that I managed to catch what Dr. Brimley mumbled to his colleague. "This is a huge mistake." He balled up his fist and coughed into it, leaving his hand in front of his mouth to cover what he was about to say. "If Becca survives this, they'll kill her for sure."

CHAPTER 3

Becca

The last thing I remembered seeing was my dad's face, and that was the first thing I saw again when I awoke. He was standing at the foot of my bed, shoulders hunched forward, stethoscope dangling from his pocket. He smiled at me, then turned to Dr. Brimley who was holding out a clipboard exploding with papers. "Not Now," he said, in a commanding but hushed tone, never taking his eyes off of me. Dr. Brimley retracted the clipboard and stepped back without argument.

I moved my legs, then pushed myself up to a seated position. The look on Dad's face, when he saw me sit up, could only be described as sheer joy. He bent down and held me in his arms, kissing my head. When he finally pulled away, I started to reach up to wipe the tears rolling down his face, but he beat me to it.

"Is everything alright?" I asked.

Dad finished wiping his eyes, then smiled. "Yes. Everything's perfect."

Before I could utter another word, nurse Olivia appeared with a small handheld mirror. "Say hello to the new Becca Tanner." She set the mirror face down on my lap.

Really? Did the procedure actually work? Hold on. I sat up straighter, eyeing the mirror. Before the procedure, I hadn't really known what to expect, but I guess I had imagined that being in a new body would feel very different. It was weird to me that I didn't notice anything strange at all. I mean, even a new pair of jeans takes a little getting used to, right?

Everyone in the room was staring at me. I noticed that

Dad and Olivia had great big smiles on their faces, but Dr. Brimley did not. He was just . . . well, he was just staring. Why didn't he look happy?

Nurse Olivia clasped her hands together and inhaled deeply. "I can't wait till you see yourself."

Dad's glasses slipped down low on his nose. He looked at me over the top of the frame. "You don't need to be nervous honey."

I picked up the mirror with a trembling hand. I couldn't be sure if the shaking was due to apprehension or excitement. It was probably both. I stared at the mirror in my hand, trying to steady it. That was when I first noticed something unexpected. My fingers looked thin, yet strong, and my skin had a golden brown suntan. Suddenly and powerfully, like a tornado, my excitement got sucked away and disappeared, leaving me with only apprehension. For the first time, I sensed deep down in my core, the full and unedited version of my new reality. I was still alive, but a major part of me was gone. I was no longer the same person. I was different, and I was afraid to face the stranger staring back at me in the mirror.

"Go ahead," Olivia urged.

Before my procedure, I had spent innumerable hours wondering about the new body I would be given. None of that had prepared me for this moment. I had no idea just how scary it would be to look in the mirror. Comparing the experience to Christmas morning had been way off the mark. Now that the moment had arrived, it felt more like Halloween. I was about to see myself wearing a mask -- one that covered my entire body, only I could never take it off.

"Honey," Dad stroked my face. "It's okay."

My hands shook visibly as I slowly lifted the mirror. The girl in the mirror came into view. "Oh my gosh!" I gasped. I reached up and touched my face, washing my fingers in uncontrollable tears. Finally I composed myself enough to speak. "Oh Dad," I cried. "I look beautiful."

Dad held me tight, and whispered in a broken voice, "You

have always been beautiful Becca, both inside and out."

SIX MONTHS LATER

So many things had changed since my procedure, but some things seemed frozen in time. I had been coming back to see Dr. Brimley each month for mandatory check-ups. I knew it was a required part of the program, but I couldn't wait to finish my final check-up and be free of hospitals for the rest of my life.

I hoped this would be my final appointment today. I couldn't imagine that he would have anything bad to say about my health, because I felt absolutely amazing.

I picked up my black eyeliner, leaned in close to the mirror and carefully traced a line along the edge of my eyelids which, at six forty-five in the morning, still didn't seem to want to fully open up and be awake.

Mom stepped into the bathroom doorway. A few strands of gray set off her blonde hair that rested above her shoulders. "Becca, your father won't be able to make it to your appointment today. He left for work in the middle of the night to prepare for an unscheduled procedure."

"Again? How many nights has it been this week?"

"You know how these things work," she sighed. "He has to go when the donors become available."

I shook my head. "Well, I never want a career where I have to be on call. I like my sleep way too much for that."

Mom reached out and tucked a loose strand of hair behind my ear, giving me a smile. Half a lifetime of raising children had produced creases around her mouth, which only appeared when her thin, pink lips turned up in the corners. I could also detect dark circles under her eyes. They weren't always visible, but this morning they were too much for her makeup to conceal. She usually doesn't sleep well when Dad is away.

"This will be the first time your dad has missed one of your appointments."

"It's okay. He doesn't need to be there anyway. I feel completely fine." I shrugged, then leaned in close to the mirror to apply a second coat of mascara. "Seriously, it's been six months."

Mom hovered there, tall body leaning against the door frame, arms folded, as her speckled green eyes scrutinized me. "Your eyelashes are so long." Her words hung in the air as if waiting for an unspoken conclusion, followed by a faded smile. "You probably don't even need mascara anymore. I on the other hand can't get by without it." She slowly turned and started walking away. "You're a lucky girl."

I set the mascara down and stepped back, looking at the explosion all over the counter -- a wrinkled up tube of toothpaste with the cap off, nowhere to be found, a half-eaten granola bar left over from yesterday, a hair straightener with an impossibly tangled cord. . . . I stared at the clutter, but my thoughts were on Mom's not-so-subtle eyelashes remark.

There wasn't any happiness in her voice when she said that. She sounded as though she was still in mourning for the loss of what we used to share. Someone else might not have noticed, but I knew her comment was not a genuine compliment. What she was really thinking was how our eyelashes were one more thing to add to the list of what we no longer had in common. Before, people said, "You look just like your mother," or "You two could be sisters." Nobody says that anymore.

I thought this day could have been great, but Mom had managed to take the wind out of my sails before I even made it downstairs. I wondered if she would ever accept the new me. Would she ever move on?

I tossed the mascara in the drawer. Why couldn't she be grateful that I am still here and that I'm not sick anymore? I grabbed my brush and tossed it into the same drawer. It landed in a crash. Why can't she see that I'm the same person on the inside? I wrapped my arms around my stomach and looked down at the crumpled up towel on the floor.

I felt my eyes welling up and quickly grabbed a tissue to catch any tears before they could fall. Mascara was going to be all over my face if I didn't stop this. I took a deep breath and waved my hands in front of my eyes.

Then my cell phone jumped to life. It was Jeff calling. I hoped this would be a good distraction.

"Hello."

"Good morning Miss America!" His enthusiasm echoed loudly.

"It's early." I pulled the phone away from my face and cupped my hand over my ear.

"I just wanted to catch you before school started, because I know you said you wouldn't be here today."

I sighed. "Yep."

"Can you still make it to the library later?" he asked.

"Uh huh."

"Can you come at four, instead of five?"

"I guess."

"Becca. You okay? You sound like someone just drank the last diet Coke in the fridge," he chuckled.

"Yeah, you sound *really* concerned about me."

"No, I am, *really*. You should see the concern all over my face."

"Well, you should see me rolling my eyes."

"Awesome!"

I almost giggled, sort of.

"Did I just hear you laugh? Yeah! Now you sound like the real Becca, the happy one."

"How keen of you to know that there are actually two Becca's," I said sarcastically. But there was more truth to that statement that he would ever know.

"Well, I'm perceptive like that. It's an extrasensory kind of thing, like telepathy."

"Congratulations," I replied with another healthy dose of sarcasm. "Your parents must be so proud to have a mutant son like you."

"Ha! That's only one of my many powers."

"What about Nora? Can she meet us at four?"

"One moment as I consult my amazing telepathic powers . . . yes, I believe she is available."

"Well, you'd better double check on that. Because I think I remember her saying something about taking care of her icky guy fingers after school today."

"Guy fingers?"

"She's going to get her nails done."

Jeff broke out in laughter. "Nora needs an intervention. I don't think there's a square inch of her that isn't painted, bleached, baked or waxed."

"You better not ever let her hear you say that."

He chuckled. "No doubt."

Mom called from downstairs. "It's time to go."

"Okay," I yelled back. "Jeff . . ."

"I heard. You need to go."

"Yeah, I'll see you later."

I dropped my phone into my purse, then reached out and began swiping all of my makeup and things into the top drawer until it was overflowing. Just that quickly, the countertop went from disaster to merely disorderly.

I paused to take one last look in the mirror. My brown hair fell past my shoulders, twirling down my chest in loose ringlets. Highlights of gold spiraled down, catching the light in the bends of the curls. I licked my finger and rubbed off some mascara that had smudged under my eyes, then grabbed my purse.

As I walked down the hallway toward the stairs, I twisted the cap off of my lip gloss and applied a generous coat. Nora said that I have lips like a movie star. Jeff put it in a much less flattering way. He said my lips looked like they had been surgically enhanced. But there was no collagen in these babies, at least I didn't think there was anyway.

CHAPTER 4

Darla

Becca knew nothing of the complications that had occurred during her procedure. Her father had never mentioned anything to her. He didn't tell her mother either. All he told them was that everything turned out perfect, just like he had promised it would.

I didn't understand why he lied to them. It was possible that he just didn't want to cause unnecessary worry, but it seemed to me that there was still good reason to be worried.

Dr. Brimley had put up a major protest. He was adamant that Dr. Tanner let his daughter die rather than use that body. But why? What was so special about that particular body? Why did Dr. Brimley say that Becca would be killed if she survived the procedure? Who was going to kill her?

I was very worried. I wanted answers to these questions.

CHAPTER 5

Becca

Doctors and hospitals had become a routine part of my life. Taken on whole, the appointments since my procedure had been far less stressful than those before. Today was no exception. The exam seemed to go fine. It probably helped that I had become so familiar with the routine.

Dr. Brimley led me to the consultation room and pushed open the door. "Becca, we're almost done for today."

I faked a smile. Oh goodie.

"Go ahead and have a seat in here while I get your mother to join us." He turned and walked away energetically.

The office was darker than I expected it to be. A few thin cracks of light escaped from the partially closed window blinds. The only other source of illumination was a skinny floor lamp that sat in the far corner of the room. The lampshade was crooked and the lamp itself even seemed to be leaning slightly to one side. It looked small and weak compared to the large, bulky pieces of furniture spread throughout the room.

I made my way to one of the overstuffed brown leather chairs facing Dr. Brimley's enormous oak desk. Most dining room tables would be envious of its massive surface area. Surrounding it, black shelves crammed with books lined every wall. As I sat there, I twisted my head to read the titles printed on their spines. This mental inventory was interrupted when I suddenly noticed how the towering shelves looked ominously similar to the iron bars of a jail cell.

I could hear Dr. Brimley talking with Mom out in the

hallway. They were on a first name basis, in part due to the frequency of my appointments, and because he and Dad worked together. Dr. Brimley did the before and aftercare exams for people like me who were donor recipients.

"Come on in," I heard Dr. Brimley say.

I looked to the doorway and saw Mom. She was smiling and had a hopeful look on her face. She sat in the chair next to me and reached out placing her hand on mine.

"So how is she doing?" Mom asked.

Dr. Brimley sat on the corner of his big oak desk. We are about the same height, but looking up at him from this angle, his withering five foot, five inch frame appeared much larger than normal. Sometimes a simple change in perspective can reveal what has been hidden, all along, in plain sight. I began to sense something discomforting in his manner I had never noticed before. What was it?

"Oh, she is just fine, Janet," he said through a plastic smile, as he pulled the stethoscope off of his neck. "Her vitals are normal, the blood work is good. Everything looks just how it should. I couldn't be more pleased with Becca's progress." He looked at Mom, then at me, his gray eyes squinting so tight from smiling that I could barely tell they were open.

Somehow, this wasn't good enough for Mom. So there I silently sat, in between the two of them. An endless parade of inane questions on one side. On the other, a feigned pleasantness with each reply.

Dr. Brimley finally brought the inquisition to a conclusion by asserting,
"In my professional opinion, Becca's assimilation of this body is so complete that it has become medically undetectable. If I weren't her doctor, I wouldn't know she even had the procedure. Oh, and of course . . ." he paused and winked at me, which was quite a feat seeing that his eyes were already practically shut. "I bet you thought I forgot." He smiled even bigger, and I'm pretty sure his eyes fully closed as he announced, "There is no hint of cancer."

Mom turned to me, still holding my hand. She squeezed it tighter and gave me a big smile. "Becca, I'm so happy." She turned back to the doctor. "Thanks Rick. It's always a relief to hear that, no matter how many times you have said it." Her shoulder length hair flipped back and forth against her face, as she shook her head. "That never gets old."

Of course I didn't have cancer anymore. It wasn't like I brought it along with me in my pocket or something. My cancer was left behind in my old body. Why did he always have to announce to Mom that I was cancer free like that? It made no sense at all.

"Well let's see, it has been six months since the procedure, so six months cancer free," Dr. Brimley said as he got up to take a seat behind his desk. I rolled my eyes while his back was turned to me and somehow fought back the huge sigh building in my throat.

Behind his desk, Dr. Brimley transformed into the small-looking man I recognized again, his blond hair turning gray in the light coming off of his computer monitor. "Becca, I want you to come back in another three months. You're doing so well, I no longer need to see you on a monthly basis. I have no significant concerns about your health or your adaptation progress in your new body." He stopped staring at his computer screen and turned his attention to me. "Do you have any questions young lady?"

I did have a couple questions: If my new body was healthy, then why did I have to come back in three months? Was there something else going on that they weren't telling me? No words came out of my mouth, but I didn't have much of a poker face.

"What is it Becca?" Dr. Brimley asked.

"Is there something wrong sweetie?" Mom chimed in.

"Well, um, with all of these check ups, I was wondering . . . do some of the other procedure patients have trouble adapting to their new bodies?"

"Hmm. That's an insightful question, but I'm afraid I

can't discuss other patients' health with you. It's against the law," he said soberly.

"Yeah, I know. HIPAA, right?"

"That's right," he said with surprise.

"Every time my dad won't answer a question, he gives me some Federal regulation as the excuse. I know them all."

Dr. Brimley nodded.

"Anyway, I was just curious."

He stood up from his chair and smiled. "Now, I'll have the nurse get you all taken care of with any final paperwork, and I'll see you back in three months." He walked to the door and opened it for us.

If the other patients didn't have problems, then I wondered why he presented my health report in such an enthusiastic manner. Did he always get this happy when his patients had good test results? He almost seemed shocked that I had nothing wrong with me. Maybe I was reading too much into this, but I wondered if good results just didn't happen for everybody.

As we began the long drive back home to the town of Clayton, North Carolina, my curiosity took a turn toward paranoia. Something hadn't been right with Dr. Brimley. I had sensed it, but still couldn't explain it. I began filling in the missing pieces with conjecture based on disjointed details. What if recipients reject their donor body after a while, like a heart transplant patient rejecting their new heart? Or what if I didn't get a new body at all, and I'm not even alive? What if I just sort of exist inside a computer somehow, and all of this is some sort of big computer program? What if . . .

This was silly. What was I thinking? I needed to snap myself out of it, or I would wind up with my own cooky government healthcare conspiracy.

CHAPTER 6

Becca

I raised up onto my toes as I swung my arms out, twirling around and around. The soles of my black flats allowed me to glide effortlessly on the dark, hardwood floors of my room. As I twirled, my hot pink skirt filled with air and opened like the petals of a blooming tulip. I spun until I got dizzy. I caught my breath, regained my balance, laughed out loud, then did it again. I felt so alive.

I heard giggling behind me, so I stopped. My little sister had silently snuck in.

"Sierra, what are you doing in here?"

She had a half naked Barbie doll in her hand and a grin on her face. Her two permanent front teeth hadn't grown in at the same rate, so one was longer than the other.

"Are you dancing?" she giggled, putting her hand over her mouth.

"Yes . . ." I did a couple more twirls, then a curtsy, holding my skirt out with my hands.

She shook her head, her long ponytail flying. "Well where's the music?"

"It's in my head."

Sierra wrinkled her little nose. "You can't have music in your head."

"Of course I can. I do it all the time."

"How?"

"It's easy. I just think of a song and sing the words in my mind."

"Why don't you sing out loud?"

Her question seemed simple, but the answer was decidedly complex. More so than the rest of my family, Sierra had been immediately accepting and indifferent to my change in appearance after the procedure. Still, she was very curious. From time to time, she would ask questions, or with wheels turning in her head, make a statement for me to respond to. This felt to me like another clarifying moment for her.

"Believe me. You don't want to hear me sing," I said.

Sierra spun and posed her Barbie doll as if dancing. "Well I can still sing good."

"I know you can. I like it when I hear you sing. Do you want to sing something for me now?"

"No." Her eyes returned to her doll. "I liked it when we used to sing together."

For as long as I could remember, singing had been a big deal in our family. Dad was a pretty good self-taught tenor, and Mom was a classically trained soprano. Between the two of them, all of us kids had inherited the singing gene. Our family traditions, outings and even ordinary trips to the store had been filled with harmonies and laughter.

I missed that. I don't sing out loud anymore. It wasn't that I didn't want to, but through sad experience I had learned that in this body, I was doing the world a favor to sing silently. And the funny thing was that now more than ever, I had things to sing about.

Our house was quieter since my procedure. I noticed that Mom held back when I was around. They all did, but nobody ever talked about it. Leave it to a seven-year-old to call out the elephant in the room. I was grateful for this body and my new life, but my singing voice was something I would always miss.

"Well, would you like us to sing something together?" I asked. "It's just not going to sound very good."

"That's okay." She turned back into the hallway. "It's time for Miss Penelope's bath." Sierra slipped from view. A second later, she popped back in with a smile on her face. "Oh, I forgot. You like your privacy." she grabbed the door handle and pulled it shut.

A full length mirror hung on the back of the closed door. I stood there staring at the girl in the reflection. The conversation with Sierra had reminded me of things I missed, but I had so much more to be grateful for . . . to discover . . . to celebrate.

I reached for a brush lying on the dresser. Curls wrapped around my fingers as I ran them through my hair. I remembered when my hair was falling out because of chemotherapy. I used to wear hats to hide my head and tried to avoid looking in mirrors.

I had two bedrooms then -- one at home, and one at the hospital. My hospital room was dull and dreary. Everything about it seemed cold and sterile. The bedding was faded, the walls were gray, the furniture looked dark and drab. So much of my time was spent there, that I often felt the room overtaking me, pulling the color and warmth out of me. When I was sick, my skin was pale and dull, as if winter's frost had settled upon me and was slowly stealing my life away. All around me, there was an absence of vitality. Even the flowers that people left behind appeared colorless, lifeless. I imagined my dull, spent body gradually becoming transparent, until I was finally erased.

With some effort, I tugged the brush through my long, thick hair, then set it back on the dresser. I swept my hair to the side and turned my head to better observe my reflection. The golden brown complexion in front of me seemed to radiate warmth and resilience. I looked and felt alive again.

I watched myself walk back and forth in the mirror. My movements were graceful and strong.

I stepped closer again to the mirror, so that I could examine my eyes. A person could express so much by the look in their eyes without having uttered a single word. My experience had shown me that sometimes eyes could reveal if a person was lying or telling the truth. Eyes could utter unspoken words of the heart, and unfortunately, they could even be the source of betrayal. Poets have said that the eye is the window to the soul . . . I agreed with the poets.

No matter how hard I tried, my eyes couldn't mask how I felt inside when I was sick. Even strangers could read me like a book. My cancer tormented me physically. Even worse was seeing how my family sorrowed when they visited me. It hurt to know that I was the cause of their suffering and couldn't do anything about it. I remembered wishing that the sunken dark circles around my eyes were sunglasses, so that I could hide the pain.

Now, the dark circles had gone. Starring in the mirror, I was amazed by the deep browns and specks of greens and grays in my eyes, framed by my long, thick lashes. I didn't want to hide them anymore.

I wondered if these eyes would betray my secrets.

Keeping a secret was hard work. I couldn't even confide in my closest friend, Nora. It was too risky. I just went to school each day, like any other high school senior, only I never told anyone that I, Becca Tanner, was walking around in someone else's body.

I stared at myself for a few more moments, then blinked and took a deep breath. Sometimes I felt like this secret I kept was like having cancer, because they both seemed to eat away at me on the inside. I had gotten rid of cancer, but this secret would never go away.

I sat down on the bed, then laid flat on my back, feet hanging off the edge. It felt safe and comfortable here. I noticed how the dark brown wooden bed posts matched the color of the floors. Black iron swirled through carved wood in the shape of leaves that ran along the baseboard and the top of the headboard. Pillows were piled at one end of the bed in shades of green and purple, small and large, some round and some square. The silky, off-white comforter was bunched up and pushed against the violet painted wall.

My eyes traveled up the wall to the clock that hung there ticking. The polished silver finish on its numbers, hands and pendulum were too sleek for the rest of the decor, but stylish nonetheless. When the pendulum swung to the left, it sparkled like a star in the night sky, as it caught the light of the sun peeking through the window.

It was after three. Time to get going. Jeff and Nora would be waiting for me.

I grabbed my backpack and hurried down the stairs. "I'm leaving," I called, as the screen door slammed shut behind me.

When I pulled out of the driveway, I noticed that I was down to a quarter of a tank of gas. I rummaged through my purse and the center console -- five dollars and thirty-seven cents, most of that in change. I knew I should get gas, but I suddenly had a king size craving for a chicken sandwich. . . and a Diet Coke. . . or a Diet Pepsi, whichever they had. Besides, there was a place to drive through on my way.

When I eventually arrived at the library, I was excited to score a parking space close to the entrance. The library was the perfect size for this small town, but the parking lot was made for a small village.

As I walked in, I passed rows of computers to my right and left. Every single computer was occupied. I think more people came to the library to get on the Internet than to check out books.

I looked straight ahead to the circulation desk. There were two librarians sitting there with bored expressions on their faces. One of the ladies was literally stretching a ribbon of bubblegum out of her mouth and then stuffing it back in. No one was asking them for help or waiting to check out a book. They must have assumed I was another Internet patron, because neither of them even looked up as I walked by.

I went to the stairs, grabbed hold of the railing and climbed up the massive, spiral staircase.

From the top, I looked out over the rows of bookshelves and watched a few children playing in the small recreation area below. They seemed perfectly happy running, climbing and reading. Little kids were always so excited about reading books.

The second floor of the library felt closed in and a little overwhelming. No matter where I ventured, I was surrounded by tall bookshelves, each row looking the same as the next one. It felt like I was standing in a big maze that would trap me for eternity if I ever forgot the secret path to the stairway.

I usually met my friends at the back right corner of the second floor. It was an easy spot for us to claim, since the computer crowd usually didn't stray this far from their cave. As I approached our usual table, I saw that Jeff was already there. He looked up from his book and waved to me. His dimpled cheeks almost overpowered his big, white smile, and his red hair looked even more like fire under the fluorescent lights. I couldn't quite make up my mind if Jeff was attractive or not. One thing was for sure, in the personality department he was a catch.

Sometimes two people meet and form an instant bond. Though the friendship is new, they feel they have known one another for a lifetime. It was like that with me and Jeff. It had been months, but I remembered my first day at West Johnston High School like it was yesterday. I entered the building without a single friend, but it didn't take long for that to change. The moment I set foot in my Civics class, Jeff enthusiastically blurted out, "Hey new girl! Come sit by me." I didn't know whether to be relieved or horrified -- should I cling to kindness or retreat from boldness? There was no manual for being the new girl.

Weeks later, Jeff confessed that he had seen me earlier that morning in the office getting my class schedule. He said we probably knew each other in a previous life, because the moment he saw me, he knew we were destined to become friends.

Most of the students didn't take notice of my arrival. At seven forty-five in the morning, they had already settled into a routine of bored indifference. An ancient overhead projector plastered the wall with detailed civics notes that day. The teacher read them word for word in a decidedly monotone voice. When I entered, he barely acknowledged me or the slip of paper the office had given me to hand him.

I remember how I nervously scanned the room, looking for an empty seat. Several boys in the back of the room were literally sleeping, sprawled out on their desks, but not Jeff. Just in case I hadn't heard him before, he sat up, signaling with both hands, "There's an empty desk right here!" Never mind the fact that this was the only empty desk in the room -- he was leaving nothing to chance. I still wasn't sure if I should sit by him or run from him, but I was glad that I decided to give him a chance.

Over the next few days at school after that, I realized what a genuine person he really was. He made me feel like I belonged, introducing me to his group of friends and taking all of the hard work out of being the new girl.

Once again, all these months later, I could still count on Jeff to make me feel both welcomed and embarrassed at the same time.

From across the second floor of the library, he sprang up from his chair with a big smile on his face and shouted, "Becca, over here!" He waved his arms wildly in the air, jumping up and down. It was definitely not library appropriate behavior, but it was typical Jeff -- goofy and fun.

I smiled, then put my finger up to my lips. "Shh!"

"Oh, sorry," he said, feigning sudden embarrassment.

"Where's Nora?" I asked.

Jeff sat down, rocked his chair back on two legs and locked his hands behind his head. "Nora isn't here yet," he reported happily. "It's just you and me."

"Where is she? I don't want to be here all night."

Jeff's demeanor changed as he landed his chair on all four legs and leaned forward, resting his elbows on the table. "We can get started on the project without her. She won't care." He pulled out the chair next to him, but before I could sit he motioned for me to stop. "Becca, are you sure it's okay that we're here alone together? Because it might look to some people like we're on a date."

I plopped down in the chair. "If this were a date, you would have picked me up at my house like a gentleman."

"If this were a date, I would have taken you someplace better than a library."

"Better than a library? Well I do declare," I said in a fake

Southern accent.

Jeff laughed so hard he nearly snorted. "You sounded just like my Mema."

One of the things I had learned since moving to the South, was that a revered grandmother was called Mema. To be compared to anyone's Mema was usually considered high praise. "I'll take that as a compliment. Now let's get started. Show me what you've got so far."

Jeff collected himself and had just started giving me a rundown of his progress when my phone started ringing. "Maybe it's Nora." I dug around in my purse, not expecting to find it before it went to voicemail. I didn't know how I always ended up with so much stuff in such a small purse. My fingers finally felt its smooth surface buried in six months worth of receipts, gum wrappers, hair ties and other junk.

The caller ID flashed. I sighed and shook my head.

"Who is it?" Jeff asked.

I hit the reject button. "It's Jason," I mumbled.

Seconds later, it started ringing again. "You've got to be kidding me," I said as I looked at the caller ID.

Jeff chuckled. "He's calling again?"

I nodded.

"Does he ever leave a message?"

"If breathing counts, then yes, he leaves lots of messages."

Jeff stuck his pencil behind his ear. "Wait a minute," his eyes lit up with mischief. "What kind of breathing are we talking about here?"

I gave him a look of irritation. "You find this humorous?"

"I'm just trying to understand. Is it heavy breathing like

this?" Jeff did his best impression of some kind of masked superhero. "Or is it more like this?" His nostrils flared and his lips flapped as he made an impossibly loud snoring sound.

"Really, Jeff?"

He pushed his chair out from the table. "No, no I've got it. Was it like this?" He stood up and started jogging in place, breathing fast and heavy.

"Uh, nice. Very nice. Now I have a creepy visual to go with the creepy breathing sounds."

Jeff sat back down, obviously very pleased with himself. I pulled the pencil out from behind his ear, tapped him on the head with it, then started turning the pages in my book.

The goofy grin fell from Jeff's face. "How often does he call you?"

"Too often," I said, still turning pages.

Jeff became silent. I kept reading, but couldn't focus my thoughts. The problems with Jason were getting out of hand. I should have never gone out with him. I wished I had listened to Jeff from the beginning. Now, when I wanted to confide in him, there was an extra layer of awkwardness.

Jeff slipped his hand onto my book, just as I was about to turn another page. He stared at me, straight-faced. I sat back and dropped my hands in my lap. Great. Here it comes. Now he's going to tell me, I told you so.

"What's going on?" he asked.

I looked down at my book trying to think of what to say. I wanted to tell him everything . . . I wanted to tell him nothing.

"Becca." he said, almost whispering. His face was full of concern.

I took a deep breath. I didn't know how it was going to turn out, but keeping secrets was hard work and I already had one too many. "Okay, fine. I've been avoiding this conversation for way too long. I know you tried to warn me about Jason right from the start, and I didn't listen." I didn't want to be lectured to, but there it was. I had opened the door.

Jeff didn't say anything. He just looked into my eyes searchingly, so I continued. "You're going to hate me for saying this."

"Becca, whatever it is, you can tell me. I could never hate you."

"The thing is, I didn't listen to you, because I thought you were jealous."

Jeff didn't respond. He sat there motionless, a blank look on his face. The silence was deafening.

"We didn't know each other very well then. We had only been friends for a couple weeks," I explained. "It just seemed like you didn't want me going out with anyone."

I was about to go on, when Jeff pushed his seat back, dropped his head to his chest and mumbled, "I see."

"Don't tell me you're mad," I sighed.

"No," he said, still not giving me eye contact. "It's not anger. It's more like sadness." As Jeff fidgeted in his seat, the wheels were clearly turning in his head. "Hasn't it been like four months since you dated Jason?"

"Sort of," I winced.

Jeff shook his head. "What does "sort of" mean?"

"It means that I'm done, but Jason won't let it end."

Jeff raised his eyebrows.

"We only went out twice. We were never even a couple," I insisted, trying to convince myself as much as Jeff. "But ever since then, he has been calling, texting and even following me.

He just won't take no for an answer. And I'm really creeped out about it." I sighed and folded my arms, still expecting the "I told you so" lecture.

Jeff closed his eyes and placed the tip of his index finger on the center of his forehead searching the depths of his own thoughts.

Finally, he looked at me. "I'm sorry," he said softly. "I'm sorry that I made you feel like you couldn't talk to me. I probably could have picked a better way to warn you about Jason."

"That wasn't your fault, Jeff. It was mine."

He shook his head. "I obviously didn't do a good job, because all you could see was a jealous and insecure jerk."

My phone began ringing again. I held it up for Jeff to see. "At least now you know why I changed my number last month."

Jeff stared at the phone, then at me. "I guess he figured out the new number."

"Yeah," I nodded. "Stalkers are resourceful like that."

"Have you tried blocking his number?"

I tossed my phone into my purse. "Oh yeah, I did. And then he started calling me from new numbers."

"I should have been paying closer attention. I should have protected you."

"I don't know if anyone could protect me from Jason. Every obstacle only makes him more determined."

"Becca?" Jeff's voice was low and cautious. "Has he done something to you? Has he hurt you?"

"No," I shivered at the thought. "He hasn't done anything more than annoy me."

Jeff exhaled loudly, but I knew he needed more assurance. I smiled at him. "I'm fine, really." I said. "He hasn't done anything to me."

Jeff's face relaxed, but his body was still tense. "So you told him you weren't interested in going out with him again and what did he say?"

"Well . . . I don't remember exactly. It was kind of weird."

"How so?"

"The first time I told him, he didn't really say anything. He just squealed his tires and drove off. But the next day he acted like nothing had happened."

"So did he ask you out again after that?"

"More times than I can count. At first, I tried to be polite, but I'm really getting sick of this."

"Well, are you sure you made it absolutely clear? Or did you leave the boundaries of your relationship vaguely uncertain?" Jeff rattled that line off as though he had practiced it before.

"Do you think this is *my* fault?" I couldn't believe he just said that to me. Whose side was he on?

Jeff paused, searching for the right words, but I thought I'd do us both a favor and stop him before he said something else stupid. "I didn't lead anyone on. I'm not into Jason and never will be. I think I've been very clear."

Jeff picked up the pencil and flicked it as if pointing toward some distant unseen target. "If he knows you're not interested, then why do you think he keeps calling you?"

"He keeps saying he just wants to talk to me."

"Oh please. I know what kind of a guy Jason is. Trust me. He wants to move his lips and wag his tongue, but words don't enter into it."

"Gross."

"The guy is clearly warped, but what I don't get is why he's still at it. Is relentless harassment supposed to win you over?"

"Maybe he thinks I'll recognize his determination as a token of love and come running to his arms."

"Have you told your parents?"

I shot him a disapproving glare.

"I'll take that as a no," he replied.

I snatched the pencil from his hand and pointed it at his closed book. "We better get going on this stuff."

Jeff opened his book and positioned it so that we could both see. He produced a spiral binder with notes already highlighted, then paused. "But what are you going to do about Jason?"

"I don't know, but can we please not talk about him anymore tonight?"

Jeff leaned over and gave me a half hug, then pulled his notes out and handed me a highlighter.

I felt a sense of relief. I had been honest with Jeff, and now I had one less secret to keep. It hadn't been an easy conversation, but it seemed like it had been an important one. I needed him to be in my corner, and he didn't let me down.

Now why hasn't Nora gotten here yet?

CHAPTER 7

Becca

We had been working on the project for nearly an hour before Nora finally showed up. She walked toward Jeff and I with her mouth open and a perplexed look on her face. Her blonde hair was pulled up in a bun so tight that her eyes looked like they had shifted another inch apart.

"I thought we were going to work on our project at five?" she said, checking the time on her phone. "How long have you two been here?" She peered over her stylish, black rimmed glasses -- they were only for looks. Nora has perfect eyesight.

I turned to Jeff. "We said four o'clock right?"

"Right," he nodded. "It had originally been five, but then we changed it to four."

Nora saddled her hand on her hip and glared at Jeff. "Well, was anyone going to tell me?" she said in a scolding manner.

"Didn't you tell her?" I asked.

"I sent her a message," Jeff's voice sounded innocent, but his body language screamed guilty. He wouldn't give Nora eye contact.

"That's funny, because I haven't gotten any messages from you all day. Was it a text, an email? What?"

"I sent you an email this morning." Jeff pulled out his phone and began swiping.

"I don't know why I wouldn't have seen it."

"Maybe you've got that bun a little too tight and it's choking off your brain," Jeff mumbled.

Nora tossed her bag onto the table forcefully before sitting down.

"It's right here."

"Show me." Nora held out her hand.

Jeff leaned over. "It's this one right here."

Nora removed her glasses to get a better look. "Oh, I see the problem." She handed the phone back to Jeff and re-equipped her glasses for dramatic effect. "You sent it to an email address I haven't used . . . since middle school," she said loudly.

Jeff smiled timidly. "Sorry. But if it's any consolation, Becca and I have made a lot of progress on the project."

"Uh, huh." Nora rolled her eyes. "Just fill me in on where you guys are at." She slid her chair over and shifted her legs out to the side to show off her favorite leopard print stilettos.

Nora always had to look good -- hair, makeup and stylish shoes were a given. She wore her clothes skin-tight, for fear that anything baggy might make her look fat. She spared no expense on her appearance.

Nora claimed she was a natural blonde, but platinum was not her natural color. She said she needed a little help with dullness sometimes so she bleached it. She was famous for fake nails and eyelashes, but underneath her overdone appearance, she was about as genuine and true as a friend could be.

We all worked on the project together for the next couple of hours, mostly managing to stay on task. We stopped occasionally to talk about different status updates and pictures people had posted on our school's so-called online homework network, which was more like a gossip network.

We finally decided to call it quits for the evening. Jeff left to return the books we had borrowed. As soon as he was out of sight, I turned to Nora. "Jeff knows about Jason."

"Oh boy," she said in a flat and knowing tone. "How did he find out?"

"Jason called me. Twice. Maybe more, while Jeff and I were waiting for you. He saw the caller ID."

"What did you tell him?"

"I told him enough. I just didn't have the energy to keep this secret any longer."

Nora cringed. "So, did he ask you a hundred questions?"

"He tried."

"Well, he seemed surprisingly calm and collected, so you must not have told him everything."

"Oh, he got upset alright, but not how you'd think. He wasn't all loud and angry. It was weird. He got really quiet, but super intense. I've never seen him like that before."

"Woah. This is worse than I thought."

"What? No. He's fine now. You saw him. We talked some more and he's good."

Nora pushed her glasses up and leaned in closer. "Trust me, I *have* seen him like this before, and he is *not* good. He may seem calm and collected on the surface, but underneath the facade he wants to punch Jason's lights out. I guarantee it."

"You think so?"

"Absolutely. When Jeff goes quiet, it's because he's plotting. He's not going to be able to let this go."

"Well, Jason's a lot bigger than Jeff," I said. "He needs to let this go or he could get hurt."

"Exactly. Which is why I need to go talk to him before he gets himself into trouble."

Maybe I shouldn't have told Jeff. I didn't think through how it might affect him, but Nora's reaction had me worried. If she was right, and Jeff got hurt trying to stick up for me, I'd feel terrible.

Nora stood up and slid her chair in, then stopped in her tracks. "Now this just isn't fair." She snatched a handful of empty candy bar wrappers protruding from Jeff's backpack. "How can the boy eat like this and never gain a pound?" She fanned out the wrappers like a Vegas card shark. Her inventory yielded a solitary Reese's cup, still intact. "This is so bad, but I'm starving. Want to split it?"

"You go ahead. I won't tell." Even if she did share, she'd give me the smaller half. I could tell by the ravenous look in her eyes that she really wanted the whole thing for herself.

Nora tossed the chocolate in her mouth and stuffed the wrappers back where they had come from. She licked her fingers to hide the last traces of evidence. "I'm going to go find him."

She disappeared into the aisles. I got up and started walking in the opposite direction, browsing the shelves.

I hoped that Jeff wasn't as upset as Nora thought. If he was, I hoped that she could talk some sense into him. Mostly, I wished that this would all go away and Jason would stop bothering me. Or that he'd be swept away in a freak tornado to someplace far away, like the wicked man-witch deserved.

I spotted a book on the top shelf that caught my interest. I tried to reach it, but came up a couple inches short. If only I had Nora's stilettos instead of these flats.

I tried balancing on my toes like a ballerina. It helped. I

could reach it, but it wouldn't budge. I attempted to wedge the tips of my fingers between the books on either side. "Come on," I coaxed, but it was no use.

In a last ditch effort, I jumped up to try and grab it. Still no luck. I dropped my arm back down to my side in frustration and looked up. "Really?" I said, as if the books were taunting me.

"Do you need some help?" a deep voice asked, almost startling me.

I turned to see who it was. I couldn't believe my eyes. Did Blake Pierce really just speak to me? I glanced to the right, and then to the left -- nobody but me. I was face to face with the absolute cutest guy in school who had previously never given me the time of day. I thought I was invisible to him.

The first time I saw Blake was at a pep rally. Nora and I were already seated when he walked in. She tried pointing him out to me, but I didn't need any help noticing. He was indisputably hot and impossible to miss.

What was a guy like this doing in a public library on a Friday night? For that matter, what was I doing in a public library on a Friday night? I must have looked pretty pathetic. A total nerd.

He leaned against the bookshelf with his arms folded -- his hard chest and shoulders dominated his large frame. I instantly felt my heart flutter.

An expression of amusement flashed across his face. Even his eyes seemed to be smiling. I wondered how long he had been standing there watching me try, unsuccessfully, to reach that book. I smiled nervously and pointed toward the top shelf.

His eyes followed, then he looked back at me. "Which one do you want?" His voice carried across the open space between us, resting on my ears, like I was listening to my favorite song.

I spun toward the shelf and pointed again. "The red one."

Oh my gosh, I sounded like a freaking five-year-old, picking out what color balloon I wanted. Before I could move out of the way, he stepped in and reached over me. The front of his shirt hung forward and brushed across my face. He smelled like . . . an autumn breeze. Woodsy. Just strong enough to draw me in, but not too overpowering.

He retrieved the book with ease while remaining flat on his feet. I took a step back and almost lost my balance, but the bookshelf seemed to reach out and catch me just in time.

He retreated a step, placing a comfortable distance between us and handed me the book. I took it from his grasp, then looked up at him, almost losing my balance again when I caught sight of his clear blue eyes up close. His head was tilted forward, mouth slightly open. His face appeared hard and strong, yet his eyes were inviting.

"Thanks," I smiled, almost blushing.

He cocked his head slightly. "Western Horseback Riding?"

I looked at the book, then back to him. "Uh, yeah." I smiled shyly.

"Do you ride?"

"Me? No . . . I mean, not recently. Not really at all."

He looked at me inquisitively.

"I went on some trail rides a couple of times when I was little."

It was hard to read Blake's expression, but I felt sure he wasn't impressed. The truth was, I felt drawn, even compelled to be near every horse I saw. I couldn't explain it, and I didn't dare try, but I had to say something.

"Sometimes when I'm out driving in the country," I said, "I'll spot some, and I'll pull over to watch for a while. I think they're beautiful."

He raised one eyebrow. "So, you're more of a horse spectator?"

"I guess." I shrugged. "For now." Was he making fun of me?

"For now, huh?" He took a long slow look, sizing me up from head to toe and back again. "It sounds like you have a plan."

"I do." I do?

"I see."

He nodded. "Well okay, then. Good luck," he said, backing away.

I couldn't believe I had just had a conversation with Blake Pierce. I was still reveling in the moment when he stopped and took a step back toward me. I quickly dropped the goofy grin off my face, wondering if he had noticed.

"Just one question," he said. "What if you find out that you were mistaken -- that you're not a horse person after all?"

"I seriously doubt that will happen," I shook my head.

"The thing is, horses are big, powerful animals with minds of their own. When you experience that for yourself, you might find that you love them, or you might not." He paused, but not long enough for me to figure out an appropriate response. "What I'm saying is, you're not gonna know until you spend some real time up close and personal . . . on the business end." He looked at me intently waiting for my reply.

"Well, I did the trail rides. Don't those count?"

"It's a start."

"And I was bucked off the last time," I added. "That wasn't fun, but I still think they're amazing creatures, so I'm pretty sure I won't change my mind at this point."

"On a trail ride?" Blake chuckled. "What did you do to get bucked off on a trail ride?" He hung on my reply as if nothing in the world was more interesting.

"I didn't do anything," I said, placing my hand on my chest. "I was merely a casualty, a victim of an irresponsible trail guide who decided my horse needed encouragement in the form of a big whack on its backside. Smack! Almost instantly, I was lying on the ground, staring up at the sky and wondering how I got there."

Blake looked surprised. "It sounds like you had a little more excitement than you bargained for."

I nodded.

"So, do you think you'll get back in the saddle again soon, or will your horse appreciation be limited to spectating for a while yet?" He folded his arms and leaned against the bookshelf.

I was exhilarated, realizing that he wasn't leaving. "Well, the unfortunate bucking incident happened a long time ago. I'm not afraid now. In fact, tomorrow I'm going to be up close and personal with several horses -- maybe even on the "business end," as you called it, though I hope that doesn't mean what I think it means."

"Oh, it probably does mean what you think it means," he said. We both laughed. "Do you have a riding lesson?"

I shook my head. "Not exactly."

Blake stared at me, and I didn't look away. He shifted his weight, then stood up straight. He seemed to tower over me, though I felt safe standing there next to him.

"You know, you're becoming more mysterious by the minute," he said.

That was the *last* thing I wanted to hear. Everyone likes to solve mysteries, but I didn't want to be interrogated. I didn't want to lie either, but my secrets needed to remain secret.

"It's okay," Blake said. "There is no rush." He seemed to discern my discomfort. "Every good thing in this world is worth a little patience."

His voice brushed across me like a warm breeze. I was pretty sure Blake Pierce had just flirted with me. I took a deep breath. "I do plan on riding and hopefully soon, but tomorrow I'll be--"

"Blaaa-ake!" a high-pitched voice called out with deliberate urgency. He turned to look.

I recognized the voice before I even saw her -- Valarie Gresham. She was in my technology class. I knew from bits of conversations I had overheard, that the two of them used to go out, but I wasn't sure if they were still together.

Valarie stood at the far end of the long aisle, looking simultaneously pouty and cute -- a look that she had obviously mastered. Her long blonde hair was perfectly straight and all one length. I swear there wasn't one split end on her whole head of hair. One side of her blonde locks hung stylishly in front of her face. She tossed it back, with a swift head flick. I'll admit it. She made me a tad jealous. Blake was being summoned by a supermodel.

I looked at him knowingly. "Thanks for the book." I held it up in a gesture of appreciation.

"Hold on." He looked up, then reached for another book on the top shelf and handed it to me. "Here's a good one."

I didn't know if he was teasing or serious, but I took the book from him anyway. I smiled softly, already missing our brief conversation before he had even gone.

"Let me know if you like that one," he said with a serious tone.

"So, you're assigning me a book report?"

He smiled, then turned and walked toward Valarie. I stood there in a daze watching him go.

They rounded the corner, almost out of sight, when suddenly he glanced back at me. Our eyes met for only a moment, before we were interrupted by a large bookshelf that seemed to step between us.

Someone cleared their throat behind me. It was Nora. She had a huge smile on her face. "I saw you talking to Blake!" she said, her voice brimming with excitement. "And right in front of his girlfriend, too. You're so bad!"

"Are they a couple? I don't think they are."

"Hmm," Nora said, putting her finger to her lips. "Let's examine the evidence. Did you see the way little miss perfect was looking at you?" She raised her eyebrows. "You were talking to her property. Her man. Those were some fierce eye daggers she was throwing at you."

"Really?"

"Oh yeah, totally Hitchcock," she said as she demonstrated the Norman Bates shower scene with accompanying stabbing violin sounds.

Nora's reenactment of the movie *Psycho* was interrupted by Jeff's thunderous library whispers that were being fired off every couple seconds.

"Becca, Nora. Where are you?"

"Over here," Nora replied with full-throated annoyance.

Jeff scurried in the direction of Nora's reply using his library fast walk -- elbows pumping, hips swaying, legs nearly straight and one foot in contact with the floor at all times. He always did this on purpose to make me laugh. I was already smiling, the laughing came easy.

"I've been looking for you guys," Jeff said, walking toward us grinning, his dimples in their full glory, bracketing his bright smile.

"We had to use the ladies room," Nora quickly replied with a deceptive smirk on her face.

The three of us headed back to our table, collected our things and made our way downstairs.

"Becca," Jeff said. "You haven't stopped smiling since you got back from the bathroom."

Nora nudged me. "I'd be smiling, too, if I were her."

Jeff's eyes searched Nora for clues to decipher her secret girl-code, but came up empty. "Okay, what are you two talking about? What did I miss?"

"Oh, nothing." Nora said in a sing-songy way.

Jeff turned to me with a bewildered look on his face.

I bit my lip. It would have been polite to give Jeff some kind of answer, but I couldn't stop thinking about Blake. I imagined smelling his shirt again. I thought about how close we had been -- almost touching. I kept replaying our conversation over and over again in my mind.

Blake sounded like he knew a thing or two about horses. I didn't get the chance to tell him that I would be volunteering tomorrow at a therapeutic horse riding ranch. I wished I had.

I wished I had asked him more questions while I had the chance. I wanted to know his story. I wanted to find out if he had a mystery. And if he did, I wanted to be the one to solve it. I hoped I would get the chance to talk to him again soon.

All the way home, and for the rest of the evening, I couldn't stop thinking of how it felt to be with Blake. He was strong, yet kind. Funny, yet sensitive. I heard the sound of his alluring baritone voice echoing in my mind like the melody of a song. The intense way he looked at me with those dreamy eyes -- that had to mean something. . . . I wondered if he was thinking about me, too.

CHAPTER 8

Darla

Last night, I followed Dr. Brimley out of the building. His long, white lab coat glowed conspicuously bright under the streetlights -- an easy target for anyone to keep track of. I thought he was about to head home for the night, but he passed his car and slunk over to a police vehicle parked near the back of the overflow lot.

The officer remained in his vehicle, face hidden under the shadow of his hat, cigarette smoke escaping from his nostrils.

Dr. Brimley walked up to the car, his hard-soled shoes striking the asphalt, from heel to toe with each step. He handed the officer a large envelope. "This is everything you'll need," he said.

As the officer stretched his hand out from the patrol car window, dark tattoos became visible on his wrist, just below his sleeve. He opened the envelope and pulled out some papers. On the top of the stack was a photo. "This is her?" he asked, holding the photo up, against the lamp light.

It was a picture of Becca! Why was Dr. Brimley handing Becca's photo to this tattooed cop?

Dr. Brimley nodded and stroked his chin, apparently pleased with himself. The officer set the papers down on the seat next to him, then flicked his cigarette out the window. He started up his vehicle and shifted it into gear. The engine's low rumble masked the sound of Dr. Brimley's footsteps as he walked away.

Had I just seen Becca's hitman? Was that officer now

going to pursue her?

Dr. Brimley pulled a phone out of his pocket and started dialing. He stood still, looked around, then held it up to his ear. "Yeah, I just gave it to him," he said.

He paced back and forth in the parking lot for several minutes. I waited, listening intently, hoping to hear something more.

He ran his fingers through his white hair, from the front to the back. "I've done what you asked me to do. What more do you want?" There was obvious distress in his voice. "I just want this entire thing to go away."

A car pulled up and parked nearby, prompting Dr. Brimley to move from his spot. "Can we talk about this later? This is not a good time," he said, peering over his shoulder.

I followed Dr. Brimley as he walked back toward the building, the phone still to his ear. "Yes, I'll get rid of it . . . fine," he said. He stuffed the phone into his pocket, before slipping through the double doors into the lobby.

CHAPTER 9

Becca

I knelt down next to my bed, flipped up the silky, violet dust ruffle and felt around for the box I knew was within reach, but hidden from view. My fingers finally made contact with its smooth surface. I grabbed hold and slid it out next to me onto the long, braided rug that stretched the full length of the bed.

I positioned it carefully in front of me, as I sat there on the floor. My hands reached for the lid, then paused. Was I ready to do this? Or would I slide it back under the bed, unopened, as I had done several times before.

Inside were painful memories from my battle with cancer, waiting to be revisited. Cancer had taken so much from me. It hadn't asked permission. It did not consult me. It took no vacations, weekends or holidays. Cancer set all the terms. I wanted so badly to have a place of refuge to separate me from the relentless grasp of my tormentor.

Now, the tables were turned. The flimsy cardboard box could do little to keep me out, yet it was powerful enough to hold those painful memories in. I had decided long before that it would do so until I found the strength to confront them at a time of my choosing. I could not wish the memories away, but I could set the terms.

I rested my hands on top of the box, but not for long. The slickness of the clear tape that held it shut seemed to be inviting me to run my fingers along its smooth wide strip. Courageous hands had found the edge of the tape and a corner that had already pulled away on its own. Almost instinctively, I started picking away at the tape. . . . It was time.

I carefully pulled the clear tape off the seams. The box howled with each tug as I ripped the tape free. I slowly folded the flaps open -- one, then another, until the contents were exposed.

There it was -- the one I was looking for. Right on top, just as I had packed it away so many months ago. I had purposely placed it on top, because I didn't want it to get crushed.

I pulled it out and turned it slowly, inspecting it for any damage. I found a couple of dented spots, but I was able to easily push them back out. The color reminded me of the sand from the beach. Dark leather straps surrounded the base. Only a couple of pieces needed untwisting. I turned it over and looked inside. My name was written on the tag.

I wondered if it would fit. After my procedure, I had gotten rid of almost all of my old clothing. My shoes were a size too big. My pants were too long. I am several inches shorter than I used to be and a few pounds lighter than I was when I was first diagnosed. I had donated everything to charity, except for the contents of this box.

I placed the hat on my head. It felt so much different now that I had hair. I stood up and slowly walked over to the mirror.

The fit was perfect. I inspected every detail starting at the very top. Then my eyes slowly traveled downward. I saw my face. Next, I noticed my long hair that cascaded down my neck and over my shoulders. This hat looked different than before, but I knew it wasn't the hat that had changed. I was the one that was different. For a split second, I envisioned how it used to look on me. I resisted letting my thoughts linger there too long. I chose instead to think of the day ahead.

I was going to wear this hat today, not because I needed

to hide baldness, but because I wanted to make new memories in it -- happy ones.

I sat down on the edge of my bed. Its softness beckoned me to lay back, to be caressed in its billowy comfort. On a normal day, I might have given in to this enticement, but not today . . . I had plans.

Today, I was going to help out with Jeff's little brother, Collin. It would be his first time riding a horse.

I set my boots down in front of me, pulled my socks up snug, then smoothed my jeans down as I slid my feet in, one at a time. My boots were dark brown, went up to mid-calf and were narrow and pointed at the toes. The sales lady told me that they would stretch and conform to my legs and feet the more I wore them. They were plain and rugged looking, as if somebody else had broken them in before me. That's how I wanted them to look, because I planned on wearing them more than once and expected to get them dirty.

I hoped Collin would enjoy riding. He has a hard time with change, and this was way outside of his normal weekend routine.

Jeff was worried that Collin wouldn't cooperate today, so he asked Nora, Stephanie and me to come down and volunteer, hoping that if Collin saw familiar faces it might make things easier for him.

I wondered how many other people with autism would be there today.

As I drove to the ranch, I traveled down some long country back roads, got stuck behind a slow moving farm tractor for several miles and saw a variety of animals. I passed by one house in particular with a large, fenced in front yard. I expected to see a couple of dogs roaming around in there, but for some strange reason, the occupants of that house decided their yard would be a good place to keep two big donkeys.

Some people say that donkeys are like horses, but to me they were nothing like horses. The horse is a happy animal. And the donkey is . . . well, the donkey is not. Every donkey I had ever seen always looked bored out of its mind. They never frolicked or pranced. They just stood there in one place, with their long, mopey ears and sad, tired faces. These two donkeys were no exception, but at least there were two of them in there to be sad and mopey together.

Another place I drove by had what appeared to be an army of angry looking goats crammed onto a barren waste of dirt. It seemed to me they had a decidedly wicked gleam in their eyes. I imagined how they were plotting to storm the fence and depose the farmer from his home. I'll admit, it could have just been that they were eyeing the lush green grass of his front lawn. Either way, it looked like they were up to something with those weird, devilish goat eyes of theirs.

At the next bend, I passed by a rundown, single-wide trailer with a large fenced-in area off to one side. There, three majestic-looking, pure white horses stood with their long manes blowing in the breeze, like waving flags. How sad, I thought. Such beautiful creatures need to run. They need to be ridden.

There was something exhilarating about watching a horse at full gallop. It seemed to me they were happiest, most alive, and most beautiful when they were running free. Along North Carolina's Outer Banks, there's a sizable population of wild horses. I read that they are the descendants of war horses used by sixteenth century Spanish conquistadors. People around here say that watching them running free along the beach is a magical experience, but one that requires patience. Simply showing up is no guarantee of seeing them. They come and go as they please. It is as if they chose the time, the place and to whom they would reveal themselves.

A few months ago, my brother Brandon took Sierra and

me to the beach at Ocracoke Island. As much as I was obsessed with spotting wild horses, Brandon was just as obsessed with racing his four wheel drive truck through the surf and doing doughnuts in the sand. The beach goes on forever and there are no fences. We covered miles of beach, but unfortunately didn't see any wild horses that day. It was disappointing, but not enough to keep me away. I plan on going back again soon. Hopefully, I'll have better luck next time.

My GPS picked up a signal again. "In one-thousand feet, your destination will be on the left," the digitized voice said. Just in time. I was starting to worry I had missed my turn. Right about then, I saw the sign, 'Hanson's Farm.' I slowed down and pulled through the gate, onto a dirt road with scattered gravel and sporadic potholes. Almost instantly, I caught up to a pickup truck, driving slowly in front of me, pulling a double horse trailer. It was impossible to see around it, but I had a perfect view of "the business end," as Blake called it, of two large brown horses. Their tails hung over the back of the trailer.

To my right and left, all I could see were trees, completely obscuring my view. The gravel road felt like it went on forever, winding around tall trees, large jagged rocks, climbing up and down endless hills.

I figured I was getting close when I saw some cows through a break in the trees revealing a large pasture. They were scattered, grazing here and there, with the largest cluster huddled together under the shade of a massive oak. I guessed they were all the same breed -- a deep brown color with white faces and random patches of white across their dark bodies. They looked perfectly content, like they hadn't a care in the world, except for the few who preferred the shade.

I rolled down my windows. A cool breeze swept across my face, carrying the sounds of the world as I passed through it. I could hear the gravel crunch underneath my tires. Birds sang and squirrels chattered in the branches on either side of me. A few cows were mooing in the distance.

White fences appeared out of nowhere flanking the road. This continued up and down several more hills before I finally saw what I had been looking forward to all week. I had arrived.

There were horses of every color and size -- black, light and dark brown, a few that were pure white. Some had patches of white and brown, like paint had splattered across their backs. Most of the horses' manes and tails were the same color, or darker than the color of their bodies, but I could see that a few were unique -- they were reversed, like photo negatives, having light colored manes and tails with darker colored bodies.

I pulled my Jeep into a roped off parking area and turned it off. From where I sat, I could see a mansion of a house off in the distance, conspicuously painted bright green. It was much brighter in color than the trees and grass surrounding it, but it was the vastness of the home, not its imperfect camouflage that set it apart on the landscape.

Not far away stood the equally impressive horse stables. Wide double doors at the entrance opened to a long and narrow structure with more stalls than I could count running along the outside wall. Several of the gate-like doors were opened on the top half, allowing horses to poke their heads out.

Closest to me, was a big red barn, almost as tall as the trees, with an iron weather vane on the highest point of the roof. To get a better look, I opened my door and pulled myself up to stand on the running board with one hand on the roll bar.

This place was amazing. I did a full three-sixty, trying to take it all in. From this new vantage point, I could tilt my head back to see the sky above the tall trees. It was worth the effort.

The sun was bright, but partially screened by enormous, fluffy, cotton-like clouds hanging motionless on the bluest sky that could ever be imagined. I was in heaven.

Back down on the ground I spotted Nora and Stephanie near the barn, draped over the fence watching the horses. I slid back down into the driver's seat and gave myself a quick once over in the rear view mirror before plopping my feet into the soft dirt outside.

I remembered that the sales lady had told me it would take a little time to break these boots in. I guess she was right. It felt like my jeans had gotten all twisted up, tucked inside. I was about to readjust things when I heard deep voices shouting in the distance behind me.

I stood up and looked in that direction, but couldn't see anything. Out of instinct, I brought a hand up to shade my eyes from the sun, but then remembered my hat in the back seat. "Yee haw," I said quietly as I placed it on my head. Now I felt the part.

It turned out that my cute cowgirl hat was both stylish and functional. With my eyes shaded from the sun, I could see two guys, each one leading a couple of horses by their reins. They looked like they had been plucked right out of an old Western movie. Real cowboys.

I sat back down and tugged my boots off to hurriedly untwist my jeans. Before I could pull the second one back on, I spotted my footprint in the dirt -- a triangle and a small square. I stared at it for a minute, experiencing unbridled joy in the realization that I was fully alive.

When I stood up, I felt my feet crush down into the soft dirt. I shut the Jeep door and flicked my hair so it wouldn't get caught as I slipped into my jacket.

I glanced in the direction of the cowboys again. They had both stopped leading their horses and were just standing there. The distance between us made it hard to know for sure, but it seemed like they were looking straight at me. I stared back at them for a moment. Had I done something wrong? Was it my boots? My hat? Or could they tell that I really didn't belong here? Ugh! Stop being so suspicious and nervous, I told myself. I smiled and waved, even though inside I felt like a big faker -- I wasn't a real cowgirl.

One of them waved back! That answered that question -- they had totally been staring at me. It was flattering, but still made me feel self conscious. I hurried to catch up with my friends, glancing over my shoulder a couple times, wondering who they were.

CHAPTER 10

Becca

As I rounded the barn, I could see volunteers already assisting riders in the main horse ring. I scanned through the crowd, side to side and back again, but couldn't spot Jeff or Collin.

All of the horses seemed exceptionally calm and well-mannered. They walked along slowly, starting and stopping on command. There was a wheelchair ramp next to the fence. I saw some volunteers using it to get a rider straight from his chair onto a horse, with minimal lifting. Each horse had at least one volunteer leading, and two more walking alongside to make sure the rider didn't fall off. It was all very well organized. The volunteers seemed to know what they were doing and the riders looked like they were enjoying themselves. I hoped Collin would, too.

"Hey ladies," I said as I approached Nora and Stephanie.

Nora stuck her leg out to show off her boots and winked. "Aren't we the cutest ever?"

Stephanie looked at me and folded her arms in a huff. "You too? What is this? Am I the only one who missed the dress farm-fabulous memo?" she grumbled.

Normally Stephanie's sarcastic remarks were followed by a smile or a laugh to indicate that no offense was intended, but today something was obviously wrong. She wasn't giving off the slightest hint of playfulness. She spun back toward the ring and stood as motionless as a statue.

I gave Nora a puzzled look and gestured toward Stephanie. She shrugged her shoulders and rolled her eyes, then twirled around to show off every angle of her outfit. The normally obsessive hair and makeup standards we have all come to expect from Nora were at an all time high today. The tightness of her clothing was also pushing new form-fitted boundaries and was in no way seasonally adjusted. I knew she had to be cold standing there without a jacket, but I wasn't surprised. She chooses skinny and cute over bundled and warm every time.

I took a couple of steps toward Stephanie. "Hey Steph, is something wrong?"

She turned her head only part way in my direction and cleared her throat. "Well for starters, I wasn't told that this place would be crawling with hot guys." She pointed at herself with both hands. "Just look at me. I didn't put any makeup on or fix my hair." She pulled off her baseball cap to show us her disheveled hair and then slapped it back on her head, pulling the visor so low that her eyes were barely visible.

Nora's eyebrows wrinkled together and her lips puckered. "What are you talking about? There are no hot guys here." She turned to me. "Trust me. I've already surveyed the options thoroughly."

"Yeah, well you might want to take another survey," Stephanie said flatly. "You missed some."

Nora snapped to attention. She held her hands out and started turning in every direction, surveying her surroundings, then stopped abruptly as if her eyes had acquired a target. Her mouth gaped open as her hands fell and slapped against her legs.

Stephanie pulled the cap down further over her eyes. "See 'em?" she asked, frowning.

Nora made the same noise she makes every time she

breaks a crash diet with a piece of chocolate. It's sort of a combination between a dying gasp, a moan and a smacking of her lips.

"What do you see, Nora?" I giggled.

"The Pierce brothers are here," she said, with overly dramatic breathlessness.

I followed Nora's laser-beam stare to the two cowboys I had seen before. They were much closer now. Close enough for me to recognize one of them. It was Blake Pierce. I didn't know his brother's name, but the family resemblance was obvious from this distance. Stephanie was most definitely, positively, one-hundred percent correct. There *were* hot guys here.

Their boots were splattered with mud and dirt, which faded into their well-worn jeans somewhere above the knee. Each wore an oversized belt buckle, which drew the eye up to their cut waists. Like Nora, they weren't wearing coats. Instead, they both wore long-sleeved thermals, with the sleeves pushed up, and a T-shirt over the top of what had to be washboard abs.

Blake's brother took his hat off and wiped the sweat from his forehead. I could see that his hair was slightly darker, but otherwise looked the same as Blake's. It was a mess too, but unlike Stephanie's -- poor Stephanie -- disheveled hair only made him look hotter.

Nora turned back to face us and broke my stare. "You need to keep your eyes on your own cowboy. Hunter is mine," she proclaimed.

"Hunter?" I asked.

Stephanie mumbled. "Hunter is the one on the left . . . Blake's older brother."

Nora made an accusatory face at Stephanie. "Why are you even noticing? I thought you were with Mark. Isn't one boyfriend enough?"

Stephanie took a deep breath and looked down. "I think Mark and I might be finished." This caught both Nora and me by surprise.

"Oh no, Stephanie. What happened?" I asked.

Her face became flushed. "I can just tell something isn't right. It's not the same between us anymore."

"Well did he do something, or didn't he?" Nora demanded.

Stephanie slumped down even farther under her ball cap. "He has been acting all secretive with his phone lately. He won't even let me touch it."

"Oh here we go," Nora said.

"He pulled it out the other day, and I asked him who he was texting, but he wouldn't tell me. Later, I asked him if I could play a game on his phone, and he made up some stupid excuse for why I couldn't see it." Stephanie's dark eyes were glossy, tears ready to fall. "When I catch him online and try to chat with him, he barely responds."

"Oh he's up to something for sure," said Nora.

"And get this," Stephanie continued. "Captain D average tells me he's too busy to talk, because he has to do homework. Like I really believe that. Plus, he leaves his status as available, so I feel like he's ignoring me and chatting with someone else."

I reached out to touch her arm and waited until she looked at me. "All you have right now are suspicions. This could be nothing. I don't want to say anything bad about him, because I know you love him, and he's my friend too, but sweetie . . . sometimes Mark is just plain clueless. That's probably all that's going on." I smiled softly at her.

As soon as I let go of her, Nora reached over, grabbed her

and spun Stephanie to face her. "Hey," she said sternly as she shook her by the shoulders. "You need to pull yourself together. There will be no more dressing all frumpy."

Stephanie looked up at Nora like a Private in boot camp.

"From now on, you're not going to see Mark or anyone else without getting yourself ready first." Nora smiled encouragingly. "Because you may be pretty, but a little eyeliner and running a comb through your hair is officially a requirement. We're not gonna have you going out in public looking like a frumpy sea monster."

Stephanie gave Nora a playful push away. "Get your hands off me you Barbie wanna-be."

Nora seemed genuinely pleased to be compared to a Barbie, but Stephanie wasn't finished. "And while we're on the subject of monsters, how about you buy just one pair of pants that won't make you walk like Frankenstein." Stephanie licked her finger, tapped it on her hip, then hissed between her teeth. "Too hot to touch, baby."

"Young ladies," someone called to us. I turned and saw a woman approaching. She was tall, with a tan face that looked rough and hard. Her wrinkles were deep-set, but her body looked as young and strong as mine. Her dark hair was pulled back in a braid. "I'm Sue Ellen, and I'm the volunteer coordinator. Thank you for coming out today."

"We're really happy to be here," I said.

"Well, follow me, and I'll fill y'all in on what we do as volunteers."

The way she pronounced volunteer sounded like there were too few syllables and some extra e's at the end. She had one of the most beautiful Southern accents I had ever heard.

There are a couple different kinds of accents I've experienced in Johnston County. There's the kind that may as well be a foreign language. Its cadence seems a little slow, like the words are being drug out. I can sort of tell where one sentence ends and the next begins, but no matter how many times they repeat themselves, my comprehension hovers around zero. Then there's the kind where I can understand about eighty-five percent of what's being said. Some of the vowels are pronounced differently than I'm used to, and there's a lot more fluctuation in pitch, especially toward the end of a sentence or phrase. It almost sounds like people are singing when they speak. I like this type. This is how Sue Ellen sounded.

We followed her over to the horses, listening to her instructions. While she talked, I looked around to see if Blake was anywhere nearby. I spotted him off in the distance putting a saddle on a horse.

Sue Ellen finished her instructions and asked us if we had any questions. Stephanie and I both shook our heads.

Nora placed her finger on the side of her face, a serious look in her eyes. "Will we be volunteering with them?" She pointed with her eyes to Blake and Hunter.

Sue Ellen laughed. "Those two are my nephews. They're usually busy doing other things around the ranch for me, but once in a while I've had them fill in when we're short handed on volunteers." She raised her eyebrows. "Any other questions?"

I placed my hand over Nora's mouth and smiled. "Nope, no other questions," I said.

Stephanie giggled. That was the first time I had seen her truly smile today.

Sue Ellen split us up, and I was assigned to assist a young girl about ten-years-old. We helped transfer her from her wheelchair onto a big, black horse named Old Bill. I was told that he was one of their most gentle horses reserved for those who have a particularly hard time staying up on the saddle. This young rider had cerebral palsy, and because she was unable to sit up on her own without support, four side walkers, including me, were assigned to help.

One of the side walkers was the rider's mom. The other side walkers were mothers, too. They all seemed to know each other and were carrying on a conversation like old friends. I just walked alongside and listened.

The rider's mom was talking about a waiting list for a new miracle cure. Everyone listened intently. Everyone but me. My heart sank. I knew instantly where this conversation was heading.

This poor mother had done everything in her power to make a better life for her child. It hadn't been enough. She knew that time was slipping away, and now she was hoping, desperately, that her daughter would be selected for a full body transplant.

She claimed to have heard that the program was expanding in North Carolina, and that each location would have its own wait-list. All of the moms seemed to be familiar with the program, but they were all short on facts and long on speculation.

It was hard to listen to them and remain silent. I could have told them that the wait list was not on a first come, first serve basis, but that the government considered other factors, like the severity of the disability, age, health and family situation. At least I believed that was correct, from what Dad had explained to me.

The mom doing most of the talking was standing on the opposite side of the horse from me. She looked a lot like her daughter. They both had long, wavy brown hair and dark brown eyes. It was obvious to me that she would have done anything for her daughter.

"We pray every night that our little Gracey will be chosen," she said. "And that she will have a suitable donor matched to her." She paused as she pushed her daughter back up onto the saddle. "This procedure is the only hope for families like us. I want so badly for Gracey to have the chance to ride a horse on her own one day and never have to use her wheelchair again. . . . I have signed up to be a donor for the program. I hope you both have done that, too. If I were to die suddenly, from a car accident or who knows what, and my body was still salvageable, then I would want my body given to someone else who really needs it, like our kids. To me, it's no different than being an organ donor. But instead of giving my heart or my eyes, I would be giving all of me."

The tall woman walking in front of me shook her head. "Well, until I see it for myself, I won't believe it. So I'm not going to sign up to be a donor," she said. "I mean seriously, how could they possibly do what they claim? I don't know anybody who has had this procedure done. I don't even know someone, who knows someone, who has had this done. And you know what, I don't think I want someone else living inside my body after I die. That's just too freaky for me. I can't help but to wonder if this isn't just some big, sick hoax."

The woman on the other side wearing an orange sweater chimed in. She didn't mind the idea of donating her body, but she wanted people to be able to choose who they donated to. "Helen," she said, glancing back at the rider's mother. "If you were to die and they gave your body to someone other than your daughter, would you think that was fair?"

The rider's mom didn't respond right away. Then finally, she took a deep breath and said, "The government is worried that if they let people choose who they donate their bodies to, that there would be mass suicides. Of course I would want my daughter to have my body, but I understand why they won't allow it."

"Well, like I said before," announced the tall lady in front of me. "I think it's all just a big racket."

I wanted to reassure them -- all of them -- that the procedure was real. I was living proof. There were risks, but Dad and his staff knew what they were doing. I wanted to give them a reason for hope, but knew that I couldn't. I didn't dare. I tried to avoid giving the slightest hint that I was interested in their conversation, because I was afraid that I might slip up and say something I shouldn't.

My family moved away from California to start over, so that nobody would find out about my new body. In California, all of my family's friends knew me as Becca, the poor girl who had cancer. Here in North Carolina it wasn't like that. People knew me as Becca -- just plain Becca -- a normal seventeen-year-old girl with one brother and one sister.

We were careful not to tell anyone where Dad worked. We'd say that he was a biologist and that he worked for a small company in Research Triangle Park, which was the name of an area between Raleigh, Durham and Chapel Hill. People around here just called it RTP or the Triangle. Every kind of high tech company imaginable, from fortune five-hundred to start-up was crammed into that patch of real estate.

The government didn't want the public to find out the names of the employees involved in the psychocedent transfer program, so they created a fake company for them to claim as their employer. There was even a fake website for the fake company.

Up in RTP, they had what looked like an actual office building. From the outside it all looked perfectly legitimate, but inside, just beyond the reception area, the facade gave way to a big empty shell of a building. It was the perfect cover in the perfect place for this kind of deception.

My dad lived a lie, just like me, but lying about a person's place of work seemed like it would be an easier thing to do than what I had to deal with. It was exhausting having to hide behind lies day after day. I was always afraid that someone would find out who I really was or that I'd accidentally say something and blow my carefully polished cover story.

While I hated having to live with these secrets, I knew that things would be even harder for me if the truth were ever discovered. If people knew who I was, or who my dad was, my life would become a media circus, or worse.

I kept hoping that maybe in time it would be different. If this procedure wasn't such a new discovery -- if it wasn't such a rare thing, maybe people wouldn't treat me like a freak. There wouldn't be so much suspicion . . . so much fear.

I continued walking in silence as the moms debated the ethics of the procedure. The rider's mother interrupted the tall lady in front of me. "I'd rather take my chances," she said. "My daughter's name is on that waiting list, and as long as there's any reason for hope, we're going to keep hoping. You can believe I'll keep calling everyday to make sure they don't forget about her."

The tall lady shook her head but didn't say anything.

"I'll tell you what," said the rider's mom. "If Gracey is ever selected, then you *will* know someone who has had this procedure done -- first hand. So go ahead, and call it crazy voodoo nonsense if you want to."

The tall lady stammered, "Now just a minute. Fact is, I've already got Kyle's name on that list." She took a deep breath trying to calm herself. "All I'm saying is that I don't think we should get our hopes up so much."

The woman in the orange sweater glanced back at the rider's mother. "What I'd like to know is, why does everything have to be so secretive about this psycho transport, whatever you call it? Have you been near Faison since they built that place?"

The other moms had heard of the facility, but had never been near it. She proceeded to tell them how her family drives that direction on their way to the beach. "I feel like I'm entering a military zone there!" she exclaimed.

"Do you really think that's where they do it?" asked the tall lady. "Why not at Duke Medical, or one of the hospitals?"

It was a reasonable question. It just didn't seem like a secret building surrounded by barbed wire was a normal place for a medical procedure. But nothing about this procedure was normal.

The woman in the orange sweater turned to make eye contact. "I don't know if it is or it isn't, but I'll tell you this; When I drive through there, it doesn't just feel like they're preventing people from getting in. It feels more like they're trying to keep something dangerous from getting out."

She wasn't far off. Dad had long feared that if his research fell into the wrong hands, it would be used for terrible purposes. Having gone through the procedure myself, I finally understood.

The government straddled a difficult line between transparency and secrecy. They had educated the public just enough to get legislation passed to fund the program and stave off legal challenges to the ethical questions that would surely come. The media called it a "Full Body Transplant." It had become common knowledge that the technology existed and that the government was determined to control it. But there was only speculation as to how or when a candidate might be selected.

The moms discussed their rights as taxpayers. They wondered out loud if it was the government's place to pick and choose recipients. Mostly, they expressed dissatisfaction at the lack of clear information and process.

"You know what I think happened," the tall lady in front of me said. "I think they started doing these procedures and realized something was wrong. They switched people into different bodies, and something terrible happened. Now they're trying to hide it. That's why they need all of this security."

I felt like I was stepping on tacks and trying not to scream. If I told these ladies that the psychocedent transfer was real and that it did work, it still wouldn't change a thing. The fact remained that their children were on an impossibly long waiting list. Their chances of being selected for this procedure were probably worse than their odds of winning the lottery and being struck by lightning on the same afternoon.

Maybe someday I won't have to keep secrets, but right now the truth was beyond impossible. The number of would-be candidates was so vastly greater than the number of donor bodies, it was like trying to drain the ocean through a drinking straw. People had to volunteer to be donors, or their families would choose for them after they died. Donor bodies had to be relatively young and healthy, which limited the supply even more. Most of the donor bodies came from people who had died in accidents, like automobile, drowning, or other injuries that could be repaired postmortem. Selection was still such a rare phenomenon that the process was anything but fair.

I looked up at this little girl on the saddle and saw how her body struggled to sit upright and stay centered on the horse. She could barely hold the reins in her hands, because her fingers wouldn't work like they were supposed to. I felt such sadness overtake me. I had to look away. Why was I the lucky one? Why not this girl? She struggled to hold on, as though the reins were the tangible manifestation of her hope, fearing that if they slipped from her grasp, her ride might be over.

We finished up and helped her back into her wheelchair. It was a relief when these moms and their uncomfortable conversation disappeared into the parking lot.

CHAPTER 11

Darla

What was so special about Becca's donor body? The answer to this question seemed to be crucial to understanding why her life was now in danger.

I searched through the entire building and every single computer, before finally finding Becca's file. Anxiously I opened it up, only to discover that the part of her file I was looking for had been left blank. There was no record of where her donor body came from; no name, no address, no cause of death . . . nothing. It was thoroughly frustrating. But just when I thought there was no hope, I found something quite serendipitously.

There was an unlabeled file lying on Dr. Brimley's desk. It had a yellow sticky note on the cover with the word, 'shred,' scrawled on it. Voices were growing louder from the corridor. I quickly thumbed through the file, but the only noteworthy thing I found was that this particular patient also attended the same high school as Becca and was in the same grade.

Dr. Brimley entered the room as I nudged the file back into its original position. I needed more time. This file very likely contained a treasure trove of information. Unfortunately, I would never know. He picked up the file and handed it to his secretary, who promptly shredded it.

CHAPTER 12

Becca

I stayed next to the horse and ran my fingers through his bristly mane. He was tall, black and shiny. Such enormous size made him look powerful, but his body wasn't sculpted with muscles like I have seen on some horses. Was he always a gentle giant, or did he somehow understand the need to be gentle with these special riders? Could he sense their innocence? I stroked his mane, wanting to show him my appreciation.

"That's right Old Bill. You are an amazing horse," I whispered to him.

A slight breeze blew my hair into my face. I took my hat off to push my hair back, then slid it on again. I heard the sound of geese flying overhead. Holding my hat on my head with one hand, I looked into the sky to admire them.

From somewhere behind me came footsteps. "Here's something you can use," a familiar deep voice said.

I turned around, trying to hide my excitement. It was Blake! He was holding a horse brush out to me. I took it from his hand and started to thank him, but lost track of the words coming out of my mouth. Had he really just come looking for me?

To say that Blake was hot didn't even begin to explain it. He had a rugged look, with a hard jawline and features. Yet, there was a gentleness in his smile and in his clear blue eyes. Staring into them, I felt like I could almost see into his soul.

"I guess you've met Old Bill," he said as he walked up to the horse and stroked the side of its face. The muscles on Blake's arm flexed with each movement.

"So, about that book you handed me yesterday. Did you just pick it randomly off the shelf, or did you really mean what you said?"

He nodded and smiled. "Yeah, you probably don't meet very many guys who are well read in the equestrian section of the library."

I shook my head.

"The fact is, I've been around horses all my life. Most of what I know has either been taught by family or learned through hard experience." He started adjusting Old Bill's bridle, then stopped and looked right at me. "But, the book wasn't random. My Aunt has the same one and sometimes loans it to her riders. If she likes it, it's a good one."

Blake started adjusting Old Bill's saddle.

"Your aunt seems very nice," I said.

"I don't know if I'd call her *very nice*."

"What kind of thing is that to say about your own aunt?"

"Don't get me wrong. She's nice, but she's also tough. Didn't you see the way she works my brother and me?" He smiled mischievously.

Old Bill stretched to nuzzle me as if to say thank you for petting him.

Blake smiled. "I think somebody likes you."

Hearing those words from Blake's lips was surreal. I needed to change this subject before I turned as red as a strawberry. "I didn't know horses could be so gentle," I said as I fidgeted with the brush in my hands.

"We only use the older, worn out ones for therapeutic riding. They also happen to be the ones the ranchers get rid of. But being mild-natured and a little tired is just perfect for this job." Blake reached into his pocket, then fed something to the horse.

"What's that?"

"Sugar cubes. Do you want to give him some?" He reached back into his pocket, then produced two glistening cubes.

I looked at Blake's hand and then at Old Bill's mouth. "I don't know about this. How will he know where my fingers end and the sugar begins?"

Blake chuckled. "All you have to do is keep your hand flat, like a plate. He won't bite. I promise. He'll just lick them right off your hand."

I put my hands behind my back.

Blake laughed. "I thought you said you were a horse person."

I worked up some courage, then held out my hand.

Blake got a twinkle in his eye. "Just so we understand each other, these are for Old Bill," he said, dropping the sugar cubes in my palm.

His teasing was only marginally humorous, but I was so nervous I couldn't stop laughing. Old Bill turned to face me. I looked back at Blake.

"Go ahead." He gave me a reassuring nod as he rubbed the side of the horse. "Flat like a plate, and he'll take it from you."

I reached out, still a little reluctantly, and placed my hand under Old Bill's mouth. He licked the sugar cubes right off, without hesitation. My hand was wet now. "Eeewww." I wiped it on my pant leg and glared at Blake.

"Think of it as a kiss," he chuckled.

"Is that what that was?" I smirked.

He stepped closer to the horse. "Are you gonna brush him?"

Blake's dreamy blue eyes were pulling me in. I had to stop myself from stepping toward him instead of toward the horse. I just stood there, motionless.

"Do you know how?" he asked.

I shrugged my shoulders.

"Give it a try."

I took a step closer to Blake, then reached out to start brushing Old Bill's shoulder. Blake was watching my every movement, but didn't say anything.

"I have no idea what I am doing here," I admitted.

He leaned in toward me. "Keep going," he said.

I turned to Old Bill again and started brushing left to right.

"You've almost got it . . . let me help you a little."

I felt him move close in behind me. His large hand reached over and gently covered the top of mine. I had a flashback to the library and him reaching over me to get that book. I had to remind myself to breathe. His hand felt rough and strong, yet he held mine with tenderness.

He guided my hand downward. We lifted the brush away from the horse and placed it back up high to repeat the arcing motion. Blake's breath tickled my neck, sending chills down my spine. Both of our arms moved as one. I had never felt so alive.

"What you want is to get all of the dust and dirt wiped off of him by using this type of motion," he said. His voice was smooth and alluring, like a familiar song I had heard many times before. The kind you fall in love with, the more it's played.

He let go of my hand and eased away. "That's right."

I gave the horse a few more strokes with the brush and then turned around to face Blake. If I hadn't been completely mesmerized by him before, I was now.

"We might make a cowboy out of you yet."

"A cow-boy?" I chided. "Not a cow-girl?"

"Around here, the term 'cowboy' is earned," he explained, suddenly sounding serious. "It signifies respect for what you can do, not for your gender." He paused and looked me in the eye. "But I'll call you whatever you'd like."

I smiled and handed the brush back to him. At the moment our fingers made contact, excitement shot through my body, as though his touch were electricity. "Well you can call me Becca."

"Not Miss Tanner?" He smiled.

"So, you already know my name. What else do you know about me?"

"I know that you have the softest hands I've ever felt."

I could feel my face getting hot. "I can't say the same about yours."

He chuckled. "I better get back over there," he motioned to his brother and another man over by the stables.

"Who's that with your brother?"

"That's my Uncle Cleatus."

"Wow, I've never actually met anyone named Cleatus

before," I giggled.

Blake grimaced. "I hope this isn't too much of a disappointment for you, but that's not his real name. He just goes by Cleatus." Blake looked down, then back at me. "His real name is Bubba." A grin escaped from his lips.

We both laughed.

"I'll see you around." He turned to leave, his boots tearing into the dirt with each step as he walked away.

My knees felt weak. I walked over to a large rock nearby and sat down, replaying every moment of our all-too-brief conversation in my mind. I smiled and tilted my head toward the sky, letting the Carolina sun beat down on my skin as I closed my eyes, basking in its warmth.

I heard the sounds of horses near and far, their hooves striking the ground rhythmically, their grunts and their neighing. The sounds traveled through the air and encircled me like an orchestra playing in perfect unison, each one striking their note at the precise moment to render their opus.

"Becca." It was Jeff calling out.

I opened my eyes and looked toward the sound of his voice. He was standing by the fence holding his little brother's hand. I got up and started walking over.

"Hey, where have you been?" I waved to his little brother. "Hi, Collin."

Collin glanced past me, avoiding all eye contact. He mostly looked at the ground and kicked his foot in the dirt. A Thomas the Tank train piece was in his hand. He had Jeff's same fiery red hair. There was no doubt that they were brothers.

"He didn't want to get out of the car," Jeff said. "There was a bit of a melt down. Luckily, I brought some Oreos. It took some time, but I think he's ready now." Jeff looked a little nervous.

I bent down next to Collin. "Do you want to ride a horse?" I asked enthusiastically. I knew he wouldn't answer me, but I hoped he could understand. I reached out and took Collin's hand, being careful not to disturb his train. The three of us walked hand in hand to the barn to get him fitted for a helmet.

Jeff sighed, shaking his head. "This is going to be the tough part. I don't know if he'll let me put a helmet on him, and they won't let him ride unless he wears one."

"Don't worry. We're not in a rush, so if it takes a while to get a helmet on him, it's no big deal. Just be careful when you snap the chinstrap, that you don't pinch his skin. I saw that happen with another rider earlier."

Sue Ellen assisted Jeff in trying to find the right size helmet. I could tell that this was going to take a while, because Collin didn't want anything to touch his ears. Jeff had to constantly chase after him and bring him back to try on each new candidate.

I walked over to where Nora and Stephanie were waiting.

Nora folded her arms, and tapped her toe slowly. "So . . ." Her eyebrows raised.

Stephanie cleared her throat. "Did you have fun over there brushing the horse?"

I tried to contain my excitement, as if it had been no big deal. "You two saw, I take it?"

Nora lightly smacked me on the shoulder. "We saw *everything*," she said slowly, exaggerating her pronunciation, as if that last word were a sentence by itself. "What did he say to you? You guys were talking for awhile."

"And is his brother available?" added Stephanie.

"We didn't talk about his brother, but we did talk about horses. He knows a lot about horses."

"Get to the good stuff," Nora said impatiently. Stephanie nodded.

I was fully aware of what "the good stuff'" was and what they wanted to hear. I just didn't want to rush into it, but I could see that Stephanie and Nora weren't in the mood for waiting. Besides, I was too excited about what had just happened to hold it in. I jumped right to the good stuff. "He held my hand. I mean, he totally held it. I had the brush in my hand and his hand was on top of mine. He was like, let me show you how to do it." I demonstrated the motion of brushing a horse.

Nora let out a shriek and Stephanie had a big grin on her face. My smile was so big that my cheeks were starting to hurt.

"I saw him come up behind you," Nora peered at Stephanie, then back to me. "I swear he looked like he was smelling your hair," she laughed.

"Did you just die?" Stephanie asked, her eyes wide. "I mean, out of nowhere, you've got Blake falling all over you." She shook her head, then abruptly stopped. "Oh, and Nora told me about the flirting in the library and how he *helped you*." Stephanie used her fingers to motion quotation marks in the air.

"He said that my hands were the softest he had ever felt."

"Shut up!" Nora said, practically yelling.

I saw Jeff turn around and look at us. Nora and Stephanie continued celebrating and congratulating me, as if I had just won a new car or something. Jeff looked away.

Nora and Stephanie fired questions at me left and right. I

answered them, but kept my voice low, and tried to get them to be a little quieter. I kept an eye on Jeff, hoping that he would get a helmet on Collin soon, and that Nora and Stephanie would stop talking about this. I looked around for Blake, too. If he overheard this conversation, I would just die.

"Oh hey." I patted Nora on the shoulder. "It looks like Collin's almost ready."

Collin tolerated riding the horse, but I never saw a smile on his face. It's hard to know what he is thinking, because he doesn't talk. If there was anyone that I wished could be cured from their disability, it was him.

Soon after Collin's ride, Nora and Stephanie left. I waited around and walked with Jeff and Collin to their car. Jeff buckled Collin into his seat, and with the click of his seat belt, I could hear a slight sigh of relief escape Jeff's lips.

"Bye Collin," I said, as I waved to him.

"Wave goodbye to Becca," Jeff said.

Collin didn't wave. He was busy rolling his train across the seat. Oreo cookies were all over the interior of the van -- just the black part of the cookie.

"He did pretty good on the horse, don't you think?" I asked.

"Riding the horse was the easiest part," he said. "It was everything leading up to the ride that was a challenge. I think I'm going to let my parents give it a shot next time. They might be able to get him out of the car sooner and with less drawn blood." Jeff's arms were scratched up. I hadn't noticed that before.

"Ouch," I said, staring at the trails of thin red lines on his arms.

He shrugged. "This is normal, really." Jeff's eyes focused

on something behind me.

"Well, you managed to go from meltdown to success, so that was pretty good."

Jeff didn't respond. He was still staring at something. I turned around to see. He was looking at Blake. I turned back quickly to Jeff, hoping that he hadn't heard me talking with Nora and Stephanie. Collin started banging his train against the window.

"That's my signal," Jeff said, finally breaking his vice grip of a stare at Blake. "Thanks for coming today, Becca," he said hurriedly as he got into the van.

"I had fun."

"I'll let you know if we need your help again," he said as he turned the key.

Jeff seemed almost like Collin just then, the way he avoided eye contact with me. He began backing out, so I turned away and started walking to my car.

"Becca," Jeff called out, surprising me.

I turned around.

"I like your hat," he said with a smile, seeming to be like his old self again.

"Thanks."

What he said jolted me to the core. I reached up and pulled my hat off my head and held it in my hands, staring down at it. The cool breeze blew my hair away from my face. I wondered what made Jeff say that all the sudden? I looked up and watched the dust flying in the air behind his mom's white minivan as he drove away.

I headed to my Jeep, hat still in hand. I looked to where Blake had been, but he was gone.

"Hey," someone said.

It was Blake's brother. I wondered what he wanted. "Hey," I replied. "You're Hunter. Right?"

Judging by his crooked grin, he seemed pleased that I knew his name. His eyes scanned me from head to toe. "I do believe this is the first time you've visited the farm."

I nodded.

Hunter leaned back against the pickup truck behind him, crossed one leg in front of the other, and pushed the brim of his hat up. "I would have remembered you . . . if I'd seen you here before."

I guessed that Hunter might be one, maybe two years older than Blake. He had a similar build and an enticing smile. But there was something about him. Maybe it was in his manner, or in the way he looked at me. I could just tell that behind the superficial charm, he had a bad boy streak a mile wide.

"Look here," he said, holding his left hand out, closing one eye and peering at me with the other one as if his hand were some sort of aiming device. "I'm gonna give you the best advice you've heard all day."

"Okay?" I replied, somewhat intrigued.

"The next time you see my brother . . . start walking in the opposite direction. In fact, you need to run."

Huh? Was this some kind of weird sense of humor? Was he being serious? I stood there, utterly dumbfounded. The expression on my face must have telegraphed what I was thinking, because he didn't wait for me to form a question.

A subtle shift in Hunter's body language conveyed his disappointment in my reaction. "Oh, I see," he drawled, spitting something on the ground, then staring at the spot in the dirt. "You're the type who has to learn everything the hard way."

I still didn't know how to respond. After a brief eternity of silence he let out a sigh. "Well go on then. I've said my peace." He looked up at me with steely eyes. "Just watch your back."

I didn't know whether to be angry, frightened, or just confused, but I gathered myself enough to blurt out a response. "What do you mean, you've said your peace? You haven't said anything, except to run from Blake and to watch my back. Is this some kind of joke? Why are you doing this?"

Hunter was wearing that crooked grin again, but this time it didn't seem charming at all. "I'm not tryin' to ruffle your feathers darlin'," he insisted, as if I was supposed to take comfort in whatever that meant. "I just don't want to see somethin' ugly happen to you."

"Hunter," I said. "If there's something about Blake I need to know, I wish you'd just come right out and say it."

He nodded his head slowly but didn't say anything.

"Does your brother know that you go around behind his back talking about him like this?"

Hunter let out a half-snort of a laugh and waved his hands as if signaling me to stop. "I'm sorry girl. I thought you knew. It's not Blake you need to be worried about. Is that who you thought I meant?"

"Well . . . who else were we just talking about?" My own words hung impatiently in the air, waiting for what he would say next.

"I'm talkin' about that viper on two legs he has for a girlfriend. Valarie. If she catches Blake talking to you . . . the way you were today, it's gonna get bad, and I mean quick."

Hunter's words landed on me like a ton of bricks. Was it

true? I knew that Blake and Valarie were still friends, but were they more than that? The way Blake had been acting, I felt like he was genuinely interested in me. Had I been wrong about him? "Girlfriend?" I asked, dreading the confirmation I now realized was sure to come.

"You do know who Valarie is, right?"

"Uh huh."

"Well trust me. She's as mean as a snake," he said as he stood there with his arms folded. "The last time she found another girl gettin' cozy with Blake, she dang near snatched her up bald-headed." Hunter nodded in the direction of the barn as he spoke, as if to suggest the site of the altercation. He cocked his head back, looking at me again. "Are you a senior?"

I nodded.

"I figured you were. . . . You ride?"

"A couple times."

"I could take you riding if you want," he said, this time flashing the full movie star smile.

Was he seriously flirting with me?

He took a step toward me. "I was thinking of goin' right now. You want to come?" he asked. His sparkly blue eyes flashed at me like his smile.

"I really need to get going. But thanks for the offer." I forced a smile, then turned to my Jeep. I glanced over my shoulder to catch him still looking at me. I didn't know if he was serious about Valarie or if he was just saying those things to send me running from Blake and into his own waiting arms. Maybe Hunter was the snake.

That night at dinner, I told Mom and Dad about the horse ranch and about Blake. I didn't tell them everything, but I told them enough. I also asked Dad if there was something he could do for Collin. I explained what a sweet little soul he had, how he was eight-years-old and had never talked.

Dad listened intently, but then took the opportunity to lecture me about keeping what he does for a living a secret. He told me that he would see what he could do, but that he wasn't making any promises and that I, under no circumstances, should ever tell Jeff or anyone else anything about my procedure.

He didn't have to worry. I understood. I wasn't going to tell Jeff about him or about me. I had already imagined several amazing cover stories I might use to give him the good news, just in case Dad ever came through for Collin. Each scenario I came up with left out any connection to the secrets my family and I shared.

If Collin did go through the procedure, and everything went well, then he would finally be able to talk. I could only imagine what it would be like to release a reservoir of unspoken words after so long. He would be able to tell Jeff and his parents how much he loves them. Jeff is such a good big brother to Collin and a good friend to me.

CHAPTER 13

Becca

People always ask the same question every Monday morning, "How was your weekend?" Saturday had been a big day for me, with plenty of ups and downs. I had a lot to think about, and hopefully a lot to be excited about. But emotional roller coasters have a tendency to leave the rider exhausted.

My Sunday started off in an exceptionally lazy fashion. I got to sleep in till almost noon. It came to an abrupt end when Mom woke me up, cleaning supplies in hand. I might have guessed. Dad had to work, so we only saw him briefly the night before. When that happens, there is often a good chance that Mom will go on a whole-house clean and purge rampage. I think it's how she releases her frustration.

Sunday turned out to be tiring after all. When the cleaning parade was finally over, I crashed onto a heap of blankets on my unmade bed. Ironically, my own room was about the only place in the entire house I hadn't been scrubbing or dusting.

The next day at school, Jeff showed up with a giant box of donuts. He caught us while we were still in the parking lot.

"Dang you Jeff," Nora moaned. "I wasn't going to eat breakfast. Why did you have to bring these?"

"I'll eat hers," Mark swooped in from three cars over, grabbing two donuts from the box.

Stephanie, trailing behind, shot him a disapproving look

as she arrived.

"Oh sorry babe," Mark said. "What kind do you want?"

"You don't even know what kind of donut I like?" Stephanie asked him, looking like she was a wounded puppy.

Nora reached in and grabbed a donut. "Here," she said, handing a glazed old-fashioned to Stephanie. "Now quit being so high maintenance."

Mark snickered while simultaneously stuffing his face with a maple bar.

"Here, I got you your favorite," Jeff said, holding out a donut to me. I almost told him no thanks, because I wasn't hungry, but I figured I had better take it anyway. I realized that he went through all of this trouble just to do something nice for me. He was always being sweet like that.

Stephanie glared at Mark after hearing that Jeff knew my favorite kind of donut.

Mark swiftly elbowed Jeff. "Dude, what are you doin' -- you're making me look bad."

"You don't like me bringing donuts?" Jeff feigned surprise.

"Man, shut-up, dude."

Nora sighed. "If he knew what I liked, then he would stop waving these little calorie bombs in front of me. I'm trying to drop a few pounds and this isn't helping." Nora let out a noise that was somewhere between a groan and a squeal, then pulled one of the biggest donuts out of the box -- a bear claw -- and started eating it.

Jeff always made sure he got a chocolate glazed with sprinkles. He also made sure it found its way to me, unharmed. In a lot of ways, he treated me better than Mark treated Stephanie.

I sometimes wondered about Mark. Maybe he couldn't help it. He really seemed to have an attention deficit problem, even with Stephanie. The only time he looked like he had it under control was when it came to baseball.

I thought that he and Stephanie made a cute couple. She had an exotic look. People tried to guess her nationality all the time. Mark had a dark complexion and dark hair too, but not as dark as hers. They looked good together.

I saw Nora go for another donut. There were no excuses this time, no hint of hesitation. She dove in like a fighter pilot.

We were all still standing around my Jeep when the first bell rang. I was looking for Blake, trying not to be too obvious. I couldn't stop thinking about him.

Nora licked some donut residue off her fingertips and leaned in close to say something in private. "I want to go back to the ranch and see Hunter. Don't you think he's cute?"

I nodded. "Sure."

"I know, right. He is sooo hot."

"Who's hot?" Mark jumped in, all ears.

Stephanie rolled her eyes. "Hunter Pierce."

Nora took one last lick of her finger to get the chocolate off. "Yeah, Becca and I can go on a double date with Blake and Hunter." She practically bounced in place. "That would be so awesome!"

Jeff's expression became hard. His jaw clenched. "Double date?"

Mark belched. "I thought Blake was going out with Valarie. Aren't they together, or did they break up again?" Stephanie elbowed him. "What? They've been on and off so many times. Who can keep track?"

"Who cares," Nora dismissed him, flipping her long,

blonde hair.

"So you are encouraging Becca to be a boyfriend stealer?" Jeff asked, seeming more than slightly bothered by this idea.

"It's none of your business," Nora snapped. "And don't be such a downer. Becca isn't stealing him. *He* was flirting with *her*." Nora flipped her hair again.

"Jeff has a point," Stephanie insisted.

Nora shot her a dirty look. "Whatever." Nora waved her hand, as if she was shooing away a bug.

I saw Blake walking toward the school's main entrance. The conversation around me faded into the background. His tall body took long strides, covering a lot of ground with each step. His wide shoulders were captivating. He looked so strong.

Then my heart sank as Valarie came into view at the top of the steps. She had obviously been waiting for him there, flanked by two of her hideously plastic acolytes. Were Valarie and Blake still a couple? In a few more steps that question might be answered. I didn't want to watch, but I had to know.

When Blake reached the last step, Valarie began doing some sort of pouty dance in place. It looked like she was saying something to him.

Blake barely lifted his hand up to acknowledge her. He just kept walking. He didn't even slow down. Valarie was really having a fit now. She plunged her fists onto her hips and glared for dramatic effect, but it was a wasted effort. Blake hadn't looked back. She turned to her friends, head bobbing, hands flying around wildly. I couldn't hear what she was saying, but it was obvious that she was upset. And I couldn't help but feel optimistic about that. If she truly was a "viper" like Hunter claimed, then hopefully Blake's response to her just now was enough to stave her off in the future.

The rest of the morning my mind was on Blake.

Everything else was a million miles away. But by the time my third class rolled around, my daydreaming had caught up to me. I was going to be late, because I had completely lost track of time in art class. The assignment was to paint a desert landscape, but my thoughts were confined to a single cowboy. In every line I painted I saw Blake. Every stroke reminded me of how our hands had moved as one, brushing Old Bill.

The bell rang, snapping me back to reality. "Oh no," I gulped, audibly. I hadn't washed out my paint brushes, and it was time to go. Luckily my art teacher took pity on me. She scribbled out a note for me to take and sent me on my way as soon as my area was clean.

I slipped into class and handed the note to my teacher, along with my homework, then headed toward an open computer.

A few steps into the row, and several steps away from my intended destination, my path was blocked. Another girl had gotten up and was heading straight toward me. It was Valarie. I had almost forgotten that she was in this class.

She walked toward me, her eyes staring straight ahead, as if she didn't even notice I existed. She was trying to pass. I was relieved. The last thing I wanted was a big confrontation. I decided that she must not know anything about Blake and I. After all, what was there to know? Blake and I had only talked a little bit. I didn't even know if he liked me. I certainly wasn't a "boyfriend stealer," as Jeff and Stephanie put it.

The rows of desks were uncomfortably close to one another. There wasn't enough room for both of us. I guess I'll be the one to squish to the side and let her pass, I thought. I tried to make myself as small as possible, melting into the desktop on my left.

She slipped by, but at the last moment jerked back toward me just enough to clobber my shoulder with her heavy, bulging backpack. The impact knocked me off balance. I fell onto the desktop I had been pinned against. Papers from the desk flung through the air, then fluttered to the floor, scattering in every direction.

"Hey!" the girl sitting at the desk yelled. "What's your problem?"

"I'm so sorry," I said, as I crouched down to pick up the papers. I turned my head toward Valarie, just as her hair was flipping back around, making it clear to me that she knew what had happened. She marched out of the classroom, but paused by the door long enough to make sure I saw the taunting smirk on her face. I didn't know where she was going, and I didn't care. But she couldn't leave fast enough for my liking.

I returned again to the papers, gathered them up, then handed them to the girl sitting at the desk. She snatched them from my grasp, unceremoniously.

I walked to the last row of computers and sat down at the only open space remaining. I couldn't believe Valarie just did that. It was clearly retribution for talking to Blake. I hadn't seen it coming. But at least now I knew. And I knew that she knew. And she knew that I knew she knew.

Once again, I found myself lost in a swirl of thoughts that had nothing to do with my current class or assignment. The rest of the hour I tried to get motivated, but I couldn't focus on schoolwork. I mostly sat there staring at my screen, trying to figure out what to do about Blake . . . and about Valarie.

The minutes ticked by. I didn't come to any conclusions. In fact, I hadn't made much progress on anything the entire hour. I was only falling farther behind on homework. I needed to pull myself together.

"Class, you've got about five minutes. Time to pack it up, and remember to save your work," the teacher bellowed.

"Tonight you need to read your chapter review and answer the study questions."

The entire class groaned, me included.

Normally, I would have been very careful to save my work before logging out. That's a mistake you only have to make once. But today I didn't have anything to save. I had literally done nothing the entire time I sat there. I drug the mouse icon over the action button, but hesitated instead of clicking on log off. Something on the bottom of the screen caught my eye. A document was still open, just minimized.

I could have easily overlooked such a small and seemingly insignificant thing. But at that moment it captivated me. It was unnamed and generic looking, but I was fairly certain I hadn't created it. So if it wasn't mine, then whose was it? And how did it get there on the bottom of my screen? Maybe it was nothing, but it may as well have been labeled 'Secret Treasure Map.' I clicked to expand it. The first line read, 'That's not your body!'

A chill ran up my spine. I minimized the document again and glanced around to see if anyone was looking. Everybody around me seemed preoccupied with their own concerns. At the front of the room, the teacher was buried by a flurry of attempted homework negotiations.

Normally, I wouldn't have dared snoop like this, but that opening line got the best of me. I simply had to know what it was about and who wrote it. I expanded the document again.

That's not your body!

It is so unfair that I have to see this fake girl parading around in her fake body every day at school. Everywhere I look, there she is, flaunting what doesn't belong to her. She probably thinks she is pretty, but my new body is so much better than my old one. I hated that old body, and I hate her for taking it. I hate being reminded that I ever looked like that.

I bet her original body was even uglier. She probably had terrible hair and a double chin. That long, curly brown hair she loves to flick back and forth took countless hours of effort and product to keep shiny and beautiful. She has no clue. I can already see split ends everywhere. Everything good about that body was because of me. I made it that way by counting every calorie and enduring crushing workouts. I give her three months and she'll be the size of a hippo. She can thank my mother for those brown eyes and that pointy little nose.

If the guys here knew that she was a fake, not one of them would go near her. People would scatter from her like she had the plague.

It's time for her to disappear from this school and from my dreams. I can't sleep with her haunting me. Fortunately, I have a plan . . .

My heart was pounding so hard, I thought it might burst right out of my chest. I reminded myself to start breathing again, then quickly looked around, trying to be discrete. Did anyone see? I turned back to the screen to continue reading.

"Becca," a soft voice said from behind me.

I clicked wildly as I attempted to hide the document from view, employing the same technique and urgency I might muster when trying to smash a spider crawling toward me. I spun around in my chair, trying to act like nothing was wrong.

It was Fiona Phillips. She leaned in, with wanton disregard for personal space. Her sage green eyes blinked impetuously. I wondered how long she had been standing behind me.

"Yes?" I replied, trying to sound calm.

"Do you have Friday's notes from English?" she asked. "I wasn't there and apparently we are going to have a quiz on Wednesday, so I need to borrow them tonight." She brushed her bangs out of her eyelashes.

I grabbed my binder and started rifling through its loose pages. I didn't have time for this right now.

"Did you hear about the group project?" Fiona asked.

"What?" I replied, still rattled from what I had just read, and hurrying to find the notes she needed.

"We are going to be assigned a group project. Did you talk about it last Friday?"

"In English?"

Fiona scrunched her nose. "Yeah . . . in English. You okay Becca?" she asked.

"Sure . . . yeah, I'm fine," I insisted. Of course, I wasn't fine, but I didn't want the conversation to go on any longer than it already had. "I just hate group projects."

"Oh, me too," she nodded. "I always get stuck doing all the work."

I practically shoved the notes in her face. "Here. Good luck," I said abruptly.

Fiona grimaced. "If you don't want to share . . ."

"No, take them." I forced a smile.

"Okay. Well, thanks. I'll get these back to you as soon as I'm done."

"Sounds good."

I knew she could tell something was up, but mercifully, it seemed, she was going to let that be the end of the conversation. I needed her to leave so I could read the rest of that note.

She turned, then paused and glanced at the computer screen. "Were you able to get very far on today's assignment?"

"Uh, not really. I'm going to finish it at home." Now please leave!

Fiona's eyes lingered again on my screen. "Okay, well thanks again."

"Sure."

The lunch bell rang. Everybody started rushing out of the classroom around me. Fiona, too.

I spun back around to read the rest of the document, but it was gone. "No!" I blurted out, slamming my free hand down on the desk. I shook the mouse, as if to conjure it back from whatever ethereal realm it had vanished into. It wasn't there. There was nothing at the bottom of the screen, and it wasn't in my documents folder. I must have closed it accidentally. I should have been more careful. Arrgh! Fiona. Why did she have to ask me for those stupid notes? Now it's gone. I flopped my head onto my hands, staring at the keyboard, then sat up with a jolt. Maybe there is something still in the paste buffer. I grabbed the mouse.

"Becca."

I knew who it was before I even turned my head. I realized that I was the last one still sitting at a computer.

My teacher was standing right next to me. "I have a meeting to go to. I need you to log off."

"Do you mind if I stay for just a few more minutes and finish something up?" I asked.

He shook his head. "It's policy to always lock up the room when faculty isn't present. There's thousands of dollars worth of equipment in here. You understand?"

"Yes, but I could close the door on my way out. And I'll be really quick," I pleaded.

"Sorry. I can't leave you unattended, and it's time to go now." He rested his hand on top of the computer screen.

It didn't look like he was going to budge on this. His eyes didn't even blink. It was like he was watching me to make sure I didn't steal a loose stapler or a stack of post it notes. I stood up and pulled my backpack onto my shoulder.

"Enjoy your lunch," he said.

"You too," I replied, in a less than enthusiastic tone.

I slowly walked out of the room. The heavy door slammed shut behind me. That was it. I wouldn't be able to get back in there before the next class. I might never know what was in the rest of that message.

I started down the hallway towards the cafeteria, staring blankly ahead, my mind in a fog. My feet were a little unsteady, so I stopped and leaned against the wall. The clutter in my purse swirled around my hand as I fished for my compact. I opened it up and looked in the mirror.

Brown eyes, check.

Long curly brown hair, check.

Pointy little nose, check.

Was that note seriously about me? It had to be. Whoever wrote it knew everything. But how could I have ended up in the body of someone who wasn't dead? It's impossible for living people to also be donors. It simply can't work that way. The whole thing made my head hurt. Still, I had actually read the note. At least the first part. This was really happening. Some living breathing girl had written that stuff. I had to face the facts in front of me. "She *is* alive," I said to myself. And what's more, she goes to my school!

Until that moment, I had always wished that I could meet the girl whose body I had been given, but thought that to be impossible since she'd be dead. I wanted to thank her for it and assure her that I would take good care of it. I was so grateful to her, whoever she was, for this miraculous gift she had donated to me -- this new chance at life made possible because of her. Now I knew that she didn't want my thanks. She could care less how grateful I felt. The truth was, she hated me, and it seemed horrifyingly clear that she wanted to hurt me in some way.

CHAPTER 14

Darla

It was me. I was the one who left that document on the computer for Becca. No, I didn't write it. All I did was make sure that it was left in a place where Becca would find it.

Everything in that document was true. I only wished that Becca had been able to finish reading it. If she had, then maybe she'd understand just how dangerous things were becoming for her at school.

CHAPTER 15

Becca

I went to the office and asked to go home from school early. It wasn't a lie to say I didn't feel well. After a brief telephone conversation with Mom, I wound up taking an aspirin and lying down in the school nurse's office for a little while. It wasn't what I wanted, but I couldn't come right out and tell mom or the nurse that some girl wanted to get even with me for being inside of her old body.

As I took a seat in my last class of the day, all I could think about was the mystery girl who was walking around here in someone else's body, too. This was crazy!

"The bell has rung students, quiet down and take a seat," called out Mr. Fitz. He wrote out 'Ethical Dilemmas' in big block letters on the chalkboard and underlined it. "Today, we're going to talk about something that has been in the news in recent months. It's called *Psychocedent Transfer*, also known as *Full Body Transplant*."

My heart sank. Please not today!

"Often, what some people hail as a useful scientific breakthrough, others see as frightening or dangerous. Full body transplant procedures have certainly been a controversial topic at both ends of the spectrum."

The typical jeers and wisecracks I had come to expect began filling the empty space between Mr. Fitz' words.

He cleared his throat. "Now, I know this may be a touchy

subject for some of you. It's possible that one of you has a friend or a relative who has had this procedure done."

"Or maybe there's a Frankenstein right here in the room," a boy in the back sneered.

"It's not impossible," Mr. Fitz calmly replied. "Although the probability of someone at this school being a donor recipient is not very high, I want you all to keep in mind that we need to be courteous to our fellow classmates. Let's keep this discussion objective and respectful."

Mr. Fitz was more right than he knew. There absolutely was someone in this class who was a recipient. For all I knew, there might be two of us.

What if she *is* in here? My eyes started panning the classroom, stopping at every girl. Could it be her? I looked at the girl across from me. She's probably too short. My eyes went down the row, hopping from girl to girl. It had to be someone who is very pretty. It had to be, otherwise there's no explanation for her wanting to switch bodies, because this body I am in is perfectly healthy.

I continued looking. Out of everyone in the room, I narrowed it down to five possible candidates based on physical features.

Maybe it was someone in my technology class, or the class just before it who used that computer. I sighed. Or it could have been anyone who stepped foot in that classroom since yesterday. That computer might not have even been touched at all before me today.

Mr. Fitz continued, "The government hasn't given out statistical information regarding the number of people who have taken part in this procedure, but they claim that they have successfully done this on multiple people."

A student in the back raised her hand.

"Yes," responded Mr. Fitz.

"Is there going to be a quiz on this?"

Everyone in class intently looked to Mr. Fitz for his reply.

He stroked his grizzled beard. "There will be participation points for the discussion, and there may be a paper involved. I haven't decided yet."

His answer kicked up a dust cloud of discontent that swelled through the classroom.

Mr. Fitz, now sitting on the top of his desk, folded his hands together. A gleam appeared in his eye. "If you are going to react that way, maybe I will give you a quiz."

The class reaction was a chorus of dissent, immediately followed by expressions of appreciation for his first proposal.

Mr. Fitz was no novice teacher. He was playing them like a fiddle and knew when to tighten the strings. Satisfaction crept over his face.

He picked up the TV remote. "As you can see, we'll be watching a video. . ." Muffled cheers arose from the students. Mr. Fitz didn't react, seemingly having predicted their response. He paused for the celebration to abate. "I will highlight a couple things before we start."

Everybody was alert and wide-eyed, plotting what they would do during the video. It seemed like several of them were interested in the video content, but there were the predictable ones who saw this as an opportunity to escape, either by socializing or catching up on some sleep. I wondered whether or not the video would tell the truth.

"Does anyone know where the facility is located that performs these procedures?"

None of the students raised their hands. Some grumbled at the stupidity of the question. I was sure Mr. Fitz knew the students would be able to answer. Faison wasn't that far away. Why was he asking this?

He pointed to a student in the back.

She shrugged. "Everybody knows it's that place down in Faison, on the way to the beach. It's no secret."

Mr. Fitz's face remained unchanged by her response. He looked around the room. "Have any of you been to this facility?"

No one responded.

"Anyone driven by?"

A few hands shot up.

"Okay. Who has seen pictures of it?"

A couple guys were eager to answer. Mr. Fitz called on one of them.

"I've driven out there several times," the boy said. "They always pull me over or stop me at their security checkpoint. You can't get in there unless they want you there."

J.D., a notorious delinquent bragged, "Well, I've gotten past the security. It was no big deal."

Scoffs of disbelief were thrown at him like wads of paper.

"Seriously, I have," he said. "I also spent the night in their jail they have out there."

It's hard to ever know if he's telling the truth. He seemed slightly convincing, but he always seemed like he was telling the truth, right up until the moment it was obvious he was lying.

"I'll prove it," he looked around at the class, a smug expression on his face, like he was about to lay down the winning hand in a big poker game. "Tell me how I know that there are three security checkpoints, and each one is patrolled by military police."

He was accurate so far.

"Behind all of that, there's like a hidden mini city in there. Some tall buildings, and they're all lettered. You know, like building A, B, that kind of thing." He poked his lips out and bobbed his head back and forth in satisfaction.

I couldn't believe it. He was telling the truth. Possibly for the first time I had witnessed an expression of actual honesty on his chubby, freckled face. I sat there staring at him, waiting to see if he would say anything else about what he saw.

He turned his head toward me. His sunken, dark eyes stared into mine. I was about to look away, but before I could, a grin emerged onto his face, followed by a sly wink and puckered lips. Eww, barf!

"Very interesting J.D.," Mr. Fitz replied. "And not all that surprising of a claim coming from you." Mr. Fitz raised an eyebrow, his forehead wrinkled up, but didn't disturb the stiff, straw-like hair piece perched on top of his head.

J.D. pulled the top of his shirt away from his puffed out, squishy chest and nodded. "Nobody can keep me out."

Mr. Fitz shook his head. "Anyway, there are a couple other government facilities that perform these procedures. One is in California and the other is in Alaska."

I haven't been to the one in Alaska, but I knew Dad had been to all three of them. I wondered which facility they got my body from. The original owner of my body could have been from Alaska or somewhere on the West Coast. I sighed. She could have been from anywhere.

Mr. Fitz paced back and forth in the front of the room. "I have one more question to ask you before we start the video. I want you to think about possible ethical dilemmas that could occur with this procedure. As of now, the effects on society are still in the early stages. But often, scientific breakthroughs that people find particularly valuable become wide spread quickly. We don't yet know the far reaching effects that this will have on our lives, or our children's lives." He stopped pacing and turned to face us. "I can assure you that this discovery will change our lives in one way or another." He turned to the TV and started the video.

I wondered what he thought about it. I couldn't figure out if he was for it or against it. There seemed to be a growing number of people who were against it from what I had heard and read. People were afraid of the unknown and that made them do and say stupid things.

I was relieved that the kids at school didn't know about me, or about Dad. But this new revelation of another recipient posed a real danger. The only thing that gave me comfort about it was knowing that whoever my body used to belong to, she was obviously trying to keep her own secret as well.

Would she risk exposing me? Maybe. She had a lot less to fear than I did. She could blow my cover and remain cloaked in anonymous deception. Given that, it became crystal clear to me what I needed to do. Until I knew who she was, there would be no reason for her to guard my secret.

There was something glaringly wrong in the fact that she transferred from her old body when nothing was wrong with it. That's not how this was supposed to work. Only the sick and disabled were supposed to be candidates for body transplants.

Could a person be so vain as to want a new body because they thought it was prettier than the one they were born with? Would anyone who works with Dad ever permit something like that to happen? There were rules after all, so how did they get around them?

I was afraid to tell Dad about this mystery girl. He had

told me many times that if our identities were ever exposed we would most likely have to move. I'd have to leave my friends and start all over again. And what about Blake?

The video ended. I turned to reach into my backpack for a piece of gum, but my eye caught someone staring at me. I looked up.

It was J.D. again. He had a slight grin on his face, exposing his shiny silver braces, that seemed to be wrestling with his jagged, crooked teeth. They looked as rebellious as he was. Even those metal wires couldn't tame them.

I turned away. I think he was trying to give me his best shot at a flirtatious smile. He needed more practice before trying that again, because he looked like he had just passed gas.

"Alright class, It's time for open discussion on body transplants." Mr. Fitz clapped his hands together and rubbed them, like he was trying to start a fire with a stick.

Please put this fire out before it begins Mr. Fitz. I took another deep breath, trying to relax. I can do this. Class will be over soon. I'll just lay low and keep quiet. I started doodling on my notebook in an attempt to be inconspicuous.

"Who wants to begin?" Mr. Fitz asked eagerly.

Hands flew up.

"Yes, go ahead."

"I think it's not right that you could date a guy and never know if he used to be all gross and ugly." The girl next to me said, wincing like she had just eaten something sour. "I don't know about you, but I would want to know if I was holding hands with someone who used to have six fingers."

Laughter erupted from the class.

I sighed. Don't encourage her.

"Alright class. Who has an insightful comment or

question to share?"

"I think it's perfectly fine to date someone who used to have six fingers," a guy in the back jabbed. "As long as the chick is hot now, who cares what she used to look like."

"Oh please," I muttered under my breath.

"Becca?" called Mr. Fitz.

"Uh, yes?"

"What is your opinion on this controversial topic?"

"I - I don't have one," I said. Couldn't he see the pleading in my eyes. I didn't want to talk about this.

Mr. Fitz turned and slowly walked away from me down the aisle, carefully searching each student's face for his next volunteer.

Thank goodness. I could breathe again.

He stopped at another student's desk. "How about you, Travis?"

Kids called Travis "Spider," and he liked it for some strange reason. He didn't get this nickname because of any amazing reflexes, or because of wearing red and blue spandex -- nope -- they called him spider because of his long, hairy toes. He helped the name stick by proudly wearing flip flops on a daily basis.

Spider cleared his throat, "Yo. It's like this. Personally, I feel that this body reassignment stuff is ethically wrong."

Mr. Fitz perked up. Finally, it seemed the discussion might get some traction. "Explain why you feel this way Travis."

"I don't want to be around cyborgs."

Several boys burst into laughter once again.

"No. I'm serious," Spider demanded.

Mr. Fitz let him continue.

"Anybody who has this procedure done is a freak in my book. I think they should all be rounded up and sent away to a deserted island or something."

"So, are you suggesting that there may be dangers that we need to consider?" Mr. Fitz asked.

"Exactly. I mean, what if they all start going crazy or somethin'? The zombie apocalypse is right around the corner people."

He got high five's from his nearby friends. Almost the entire class began chanting, "Spid-er, Spid-er, Spid-er."

The bell rang. I got up and bolted out of the classroom, feeling like I was about to run out of oxygen in there.

CHAPTER 16

Becca

I scanned across the waves of bodies spilling out into the hallway, like a mariner searching for a lighthouse amidst the storm and surge. At last, a friendly face. I spotted Nora making her way toward me.

It was often easy to take a friend for granted. At that moment, however, I felt particularly aware of just how important my friends were to me. Nora was my lifeboat, here to rescue me. Without her, I would have been alone, tossed into the heaving crowd.

She had no idea what I had been through today, and I wouldn't be able to tell her, at least not like I wanted to . . . not like best friends normally do.

Keeping secrets from my closest friends was the hardest and loneliest part of my life. All I wanted was for us to get out of here.

As Nora gave me the rundown on how much homework she had, her words melted into the conversations and shouts, coming from the other students making their way through the high school's turbulent hallway.

I couldn't help but to scrutinize every girl who passed by. Someone, possibly in this very hallway, right now, was the one who wrote that note about me on the computer.

A girl wearing sunglasses walked by. They were those dark, over sized ones, covering half her face -- the kind people wore at the beach. Was she staring at me just now?

Two tall, thin girls with long brown hair appeared as the crowd parted around them. Both were smiling wickedly. One made eye contact with me, as the other whispered in her ear. They laughed like hyenas as they passed. Were they laughing about me?

I felt helpless, like a hunter's prey. Every pretty girl who looked or did anything even slightly out of the ordinary was a predator.

The situation was impossible. It could have been any one of those girls, and I had no way of knowing which one of them it was. I wished I could read people's minds.

Nora placed her hand on my shoulder. "Something bothering you?"

I tried to snap out of it. I stared at her blankly, searching for something to say. Suddenly her eyes widened, and her expression changed from one of concern to excitement. She looked right through me as if I were invisible.

"Look," she whispered, "Here he comes."

Blake was walking toward us. He was hard to miss. Even though he was the same age as the rest of the seniors, there was something mature, almost adult about him. He walked through the hall like a man in a sea of boys.

Nora fluffed her blonde hair and instinctively tried to suck in her stomach. "Hi Blake," she cooed in the most angelic sounding voice she could produce. She fluttered her eyes with enough intensity to send a message in Morse code.

Blake turned his head, his square jaw coming into full view atop his broad chest. He gave a little head nod to Nora, then settled his gaze on me. "Ma'am," he said.

I stood there staring back at him, speechless. No one ever

called me ma'am. Was there even a proper response to that?

Suddenly I felt awkward. I didn't know how to stand, or where to look. Only forty-eight hours earlier at the ranch, we had been laughing and talking. Everything had been so natural and comfortable. Now, I didn't know what I was supposed to do. I wanted it to be like it had been on Saturday, but it felt different with everyone else around. Nora carried the conversation. I stared at Blake, barely speaking, like we were practically strangers again.

After a few salvos of meaningless banter had been exchanged, Nora draped her arm over my shoulder. "So Blake, Becca and I were wondering if we could come by the ranch sometime and, you know . . . get better acquainted . . . with the horses."

I laughed uncomfortably, feeling almost paralyzed by the awkwardness swirling around me. I couldn't believe she just said that to him. Why didn't she ever consult with me first?

Blake scanned my face. The corners of his mouth turned up. Then he eyed Nora. "You're interested in horses?" He seemed more than mildly skeptical. Maybe it was due to her impossibly tight skinny jeans and four inch heels, or maybe it was her ridiculously long, manicured nails.

Nora nodded, "Oh yeah. Didn't you see that I was wearing those super cute boots last Saturday? I looked really good in those," she said, half teasing.

"Hmm. I think I do remember that," Blake acknowledged.

I could sense his sarcasm, but it flew right past Nora.

"Well, they're more than a fashion statement. They're also functional," Nora chirped, anticipating Blake's approval.

He raised an eyebrow and checked my reaction, then

turned back to her. "It's about the boots, then. Good to know."

"That and who's in 'em!" Nora winked.

Blake focused his attention on me. "I'll check with my aunt about a visit. She's the one who runs the place. You did want to come, right Becca?"

"I would love to come. Your aunt and uncle's ranch is amazing," I said, making sure I sounded excited enough, so that he wouldn't doubt my sincerity. What I said was truly how I felt, with one small exception; the thing I really found amazing was the effect Blake had on me every time I was near him. He was my entire reason for wanting to go. The horses and the ranch were merely a nice bonus.

"Of course she wants to come," said Nora. "Becca likes horses more than I do, and that's saying a lot."

"Alright, I'll let you know," Blake said, keeping his eyes on me as he backed away. "See you two later."

"Bye," I said, still not fully processing what had just happened.

Nora waved, using her signature shy girl wave. It didn't fit who she was at all, yet somehow it seemed to work on most guys she flirted with.

Blake disappeared down the hallway.

"Nora, what is your deal?" I whispered.

"What?"

"I don't need you to help play matchmaker. Give me some warning next time."

"Sorry. I didn't plan that. The thought just popped in my head when I saw him. Besides, it worked didn't it? And anyway, I didn't do it just for you. I want to see Hunter again."

I wondered if I should tell her that Hunter had been

flirting with me. If I told her, she might be upset. If I didn't tell her, then she might get hurt. It was complicated, but I chose not to tell. I decided it was highly doubtful that the two of them would ever become a couple. Hunter didn't seem like the boyfriend type. I also knew that Nora was definitely the type who had to figure that kind of thing out for herself.

Besides, I had my own complicated situation. Blake didn't exactly seem to be on the market. It was clear that Valarie still had her territory marked. If Blake hadn't broken things off with her, then maybe he had just been flirting, like his brother. Or maybe he only wanted to be friends.

"I don't know what Blake even wants from me," I said, in frustration. "I think he's still with Valarie."

"Umm, hello. Earth to Becca," Nora scoffed. "Didn't you see the way he looked at you just now? He's got it for you bad!"

"You really think so?"

"Girl. Yes!"

"Well, maybe," I conceded, hoping desperately that she was right. "But even if he likes me, I don't think he has broken things off with Valarie. They're still an item."

"Who told you that? Valarie?"

"Not in so many words. But she practically took me out with her backpack today."

"Are you kidding me?"

"I'm serious. She totally knocked me over onto this desk." I mimicked the swinging, the impact, and the papers.

"Oh my gosh Becca. It's just like I said. She's completely Hitchcock. She's Norman Bates with a knife in the shower."

"Are you really going to crack jokes about insane killers right now?"

Nora shook her head. "I don't know. All the evidence suggests that you are something of a magnet for psychos. First Jason, now Valarie." She counted on her fingers, dramatically extending one, then another. It looked like she had a third and a fourth cued up behind her spring-like thumb, but ran out of names and dropped her hand.

"You are supposed to be cheering me up, not kicking me when I'm down," I chided.

"Oh pa-lease. I guarantee you Blake has already dumped that chick. She's a hot mess, and everybody can see it. Sooo not his style."

"I don't know, Nora."

"Trust me. He probably broke things off with her over the weekend, which explains why she attacked you today." Nora's eyes got wide as she caught sight of someone approaching behind me. "I can't believe this. Speak of the devil."

"Please tell me it's not her," I whispered.

Nora scowled. "It's not her . . . it's him."

I turned to see Jason approaching at full stride, with J.D. in tow. His letterman jacket rubbed uneasily on the sweat stained T shirt underneath. Gel spiked hair rode motionless atop his head, scraggly goatee on his chin. I would have found him singularly repulsive just then, if not for his much pudgier and even less attractive doppelganger. J.D. and Jason were like each other's evil twin. They had the same basic look, but different body sizes. The two of them together reminded me of a before and after photo gone terribly wrong.

J.D. jiggled his eyebrows at Nora, smiling at her with that crooked, metal grin of his. Gag. How could either of these guys possibly think that we would be interested in them? I didn't want to see anymore sly winks or kissy lips from J.D. or hear anymore about him breaking through security at Dad's work.

My patience was equally exhausted with Jason. Under no circumstance, did I want to give him the illusion that he and I were ever going to be anything more than a bad memory. Keep walking boys, just move along.

"Becca," Jason said, coming to a standstill in front of me, his head tilted to the side. "How's it going?"

Oh joy. He wants to fail at impressing me in some way, and rekindling the love I *never* felt for him.

"What do you care?" snapped Nora.

"Is your name Becca?" he fired back, glaring at her.

Nora rolled her eyes. "She doesn't want to talk to you. Get a clue already."

"Hey Nora," J.D. jumped in. "Sup?"

"Hey," she said with as little enthusiasm as possible.

Like clockwork, J.D. busted out his signature kissy-lips face for Nora. He probably thought it made him look more attractive, but it only brought attention to his disgusting mouth and overall crudeness.

Jason stepped in front of J.D. "Becca, we're going to get pizza. Do you want to come?"

It was truly astonishing. He was acting as if none of the messed up history between us had ever happened.

"Um, I don't think so," I said, shaking my head.

"Come on. I'll even buy."

I almost had to laugh at the sheer stupidity of that statement, but I was too uncomfortable to let my guard down for even a moment. "In spite of how shockingly generous that offer is, coming from you," I jabbed, "I'm afraid the answer is still a definite no."

"Jason, don't you listen? She wants you to stop texting and calling her every waking minute of the day. You're an embarrassment," Nora said, overemphasizing her pronunciation, as if to help him comprehend such a big word. She turned to J.D. "And as for you," thick disdain in her voice. "Never gonna happen."

I couldn't see J.D.'s reaction. At that moment, Jason decided to step even closer to me, officially crossing the boundary that even a casual observer would clearly identify as my personal space. His big, football lineman body made me feel helpless, like I was about to be tackled and crushed.

"Becca," he said slowly. "I really want to talk to you." His voice was low, attempting to sound sincere, but there was something wild in his eyes that made me want to run.

"Jason," I said, as firmly as I could, "Please just drop it. I don't want to talk." I looked him in the eye and repeated, "Please," as I reached for Nora's arm. "Let's go, Nora."

We began walking down the hallway and turned toward the exit that opened to the parking lot, but the two of them didn't give us much space. Jason and J.D. mirrored our movement step for step. Possible scenarios began playing out in my head: What would we do if they followed us all the way to the car and tried to get inside with us? Nora and I instinctively picked up our pace.

When we reached the car, Jason and J.D. were still right on our heels. At the last moment, they walked right past us, so close that Jason brushed against me. It was all I could do to hold back the urge to scream at them.

Nora quickly got in my car and closed the door. "Those idiots! Are we supposed to be impressed now?" I hadn't seen her this upset before.

"You okay?" I asked.

Nora shook her head. "Do they think we're going to run into their arms now and beg them to go out with us?"

Something Dad had tried to teach me years earlier came to mind. He warned against the use of manipulation under any circumstance. His lectures often quoted the great philosophers like Machiavelli and Cicero on these kinds of topics. In Dad's distilled version, manipulation is a tool used by tyrants and bullies. He explained that even a tyrant wants to be loved, but if he can't get love he will settle for being respected. If he can't get respect, then he will settle for being feared. And if he can't elicit fear, he will ultimately settle for being hated.

Jason and J.D. were presently embarking on a dark path. They had just settled for being feared. For Nora and me, that meant things were only going to get worse. J.D. would follow Jason blindly, and Jason would never give up. Bullies and tyrants seldom, if ever, relent.

Nora and I watched as they tore out of the parking lot in Jason's truck.

"Maybe we should have stayed in the building," I said, "I'm so sorry, Nora."

"Why are *you* sorry? You didn't do anything wrong."

"I feel like this whole thing with Jason is my problem," I confessed. "And now I'm dragging you into it. I just wanted to get away from them. I didn't realize they would practically chase us all the way to our cars like that."

Nora stared out the window for a long while before finally collecting herself. "Well they're gone now. The jerks. I'll see you tomorrow." She opened the car door and slid out, but leaned her head back in before closing it. "Maybe you need to stand up to Jason once and for all. Maybe you're being too nice and it's giving him the wrong impression." She closed the door and hopped in her yellow convertible, one space over.

I didn't think I was being nice to Jason. What else could I have done? Did she expect me to spit in his face or kick him in the groin? Did she not notice how much bigger than me he is?

I started my Jeep and wound through the Senior parking lot toward the school exit, nearly getting hit by some kid in a hatchback. I slammed my hand on the horn, and my foot on the brake, just in time to avert disaster. We both got out of our cars. There couldn't have been more than a millimeter of space between our vehicles.

The excitement was cut short when I spotted Valarie and a couple of her friends talking to Blake and another boy near the end of the parking lot. Blake was flipping his keys in his hand. His tall body leaned back against his silver Mustang. He had on worn blue jeans and a comfy looking shirt. His wind blown hair almost disappeared in the bright sun. Seeing him like that reminded me of all those hot looking pilots in that eighties movie, *Top Gun*. Yep, that was exactly what he looked like.

I sat back down behind the wheel, greeted by a mess. The contents of my backpack had flown everywhere when I slammed on the brakes. I bent down to start retrieving debris, inspecting, brushing off and returning each item to my backpack where it belonged.

With everything more or less situated again, I reached blindly for the door handle to pull it shut. Strangely, the door wouldn't budge. I turned my head to see what the problem was. The near collision, followed by the clean-up effort, had been unexpected diversions. I had been lulled into complacency, disarmed, and was once again vulnerable. The timing couldn't have been worse. Jason was back.

He had his left hand on the top of the door. With one last step, he closed the distance needed to place his body in between, completely blocking the door. He leaned forward, with his right arm draped over the roof of the Jeep. "Wow, sorry. Didn't mean to startle you," he chuckled.

"What are you doing here?"

He smirked. "How about a *nice to see you again*?"

"What do you want?" I demanded.

"I want to know what I did that was so terrible to make you totally write me off. You dropped me like I was a piece of garbage, without any explanation at all. What did I do to deserve that?"

I wasn't about to be goaded into another one of his manipulations. "Jason, it doesn't matter. You are just not my type. Now move."

"It does matter," he said, not moving. "Did I take you to the wrong movie that night? Was that it?"

"I said move!"

"Just give me a chance. One more date. I promise, I'll treat you like a princess." His voice wasn't whiny, but there was a decidedly childish quality to it. I saw and heard him for who he was -- a manipulator. Nothing that came from his mouth was sincere. There were only moves and counter moves in his deceitful game.

"We will never go on another date again. You will never be my boyfriend. Get out of the way!" I said, almost yelling.

He leaned in closer, once again crossing the boundary of my personal space. "I'm not going to move, because you're not listening to me." His calculated calm exterior strained to contain a growing rage within. I saw a wild and dangerous gleam in his eyes.

My heartbeat was palpable. What if he tries to get in, pushes me over and drives us to the back of the parking lot or someplace worse?

"You need to listen to me, Becca . . ."

I turned the ignition, threw the gear shift into reverse, locked my eyes on the rear view mirror, then pushed down on the gas pedal. The Jeep lunged backward several feet. Jason shuffled alongside, still holding onto the door. I thought for sure that would get him to relent, but instead he seemed to take pleasure at my reaction to his antics.

"Hey! Don't you run me over. I'll call the cops," he laughed, wickedly.

I hit the brakes, having retreated just far enough to change direction and swerve around the hatchback in front of me. Jason stepped back, fully extending the door, then slammed it shut with tremendous force. The entire Jeep shook.

"You know, it's not safe to drive with a broken mirror," he jeered, hurling his fist downward and striking the side view mirror, knocking it out of alignment. Without even thinking, my right hand found the pattern, up, left, left, up. The transition was instant. The Jeep's rear tires squealed as I dropped the clutch and stomped the gas pedal to the floor, pushing me forward.

He tumbled to the pavement as I pulled away. The Jeep's engine roared in approval.

I knew I hadn't hit him. Why did he fall down like that? Should I stop, or was this just another ruse? I was afraid and didn't know what to do. My hands were tight on the steering wheel. I kept driving, checking my rear view mirror every few seconds. He wasn't following me. Through the traffic light. Up the hill. Left turn. I started to breathe again. Sharp right. Heart racing.

With sufficient distance between us, I pulled over at the first opportunity, camouflaging myself among the other vehicles in front of the Piggly Wiggly until I calmed down.

The next day at school, I was on edge again, trying to avoid contact with Jason while simultaneously looking for my mystery girl. It wasn't that I did anything terribly out of the ordinary. I simply started paying more careful attention to the clues and behaviors around me.

I promised myself that I wouldn't let the search become my ruin. I needed to keep a level head and remain on guard to prevent another run-in with Jason. Still, it was hard to prevent the implications of that note from consuming my thoughts. I was no closer to finding this girl, and the danger she represented was staggering.

I had managed to avoid Jason all morning, at least in person. But that didn't stop him from blowing up my phone with text messages:

> *3:25 AM.*
>
> *Jason: Hey, sorry I got upset yesterday.*
>
> *3:48 AM.*
>
> *Jason: Becca, can we talk? I promise I'll be a gentleman.*
>
> *5:17 AM.*
>
> *Jason: You looked really pretty yesterday.*

... and so it went. I never responded back to him.

When lunch rolled around, Nora couldn't wait to tell everybody the story of Jason and J.D. following us out to the parking lot. Jeff came unglued. Mark literally had to hold him back from rushing off to find Jason and confront him. Thank goodness Mark was there.

I was pretty sure that if Jeff had found Jason, it would have been bad. Jason would have clobbered him. The two of them were probably about the same height, but Jason was way more filled out, with great big biceps and pecs, plus an extra forty pounds of fat on him. Years of conditioning as a football lineman, plus an extensive body of work as a class A bully, would no doubt be an insurmountable advantage.

Jeff had muscles too, only his build was much leaner. His legs were really ripped and defined from playing soccer, but not so much on his upper body. He had a visible six pack, but only because he had practically zero body fat. I saw how cut his abs were one day when he lifted his shirt to wipe the sweat off his face during soccer practice.

After school, Jeff walked with Nora, Stephanie and me out to the parking lot. I told him he didn't have to do that, but he really looked worried, so I didn't argue the point. I wished that Mark would have come along too, just in case Jason paid another surprise visit.

We stood next to my Jeep watching Jeff inspect the loose side mirror.

"Oh, guess what I heard," Nora said. "Poor helpless Valarie had car trouble this morning." She exaggerated a slow motion wink. "So she called Blake and asked him to give her a ride to school."

Everyone looked at me for a reaction.

Nora continued. "He was already at school when she called him. She wanted him to leave campus to go get her."

"Oh she is shameless," Stephanie gasped. "He didn't do it did he?"

"Word is, he did. But that's not even the best part. Mandy, in my bio class, told me that Valarie was planning to get Blake to ditch school and stay at her house with him . . . alone."

"But they were both at school today, right?" asked Stephanie.

"Yep. So only part of her horrid little plan worked."

"Uh . . ." Jeff interjected. "You know Nora, people do have car trouble now and then. It is an actual phenomenon."

"Pa-lease," she snapped. "You know nothing about women." She wagged her head at Jeff while speaking, like it was a giant finger scolding him. "You should actually be taking notes, not debating me on every single thing I say."

Jeff looked away, shaking his head.

"Right there. That's what I'm talking about. If you would pay attention to what I'm telling you once in a while, you might actually get a girlfriend of your own some day."

A defiant look formed in Jeff's eyes. It was the same look he gets in a soccer match when an opponent beats him one on one. I jumped in to prevent the train from derailing any further. "Did Mandy say anything else?" I asked.

Nora smiled. "She said she's pretty sure Blake delivered the *let's just be friends* speech a while ago." She looked straight at Jeff. "That's why Valarie has been working overtime trying to win him back."

Jeff appeared to be ignoring Nora. His eyes were searching the parking lot. I wasn't sure if he was even listening to us anymore, but then he pointed and said, "Oh look, there goes mister wonderful right now, with his little liar girlfriend right next to him."

Blake's shiny silver Mustang blinded me, as it caught the glare from the sun. I could hear the distinct low rumble of its engine approach, as he followed the line of slow moving cars exiting the parking lot. By the time the Mustang was next to us, the bright glare had subsided and was replaced by a sight far worse -- Valarie.

The expression she wore said everything. It was something like the look of triumph a conqueror might wear, at having vanquished a rival. But it was more than this. It conveyed the sort of ugly satisfaction that comes not from defeating an opponent, but from rubbing it in their face.

"Oh my gosh," Nora gasped. "Did you see that look she just gave you?"

Jeff searched for my reaction, but didn't say anything. All of his irritation with Nora melted away. His body language and expression made it instantly clear to me that he was concerned for my feelings above anything else.

I wasn't wounded in the ways they probably expected. I didn't feel jealous over Valarie riding in Blake's car. What I felt was something else.

I didn't want Blake to be with me because of guilt, or a sense of duty, or because of any trickery. Manipulating him into being with me held no allure at all. I wanted him to choose me . . . because he wanted to, and for no other reason.

If Valarie made up the story about her car being broken down just to get Blake to spend some time with her alone, then there was nothing for me to be jealous about.

What was frustrating was having to watch this go on, and wait to see it play out. Blake seemed oblivious to the intricate web she was spinning around him, hoping that she'd be able to trap him for good. Why couldn't he see her scheming the way I did?

"Hey," Jeff said. "Do you guys want to get out of here? We could go get some ice cream or something."

Nora sighed. "Really Jeff?"

"Why not? I think DQ has a new flavor this month."

"I can't keep eating all of this junk food like you do." Nora playfully poked him in the stomach. "Where do you put it? You should be like five-hundred pounds by now."

"I can't," I said. "My mom asked me to run something out

to my dad's work."

"Me either," Stephanie groaned.

"Jeff," Nora said, with a pouty face. "I'll come, but only if you'll split something with me." She started searching through her purse for her keys.

While she was looking down, Jeff rolled his eyes at me. I smiled. I knew exactly what that look meant. Nora wouldn't eat just half of whatever they ordered. She'd do a lot more damage than that.

"Okay," Nora said, exhaling as if she had just come up for air after free diving into the depths of her purse. "I'm ready," she jiggled her keys. "Let's go."

"See you guys," I said.

Stephanie said her goodbyes and hurried off. Jeff's feet were anchored in front of me.

"Well come on," Nora grabbed him by the arm.

He shook his head.

"Oh." Nora sighed. "Becca, he's not going to leave until he knows you have safely driven out of the parking lot without any threat of Jason around."

Normally, I might have been irritated with Jeff for treating me like I was weak and helpless, but the way he was looking at me, at that moment . . . there was something uncommonly noble, and pure about it. His chocolate brown eyes seemed even more sincere than usual. Jeff was a genuinely good guy.

I hadn't ever seen him look at me quite that way before. It felt nice. Possibly, for the first time ever, I had seen him as someone other than a brotherly figure, no longer relegated to the friend zone that I had always placed him in. My eyes left his gaze. They had already lingered there too long. I wasn't supposed to be thinking of Jeff that way, and refused to give myself permission to do so. I quickly turned and got into my Jeep. As I drove out of the parking lot, those thoughts about Jeff remained behind, trapped within the tall fence that surrounded the school campus.

CHAPTER 17

Becca

I loved driving my jeep. It suited me. It wasn't too fancy, but versatile and comfortable in a favorite pair of jeans kind of way. When I had cancer and was stuck in bed for what seemed like eternity, I always dreamed of being able to get outside and go somewhere, anywhere . . . maybe up into the mountains, or to the beach.

For some reason, in this little fantasy of mine, I pictured myself behind the wheel of a red Jeep with the top down, the wind in my hair and the warmth of the sun soaking into my skin. It's funny because I had never ridden in a Jeep, or any other kind of convertible, but I somehow knew exactly how it would feel, and I longed for this dream to become reality.

When I was fifteen, I had come to accept the likelihood that there were many things I would never have the chance to experience first hand: Driving a car, going on a date, having a first kiss . . . and so many other firsts were for me, going to be nevers. After we moved to North Carolina and I started this new life, I slowly began to give myself permission to hope for these things again.

A couple of weeks after I got my driver's license, Dad handed me a set of keys and told me to go look in the driveway. There it was -- my red Jeep. It wasn't new, but I have never thought of it as used. I've always preferred to think of it as broken in.

It was perfect. When I saw it I cried uncontrollably. I was

overwhelmed with gratitude, and joy, and with the realization that I was going to have the chance to live my life after all. My emotions had been subdued for so long, that when the release finally came, it was like a dam bursting. I found it impossible to explain these feelings to my parents through my tears.

Fortunately, I didn't have to. Mom took my hand and began crying herself. Dad gave us both the biggest hug and kissed me on the forehead. No words were spoken, but in that moment I understood that this red Jeep was much more than a car. It represented all of their hopes and dreams for me, as well as my own, which had nearly been lost. It symbolized my new life.

Driving myself to the middle of nowhere was one of the many dreams I couldn't wait to finally experience. In North Carolina, I soon learned that lots of places were in the middle of nowhere. As I looked past my hands gripping the steering wheel, over the dash and through the windshield, I marveled at the wide expanse of the Carolina landscape. A lone road sign went sailing past me, indicating that I was exactly halfway to the middle of nowhere, which was where Dad worked.

The endless sky above me was filled with swirling blues and purples. I watched as it slowly retreated from thick darkness encroaching on the distant Eastern horizon. It was beautiful. As dusk arrived, I pulled over to the side of the road and soaked in the last moments, staring up into the sky. I grabbed my ball cap and pulled my ponytail through the back before slipping on the big comfy sweater I swiped from my brother. The evening air was a little too cold for me to be driving with the top down, but I couldn't help myself.

Dad worked in the tiny town of Faison. It had exactly one stop light. On the right was the grocery store. Across the street was an old time drugstore that had probably been there since North Carolina was a colony. Next door, and very out of place, was a brand new service station. It looked inviting, but

I'd never stopped there. The price of gas was crazy high. Come to think of it, I'm not sure I had ever noticed a customer at that service station.

Just past the stop light, stood a spacious hotel. Its large parking area was flanked by fast food restaurants and a few small businesses. This may sound like a forgettable and insignificant place to visit, but concealed nearby was a heavily guarded government-run mini-city where thousands of people worked daily.

Faison used to be a quiet farming town with quaint southern charm, where everybody knew their neighbor's business and their children's names. An old sign painted on the drugstore wall used to read, 'Welcome to Faison, where there are more acres than residents.'

Ever since the government bought up all of the farmland and turned it into a secret research facility, people started joking, "Welcome to Faison, where there are more cameras than people." From stationary units on the ground, to drones in the sky, the saying was true. The government had every inch of this place under surveillance.

All of the old timers were gone. It was no secret that the government employed everyone who still lived in Faison. Ironically, now it was the government who knew everybody's business, their children's names, and probably even monitored what they ate for breakfast. This town, once small and quaint, was now the hub for one of the government's most guarded research programs, and it was all because of Dad's breakthrough discovery -- psychocedent transfer.

"Fame is a cruel punishment," Dad often said. He had gone to great lengths to remain in anonymity. By now, most of the world had heard of psychocedent transfer, but they'd never heard of its inventor. No matter whether they loved it or hated it, most people credited the creation of this procedure to the government.

In the eyes of the world, Dad was a faceless man behind the scenes. Just the opposite was true in Faison. Around here, everyone knew him and a lot of people respected him. But there were still those who remained skeptical. Transferring a human's soul from one body to another, had become a divisive topic.

I didn't think that Dad ever anticipated that his work might result in anger or outrage. Confronting criticisms and recognizing that his work had been the genesis of an ethical dilemma on an epic scale had weighed heavily on him.

For most people, the discovery and dilemma were still abstract ideas, but in Faison, there was no mistaking the tangible realities. Each day, as Dad drove to work, he was reminded of the men, women and children who had been uprooted and displaced. The fertile farmland which had given life to new crops and new generations of farm families for nearly two centuries, now sat idle. The lives, the history, the dreams of the people and their connection to the land had all been replaced by the interests of a single government program.

It didn't happen overnight. It took many months for this transformation to fully manifest itself. To the casual observer, only noticing the world from one moment to the next, this kind of government intrusion is inaudible, invisible, and impossible to comprehend. Only by taking a step back does the big picture come into focus.

The size and weight of this program crushed everything in its path. Once in motion, the government was a relentless, unstoppable force with its own gravitational pull on whatever remained standing nearby.

At some point, Dad came to realize that regardless of how noble his intentions had been, the reality was that he had become trapped himself, under the very forces his discovery had caused to descend upon this little town in the middle of nowhere.

In Faison, everyone from the person flipping burgers at the fast food restaurant, to the drugstore clerk ringing up people's energy drinks and aspirin, were all government employees. The town had been completely taken over. Not a single tobacco or cotton plant grew in the rich soil. No corner farmer's markets. No ma and pa shops.

Once the residents saw what was happening to the place, they chose to leave. Everyone was paid a hefty sum for their land, but the complete takeover of this place had to have been devastating for them.

The only hotel in Faison was built by and for the government. It was never intended to be used by the general public. Dad said that the hotel was closed to visitors for security reasons. The only approved hotel guests were government employees, procedure patients and their families, and VIP guests -- high ranking government officials, foreign dignitaries and the like.

My family and I stayed at the hotel for exactly forty-eight hours after my procedure. All donor recipient patients had to stay there after their procedures to be closely monitored during recovery. Sierra had initially been excited about staying in a hotel that had both an indoor and outdoor pool, but her enthusiasm evaporated quickly when she discovered that there was no slide or diving board. I couldn't go swimming, because the swimsuit I packed was too big for my new body and it didn't seem like the type of place where I could wear a T-shirt and shorts to swim in.

Every inch of the hotel was extravagant. In the lobby, there was a shiny black grand piano. Someone was usually playing it. The beautiful sounds of classical music filled the air in the spacious lobby from sunrise to sunset. The large, ornate chandelier that hung from the skyward ceiling had hundreds of crystals that glimmered and sparkled like they were dancing to the music.

We ate all of our meals at the little restaurant located right inside the hotel. It was the fanciest place I had ever seen. The wait staff all wore suits with black ties and never let a glass go empty, or a used plate intrude too long. Each place setting had more pieces of polished silverware than a single person could possibly use.

It was in that restaurant that I ate my first meal after the procedure. I looked over the menu carefully, considering all of the delicious foods that I had craved, but that my body hadn't been able to tolerate for a very long time, due mostly to the aggressive medications I had been taking.

I settled on a steak, ordering the best cut on the menu, medium rare. When our meals arrived, everything looked perfectly delicious, but from my first bite, it was a disappointment. It didn't taste nearly as good to me as I had remembered steak tasting. The flavor was weird. The texture wasn't quite right either. Medium rare actually seemed kind of gross. How had I ever liked that?

I sipped my water and stared at the juicy lobster Mom had ordered. Funny, I used to loathe seafood, but now my mouth positively watered for it. Mom ended up trading meals with me when my steak arrived. That was the night lobster became my new favorite.

Dad arranged for me to get a massage at the hotel's full service day spa. I used to be very ticklish, but after my procedure, I didn't seem to have that problem. Mom, Sierra and I got manicures and pedicures. I stared at my hands and feet that day, probably more intently than the woman doing my nails. I was trying to memorize what they looked like.

It must have been frustrating for the lady trying to apply

the hot pink nail polish on twenty moving targets, but I felt like I had to keep wiggling my fingers and toes to make sure that they were really mine. Mom gave the lady a generous tip for all of the smudges she had to fix.

On my drive to Faison, I always knew I was getting close when I started seeing Department of Homeland Security officers parked on the side of the road about every couple miles. Their dark blue SUV's, with black wheels and no hubcaps, were obviously out of place on this landscape.

This was the part I didn't like about the drive. I knew those officers didn't write speeding tickets, but seeing them there always made me feel anxious. Instead of enjoying the painted sky, my eyes kept checking the speedometer and rear view mirror.

Even though I had been there several times before, the entrance to the government facility was far too easy to miss. I had done that the last time I had driven by myself. There simply weren't any obvious landmarks -- no neon signs, and not a single building visible from the road. There was only this unassuming little side road off of an old country highway, unremarkable except for the fact that its asphalt was a slightly darker shade than most.

After making the turn, a small square sign with government lettering came into view. It was impossible to read such tiny print from a moving vehicle, but it confirmed that I had made the correct turn.

As I headed down that darkly paved road, an unmarked Homeland Security vehicle crept up alongside me. The tinted windows were so dark that I couldn't see who was driving. It stayed in my blind spot and remained there until I stopped at the first security checkpoint.

I didn't understand why we had to do this same dance every time. I arrived at the first checkpoint and handed the guard my visitor ID card, issued to me months ago.

The first and last security checkpoints were small. The kind with a building big enough for two people but no more than one chair. The entrance was gated off, and everyone who entered had to stop because it was always barricaded. This first security screen didn't bother me much, because they just swiped my ID card, made sure my face matched the picture, and then raised the gate and retracted the spike strip on the road so I could pass.

As I pulled through the gate, the unmarked vehicle stopped. Its headlights illuminated the inside of my Jeep as it turned to head back in the opposite direction.

After a bit more driving, my next stop came into view. Armed military police stood out in front of me, signaling me where to pull over. This was the main checkpoint. The one I hated. There was a gated entrance, just like at the previous checkpoint, but the building here wasn't small. It was two full stories and as big as a typical corner pharmacy store. The walls appeared to be made of cinder blocks, painted white and there were hardly any windows. It looked like a storage building, rather than a place intended to be inhabited by people for any duration.

As I pulled up, I rolled down my window, and for some reason I smiled at the man in the uniform. I think it was my nerves getting to me. I wasn't happy to see him. Not in the least.

"Leave your vehicle running, Miss, and please step out," directed the man in the uniform. He opened my door and motioned me into the building. "Right this way."

As I entered through the large, metal double doors, I glanced back at my Jeep. The bomb sniffing dogs were already inspecting it. I sat down to remove my shoes, then plopped them onto the conveyor belt to be X-rayed.

I handed a lady my purse and she began going through it. When they inspected bags and purses, they took everything out. They opened little zippered pouches, took off caps of lipstick, smelled any lotions or hand sanitizer. Seeing all of the trash being pulled out of my purse made me really wish I had cleaned that out before I came. I didn't know how I had fit it all in there to begin with.

I walked through the metal detector, almost holding my breath. Thankfully, it didn't beep.

Another uniformed officer handed me back my shoes. "Here you go Ms. Tanner," he said.

I nodded in response, then sat down to put my shoes back on, noticing the pristinely polished combat boots he was wearing. His boots had way too many holes to lace up.

I walked over to the woman who had been going through my purse. She didn't have any makeup on and her hair was cut short. Her shoulders were broad. The features of her face seemed hardened -- dark eyes, straight mouth, muscular jaw.

"All set," she said, surprising me with an unexpectedly delicate, high-pitched voice.

I paused, curious at her rugged outward appearance in contrast to her delicate inner voice, then realized that I had been staring at her a little too long and forced a smile as I reached across the table.

She handed me my purse, but then stopped and pulled it back slightly. "Didn't I see you here a few days ago?"

"Yeah, I came with my mom for my doctor appointment," I replied.

She looked me up and down, her eyes scanning over me with what was probably the same look I had just given her, then handed over the purse. "Welcome back," she said.

I clutched the purse under my arm and headed out of the building at a much quicker than normal pace. One armed soldier had remained next to my Jeep, his eyes following me with intensity and purpose as I approached.

He reached to open my door, his large hand swallowing up the entire door handle. "Have a nice day," he said, stepping out of the way. I climbed inside my Jeep and he shut the door.

It always happened this same way. I wished they wouldn't say anything at all during the whole routine, because when they tried to act polite, it sent me the opposite message. It was like they were reading from a script and this was their millionth time through it. They could care less if my day was nice or horrific. They were just repeating their lines.

I was told there was a separate entrance for employees. I'd never seen it, but Dad said that it was almost as bad as the visitor's entrance. I didn't know if he just said that to try to get me to stop bringing up my disdain for the security situation.

I could hear a clear, patterned, loud noise being repeated as I started driving again. It almost sounded like a machine gun firing. Then I saw its silhouette through the bright spotlights fracturing the darkness ahead of me. A helicopter was coming in for a landing. Its rotor blades beat against the air in a violent, rhythmic pattern. I watched as it lowered straight down in a slow, easy descent.

I passed one more small security checkpoint, but they didn't make me stop. The guy at the gate waved me right on through.

I took a deep breath and relaxed my grip on the steering wheel. I could finally see office buildings coming into view. Street lights guided me the rest of the way in, under what was turning out to be a dark overcast night without a hint of light from the moon or stars.

There were buildings that spanned as far as I could see to

my right, my left and in front of me. They varied in size, shape and to some extent in color. Each time I visited there seemed to be a new building under construction, threatening to outdo the one built before it. The most recent building had a roof garden and was completely environmentally self-sustaining with the latest in technological and environmental research.

Buildings were identified with letters from the alphabet - A through L. The building my dad worked in was building E. It was a big black building with dark windows on every side, fifteen stories tall.

It seemed strange that all of these buildings and all of these people were necessary for carrying out Dad's work. I suspected that there had to be other things going on here. When I asked Dad about it, he said that the government had a lot of projects and that he didn't even know what they all were.

Not only were there office buildings and laboratories on the campus, there was also a designated housing area where top employees could live if they desired. Dad said that he didn't hesitate to turn them down when they offered to build him a home. They tried to convince him that it would be the best place for his family to live, but he told them that they would have to chain him to the home to make him stay, because nothing short of that could make him do it.

For the employees that didn't hold prestigious positions, there were government sponsored housing options available in the towns nearest to Faison, which consisted of apartment-type homes. They were small and plain, yet highly affordable and convenient.

Since the employees had to spend so little on rent, a lot of them drove expensive cars. The parking lots here were full of luxury vehicles and exotic looking sports cars. That probably explained why J.D. had been snooping around Faison. He was probably looking to steal car stereos or hubcaps or something.

The government tried to supply everything the employees might want or need, right on campus. If my family did live here, within Faison's walls and gates, we wouldn't have had to leave the fortress for much at all. There was a school, day care, medical and fitness center, a small grocery store, several cafes, parks, and a small cinema. Mom was almost convinced to live here, but Dad never was. I was with Dad on this one. No matter how perfect things seemed to be, it couldn't make up for the sense of confinement and lack of privacy. It may as well have been a prison.

It was hard to see at night, but the office buildings were surrounded by lush, green grass and perfectly trimmed hedges. The landscaping was intricate and precise. When the facilities workers cut the grass, they left perfect diagonal lines on lawns that remained green year round. Unique fountains, scenic walking trails and outdoor sculptures complimented the wide variety of trees and plants on the beautiful grounds. Colorful flowers were always in bloom. Workers would remove the old flowers, even before they withered, and replace them with new blooms, selected specifically for each season.

Other than the security checkpoints and surveillance, this place appeared to be utopia. Since it was such a beautiful place, then it should follow that I'd feel peace and serenity here. In theory, it should have been comforting to know that all of the extreme security measures were keeping the bad guys out. But I never quite felt relaxed until I left, for some reason.

Call it paranoia, intuition, or whatever, but each time I came through those checkpoints I feared that I might be trading unfettered freedom for blind security, for the very last time. It was hard to get inside this fortress. If the people Dad worked for had a reason to do so, they could easily make it impossible for anyone to get back out.

I drove up to Dad's building and headed inside, feeling more at ease because I would soon be with him. The first thing I usually noticed when I stepped into the lobby were the black floors, because the room was enormous and there weren't enough pieces of furniture to fill up the space. The floors reminded me of the exterior of the building -- hard, strong and dark.

The lobby's ceiling reached all the way to the top story. Heavily tinted windows ran along the wall opposite the entrance, from floor to ceiling. During the day, the bright sunshine and lush green vegetation outside always looked dark and gloomy from the inside. The lobby was the intersection point for the two sides of the building, connected by expansive balconies, which served as walkways connecting the east and west wings.

The furniture was modern-looking, made of leather and in bright primary colors. Modern paintings hung on the walls. The subjects painted were unidentifiable and foreign looking, like something from a nightmare. At the center of the lobby was a large fountain filling the air with sounds of violent, crashing water.

"Hello Ms. Tanner," the receptionist said, as she watched me sign in on the visitor's log. She handed me a temporary ID badge, unique to that building. "Good to see you again."

"Thanks," I said as I clipped the badge to my shirt.

"I'll let them know you're on your way up." She picked up the phone, wedged it between her chin and shoulder and pressed a couple buttons, never seeming to take her big round eyes off of me.

My shoes clacked against the hard floor as I turned and walked, echoing almost as loudly as the sounds coming from the fountain's crashing water. I pressed the up arrow button and stepped back to wait for the elevator doors to open.

Back toward the building entrance, the receptionist was still staring at me, her narrow, pale face in full view. When we made eye contact, she adjusted the serious expression on her face to a kindly smile, but her eyes remained fixed on me like one of those surveillance cameras on the grounds. The awkwardness of her undivided attention made me feel uncomfortable, just like everything else about this place, with the exception of Dad and the top floor where he worked.

This place was eerily absent of activity tonight. It seemed as though the receptionist and I were the only two people in the building, yet the parking lot still had some cars in it.

Inside the elevator, I pressed the button for the fifteenth floor. It took me straight up, not stopping at any other floors, announcing my arrival with a soft ding. The doors parted and I felt as though I was stepping outside into nature's arms, as my feet sunk into the lush forest green carpet.

Flowering plants and vines hung at different points from the ceiling, billowing over from their containers. Some plants were in decorative pots mounted on the walls -- wide, tear-shaped leaves draped over the sides. The darkening sky rested heavily against the dome shaped skylights that lined the ceiling.

I walked through the hall and toward Dad's office. The secretary wasn't at her desk, so I passed right by and knocked on Dad's closed office door. There was no response, so I turned the knob to see if it would open. It was locked. I pushed against the door and turned it again, but still no luck.

"Where is he? He knew I was coming," I grumbled to myself. I plopped myself down in the secretary's chair, thinking I would just wait until Dad came back from wherever he had gone.

I shoved away from the desk, then spun myself in a

circle, pushing with my feet. After a number of revolutions, I noticed some filing cabinets against the wall. I spotted a particularly tall inviting one in the corner. All of Dad's patient files had to be stored somewhere. I guessed they were in those drawers. When he was about to see a patient, he would ask his secretary for their file, and she would retrieve it for him, from that very spot.

If I were right, then the girl at my high school who wrote that note would be in one of the files. The details of my mystery girl's identity were literally within reach! I knew I shouldn't snoop, but this was too incredible. It had to be fate or something. I pulled on the drawer, but it wouldn't budge. Dang it.

Still, my mind was now racing with possibilities I had not previously considered. What else might be inviting itself to be perused?

I slid over to the secretary's computer, grabbed the mouse and clicked. She was still logged in. I opened the documents folder, scanning quickly through all of the file names, looking for anything that might point me toward patient records. My heart started to race.

I kept one eye on the screen and the other on the hallway, waiting for anyone to round the corner. Dad's secretary might be back any second. She wouldn't have left herself logged in if she didn't intend on being right back.

There were so many files to scroll through. Would I even find anything? The rush of adrenaline pulsing through me intensified. I couldn't let myself get caught. I had to be quick.

Even though I hadn't planned on snooping, I knew in the back of my mind that this was my best chance for finding out who wrote that message on the school's computer. I wouldn't have to look at everyone's personal information. The date of the mystery girl's procedure had to be the same as mine, or very close to it. Once I found a list of patients, all I would have to do is search the dates for the month of October last year, looking for any familiar names.

I came across a file titled, 'Patient Background,' and immediately clicked it. Yes! Names were listed in alphabetical order, according to last name. I scanned down the list of names. My hands started to tremble. My breathing was quick. Anderson, Ashworth, Baker, Cannon, Cole, Curt, Damon, Delaney, Everson, Jackson, Jones . . . none of those sounded familiar. I kept reading. Kemp, Kimbrel, Kirk . . .

I heard the elevator ding. I quickly started closing the windows I had open. My hands still shaking, heart pounding in my chest. Please don't come around that corner. I closed the last folder and darted across the room, toward Dad's door, putting distance between me and the evidence.

A short, older woman appeared. "Oh!" she said, surprised. "Hello. You must be Becca. I'm Natasha," her head nodded as she spoke. She placed her hand on her chest. "You gave me a little startle. I didn't know you were in here," she said as she walked over to her desk to set her mug down. "Your father said that you would be stopping by tonight to drop off some papers, but it's so late that I didn't know if you were still coming."

I pointed to his door. "My dad isn't in his office."

She tilted her head. "He is very sorry that he couldn't be here to see you. He was called into a last minute meeting." She pulled out her chair and sat at her desk.

I wasn't surprised to hear this. It's not the first time that I had come out here and not seen my dad. When this sort of thing happened, I always tried to remind myself of all the good he had done, and all of the other people he helped.

"Your father left this envelope. He said it's for your mom." She held out a large manilla envelope stuffed with papers. "Too bad you had to drive all the way out here just for this, but unfortunately he's going to be working through the night."

"Okay, well, thanks. . . . I better get going." I couldn't wait to get out of there. My heart was still pounding like a drum.

She looked up at me. "Uh hun, was anybody else in here when you came in?"

She must have seen something out of place! I managed to give my shoulders a half shrug. "I-I just got here."

"Right," she said. Her look was more serious than before. "Can I get you anything . . . a drink, or a snack?"

I wasn't sure if she wanted to keep me there and was bribing me to stay, or if she wanted me to leave and was offering me parting gifts. I saw a flash of lightning out the window behind her.

"No, thank you," I said, already heading toward the elevator.

She called to me, "You look like you're doing quite well, Becca." I turned back around, curious why she said that. "You are one of the reasons why he works so hard, you know. You are a testament to all the good your father does, and I am so glad that I can work with him. He's a wonderful man." Her eyes scanned over me.

Lightning flashed again, this time I saw a streak of light zig zag across the sky.

I nodded, then continued backing toward the elevator again. Just as I pressed the down button, a loud boom of thunder shook the building.

"Oh dear," she said. "That was close. Be careful on your drive home. It sounds like a nasty storm out there."

"I will," I said mashing the button again. Elevator, hurry

up!

Another loud strike of thunder crashed.

"Oh my poor Charlie," she called out. "He's going to be so scared. I need to get home to him." She ran back toward her desk, still talking loud enough for me to hear. "Charlie's my dog. He absolutely hates thunderstorms, he just--" She stopped mid-sentence. "What is this? Wait a minute. This doesn't look right. Why is this here?"

Crap! I hurried to smash the button again. Did she know? Was she going to call security on me?

Then the elevator arrived. I quickly slipped through the parting doors, veering straight over to the first floor button and started mashing it wildly until the doors closed.

Racing through the lobby, I tossed my visitor's badge onto the now vacant receptionist's desk, and hurried toward the door. The heaviness of the air met me as I exited the building. It felt much warmer than before, because the humidity had settled in. There was still no moon out tonight. The clouds must have been really low. I saw another flash of lightning fracture across the sky in the distance. My hurried walk turned into a full sprint. I struggled to breathe in the thick air, as my feet pounded against the hard asphalt.

CHAPTER 18

Becca

Dropping my Jeep's convertible top down and driving with the wind in my face always felt exhilarating. Trying to put the top back up . . . that was an entirely different kind of excitement, particularly with a thunderstorm approaching and maybe even someone from security on his way.

It normally took me a solid five minutes or more to get the top fastened, zipped, snapped, latched and velcroed in place. I had done it enough times that I could complete every step in order, from memory, but that didn't mean it was easy. Most steps required both hands and had to be performed while standing outside the vehicle.

Even under ideal circumstances, I would have been hurrying to get out of here, but there was nothing like the motivation of a thunderstorm and Dad's suspicious secretary to encourage a record setting time. The first drops of rain arrived as I was finishing up, dampening my hair and clothing, but the Jeep's interior remained dry, and I was on my way.

Once through the security checkpoints and out of Faison, I drove as fast as I could, trying to stay ahead of the storm, only slowing down when I saw a Homeland Security SUV, or another vehicle on the road.

Judging by the frequency of lightning flashes in the storm behind me, I knew the rain I was currently catching was only the warm up phase. The main event was still headed my way, and it would be much worse. Soon, it would fall in buckets, roads would flood, thunder would crash and lightning would strike wherever it pleased.

A deafening boom and another flash of lightning exploded. This one didn't leave a streak across the sky. What I experienced was a brilliant bright flash all around me, like someone had flicked on the light switch in a dark room, then immediately turned it off again. I cranked up the radio, against the deafening noise of the rain hitting the top and metal surface of the Jeep. Crashes of thunder still pounded through the music and shook the air around me.

There were no more streetlights. The lines on the road retreated from the heavy rain, making it hard to see where I was going. I turned the high beams on, hoping they would help to reveal my path ahead. The light coming from my headlights reflected off of sheets of rain that seemed to be hanging, suspended in the air in front of me, like silver strands woven upon a black canvas.

Driving down this stretch of lonely back roads in the daylight, with the sun shining, would have offered up an endless vista of picturesque farmland. It was still too early in the season for crops to be planted, but when the farmers prepared the soil in this part of the county, I could see row after row of perfectly mounded soft dirt, laid across the abounding flat expanse.

Every few miles there were abandoned homes and barns along the roadside. It was hard to believe that these rickety old structures remained standing. Windows were missing, broken or boarded over. Holes in the roofs and spaces between the boards of the exterior walls had been overtaken by vegetation.

Whenever I drove past these old buildings, my mind's eye filled in the missing and broken parts, renewing them to what they might have looked like when they were still young and vibrant.

These broken down homes and barns didn't leave the landscape looking unsightly. Rather, there was something beautiful about their condition. There was a story behind each of these places -- a history that was probably once grand. Families, and maybe even generations had lived their lives within these walls, and under these once safe and sturdy roofs.

I wished I could enjoy that view right now. With the thick darkness around me, all I had to look at were the things coming and going nearby, like the repetitive yellow dashes on the road, sporadic sets of white headlights, blurry, red tail lights, and the occasional reflective glimmer of a passing road sign.

A loud clap of thunder cracked, temporarily silencing the music from my radio. I was reminded of Dad's secretary and the frightened dog she wanted to get home to. If only I had been given a couple more minutes on her computer, I might have found the name I was looking for. I hoped she didn't suspect me of snooping around in her documents, and if she did, I hoped she wouldn't say anything about it.

A knot in my stomach kept twisting tighter and tighter, knowing that the longer it took for me to find out who this mystery girl was, the closer I would come to having my secret exposed. The things she had written were full of anger. She seemed determined to do me harm. But to what lengths would she actually go? The not knowing felt like torture.

I didn't understand how she could want to hurt someone who she had so much in common with. She had lived in this same body for seventeen years. Didn't she feel any kind of connection now? All of her old memories -- birthdays, vacations, school, friendships. Every cherished memory had taken place in this body. I hadn't been there, but this body had, and now it was part of me.

There must be some small portion of love she still has

for this body, I would hope. But that all depended on the type of person she was on the inside. Was it delusional to entertain the thought that maybe she didn't really mean all the things she wrote? Maybe she was all talk. Maybe she was just blowing off steam the day she wrote those things. I had to consider the possibility that she was actually a good person, and would never really do anything to harm me. She wouldn't actually be plotting revenge, just for being in the body she hadn't wanted. Right?

Thoughts of this mystery girl quickly left my mind when I saw a vehicle approaching from behind me at an alarmingly fast rate. I checked my speedometer to make sure I was driving under the limit. When I looked up again, the vehicle was already on my bumper. I slowed down a little, not sure if it was a cop.

There weren't any oncoming cars, so whoever it was had a clear shot to pass me on the long straight stretch of road ahead. I slowed down even more, but couldn't coax the driver into passing me. Turn after turn, they stayed right on my bumper, uncomfortably close.

My eyes bounced between the road ahead and the rear view mirror, over and over again, but I couldn't make out what kind of vehicle it was. It was too dark, and my Jeep didn't have a rear wiper to clear the window.

I slowed well below the speed limit. With every curve in the road, my unwanted company remained practically glued to my rear bumper, never falling too far behind, and sometimes getting so close that I lost sight of the headlights below my rear window.

My heart thumped faster, harder. I knew something was wrong. Whoever this person was . . . they were trouble.

I kept driving, turned off my radio so I wouldn't be distracted, and checked my doors to make sure they were locked. I felt around for my phone inside my purse, trying not to take my eyes off the road. After some digging, I grabbed hold of it and set it in my lap.

Several more miles flew by and the vehicle behind me didn't budge. I had sped up, slowed down . . . nothing got this guy to leave.

The windows were getting foggy, so I turned on the defroster. Rain poured out of the sky in buckets. My wipers were already on full blast.

Thunder crashed loudly. I jumped, causing the vehicle to swerve, then struggled to regain control due to the high water on the road.

Home was still miles away, but what was I going to do if this vehicle didn't leave me alone? I couldn't pull into my driveway and let this maniac behind me see where I lived. I thought of stopping at the fire station near McGees Crossroads, but remembered it was a volunteer fire company. This time of night there would only be vehicles, no people. I couldn't think of a single well lit gas station or busy store to stop at -- not down these roads.

I took a deep breath, but it didn't help to calm my nerves. I could feel my neck tensing up, my hands ached from how tightly I had been gripping the wheel.

A flood of light shot up behind me. It wasn't coming from headlights. My pursuer had turned on some sort of light bar mounted on the roof. It was so bright that I couldn't see anything out my back window. The glare from my rear view mirror was blinding. My foot smashed harder onto the gas pedal.

The driver behind me started flashing his lights on and off. My eyes strained to stay focused. I could hardly tell where the edge of the road was. The Jeep jolted forward to the left. He hit me! I gasped, gripping the wheel and fighting to straighten back out.

My hand trembled as it reached for the cell phone in my lap. My left arm strained to hold the wheel steady while I dialed with the other hand. I put the phone on speaker, and waited. But the call wouldn't go through -- no signal.

He laid on his horn. My arms jerked, and the phone flew. My Jeep hydroplaned across the shoulder of the road, massive amounts of water spraying up. The tires tore into uneven ground, causing the Jeep to bounce uncontrollably. My whole body slammed against the seat belt. I pulled the wheel hard to the left and slammed on the brake. The Jeep bounced along, then jumped as the tires made full contact with the road again, causing it to go into a hard spin on the wet pavement. After a near full rotation, the tires regained traction in the middle of the road, miraculously facing the right direction.

My heart was racing, and I was practically gasping for air. I glanced down, over and over, until I spotted my phone as my shaking foot held down the gas pedal. I gripped tight to the wheel and leaned over toward the passenger side floor. My fingers made contact, and I grabbed it. I hit redial. Oh please, let this call go through!

After several seconds, the phone finally rang.

"9-1-1, what is your emergency?" the operator asked.

"I'm being followed. Someone is chasing me in my car, trying to run me off the road. They are right behind me. I need help!"

The operator started asking me questions, and I was trying to answer her with as much information as possible, but I didn't know how to tell her where I was. I had been so distracted, that I hadn't paid attention.

Then the realization hit me -- there probably wasn't a cop around for miles. My heart sank.

"Ma'am? Ma'am? Are you there?" the operator asked.

I knew I was going to have to do something myself. But what? I couldn't outrun this guy. There was nothing I could do to get him off my tail.

Then the vehicle started to make a move, like it was going to pass me. Adrenaline pulsed through my body.

"Hold on," I said to the operator, then set the phone down in my lap. What was I going to do if the driver pulled up next to me? He'd be able to see me, and there wouldn't be anything I could do to get away.

The vehicle switched into the other lane. It sped up, almost next to me. I looked over, but he stayed back just far enough to remain in my blind spot. I slowed down. He slowed down too, never moving from that spot.

I saw headlights approaching in the lane that he was in. He stayed there. What was he doing? The oncoming vehicle blasted its horn. My heart pounded in my chest. I punched the gas, trying to get away from the impending disaster. Both vehicles laid on their horns, but the driver beside me still didn't move.

The oncoming lights were getting closer. I started screaming, as I pushed the gas pedal harder, but it was already to the floor. The car ahead flashed its lights. The engine next to me continued to roar. "Get off the road!" I yelled to the driver up ahead, knowing he couldn't hear me, but I didn't care. "He's going to hit you! Move!" Suddenly, lights flashed up, blinding from behind me. My pursuer finally moved out of the way and was back on my tail. The oncoming car sped past, horn blaring. I could barely take in enough air with each breath, yet I managed to exhale in relief.

Immediately, the vehicle behind me jerked back over to my blind spot, then swerved back and forth from lane to lane behind me. I kept my speed constant, not knowing what else to do. This guy was toying with me, not trying to pass, never getting more than a couple feet away from my bumper. I was afraid of what he would do next.

I grabbed my phone and wedged it into the crack of the passenger seat, then gripped both hands onto the steering wheel. I maintained my speed until he was in my blind spot again, then I slammed on the brakes and turned down a side street.

He hadn't been able to react in time and sailed past me. Finally! But, I wasn't about to wait around to see if he was coming back. I had turned into an unfamiliar residential neighborhood and knew I had to be careful not to get lost. I didn't want to end up being cornered somewhere if he did come back.

After a couple of quick turns I pulled over, hoping my Jeep would blend in with the other cars parked on the street. I turned everything off, including my wipers. It was still raining, but being able to see clearly wasn't the most important thing at the moment.

I picked up the phone and started talking to the 911 operator again.

It didn't take long before headlights approached from behind, so I slid down in my seat just far enough to peek over the dashboard. Rain pounded on the roof. It seemed as though blankets of water had been draped over my windows, taking any visibility away. I put the phone down again and sat there, quiet. Waiting. Listening.

The distinct rumble of the vehicle's loud engine let me know it was getting closer. My chest tightened. I slipped down even lower in my seat. The engine roar kept growing louder. I sat in pitch dark silence, practically gasping for air. The engine was so loud now, that I knew he was right next to me. I fought the urge to scream. If he was coming to get me, I wanted to jump out and run, but I couldn't risk him seeing me. He might not have known that I was still inside the Jeep. All I could do was wait.

I sat there, trembling in fear, slouched down, practically on the floor. The louder his engine got, the harder I shook. I hated not being able to see. What if he was getting out of his vehicle right now and heading over here?

Ever so gradually, the sound of his engine started to fade, and I gasped for air again. He had passed, but hadn't gone far. I could still hear him. Waiting. Had he blocked me in? Was he coming for me now?

I grabbed the steering wheel and pulled myself up, just enough to see out my front window. The blurry red tail lights of his vehicle were only a couple houses in front of me. From this angle, I could see that it was some sort of dark colored truck or SUV with big lights on top.

My pursuer was slowly disappearing into the rainy night. But just as I was starting to feel hope, the blurry red tail lights flashed bright. I sat up in my seat, securing my grip on the slippery steering wheel.

His brake lights went off and his backup lights came on as he sped toward me in reverse.

I screamed. Nobody could hear me, except the lady on the phone.

I cranked the ignition, then the wheel, and punched down on the gas pedal. Tires spun and squealed until the Jeep gained traction. I made a U-turn, smashing against the curb, going up and over, tearing into the lawn, then plunging back down onto the street again. My foot shook as I kept the gas pedal floored, hoping to outrun him. I drove out onto the main road as fast as the Jeep would go.

I didn't look in my mirror any more. All I wanted to do

was get away.

The Jeep flew like a rocket, almost hydroplaning a few more times. Either I would keep speeding and possibly get in a wreck, or slow down and get caught by the guy following me. I chose to keep speeding.

I took a deep breath, wiped the sweat away from my forehead, then finally looked up in the mirror. All I saw was dark. No more headlights.

Several more minutes passed.

I watched intently in my rear view mirror. Lights approached, so I sped up again. My heart pounded in my chest. The lights turned. I breathed deeply, full of relief. Every vehicle on the road was him. This was what terror felt like.

Another vehicle approached. Its speed was incredibly fast. The headlights flashed bright. It pulled right up onto my bumper. I started to panic. Lights on the roof blazed again -- the same ones! It was him! My foot slammed down, trying to press the gas pedal through the floor. Then everything behind me went dark, like he had turned off all the lights on his truck. I couldn't see him.

Was he still behind me? I passed a streetlight, watching in my rear view mirror. It illuminated everything around me. There was no sign of him. He had vanished.

I eased up on the gas and continued toward home, unable to fully calm down. Only a couple of miles to go.

Up ahead, the signal turned red, and I came to a stop. There were more cars on the road here. I nervously inspected each one of them.

Relief finally washed over me, when I reached the last intersection before heading into my neighborhood. I stopped at the stop sign, looked around, then went.

From the left side of my car, out of nowhere, came the terrible engine noise of my pursuer's truck! I whipped my head toward the sound. The truck's engine roared, then lights glared, hitting me straight in the face. I stomped the gas, as his horn blew. I braced for impact, holding my breath, closing my eyes.

His horn screamed past, just behind me. I opened my eyes, then exhaled, absolutely stunned that I was still in one piece. I thought I would die.

Still in shock, I sped down the street to my house. My pursuer must have already known where I lived. He had planned to ram me at that intersection. He knew exactly where to wait and got there before I did.

Was I even safe in my own home?

This couldn't have been a random chase. I felt certain about that. What I wondered was, exactly how long had he been following me. Did he tail me on my way to Dad's work? Had he been behind me the whole time? My stomach was nauseous. What did this all mean?

I turned down the second street to the right, my street, and sped to the end, where our three story, red brick house sat, at the center of the cul-de-sac. The exterior lights were on. A police vehicle was parked in front. My shoulders finally relaxed, jaw unclenched. Mom was standing under the porch with the policeman. I couldn't believe it was finally over. Mom came running out to the car. We hugged for a long time.

I wasn't able to give the officer a definite description of the vehicle that had chased me, except that it was a truck and could have been dark blue or black. One thing I knew was that the engine had a distinct, loud sound. I knew I could recognize it if I ever heard it again.

The officer's radio started buzzing with chatter. He reached over to his shoulder and turned the volume down. The sleeve of his shirt crept up on his wrist. A portion of his skin that had previously been covered by his long sleeve was now in view. His skin was full of tattoos. My eyes followed to his other hand, as he lifted up his pad of paper. Similar tattoos were on his other wrist as well. A small gust of wind blew through the air, sending the scent of cigarette smoke off of him and over to me.

The gaze of the officer's dark eyes was unsettling to me. I folded my arms across my chest, trying to fight off the uncomfortable feeling. Was he interested in me . . . or was it something else?

When I finished answering his questions, I went inside and took a long, hot shower. I wrapped my wet hair up in a towel and put on my most comfortable pajamas but still couldn't relax.

"Becca," Mom called as she knocked on my bedroom door.

"Yeah?"

"Your father called. He wants you to wait up for him. He should be home soon."

"Okay."

I knew Mom had already talked to him on the phone and told him everything that happened. Why did he still want to talk to me?

I took the towel off my head and twisted my hair up in a bun to keep it from getting my clothes wet. I could feel my stomach knotting up again. What if his secretary said something to him . . . what if he knew that I had been snooping on her computer?

I went downstairs and turned on the TV, trying to take my mind off of things. It was almost eleven o'clock. Mom walked in wearing her pink fluffy robe with a bowl of popcorn in her hands.

"Are you hungry?" she asked.

I was too nervous to be hungry. I shook my head, then looked at her. "Do you know why Dad wants me to wait up for him?"

She sat down next to me. "He probably wants to see that you're alright."

"But didn't you already tell him I was fine?"

Her eyebrows furrowed. "Are you too tired? Have you already taken your nighttime pill? I know how drowsy that makes you."

I wished I had taken it. "No, not yet."

"He told me he canceled whatever he had been working on. He's already on his way home. But I'll tell you what, if he doesn't get here in the next half hour, then you can take your pill and go to bed. I'll let him know you were too tired."

Mom sat with me until her popcorn was gone, then we went into the kitchen to empty the dishwasher and talked a little more. The rain was coming down hard outside, but I hadn't noticed any more lightning.

We were still in the kitchen when I heard the front door open, and the knocker clang against the metal as it shut.

"I'm home," Dad called out.

He walked into the family room, a concerned and tired expression on his face. His pale blue eyes were surrounded by fine red lines. He sighed in relief when he saw me and gave me a big hug. My wet hair pressed against his cheek. I felt my stomach ease up. Maybe he did just want to make sure I was alright.

He took a deep breath, then kissed the top of my head. He asked me a few questions, wanting to know if I was sure

I couldn't identify the person who had followed me. I kept telling him that it was too dark. Finally satisfied with the explanation, he walked over to the closet and hung up his coat. He slid off his shoes, groaning in relief, then sat down in the oversized recliner across from me.

He appeared as though his job was aging him faster than the hands of time would do on their own. His hair seemed to be thinning more. I could see the shiny bald spot on top of his head peek through as he bent over to peel his socks off. The original jet black color of his hair made the patches of gray stand out -- his sideburns were almost completely white. He looked like he hadn't shaved in days.

Before he reclined his chair, he leaned towards me. "Becca," he said. "If something like this ever happens again, I want you to call me, not the police. My job comes with certain perks and one of them is top of the line security. I can send agents to help you. They'll do a much better job than the police. They have more resources at their disposal. The government takes any threats to employees and their families very seriously." He shook his head, then reclined his chair. "I was afraid this kind of thing would happen." Dad stared off, deep in thought. "I don't know if I'll be able to keep all of you safe. Maybe it was foolish of me to think we could live a normal life."

"It's not foolish," I said, hoping to derail his current train of thought. "We are living normal lives. And I don't want anything to change about that. Whoever followed me tonight . . . it might not have had anything to do with what you do for work." I fidgeted a little with the pillow behind my back, thinking about what to say next. I knew I had to contain this before drastic decisions started being made. "Dad, it wasn't that bad. I probably overreacted." I shrugged my shoulders. "It might have been a couple of kids out for a joy ride."

I really didn't believe that. I didn't think I had

overreacted at all to what had happened. I had every reason to believe I was going to be abducted, maybe killed, or at the very least injured in an accident . . . but right now I was more terrified of something else -- Dad moving us away, to live in Faison under lock and key, or somewhere worse.

Dad pointed at me with all ten fingers at once. "You need to promise me you'll call me if something like this ever happens again, Becca. If I'm not available, then tell my secretary it's an emergency. She'll know what to do."

Mom came in and sat next to me on the couch. "Your father's right. We need to make sure that you kids are protected by the most capable people."

What could I say to calm their fears? I didn't want to lie, but I also knew that if there was a next time, I probably wouldn't call Dad. I'd rather try to handle the situation on my own. I should have never called the police. All that did was point them in a direction that was every bit as frightening to me.

I shook my head. "I am aware of the security you have at work, Dad. I was reminded of that tonight when I went to see you. I think every inch of my purse was searched with a magnifying glass, not to mention the intense examination my dangerous looking shoes were subjected to. Luckily, it turned out they weren't a threat, so I didn't have to go barefoot."

Mom folded her arms, her hands disappearing into her fluffy robe. "This is serious, Becca." She turned to Dad. "I'm not sending her out on any more trips to your work again by herself. I should have never sent her tonight."

Dad looked even more tired than before. I knew he was ready to call it a night, and so was I. They hopefully weren't going to make any rash decisions tonight, like moving, or keeping me from driving places by myself.

"I'm really tired," I said. "Can I go to bed now?" I wanted

to move on from the topic. The only thing I could do was to excuse myself so that I could go to sleep. Dad would understand that, and he'd probably even be relieved at the suggestion.

"Go ahead, honey," he said. "I know it's late. . . . Don't forget to take your pill."

"I know," I said. I hugged them both goodnight, then headed back into the kitchen.

As I filled up a glass with water, I could hear my parents talking in the other room. I swallowed my pills, then stood close to the doorway to listen.

"Do you really think that what happened to Becca had something to do with work?" Mom asked.

"I didn't want to worry you, but there have been some incidents involving other researchers."

"What kind of incidents?"

"Now, don't worry. Nobody has been hurt. There have just been some minor things like mail stolen from mailboxes, computer hacking attempts, that sort of thing."

"Why didn't you tell me sooner? Are we still safe here? What are we going to do?"

"Nothing has happened so far. We have a good alarm on the house. The mailbox is locked. I've got firewalls on the computers."

"But what about what happened tonight with Becca? What if--"

"Janet," Dad said calmly. "What happened tonight was probably nothing. Becca knows now to call me if anything suspicious like that ever happens again."

I felt relief hearing Dad say that. I wasn't sure if he truly believed that everything was okay, or if he was just saying that to calm Mom down, but either way, it was good to hear. I knew I would have to be extra careful not to upset the fragile balance between safety and security that existed within our family. Mom and Dad needed to believe that I was not in any danger. And I was going to make sure that happened, even if it meant that I had to keep more secrets.

CHAPTER 19

Darla

When I learned Becca had been subject to a high speed pursuit on her way home from Faison last night, I understood why her father arrived at work early this morning, looking so upset.

He gave his secretary strict instructions to prioritize calls from his family over all else. Next, he placed his personal security team on high alert, warning of a possible threat to his family. He even arranged for twenty-four hour surveillance outside the family home.

By seven this morning, the security detail assigned to Dr. Tanner had already been beefed up, but this wasn't due to his request. Rather, the order had already come from higher up.

A special meeting was held. Afterward, I overheard him talking to Becca's mom on the phone. He told her that the government was practically insisting that they move their family to Faison, but he had managed to convince them that the increased security would be enough, for now.

I wondered if Becca's father knew that the government would try to move his family after finding out about the incident. From the onset of the meeting, he seemed overly anxious to present an image of calm and control. It was as if he was anticipating how his bosses would react and was trying to assure them that further action was not necessary. I wondered if he was motivated by Becca's desire to stay put, or if there was some other reason he didn't want to move his family to Faison.

I also wondered if the increased security would be enough to keep her safe.

CHAPTER 20

Becca

"The great thing about mornings is that they usher in a fresh start. No matter what happened yesterday, each new today begins fresh and full of possibilities. What lies ahead is still unknown, waiting to be discovered." That was the quote hanging on my bathroom mirror.

My morning had been surprisingly uneventful. I was having a good hair day. The first outfit I picked out was a winner, and I remembered both my lunch and my homework. Even traffic was uncommonly cooperative. The other drivers on the road were courteous, and most of the light signals I came to were green. To top things off, the sun spread out across a great big clear sky. All of that should have made for the start of a perfect day . . . only it didn't.

Last night, I woke up about every hour -- tossed and turned, faded in and out of sleep. There was no need for the alarm to wake me this morning, because from about four until six, sleep managed to evade me all together.

I was still on edge. Afraid. My neck and shoulders ached from the tension I had been carrying, and due to lack of sleep, I was drained of energy. To sum it up, I'd have to say that I felt pretty much violated and completely stressed over the events of the previous evening.

While driving to school, I think I spent more time looking in the rear view mirror than at where I was headed. Every time I saw a dark colored truck on the road, or heard a loud engine, my heart jumped and so did the Jeep's gas pedal.

I didn't feel ready to hazard another day at school, dodging Jason and hunting for my mystery girl. At least not by myself.

A couple of miles from school there was a small cafe where Nora and I often stopped for something quick to eat. Instead of our usual booth, I sat at a small table for two in the corner, facing the door. I didn't feel nearly safe enough to leave my back turned to the other customers coming and going.

On the table in front of me was a plain bagel, toasted, with cream cheese and a diet Dr. Pepper, both of which had barely been touched. An open book lay next to my food. I wasn't reading. I tried, but just couldn't concentrate on it. My eyes scanned the words, but my brain refused to process them.

Though I had a rough idea what the truck from last night looked and sounded like, I had absolutely no clue who had been driving it. And that's what was so deeply troubling to me. I felt like I was going to lose my mind.

Every person who entered the cafe, every sound, every movement, caught my attention. I hyper focused on a myriad of unimportant things.

Most of the people who visited this little cafe were probably following their normal daily routine. Some were headed to work. Others, like me, were on their way to school. But I had no way of determining friend from foe. A kind smile was no indicator of true intentions. I stayed alert.

On the door a little brown bell hung from a frayed string. It swayed back and forth, announcing each patron's entrance or exit.

A short man with slicked back hair strolled in. His phone was glued to his ear. Beneath it, a shiny gold watch peeked through his sleeve.

A few seconds later, the bell rang again. A woman burst through the door, seemingly in a big hurry, wearing a tight fitting skirt that came to her knees. She got her order to go, like the man on the phone.

Across from me and down a table, two ladies wearing workout clothes were deep in conversation. Whatever they were discussing had fascinated the woman in the skirt enough to eavesdrop openly while she waited for her order.

The smell of fresh baked bread and pastries filled the air and wafted onto the street outside, keeping a steady stream of customers filing in and out through the heavy double doors every couple of minutes. A brisk pace was nothing unordinary for the employees who buzzed around behind the counter like bees in a hive.

Through the window, I saw a blonde approaching far down the sidewalk. Her head was turned toward the street, so I couldn't see her face. I hoped it was Nora. She was supposed to meet me here and was already ten minutes late. At a distance, the blonde's height and body shape looked like a match, but her walk was odd. Nora had a bad habit of squeezing into shoes she said were too cute, when what they really were was too tight. So, I couldn't confirm or reject on the basis of a funny walk.

At last the blonde turned to face the doors as she pushed them open. Nope. It wasn't her. I slouched back down into my chair and decided to give the book another try.

I managed to read through a couple pages without any distractions. That was, until I heard the bell, followed by a commotion at the door. I looked up.

A feeling of dread settled upon me as I watched, not one or two, but an entire group of well-dressed girls make their way through the double doors. They were noisy and flashy, like a flock of pink flamingos, but without the natural grace. It didn't take long before they caught sight of me, and their noise turned to hushed whispers. The girls practically froze in their tracks, until Valarie pushed her way to the front, a confused look on her face, as she lifted her sunglasses up onto her head.

One of the girls in the group pointed at me accusingly, like she was tattling to her teacher. Valarie's eyes halted and rested on me with a thud. Her rose colored lips pursed together so tight, they practically vanished from her face, while her big beautiful eyes narrowed disdainfully, transforming into a thin glob of clown-like mascara and eyeshadow.

Ugly gossip was being disseminated back and forth between these girls faster than the announcement of a new fashion trend, but Valarie didn't speak a word. She stared at me with an expression on her face so ferocious, I thought for sure she was about to come charging at me, like some wild animal, with the entire pack by her side.

If only the book in front of me was titled, 'What to do when a group of mean girls are giving you dirty looks and you are by yourself.' But I wasn't that lucky.

I had to think of something quick. Only two possibilities came to mind:

Option one -- look away and pretend that I didn't notice them.

Option two -- stand up, march right over there and have it out with Valarie in front of everyone.

The choice looked like it was going to be made for me. It quickly became clear that Valarie and her friends had no intention of ignoring me, or allowing me to ignore them. Option one was not a realistic possibility.

I reminded myself that Valarie had this coming to her. I wouldn't be in the wrong for blasting her with whatever came out of my mouth. Could I summon the courage for option two?

If it weren't for the fact that there was only one of me, and a whole pack of them, I might have actually been brave enough. But standing up against all those girls at once was terrifying.

Still, I couldn't just back down like a complete coward. I stumbled upon a third option -- a middle path, and stared back at them, determined to convey an expression of unflappable indifference on my face.

Outside I was all steely resolve, but inside I was as fragile as a glass house. On top of the unwanted and unpleasant emotions I had been battling recently, this latest confrontation with a pack of mean girls was propelling me dangerously toward a tipping point.

As casually as I could, I lowered my book, keeping my

eyes on the group of girls, staring through them, not at them. I tried my best to keep my expression blank, aloof, bored. The truth of the matter was, I felt extremely intimidated, and no matter how hard I tried to fight that feeling, I couldn't shake it. I had to look away or risk them detecting a crack in my facade.

I pretended to keep reading my book, catching glimpses of them now and then, hoping that they would hurry up and order their food, so that they could leave.

One of the girls grinned wickedly and began whispering something in Valarie's ear. Devious smiles appeared. Then more words were exchanged. Heads nodded.

Valarie pulled her dark sunglasses back down over her eyes, flipped her long blonde hair and turned to walk to the counter, rummaging through her designer purse for some money. The mean girls followed, all except for one -- she was headed straight toward me.

At first, I thought she had a surprised look on her face, but upon closer examination, I realized that her eyebrows were drawn on that way -- high and arching, like two parenthesis that had fallen over. Despite her misguided makeup job, she was quite cute and had a friendly smile. Yet it was as out of place as her eyebrows. I was confused. What did she want?

"Can I sit here?" she asked, pointing at the chair.

I lowered my book. "Sure."

She pulled out the chair, metal scraping across the tile floor, like nails on a chalkboard. "I saw you the other day at the horse ranch," she said as she sat down.

I remembered seeing her there as well, but I didn't know that she was Valarie's friend. "Oh, yeah. Right. I saw you, too," I acknowledged, trying to sound aloof and unconcerned.

"Blake's got an absolutely amazing place there. Don't you think so?"

I nodded, hesitantly. The ranch wasn't Blake's, and I didn't know if she was confused on the matter, or if she was just using that as a segue to talk about him. Either way, I wasn't about to correct her. All I wanted was for this conversation to be as short as possible. I had monumental doubts about her motives, no matter how inviting her smile.

"We go there all the time," she said. "I hear you're new to North Carolina. So . . . where are you from?"

Where was she going with this? It seemed like a harmless and normal conversation, but I still didn't trust her. "I'm from Southern California."

"Oh cool. The beaches there are so awesome."

"They're pretty nice here, too."

Her eyes quickly scanned over the book in my hands, then to the food in front of me. "So, I've seen you hanging around a couple guys at school." Her forehead creased, yet her eyebrows seemed to stay put. "The one guy has red hair, and the other one has dark hair. I think his name is Mark."

"Yeah, Jeff and Mark."

"Are y'all just friends, or is one of them your boyfriend?"

"We're good friends."

The girl leaned in, as if to tell me something in confidence. "It's just that," she paused and glanced over to her friends. "You see that girl over there with the tan jacket, Valarie?"

"I know who Valarie is."

A slightly mischievous smile spread across the girl's face. "Well, since you're new here and all, you need to know that Blake belongs to Valarie."

"Belongs to . . . as in . . ." I stammered.

"As in they are the absolute cutest and most romantic couple in the entire school." Her words took on a serious, *you better watch it*, sort of tone.

"Strange. I heard they broke up. Valarie didn't mention it?" I baited.

"Oh sweetie. You just don't get it. People like Valarie and Blake aren't like you and your guy friends. What they have is way more intense."

"So you're saying they did *not* break up?" I asked.

"They do it all the time. Break up to make up. Ever heard

of it?" she grinned. "But they always end up back together. Their relationship is . . . complicated."

"Sounds more like arduous," I said, flatly.

She stared back at me with a look of confusion on her face. "So anyway . . . they've been seeing each other going on five months now."

I was surprised. With all of this fuss, I would have guessed they'd been together much longer.

"That may not sound like a long time, but they hang out together almost every day, so it's really more like they've been together for years."

Years? She's gotta be kidding.

"They're even talking about going to the same college after they graduate." She quickly glanced at her friends again. "It looks like we're fixin to leave." She stood up and sighed. "Listen, you seem like a nice person, so I want to do you a favor and give you some helpful advice."

Advice, huh. Now I was really curious. "Go right ahead," I said pleasantly.

"If I were you, I'd stay far away from Blake, especially since you know now that he is *not* available." She leaned in. "You don't want to get on Valarie's bad side . . . trust me."

I didn't trust her, and I didn't want to believe anything she had just told me. "Why are you telling me all of this, and not Valarie?"

She wrinkled her nose. "I'm trying to do you a favor here. I just told Valarie that I was gonna find out if you liked Blake. She'd kill me if she knew I was warning you about her plans."

"What plans?"

"I don't know any specifics," she whispered, "but everything Valarie does, she does big."

"And what does big mean, exactly?"

"Well, the last girl who tried to get between her and Blake got destroyed, at school, on social media, you name it. By the time Valarie got done, that girl didn't have a friend in the world."

"Valarie's plan is to turn my friends against me? That'll never happen."

"Look, Valarie is very skilled at doctoring photos and knows her way around a computer and the Internet better than anyone I know. If she wants you to suffer, she can make your own family hate you."

"Hmm, thanks for the warning. I think."

"Just do yourself a favor and forget all about Blake Pierce."

I sat up straight and looked her in the eye, so that she would understand the seriousness of what I was about to say. "Unfortunately for Valarie, I have an exceptionally good memory, like an elephant. I don't forget the people I care about, and I'm certainly not going to forget about Blake."

Her arched eyebrows somehow became straight, and the friendly smile disappeared from her face. "Elephants are fat, wrinkly and ugly. I guess that means you are, too." She spun around and headed out the door to catch up with the rest of her friends.

I bit my lip to restrain myself from quipping back with a response. I wished that I hadn't described myself as an elephant, but the words seemed to come flying out of my mouth before I could stop them.

I sat there contemplating everything that had been said, and what had not....

The bell jingled again. It was Nora.

CHAPTER 21

Becca

Nora approached me, her expression dripping with anticipation. "Tell me what happened last night. Don't leave out any details."

I didn't want to talk about last night anymore. I wanted to talk about what had just happened with Valarie and her horrible friend. So, that's where I began, and I told her everything, except for the remark about the elephant.

"Hmm," Nora propped her chin on her fist, deep in thought. "She might be bluffing," she finally announced, as if these four words were the complete summary of her analysis.

"Who? Valarie or her friend?"

"Both."

"How so?"

"That girl said exactly what Valarie wanted her to say. I guarantee you that she was instructed on what to tell you. All that stuff about betraying Valarie's confidence, like it was some kind of secret warning . . . I mean really, since when have any of Valarie's friends been nice?"

"I know. Plus, she really didn't tell me anything that I couldn't figure out on my own."

"As far as Valarie ruining your reputation, I highly doubt she could do that."

I hoped Nora was right. It was wishful thinking, but the alternative wasn't pretty.

"If I were Valarie," I said. "I'd want Blake to love me because he wanted to, not because I got rid of the competition."

"Ain't that the truth." Nora broke off a piece from my

bagel. "I think that Valarie's little minion was also lying about something else. Those two aren't getting back together, and Valarie knows it. They broke up for good, and she just doesn't know how to deal with it."

"I'm not sure about that," I countered, "because almost every time I see him, she's there, somewhere, hovering."

"Well she is a vulture, and that's what vultures do." Nora took another piece of my bagel. "Tell me about what happened last night."

I told her about the truck following me. All of the details -- bright lights, dark roads, trying to hide in that neighborhood. I felt the emotions of that moment rushing back, like I was experiencing that same panic again, only with slightly less intensity. I stopped a few times to take a drink and regroup. I told her how the truck drove past me, then started backing up, how I tried to escape, but the tires of my Jeep spun out and I almost didn't get away.

"Do you think it was Jason following you?" she asked.

Here I was, at the part of the story I couldn't reveal to her because of my secret. I wished I could tell her about Dad, what he did for a living, and that people wanted to steal his research, but I couldn't tell her.

"I have no idea who it was," I said. That was true. I didn't know who it was. "It didn't look like Jason's truck."

"Who else could it have been?" she asked. "He's the number one suspect as far as I'm concerned. It's not like he doesn't know how to borrow another person's vehicle."

"True."

"Remember how we saw him driving by the hair salon when we were getting our hair done a couple months ago? He drove by like he was scoping the place out, back and forth, squealing his tires, sticking his fat head out the vehicle's window. Remember how his bugged out eyes were all crazy?" She pointed her finger at me. "He was driving an ugly green SUV that day."

I sat there tearing the rest of my bagel into small pieces.

She made some good points. Maybe it was Jason.

"Why is he so obsessed with me?"

"I'll tell you why." Nora raised her eyebrows. "It's because he's crazy. And as I always say, don't ever try to understand or reason with crazy. The guy has been stalking you for months, and if it was him who followed you last night, I'm worried about what he's going to do next."

I had already been wondering that myself, but hearing Nora say it legitimized my worst fears.

Nora pulled out her phone and looked at the screen. "We've got to get going. I can't be late for school again this week."

"Alright," I said, summoning the will to get up.

Nora bounced over to the counter. "I'm going to get a bagel real quick, if they have non-fat cream cheese. Wait for me."

I took a deep breath and tried to clear my thoughts. It was no use.

At school, the probability of running into Jason, or Valarie, or one of her horrible friends, or the mystery girl who wanted to hurt me, had to be astronomically high. More likely than not, I would tangle with more than one of them before the day was done. The only questions were who, when, and in what order.

Nora and I headed out to our cars, giving me my first answer. Valarie and her friends hadn't left yet. They were all huddled close together in front of her red BMW.

"Oh look, it's the wicked witch and all her flying monkeys," Nora whispered.

Nora had parked right next to me. When we got to her car, she placed her food on the roof, so she could search for her keys. "Dang. All of those girls *are* staring at you. They must *really* hate you." It was as if she hadn't believed my story until verified by independent visual confirmation.

I hurried into my Jeep, anxious to break away from their stares. Nora followed right behind me in her car, all the way to school. We met up with our friends in the parking lot, and I told them about what happened last night and at the cafe.

Mark reached toward Nora's bag of food. "Are you going to eat that?"

She snatched it away. "Don't even think about it."

Stephanie smacked his shoulder. "Didn't you hear what Becca was just saying? She was chased by some crazed maniac and all you can think about is food?

"What? I'm hungry," said Mark, holding his hands out in a gesture of innocence.

Nora pulled a bagel out and took a bite.

Jeff's expression was one of troubled concern. "Becca, are you sure you didn't get a good look at the truck, or the driver?"

Nora held up her bagel as if she was holding up a finger to get him to wait a minute while she finished chewing. "Jeff, she already explained that," she mumbled, still trying to finish her bite. "Please don't ask dumb questions."

"It's not a dumb question, and I'm just trying to help," Jeff retorted.

"Well, Becca's not an idiot. If she saw who the driver was, then she would have remembered it the first two times she told the story."

"So touchy today," teased Mark, grinning through a toothy smile.

"I get grouchy when I haven't eaten, okay," said Nora, taking another bite.

Stephanie wrapped her arm around Mark's, leaning her head against his shoulder. "I'm glad you're okay, Becca."

"Thanks," I said.

"What were you doing driving around in the middle of a storm, anyway?" asked Mark.

"I was running an errand for my mom."

Jeff's arms were folded, his face hard. "Do you think it was Jason?" he asked.

"I'm sure it was him," said Nora, taking another bite.

Mark placed his hand on my shoulder. "But you couldn't

tell if it was Jason's truck?"

Nora moaned. "I thought we went over this. Geez."

"It wasn't his truck," I said. "This truck had those lights on the top of it. The kind that are attached to the roll bar. The real bright ones."

"Who else could it be?" asked Stephanie, slipping her hand into Mark's, pulling him away from me.

We all started walking toward the building. Once inside, everyone went their separate ways, except for Jeff. He turned down the same hall as me. I noticed that he got a haircut recently. I liked it better this way. It was short, except for on the top, near the front. He had it sticking up somehow, only it looked like it did this naturally, because there wasn't any obvious trace of gel or hairspray in his red hair.

Jeff caught me staring at him and gave me a curious look. I scrambled to think of something random to say. "So, how's Collin?"

"The usual. Sometimes sweet, sometimes sour. My mom keeps getting calls to come pick him up from school."

"Why?"

Jeff grimaced a little. "He's a biter."

"Oh."

Jeff shrugged his shoulders. "He has autism. It's not like he has rabies or anything . . . and it's not all the time. He tends to do it more when he gets upset."

"Does Collin ever bite you?"

"What do you think?"

I realized my question was dumb before he had even answered, but I couldn't take back what I had said. "Uh, yeah, never mind."

Jeff looked at the ground.

"Hey," I said. "At least he didn't bite the horse that day."

Jeff didn't respond. I wondered if I had said the wrong thing again. Then I saw his dimples, followed by a big smile. Before long, he was laughing, and so was I. Jeff's laugh was always loud and infectious. I loved it, and I really needed this. It felt like such a huge release. I wanted to stay in that moment. I didn't care if we ever made it to class.

"Do you need to stop at your locker?"

"No, I don't need--" I stopped mid sentence, suddenly realizing that I did need something. "Oh shoot!"

"What?"

"I left my homework out in my car."

"You can run for it, but you won't make it back in time. Want me to go?"

Jeff was always the perfect gentleman, but I didn't want him to do that. I told him I'd figure something out. Luckily, my first block teacher was in a good mood and wrote me a hall pass. The tardy bell was already ringing when I exited the front doors, headed for my Jeep. A couple of stragglers raced past me, on their way inside, but I was otherwise alone.

My parking spot was about as far away from the building as it could possibly be. I tucked the note into my pocket and started walking, wondering if I would spot Blake's car but didn't see it.

When I reached my Jeep, I opened the passenger door and used the seat as a makeshift counter, separating the loose papers from my binder into piles as I searched for my homework assignment. One of the piles spilled over the edge of the seat and onto the floor. With a little more digging, I spotted my assignment and set it aside.

While I was busy collecting scattered papers and stuffing them back in my binder, the noise from a vehicle's engine grew louder in the distance. I hadn't paid it much attention at first, until I felt the unexpected sensation of goosebumps on the back of my neck, and something deep down in my core began to tremble. A wave of impending doom settled upon me -- darkness, heaviness, panic. The sound from the engine was unmistakable.

Because of where I had parked, the entrance from the road to the student parking lot would bring the vehicle directly past me. Frozen in place, next to my Jeep, I forced myself to turn and look in the direction of the sound. There was no uncertainty about what was headed my way.

It was a big, black, four wheel drive truck, with tinted windows and a roll bar with lights on top. This was the same vehicle that had followed me the night before. I climbed inside my Jeep, shut the door and once again crouched down to avoid being seen.

Papers rattled in my trembling hands as I watched the truck approach. My heart pounded in my chest. As it passed by, I ducked out of sight, popping back up when I was certain it had passed. The truck was pulling around to the front of the school.

I slipped out of my Jeep and crept around the back, leaning tight against the spare tire, trying to stay hidden. The truck had come to a stop, but my heart was still racing. I darted to the next row of cars, then another. The truck's engine roared as it sped away from the curb.

A girl! Whoever was driving had dropped off a girl with long, straight dark hair. She didn't look familiar. Her back was to me, and from clear across the parking lot it probably wouldn't have helped even if she had been facing me. She was much too far away to catch any detail. All I knew was that she had gotten out of that truck and was headed through the front doors of the school in a hurry.

I watched her disappear, then turned my attention back to the truck. It was now at the opposite end of the parking lot, heading around the carpool loop. Staying low, I peeked through car windows, watching until it drove out of the lot toward the exit.

I sprinted back to my Jeep, grabbed my homework assignment, and ran as fast as I could toward the building. I had to find out who that girl was.

Homework in one hand and keys in the other, I crashed through the school doors, into the lobby, where three hallways intersected, between massive trophy cases. She could have gone down any one of them. Or maybe, she went to the attendance office. She was tardy, after all. That was it! I ran to the office. A couple of girls were standing at the counter -- hair too short, too blonde. She wasn't here.

I ran back out and scanned the hallways again. There was no time to waste. I went with my gut and took off down the one to my right.

At the end of the long hallway, I had to catch my breath and make another decision. Right or left? There was no sign of the girl in either direction. I wanted to scream. I had lost her.

It was then that I heard a classroom door click shut. It was definitely on the left, only a couple doors down. I ran to it, flung it open and stepped inside.

My eyes urgently scanned over the entire class. The teacher looked up at me. "Miss," she said. "Do you need something?"

I didn't respond. My focus went from person to person. Dark hair. Long, dark hair, I said to myself, searching feverishly for a match.

"Becca," somebody called to me. "What are you doing in here?"

It was a girl I knew from art class, but she didn't fit the description. I moved on.

"Excuse me," the teacher called out, with greater intensity than before.

"Sorry," I said. "I was looking for somebody."

The teacher stood up and started walking toward me. Just then I spotted the girl with the hair. Once again, her back was toward me, turned around in her seat.

"You need to get to your own class, young lady," the teacher demanded.

I ignored her and walked toward the girl, determined that nothing would stop me. I had to see her face.

"Young lady!"

Only a few steps from the girl my heart sank. She had on red pants. Red. The girl I saw getting out of the truck wasn't wearing red. She had on something much darker.

"Did you hear what I said?" The teacher was headed straight toward me.

"Sorry. Wrong class," I blurted out as I turned and hurried out the door.

Once in the hallway, I ran. I didn't even know where I was going, but I was too upset to do anything else. It was pointless to keep trying. I'd never find her. Long, dark hair -- some description that was. It probably matched a third of the girls that went to this school.

I headed back to class, thoroughly dejected, and took my seat.

"Where did you park? Virginia?" my teacher asked.

"Yes," I replied, to the delight of some jeering classmates. They had no idea the kinds of problems I was dealing with.

All I had wanted was to be like them -- carefree, enjoying a normal life like a normal teenager. Well, I was anything but carefree, and about as far from normal as I could imagine.

As my eyes panned across the room, I stopped feeling sorry for myself. All my senses came alive again. There were two girls in that classroom with long dark hair -- Tiffany Greyson and Fiona Phillips. Could one of them be her?

CHAPTER 22

Becca

I drug myself up the stairs to my bedroom, dropped my backpack in the middle of the floor, and with my last ounce of strength pushed the door shut, before collapsing onto the bed. It had been an exhausting day.

Luckily, Jason wasn't at school today, but I still had Valarie and her friends to contend with. Even more dangerous, was the mystery girl, whose unknown plan and identity loomed larger with each passing day. On top of everything else, I now knew that menacing black truck was no coincidence. Whoever had been driving, was just the latest in the growing list of people who wanted to torment me.

I had seen the dark haired girl being dropped off. Had she seen me? Did she know about me? Could she be the same girl who had written that note on the computer? At the very least, she was connected to the driver of that truck -- someone who terrified me, and she was right there at my school, just like the rest of them.

Going the entire day, being constantly on guard at every turn, and from so many directions, consumed all of my energy, and required every last drop of courage I could produce. I was relieved to be home.

I had barely closed my eyes, when my phone started to ring. It was Jeff. I didn't want to talk at first. I thought what I needed was quiet and rest, but as usual, it didn't take Jeff long to have me laughing out loud. I forgot all about being tired.

Whenever I was with Jeff, my troubles always seemed to be a little less daunting. They didn't go away, they just felt less insurmountable. I found it strange how our simple conversations, about a whole bunch of nothing, could have such an effect on me.

Rolling onto my back, my stomach started growling. I looked at the clock. It was a little past six. I realized we had been talking for over an hour, and I was kind of surprised that Mom hadn't called me down to help with dinner.

"Have you eaten, yet?" I asked him.

"Yep, right before I called you. My parents had this church thing to go to, so I made mac and cheese."

"You cooked?" I laughed.

"I'll have you know, I make excellent mac and cheese. You should come over, and try it sometime."

"So did you make it from scratch or from a box?"

"From scratch, of course." Jeff began explaining the finer points of his mac and cheese preparation technique, like a gourmet chef.

Part way through his story, I caught a whiff of Mom's homemade rolls beckoning me from the oven downstairs. Jeff's words became background noise. All I could think of was taking a bite of a hot, fresh roll, and how delicious the melted butter would taste on my tongue. Just as I was about to interrupt him to say goodbye, an almost forgotten thought pushed everything else aside, even the rolls. I couldn't get off the phone. Not yet.

I went over to my desk, opened the top drawer and pulled out a sheet of paper and a pen. Along the top I printed 'Possible Mystery Girls,' then underlined it.

It had occurred to me that my mystery girl might be

right in front of me, but I wasn't even seeing her. I needed to consider evidence and suspects in a much more objective way.

Did she have long dark hair, like the girl who got out of the truck? Maybe, maybe not. The only thing I knew about her, was that the mystery girl had described herself as pretty. She thought her new body was more attractive than her old one -- more attractive than mine. I had been scrutinizing all of the prettiest girls in school, trying to decide if any of them could be her. But what if *my* idea of pretty was too narrow, or too broad. I could very easily be overlooking someone who was a prime candidate, or wasting time considering girls who shouldn't even be on my list. What I needed was an outsider's perspective in this search.

"Jeff, I have a question, and it's not about your mac and cheese."

"Okay?"

"Well," I paused, unsure how to ask the question. "I guess it's more of an opinion, really, but I need to know who you think the most beautiful girls in school are."

Silence. Nothing but a lot of silence.

"Jeff, you still there?"

"Oh, I'm still here," he mumbled, "I'm not answering you, on purpose."

"Come on," I coaxed.

"No. No way," he said, emphatically.

Why was he refusing to cooperate all of a sudden? I knew that any guy could rattle off a dozen names of attractive girls without even having to think twice about it, but he couldn't give me one?

"What's the big deal? I'm not asking you to rank the entire school. Just give me your top five list of the most beautiful girls. Now, go."

"Why do you want to know?"

"Because I'm curious."

He sighed, paused, then sighed again for what seemed like the thousandth time.

"I'm waiting."

"Is this some kind of a trap?" he asked. "You're not going to blackmail me later?"

I laughed. "No, you goof. I just want to know what you think. Are you going to tell me or not?"

"I don't know," he groaned. "This seems kind of weird."

"Weird? So you're saying that I'm weird?"

"No! No, I'm not saying that."

More silence.

The trouble was, Jeff wasn't saying anything at all. I needed his help, and he was the one getting all weird about it, not me.

"Fine," he huffed. "Megan Jones, Cari Petrich, Fiona Phillips, Nora and of course . . . you."

He sure busted those names out quickly. I wished he hadn't wasted two picks on me and Nora, but I wasn't going to press him for more.

His response was actually helpful. I hadn't considered Fiona Phillips. She was the one who had interrupted me when I was reading the mystery girl's note in the computer lab. I was so distraught that day, that I had completely forgotten about her being there until just now. Fiona also happened to have long, dark hair, like the girl I saw getting out of the truck. As for Megan and Cari, I didn't know if either of them were taking technology courses this semester, but Fiona, Fiona was definitely a person of interest. I wrote their names down, with Fiona's at the top.

It was a good start, but I couldn't help noticing that Valarie's name was conspicuously missing from Jeff's list. "Thanks," I said, "but I think you forgot somebody."

"No I didn't."

"Sure you did. I'll give you a hint. She is horrible, and her name starts with a V. V as in vicious."

Jeff laughed. "Is this my list or yours? Because if you're talking about Valarie, that girl is nowhere near my top five. She's *way* down the list. In fact, if this is my list, she's at the very bottom of the last page . . . on the back."

"Really? You don't think Valarie is attractive?"

Jeff buzzed his lips to emphasize his complete disapproval. "That girl is so mean and nasty."

I planted my forehead in my palm. At no point had I asked him to include a personality assessment in this survey. Leave it to Jeff to read between the lines and give me a list based on inner beauty. "Valarie's meanness has nothing to do with what I asked you."

"To me it does."

I knew he couldn't see me through the phone, but I gave my screen an irritated look anyway, as if mental telepathy would convey the idea I was trying to get across to him.

"I see her every day in English class," he continued. "She thinks she's some kind of queen and everyone else is either a peasant or worse."

"And because of that, she's ugly?"

"Uh, yeah."

"Okay. But that's not the list I was asking for, Jeff."

"There's a lot more to beauty than a person's appearance."

"Yes, yes, but I asked you who the prettiest girls were."

"No. You asked me to list the most beautiful girls in school, and that's the list I gave you. Valarie's not on that list."

I didn't know how to respond.

"You have to agree, she's as mean as they come, right?"

"Oh, I think she hates me," I said.

"I know she does," he replied without a moment's hesitation.

"How do you know?"

"Uh . . ." He went silent.

"Jeff?"

"I guess I sort of overheard something. I just got bits and pieces, but Valarie and her friends were kind of mentioning your name, and something about you being after Blake." He let that linger for a moment before continuing. "Oh yeah, she also said that you think you're quote, *all that*."

"Lovely," I sighed.

Someone knocked on my door. "Come in."

Sierra's little head peeked out from behind the door, with one of her pigtails dangling across her face. "Mom said to tell you to come down for dinner." She quickly disappeared back behind the door and pulled it shut.

"I gotta go, Jeff."

"I heard."

"I'll see you tomorrow."

"Wait. Becca?"

"Yeah?"

"I just have to tell you one more thing. You know all that stuff I was saying about inner beauty?"

"Yes."

"If I put all of that aside, you're still way prettier than Valarie, even on her best day."

"Wow . . . thanks." It felt great, being complimented like that, but I knew he was just saying that because we were friends. By any objective measure, Valarie was gorgeous, and I was just average looking.

"And as for Blake and Valarie," Jeff continued, "I don't know what he ever saw in her, but if that's the kind of girl he likes, he's making a monumental mistake. I guess that's what I needed to say. Now go eat your dinner." Jeff hung up the phone.

I didn't know what Blake saw in Valarie either, but it gave me some hope to know that Jeff could look beyond her outward appearance, to see who she really was. I just hoped that Blake could see it.

I headed downstairs, into the dining room, to find my whole family, including Brandon already sitting at the table eating.

"Hey sis. I brought home some of my laundry for you to do," he winked.

The only reason Brandon ever came home from the dorms was to eat and do laundry. "In your dreams." I walked toward Sierra who was patting the chair next to her, inviting me to come and sit beside her. "Did Dad actually make it home in time for dinner? What's the occasion?" I joked, as I scooted my chair in.

There was a little mischief in his eyes. "I snuck out and sped away before they could stop me."

Mom must have known ahead of time that Dad would be home early. She had set the table with the good dishes -- her great grandmother's china. She pointed toward a plate at the center of the table. "The steaks on the left are rare, and the others are medium or well done."

I poked until I found a well done steak that didn't appear to have come into contact with any of the juices from its lesser cooked neighbors.

Sierra raised her hand. "Where are the corn holder thingies?"

I looked over at her plate. Her corn on the cob was swimming in an impressive pond of melted butter. She must have used up a half stick.

"I'll get them," Mom said, as she headed to the kitchen.

Sierra instantly recognized Mom's departure as an exploitable lapse in parental supervision and made her move for the salt shaker. She began vigorously distributing its contents across the surface of her butter pond.

"Becca," Dad said. "Help her with that."

I took the shaker from her, turning it right side up. "That's plenty."

She scowled. "I know how to do it."

Brandon chuckled. "Let her dump as much on as she wants. I can't wait to see her take a bite."

Mom came back in the room, corn-spears in hand. "No, let's not let her do that."

Dad turned his attention to Brandon. "How's school going?"

Brandon was finishing up his freshman year at Duke, but unlike Dad, he wasn't going on a scholarship. The topic of his grades came up frequently whenever he visited, but he usually managed to escape without giving many details.

This time, Dad had him cornered at the dinner table, but the conversation took an unexpected turn in the direction of career possibilities after college -- specifically, jobs within Homeland Security. Dad thought he could pull some strings and get Brandon introduced to the right people for a summer job. "A foot in the door," Dad called it.

We finished eating dinner, and Brandon escaped without committing to anything. Finally, it was my turn. "Dad," I said. "I have a question for you about work. Do you ever do the procedure on people who don't need it?"

"I'm not sure I understand what you're asking?"

"Are psychocedent transfers ever performed on people who aren't sick or disabled?"

He shook his head. "It's still a rare thing. There simply aren't enough donors to meet demand. Maybe someday things will change, but so far the program has only been extended to a tiny fraction of candidates -- those with the most serious terminal illnesses, disabilities or traumatic injuries."

"But what if someone lied to you about being sick, and all they really wanted was to be skinnier, or taller, or maybe prettier?"

Dad placed his elbows on the table and laced his fingers together. "I think I see where you are headed with this. Do you remember all of those examinations Dr. Brimley performed on you before your procedure?"

"I couldn't possibly forget."

"Well," Dad explained, "Every donor and every prospective recipient goes through something very similar to what you experienced. It wouldn't be possible for someone to sneak past."

"So, there are never exceptions?"

"There are differences, of course, depending on the unique circumstances of each patient." Dad leaned back in his chair. "But the answer to your question is no. There aren't exceptions. Before a prospective recipient is selected, we know everything there is to know about them. They are checked and double-checked at every stage. There are no secrets, and no surprises."

I wanted to believe Dad. I trusted him, but what he was telling me didn't make sense. Donor bodies came from people who recently died. Recipients supposedly had serious medical issues. But this body that I had been given was in perfect health, and its previous owner wasn't dead. She was very much alive, walking the halls of my school and plotting to get even with me for a reason I couldn't understand.

If Dr. Brimley was the one verifying the conditions of donors and recipients, checking and rechecking like Dad had described, then he was falsifying patient records. I was walking proof of it. But why would Dr. Brimley lie? Why would he say someone was sick when they weren't?

Mom started clearing the table, going back and forth to the kitchen.

Brandon got up to help her. "You of all people jumping on the conspiracy bandwagon, Becca?"

"No. It's not that. I was just wondering."

"When you get to college you'll find out that a good thesis depends on credible sources. It just so happens, the most credible source in the world is our dad."

Maybe so, but the mystery girl's note seemed pretty credible as well. She knew everything. Was it possible that things were happening Dad wasn't aware of? Doubtful. After all, he ran the place. If anything was going on, he should at least have some kind of suspicion.

It was part of everyday life for my entire family to keep our secret -- my procedure and Dad's identity. I had a few extra secrets that none of them knew about. Maybe Dad had a few of his own as well.

I hoped that our conversation would have gone a different way. I wanted to confide in him, but if I told him everything that had been going on, I was afraid he would freak out like Mom.

The last thing on earth I wanted was to start over in a new place, trying to make new friends. I had to find out who this mystery girl was, before she sealed my fate, if it wasn't already too late. It was just a matter of time before everyone at school would know about me. She had a plan in the works. I didn't know what it was, but I couldn't risk being exposed. She could do it tomorrow, or maybe she had already started a rumor tonight.

Mom picked up the last plate of food from the table. "I know we had a late dinner, so we can leave the rest of the clean up for tomorrow," she said. "Sierra needs to get ready for bed."

I got up from my chair and picked up my plate to take into the kitchen before I headed upstairs.

"Don't forget your pills," Dad said. "It's very important that you don't forget. Remember what Dr. Stella and Dr. Brimley said. You have to take both every day."

"I won't forget."

It seemed like I heard that same reminder daily from either him or Mom. Next thing I know, Sierra's going to be saying it.

I set my plate on the kitchen counter. Should I even trust Dr. Brimley? I had a bad feeling about him at our last appointment. Dr. Stella was no better. I hadn't trusted her from the start.

What if these pills were actually bad for me in some way? After taking them, I always felt tired and weak. I hadn't remembered one single dream since I started taking them -- since my procedure.

In the mystery girl's letter, she wrote about how she still dreams at night, and how she didn't want to dream about me anymore. How was it that she could dream, and I couldn't?

I opened each bottle of pills, taking a little blue one, then a yellow one in my hand. I walked over to the doorway, then peeked around the corner to see where everybody was. They had already left the dining room.

I headed over to the trashcan and stepped on the lever to open the lid. From my open palm, the pills stared back at me. Sierra walked in, giving me a startle. I jumped back from the trash can, concealing the pills in a fist.

"Mom said for you to tuck me in and read me a bedtime story."

"Okay, I'll be right there."

She slowly turned and walked away, shoulders shrugged forward, feet shuffling across the floor. She'll probably fall asleep as soon as her head hits the pillow.

I opened the trashcan again and quickly threw the pills in, then turned to walk away but stopped. I needed to make sure they were out of sight. I opened the lid again, this time doing a thorough visual inspection of the contents. I couldn't see them. I removed my foot from the lever and the lid dropped back down. How long would it take for me to fall asleep? It didn't matter. Even if it took hours, I had made up my mind. I was never going to take them again. They would find their way into the garbage, down the drain, or wherever, if that's what it took.

CHAPTER 23

Darla

I overheard an intense exchange between Dr. Brimley and nurse Olivia. Unfortunately, I only caught the last part of their conversation. Dr. Brimley was angry and nurse Olivia was definitely scared.

I saw his ears turn red. He shot up from his chair, marched over to nurse Olivia, then stood in front of her at an uncomfortably close distance. "You don't know what you're talking about," he said through gritted teeth.

Nurse Olivia held out a file folder, thick with papers. He snatched it from her hands and quickly thumbed through the pages.

"Look at the last page," she said, with deliberate calm. "There is no record of her donor body. Where did it come from? Did it just show up out of thin air? I don't know if you remember, but this is the third time I've come to you with this kind of problem. Something's not right."

Dr. Brimley didn't look. He abruptly shut the folder, then slapped it down onto his desk. "This is a simple mistake. A clerical error." His eyes narrowed. "Nothing more."

Nurse Olivia's mouth was agape, a shocked look on her face. "A clerical error?"

Dr. Brimley reached out and clamped his fingers onto her shoulder, staring at her square in the eyes. "This discussion is over. Do you understand?"

Nurse Olivia hesitated, then nodded, a frightened expression on her face.

Dr. Brimley pulled his hand away, but he wasn't calming

down. "I'm glad you understand." He sat down at a desk and began typing violently on the computer keyboard, no longer giving her eye contact. "You can leave now."

Nurse Olivia quickly left the room. I followed her down the hall. Moments later, another nurse asked her if something was wrong. Nurse Olivia shook her head and said, "Oh nothing, the procedure today was just intense."

The other nurse agreed, then went on about her work.

I never did find out who Olivia and Dr. Brimley were talking about. That folder of papers on his desk had mysteriously disappeared.

What I couldn't stop thinking about, was Olivia's claim that there had been missing information for three donor bodies. Three!

CHAPTER 24

Becca

I stood at the kitchen counter, barely awake, waiting for my toast to pop. It had been a long night of tossing and turning, unable to quiet my thoughts. The last time I remembered looking at the clock, it was two-thirty, which meant I had gotten no more than fours hours of sleep.

Mom was peeling potatoes next to me.

"Are you making hash browns?"

"Not so lucky. These are for dinner. I thought I would throw a few things in the crock-pot to simmer." She looked up from her peeling. "Did you remember you have an appointment with Dr. Stella after school today?"

"I know, and I promise I won't be late this time," I said, trying to sound sincere. The truth was, I didn't want to go to my counseling appointment today, or any other day, ever again.

"That reminds me," Mom said. "We need to get your prescriptions refilled."

"Oh yeah. I forgot to tell you I was almost out of my pills." The thing about keeping secrets is that they can quickly spin out of control. If I was going to keep this charade up, I would need to remember little details like this.

"Dr. Stella might have to authorize a new prescription this time. I'll have the pharmacy call her office and take care of it."

"Why don't you just tell her I'm doing fine and that I don't need to come in today?"

"Becca, we've talked about this."

"I know, but I seriously can't stand her."

Mom shook her head. "You know this part is not negotiable."

I wondered if she would feel the same way if she knew about my mystery girl, and where my body really came from, but I couldn't tell her, and the conversation with Dad at the dinner table last night had only made things worse. His explanation hadn't been comforting at all, and only raised more questions.

I had every reason to believe that Dr. Brimley was involved in my mystery girl's scam to switch bodies. Since Dr. Stella also saw the same patients before and after their procedure, that meant she also had to be involved in the cover up.

Mom tossed a hand full of potatoes into the crock-pot. "I know you don't like having to answer her questions, but try to remember she's just doing her job."

"It's not just the questions, Mom . . . it's the neurological evaluation. She puts that thing on the back of my neck every time, and it makes me feel like I'm going through the procedure all over again."

Mom looked into my eyes. "Sweetie, I have no idea what that must be like for you, but I do know one thing. Your father loves you. If there is a better way, he'll find it, but until then, there's no other way to monitor patients. You have to be hooked up to a DNI transmitter. Your dad, Dr. Brimley and Dr. Stella are all in agreement on this. I'm sorry, but you have to do it."

"Am I the only person who can see that I am fine?" The

stress and frustration I was feeling nearly brought me to tears, but I held them in. "I don't need to be monitored. There's nothing wrong with me."

"You may be right," Mom nodded. "But we're not going to take any chances. Besides, they need the data, Becca, and that is what we agreed to when you were selected as a recipient. Think of it as your contribution to further your dad's research. You are helping other people."

"I think this family has contributed more than enough to this research already," I grumbled.

Mom gave me *the look*. I knew I had better drop the subject, before she moved on to the next level, which was *the look*, plus a longer lecture by her and Dad.

I sat at the table and finished my toast without saying another word, listening to Sierra ramble on about the different marshmallow shapes in her cereal until it was time for me to go to school.

Before I could back my Jeep out of the driveway, I had to stop and roll down my window to adjust the side mirror. The inside controller didn't work anymore, and the mirror itself didn't stay in place ever since Jason broke it. My day had barely started and already I was reaching my limit.

I tried to focus on something productive, going through the list of possible mystery girls in my mind as I drove. Now that I had a list, what I needed was a plan of action.

Just outside the school campus, I caught a red light. With fateful timing, Fiona Phillips pulled up behind me. She must have seen me looking at her in the side mirror, because all the sudden, she gave me a strange look. It was kind of a knowing smile, yet at the same time it seemed patronizing and belittling. She flew past me when I turned into the parking lot, and I lost sight of her. No problem, I thought. I knew where to find her.

My friends were standing in our usual spot, under a big oak tree next to the tennis courts. As I walked toward them, they all turned and stared at me. Even Nora. Something wasn't right.

Jeff could usually be counted on to watch for me, but there was a different expression on his face today -- no smile, no welcoming nod of the head, just a cold, blank stare. Why was he looking at me like that? Why were they all staring at me?

I got out of my car and slowly walked toward them, glancing down at my clothes. Everything seemed fine. My jeans were zipped up, my shirt was buttoned correctly, shoes matched.

Stephanie whispered in Mark's ear, her dark eyes never leaving me. Mark folded his arms. His mouth became straight, tight.

Had the mystery girl exposed my secret? Did they all know that I was in someone else's body? Someone please smile, wave, say something. I didn't know if I could deal with this. What was I going to say to them? What would they say to me? Would they even give me a chance to explain?

Nora was my best friend. She always took my side, no matter who was against me. Would she still want to be my friend? And Jeff. Would he turn his back on me, because I had lied? Would Stephanie and Mark still want to hang out with me, even though it would mean social suicide?

I stepped up onto the curb, stopping several feet away from them. My heart was racing. "Hey guys. What's going on?" I asked hesitantly, looking to my best friend, hoping she would forgive me.

She stepped forward, her hands wedged into the front pockets of her jeans. Her eyebrows drew together. "So tell us."

"Uh, tell you . . . what?"

Stephanie sighed. "Becca, we've been waiting for you to get here."

My stomach started to feel queasy. I wasn't sure if I would be able to keep my breakfast down. "W-why? What's going on?"

Stephanie's eyes widened. "Everyone is talking about it."

The nausea was almost at full force and now the world seemed to be spinning. Please don't let this be happening. Please, no.

Nora shook her head, "Not everyone. Stephanie is exaggerating a bit, but a lot of people are spreading rumors."

I felt my knees start to tremble.

"So . . . are you gonna tell us?" asked Stephanie.

"Did anyone follow you or chase you again last night?" Mark grinned. "We've been waiting to hear."

I took a deep breath, then exhaled in relief. "That's what this is about?"

"I guess that's a no," Mark replied, looking a little disappointed. "No car chase? No late night road rage psychos?"

"I hate to tell you this," Stephanie began, "but somehow the story you told us about that truck tailing you has spread around the school. Everyone is talking about it, but with some uh . . . embellishments."

Mark grinned. "I heard that someone shot at you, and shattered your back window."

Jeff looked over at my Jeep. "I guess whoever told that version missed the fact that the back window of Becca's Jeep is plastic, not glass."

"Well, the version I heard," Stephanie started, "was that

you ran somebody off the road in a major road rage incident, got arrested and then lied to the police."

"Nice one," Mark held up his hand to give a high five.

"But Becca, I know that's not true. That's not the story you told us," Stephanie said.

"Congratulations Becca, you're the latest gossip topic," Mark chuckled.

"Such idiots at this school," Nora sighed purposefully.

"I don't understand how this happened?" I said. "I only told you guys."

Jeff looked around the group, then at me and shrugged his shoulders. "I didn't tell anybody else."

"You *know* I didn't say anything," said Nora.

Mark realized everybody was staring at him next. "Wasn't me."

Stephanie looked at the ground.

"Stephanie?!" Nora fumed.

"I didn't know I wasn't supposed to tell anyone. I didn't think it was a secret."

Nora glared at her. "So who did you tell?"

Stephanie hung her head, avoiding eye contact. "I don't know. Just a couple people in my Marketing class."

Mark shook his head. "Babe. You obviously told the wrong couple of people."

"I'm so sorry," Stephanie pleaded, finally looking up at me.

"It's okay," I said. "Don't worry about it. Really. I can think of way worse rumors."

The conversation continued, as we all headed toward the

building. I had imagined the worst, and glimpsed the fallout I would face if my secret were ever revealed. It left me a little shaken up, but considering what could have happened, I welcomed this lingering feeling of uneasy relief.

I entered my first class and turned to walk down the aisle toward my desk. That's when I saw him. I stopped in my tracks, and quickly glanced around the room to make sure I was in the right place. Students, teacher, room layout -- everything looked correct, except for the guy sitting two seats behind my desk. It was Blake.

His blond hair was sticking up on top in every direction, yet falling perfectly into place. My eyes traced along his hard jaw, then up to his lips. He was looking down at his paper, so I let my gaze linger. He must have transferred into this class. At least, that was what I hoped had happened.

Blake still hadn't seen me. His eyes remained on his paper, his pen speeding from one line to the next.

The tightness and warmth in my cheeks let me know that the involuntary smile spreading across my face was probably more than I wanted to reveal. Any second, he was going to look up and see my hopelessly smitten, thoroughly ridiculous grin. I tried to force my mouth and cheeks to relax a little, but it was impossible.

I hurried to take my seat, trying to turn away before it was too late. Just then, he looked up, directly at me. Busted. The bell started ringing, as if to celebrate the moment his dreamy blue eyes caught me staring at him. Mercifully, he immediately looked back down at his paper again and started folding it up.

I slid into my desk, eyes forward. I could feel my face going from warm to hot. Why didn't I say something? Why did I keep making things awkward between us? Then it occurred to me, he hadn't said anything either. Maybe he hadn't noticed me. It did feel a little like he looked right through me. He could have been in one of those momentary trances, the zoned out, concentrating really hard kind.

The teacher began speaking, but all I could think about was how Blake might be looking at me. There he sat, only a few feet behind me. I couldn't see him, but he could see me. Every movement I would make, every time I brushed my hair back behind my shoulder, raised my hand or leaned over to get something out of my backpack, he would see it all. I wasn't sure how I felt about that.

The teacher called him to the front of the classroom. I kept my head forward, but my eyes looked to the side, impatiently waiting for him to pass by. I heard his steps, then saw his jeans, the lower part of his gray shirt. His right hand inched toward me. A tingling sensation shot through my arm like electricity, as his fingers brushed against mine, leaving behind a folded up piece of paper. I trapped the note between the desktop and an open palm, then slid both hands back toward me and lowered them into my lap as he kept walking.

At the front of the classroom, Blake glanced back at me while the teacher engaged him in a one-sided conversation. Did he want me to read the note right now? I held the paper tight in my hand, wondering what it said. I was about to unfold it, but he started walking back toward me, and I froze.

His eyes met mine, but I couldn't read his expression. There was no smile, no anything. His face was completely blank, giving me no clues about the contents of the note or his feelings. I hoped for a sweeping romantic declaration, but I was also braced for disappointment. Either way, I couldn't wait another second to find out.

As soon as he passed, I opened the note, keeping it low and hidden in my lap. I glanced to the left, and to the right. No one was watching.

Of all the things I could have imagined or hoped for, at

no time did a sketch of a girl being bucked off a horse enter into my thoughts. Blake had drawn me a picture. Was that supposed to be me? It was hard to tell. In fact, I couldn't even be sure if it was a horse. Blake had a lot of attractive qualities, but artistic ability was not among them.

I spun around in my desk and stared at him. It wouldn't take long for the teacher to say something, so I had to make this moment count. Without words, I needed my expression to convey that I was hoping for something more. Blake must have understood. He immediately replied with a hand signal that could only mean one thing.

I turned back around and flipped the note over. There, in small block printing was a phone number and the words, 'text me.' I still didn't know what he wanted to talk about, but who cared. I just got Blake Pierce's phone number!

When class ended, I hesitated in packing up my things, hoping that Blake would stop and talk to me, but another guy near the front of the class had already started up a conversation with him, then a second guy joined in. It would have felt awkward to interrupt, so I didn't.

With the benefit of the full class period to think about things, I had tempered my enthusiasm with a dose of reality. This phone number might not mean anything. If Blake was still seeing Valarie, then I was not about to be his second girlfriend, or some secret fling on the side. I really hoped he didn't think I was that type of girl.

There was no shortage of girls trying to get Blake's attention. He was fun to talk to. It seemed like everyone knew him and genuinely liked him. All the girls agreed he was completely and in every possible way handsome. He was everything I envisioned having in a boyfriend. He was perfect, except for one thing, Valarie.

I had stayed after school to make up a test. After that, I was supposed to go straight to my counseling appointment.

As I sat at my desk, staring down at the yellow number two pencil in my hand, Blake consumed my thoughts. With every multiple choice question, option D read, 'none of the above,' but I changed it in my mind to D, 'Blake Pierce.' I wanted to choose D for every answer.

The closer I got to the end of the test, the harder it became to resist the impulse to rush carelessly through the questions. I paused, staring at the dulled point of the pencil I had sharpened just before beginning. I pressed it down, carefully bubbling in another row on the answer sheet. There was only one more question to go, then I could get out of here. Sadly, I was sure everyone else was long gone by now.

I had hoped I would get a chance to see Blake before he left for the day, but this test had taken much longer than it should have.

I still hadn't sent him a text message. I couldn't figure out what to write. Nora and Stephanie gave me some suggestions during lunch, but nothing sounded right. We did agree on one thing. The hottest guy in school had just given me his number. My very first text to him could not begin with 'Hey' or 'What's up.'

Mark tried to help too, which got a little out of hand, so I had to put my phone away. Stephanie finally gave him her chocolate chip cookies to shut him up.

I thought I'd figure something out before the day was over, but it hadn't happened. Blake was gone, probably wondering why I hadn't texted, and I still had no idea what to say.

I focused on my test again, filled in the last bubble on my answer sheet and handed it in. I was free to go -- free to go see

Dr. Stella. Oh the dread.

I stepped out into the empty hallway. The teacher was right on my heels. I guess I had kept him longer than he expected. He locked his door, then turned and headed in the opposite direction.

A custodian walked toward me, pushing a large broom. A fully packed ring of keys hung from his belt and jingled with each step he took. He smiled and nodded, then continued on.

The hallway was an obstacle course composed of drink spills, loose papers, a torn pep rally banner, food wrappers and other wadded up pieces of trash. Cinder Block walls were plastered with posters and flyers. Random locker doors had been left open. A long row of fluorescent lights ran down the center of the ceiling giving off a glow slightly more powerful than the humming sound they emitted into the otherwise silent space. One of the lights flickered ever so slightly. The others remained steady.

I continued down the hall until the end, then turned the corner and stopped abruptly. Ominous thick darkness hung before me like a curtain. A still small voice whispered from somewhere deep in my soul. It told me to turn around and find another way out.

Reason and experience told me to ignore the warning and keep walking. After all, I had been down this particular hallway thousands of times before. Still, something wasn't right. Maybe it was the decreased visibility, or the eerie silence. It could have just been the overwhelming vacancy of the place. Whatever it was, it had a forbidding feel about it.

The idea came to my mind again, more powerfully this time -- *you are in danger.* I looked over my shoulder, back down the hallway I had just come through, my eyes searching for whoever was behind me. But then, the lights shut off. Darkness surrounded me.

"Hey, I'm still in here," I called out. "Turn the lights back on."

My cry echoed faintly. For several unsettling seconds I waited, frozen in place, hearing nothing but my own heartbeat. The lights remained off.

"Hello?" I called out again.

An eerie feeling seemed to be all around me, and I didn't want to linger any longer than I already had. I started down the black hallway, my shoes echoing as they struck the hard tile floor.

A locker door slammed shut somewhere in the distance. My whole body jumped. I snapped my head around to look but could see only darkness. I took a deep breath to try to calm my nerves. Some other straggler down the hall was probably just getting their homework from their locker, I told myself.

I turned back around and continued walking. The steady sound of my own footsteps filled the dead air once again.

Along with the normal things I always lugged around, I had to bring home two of my textbooks tonight, each one as thick as a dictionary. With a little hop and a tug, I adjusted my backpack on my shoulders, trying to find a comfortable position.

At that moment, I realized something else wasn't right. There were more footsteps than my own.

I stopped walking and listened. I could hear the extra set of footsteps echoing from somewhere behind me. I spun around and stood perfectly still, expecting to see someone come walking around the corner, but the footsteps had also stopped. All I saw was an empty hallway -- classroom doors closed, lockers shut and darkness from end to end.

"Is anybody there?" I tried to call out, but my voice cracked and was barely more than a whisper.

Nobody responded.

I cleared my throat. "Hello?" I tried to speak with confidence, as if I wasn't scared, but again failed miserably.

There was still no reply. The hallway was strangely silent.

I quickly turned around and started walking at a faster pace than before. Please just be nothing, I said over and over in my mind.

The footsteps started up again behind me, only they had picked up in pace matching mine. Once more, I stopped and spun around, my eyes searching through the darkness. Be brave, I told myself. Scare whoever this is away, while you still can.

I inhaled, clenching my fists, ready to take another stab at deterring whoever this was. "I know you're there. Why won't you answer?" I waited, listening, feeling hopeful that my confrontation had scared them off.

But I couldn't ignore the apprehension that was growing inside me.

"This isn't funny!" I shouted as sternly as I could manage, my heart now pounding in my chest.

I tried to think calming thoughts: Maybe whoever it was had stepped inside a classroom and couldn't hear me. Or maybe they had earbuds in and were listening to loud music.

I turned and started walking again, this time at a deliberately easy pace, taking slow deep breaths. I hadn't gone far, maybe a half-dozen steps, when the noise started up again. My entire body was electrified as I listened to the heavy footsteps.

I thought I heard a voice say my name. "Becca." The sound was faint, barely noticeable, yet it was distinct to my ears. Goosebumps raised up on the back of my neck.

I looked straight ahead, feeling almost numb, like I was in the beginning stage of shock, but somehow my legs kept moving. My first instinct was to flee, to get out of there as fast as possible. But at the same time, a debilitating sinking sensation was growing inside me, leaving me with a paralyzing and overpowering feeling of dread for what was about to come.

I was afraid to go another step but even more afraid to stop. I walked faster. The footsteps behind me seemed to be coming quicker. My heart pounded in my chest. My feet hammered against the floor. All I wanted to do now was escape to the light and freedom outside these walls. I was no longer interested in confronting whoever this was, not anymore.

Faster, just go faster, I thought to myself. Before I realized what I was doing, I had started jogging . . . and the footsteps behind me were coming just as fast.

My heavy backpack slammed against my back over and over again. The footsteps echoed like thunder behind me. There was no reprieve from the darkness.

Fueled by desperation and fear, combined with adrenaline, I managed to quicken my pace to a sprint.

My breathing was quick, almost near gasping. My lungs burned as I tried to take in enough oxygen with such short and rapid breaths. I wasn't winded from exhaustion. This was due to fear. I was practically in full freak-out mode. I wanted to scream, but I didn't think I could get the sounds to come out of my mouth.

The heaviness of my backpack pulled me in the opposite direction. I needed to go faster. I wanted to leave it behind, but knew how disastrous that would be -- my car keys were inside.

Closer, quicker, the footsteps behind me came.

There was a right turn up ahead, and I was approaching it fast. I knew I couldn't maintain this speed -- I might slip and fall. I slowed down, preparing for the turn.

Rounding the corner, I glanced over my shoulder. Then my body slammed into something. I gasped as it hit my stomach. The speed of the collision caused a loud crash. I stumbled, trying to keep myself from falling. Looking down, I saw a large trash can rolling toward the wall of lockers.

Thunk-tap, thunk-tap, thunk-tap. The sound behind me was almost painful to hear.

Back on my feet, there was another turn coming up. I only slowed slightly, then the slickness of the floor made me lose traction. I wobbled and stumbled a couple steps but somehow kept going.

The footsteps were getting louder.

My whole body felt tight and cramped -- my shoulders, my legs, arms. I could feel my fingernails digging into the palms of my hands. I ran to the nearest door, slammed my hand down onto the handle, but it was locked. I tried the next one, still nothing.

There was another door across the hall. I turned the knob and it moved! I yanked the door open, spinning around quickly to push it shut, leaning with my whole body and pushing. The door latched into place, and I twisted the lock shut. As soon as I heard the deadbolt click, the doorknob jiggled.

Gasping for air, I backed away, then looked around the room. Everything was dark, even darker than in the hallway.

I knew this was one of the science labs -- rows of tall counters, stools, and shelves filled with beakers, flasks and other equipment. I had been in this room before and knew there was another door. I ran over to it, turned the handle, but it was locked. I slipped my backpack off and fumbled for the zipper, scrambling to find my phone. Just then I heard pounding. I looked up and utter dread washed over me. . . . I saw my mistake. Next to the door, was a frosted glass window. The faint silhouette of my pursuer appeared behind it. He slammed his fists against the glass with tremendous force. I had chosen the wrong place to hide.

CHAPTER 25

Becca

The battery on my cell phone was completely dead.

On the other side of the window, the pounding continued but was quickly growing louder and more violent.

I ducked behind the nearest counter, stashing the phone in my backpack again, then laced my arms through the straps.

With a deafening crash, a burst of shattered glass sprayed through the air. My entire body flinched. Moments later, the lock on the door clicked, its tiny sound slamming against my ears. And I knew . . . he was coming.

My hands squeezed tightly around my legs, as I listened to the door slowly creak open. The thick darkness parted. I snapped my head up, catching sight of a hazy beam of light, gradually projecting across the floor and part way up the wall.

Every muscle in my body was tense. The sound of my own heartbeat boomed so loudly in my ears, I feared it would give me away. From my hiding place, all I could see was an eerie, dark silhouette. The shadow stood there, looming in the gray light coming from the doorway. I swallowed, feeling my throat strain to obey, as the image of the shadowy figure began to move.

I listened to the crunching and popping of the shards of glass beneath his feet. He was entering the room, but which way would he go?

My breathing became almost uncontrollable now -- my

chest rising and falling fast. I watched as his shadow grew bigger, almost filling the entire space on the wall. Then, he stood still.

Several long seconds went by.

I heard the doorknob jiggle, more glass crunched under his feet. Slowly the hazy light retreated, as the door began to shut. Then the light and shadow both disappeared. The room became silent, except for the beating of my heart.

I waited, motionless, for what seemed like hours. I wasn't sure if he had left, or if he was still in here somewhere.

My legs had fallen asleep, but I remained like a statue, sitting there on the hard floor, until I couldn't bear it any longer. I carefully shifted to a crouched position, trying to relieve my legs and feet from the tingling and pin pricking sensation.

I picked up my foot, hovering it barely above the ground, inching it forward, one small . . . slow . . . step. Then another slow and careful step. I planted my hands onto the ground and leaned forward, until I could see the doorway. My eyes searched through the darkness. Please be gone.

Through the broken window, just enough light trickled into the room for me to barely make out the teacher's chair. Behind it, I saw a tall bookshelf. Next to that, a small table. I strained to see through the darkness for more, but it was useless. Even if the lights were on, there were still too many places for him to hide.

It felt like the room was closing in on me, getting smaller, more cramped. The air even seemed thicker. It was hard for me to breathe. I couldn't stay in here. I was growing too desperate. The longer I waited, the more my chest felt like it was being squeezed, and my heart felt like it was ready to explode.

I didn't know if I was compelled more by courage or fear, but I was determined to escape and too afraid to wait any longer. Carefully, I started to stand, avoiding any sudden movements. My eyes were wide, ready to search for the quickest path to the door. Just as my head was about to clear the counter, a sudden burst of melodic chiming filled the air. It was his phone. Immediately, I ducked back down, practically gasping, as I tried to recover from the sudden rush of adrenaline pulsing through me.

The ringing noise stopped.

I heard his footsteps. They were slow, deliberate.

I turned my head, following in the direction of the sound. He gradually made his way over to the left corner of the classroom, then stopped.

I raised up onto my toes. He had given me an opening. I was now closer to the door than he was. I shifted my weight forward onto the balls of my feet and inhaled, summoning every bit of courage inside me.

Just as I was about to make my move, a flurry of quick footsteps held me in place. He was running back toward the door. I cowered down, behind the counter once again, listening to the sounds of the glass crushing under his feet, until he again stood still.

I was positioned diagonally across from the door, practically in the center of the room. I knew exactly where he was. I could hear him breathing. The distance between us was much too close for comfort, yet the door he stood in front of seemed impossibly far away. There was only one way out, and I feared that I had missed my only chance of escape.

Slow footsteps came again. This time, they were heading off to my right, along the wall and would soon be behind me. I knew I couldn't stay here. Once he moved far enough toward the back of the room, I would be in his line of sight, with only the darkness to conceal me.

I kneeled down and placed my hands on the floor. With each step he took I crawled, trying to match my movements with his, masking my own noise beneath his loud footsteps. I rounded the corner of the counter, out of his view, then sat down, heart pounding in my chest, waiting for his next move.

I heard him pivot, his shoes sliding on the hard floor. He started back toward the door again.

I leaned forward to crawl back to my original spot but couldn't move. My backpack was caught on something. I quickly slid it off my shoulders and felt around to find what it was caught on. A strap had become wedged under a loose board at the base of the counter. I gently slid the strap out until it was free, then quietly pulled my backpack onto my shoulders once more.

For some reason, when he reached the opposite wall, he turned and started off on the exact same path again, moving slowly to the back right corner of the room. Only this time, when he got to the halfway point, he stopped.

I was about to sneak over to the next counter, which would get me closer to the door, but just as I began to crawl, a sharp sting pierced the palm of my hand. I bit my lip in pain. Somehow a piece of glass must have landed all the way over here.

The footsteps continued again. I sat there and listened, with my pricked hand pulled into my chest.

I had no idea what he was up to, but he kept retracing his steps -- walking toward the door, then straight back toward the opposite wall. Was he toying with me, trying to coax me into running? Or was he still trying to figure out where I was?

All I needed was some distance between us -- enough so that I could make it through that door and then run for my life.

But if I couldn't get that, maybe I could slow him down instead. I remembered the loose board right behind me. If I could pry it free, it might make all the difference. I turned to it and wedged my fingers underneath.

Loud crashes filled the air, and I jumped. He had knocked the stools off of one of the counters, and they all went tumbling to the floor. I pulled harder at the piece of wood, but it wouldn't break free.

I heard a couple steps, a pause, then the crashing of more heavy, metal stools raining down from another countertop.

He took a few more footsteps, traveling toward the door. Stools went crashing again. Now, I knew what he was doing. He was going to move to every single counter, one at a time, until he flushed me out.

I tugged at the loose trim, placing my feet against the base of the counter and leaning back with all my body weight.

To the next counter he went, this time a row closer. The stools came crashing, my heart beating so hard, it felt like it would burst.

The next counter's stools went crashing to the floor. Then the next. I bit my lip again, to stop from screaming. He had one more to go, then my row was next!

I readjusted my grip at the end of the wood for maximum leverage, and pushed with my feet, trying to peel the wood back with all the strength I could summon. The stools from the last counter hit the floor.

The piece of wood trim snapped free, causing me to tumble backward. He advanced to my row, one counter over to my right. I scrambled around to the opposite side of the counter, the long thick piece of wood in my hand.

Stools went crashing. My counter was next!

I peeked around the corner, still crouched low to the ground. I watched his feet. That was all I could see. One step, then another. He was almost right next to me! I held my breath, gripped the board tight. I heard the stools shift as he grabbed hold to yank them down. Cocking the board back, I raised up onto my knees, then swung it like a bat, aiming for his legs.

The force of the impact sent a vibration up through my arms. A sharp pain flashed in my hands and fingers from having gripped the board so tight.

Above me was an explosion of crashing stools, mixed with a loud grunt. I dropped the board and sprang to my feet, bounding toward freedom. My fingers fumbled frantically for the door knob. I yanked it open, then flew down the hallway. The stairwell was just ahead. I stayed tight to the inside corner for the sharp right turn.

My hand hovered over the railing, as my feet pounded down the steps. Under the dim emergency lighting of the stairwell, my eyes concentrated on each step, hoping that my aim would be right. I knew that I was pushing a thin line between what I could safely manage and what would make me fall.

I made the turn at the landing, illuminated by the eerie green glow of the exit sign over the doorway below, but still had another flight of stairs to go.

From the hallway above, footsteps came thundering toward the stairs. There was a momentary silence, then a loud slam right behind me. He had jumped. I gasped, as the echo in the stairwell ricocheted off the walls all around.

I knew what I had to do, but wasn't sure if I'd make it. With all my power, I leaped into the air, skipping over the steps below. My landing was hard. The impact stinging, like the floor had stabbed me up through my shins. I stumbled forward, catching hold of the door frame to regain my balance.

Another loud crash exploded right behind me. He had landed his last jump. I gasped, hardly able to catch my breath. It felt like someone had taken the oxygen right out of the air. I fought through the pain and the dizziness, steadying myself on the wall, then pushing off and heading down the hallway.

Up ahead, I could see light coming from two narrow windows that bordered the exit doors. Safety was within sight, but my legs weren't moving fast enough. Each step was like sludging through thick mud, and it was only getting deeper.

The scent of cigarettes on his breath reached out from behind, letting me know just how close he was -- maybe close enough to grab me. I had made it this far. Please don't let him catch me now.

His heavy breathing seemed like it was right in my ear, but I couldn't run any faster. I was pushing as hard as I could . . . only a few more steps to go.

I felt him swipe at my hair. Instinctively, I snapped my head forward and lunged for the door, but my hair was caught on something -- maybe his ring or his watch. A loud shriek escaped from my lips, as a few strands of hair ripped from my head, the force causing me to lose my balance.

My body began to spin toward the ground. I collided against the push bar of the door. It swung open, and I spilled out onto the concrete sidewalk, eyes blinded by the flood of light outside.

I heard the sound of the heavy door slam shut behind me, and cars rushing by on the nearby road. There were muffled voices off in the distance. My eyes began to focus.

I found my footing and ran further, constantly looking over my shoulder. At the parking lot, my legs slowed, but my eyes still darted around wildly. All I could see were the two shut doors, an empty bench, and nothing -- there was nobody.

My body wasn't able to stop. I walked in a circle, trying to catch my breath, but the pounding in my chest wouldn't go away. I kept watching the door.

Finally, I took a deep breath. The cool air filled my lungs. Then I turned, scanning the parking lot behind me.

Just past the far end of the building, was a drop off. Down the hill, obscured from view, was the track and football field. The muffled voices I heard were coming from that direction, and growing louder. Two girls appeared, both with red faces, wet hair, shirts stained with sweat. They had obviously been running. Whoever had been chasing me must have looked the same.

I watched for anything strange -- like a gaze that lingered a little too long, but other than the sweat, there was nothing particularly menacing about them.

Then more students came after them, staggering up the hill. I scrutinized them as they headed past me toward the locker rooms. It was obvious that all of them had been running. I examined their feet, looking for hard soled shoes, until the last person had passed by.

I reached up to the spot on the back of my head where my hair had been pulled, then inspected my fingers. My head wasn't bleeding, but the palm of my hand was. The cut was just superficial, but it still hurt. I gently pressed down on it, feeling for more glass, but found none. I didn't have anything to wipe it with, so I folded up my sleeve, using the inside of my shirt to wipe the blood.

With my backpack on the ground, I searched until I found my keys. I wanted to have them already in hand when I approached my Jeep, just in case.

I had to walk all the way around the large building to

get to the student parking lot. I kept my distance from the building and repeatedly looked over my shoulder to make sure I wasn't being followed. My hands were trembling, so I crossed my arms over my chest, and tucked my fingers under to try to make them be still.

The student parking lot was nearly empty. In the distance, someone was standing near my car, staring in my direction. I stopped, reaching my hand up to shade the sun from my eyes. I recognized the car parked next to mine -- it was shiny and silver. The tall figure next to it didn't move. I continued walking toward him, but slower, waiting for his face to come into view.

Was this really happening -- it was too unbelievable. What was Blake still doing here?

CHAPTER 26

Becca

It looked as if a piece of the sky had been captured in Blake's blue eyes. "You never sent me a text," he said smiling.

"I was going to send one as soon as I was done with my test." I managed to smile back at him, trying to act like nothing was wrong. "But my battery is dead."

Almost every ounce of my energy had been spent. What I had left, I was using to put on an act for Blake. And I had no idea why I was doing this.

He stroked his chin, with a sly grin on his lips. "I was beginning to wonder if I had frightened you off."

"I've just been . . . busy today."

He made a quick glance around the empty parking lot. "I guess so."

There was nothing I wanted more than to be with Blake, but I was starting to feel weak and a little faint. I adjusted how I was standing, hoping that would help, but everything seemed to be spinning, and my vision was going black. I dropped my backpack to the ground, staggered toward the car and leaned against it.

"Are you okay?"

I thought I could fake it and ignore what had just happened in there, but I couldn't. The sound of those heavy footsteps behind me were still echoing in my mind.

"Becca?"

"I feel like I'm gonna . . . pass out," I said, between labored breaths, turning to sit on the Mustang's fender.

Blake moved a step closer and crouched down in front of me, looking into my eyes. "Do you need to lie down?"

I took a couple deep breaths. "No. I just need to sit for a minute." I really didn't know if that would help. I hoped it would.

"Are you sure?"

"Yeah, the spinning has stopped."

"Are you sick?"

"No."

He waited, with concern written all over him, as I sat there, trying to recuperate.

"What happened to your hand? You've been bleeding."

I nodded. "Somebody was following me in the building. They were chasing me."

His back became rigid. "What? . . . Who?"

"I don't know. I tried to see who it was, but it was dark."

"This happened just a few minutes ago?" he asked, looking toward the building.

I nodded.

"Wait here. I'll be right back."

Blake stood up, and I quickly reached out for his arm. "No, don't."

"I'm going to go find the idiot who chased you." Blake's jaw was clenched, his eyes full of fire.

"No." I looked up, pleading with him to stay. "I could

really just use your company right now."

He stared into my eyes for a moment, then sat down next to me, scanning the parking lot. "So what happened? The guy chasing you . . . he hurt you?"

"The cut was from broken glass. He didn't do that."

Blake watched intently as I blotted the blood with my sleeve.

"He did pull my hair, but I was able to get away."

That was plenty for Blake. His eyes narrowed and he leaned forward. "Are you sure you need me to sit here with you? Because--"

I wrapped my arm around his, pulling him back. "No. Stay here. . . . He's probably gone."

"What did he look like?"

"I didn't really get to see him. It was dark and he was behind me mostly."

Blake visually inspected the cut on my hand. "Tell me everything you remember about him."

"Just that he smelled like cigarettes. Like I said, I really couldn't see who it was."

"What's going on, Becca? I heard about you being chased while you were driving a couple nights ago." The tone of Blake's voice was deeper, and his words were deliberate.

"You heard about that?"

He nodded his head. "Yeah."

"Either someone is playing a sick practical joke on me, or . . . I just don't know."

"You have no idea who might be doing this?"

"My friends think it's Jason."

"Jason," he paused. "Jason Romanowski?"

"Yes."

"Why him?"

"Uh . . ." I hesitated. "We sort of . . . used to . . ."

"You two were seeing each other? Wow!"

"Really? You have to throw in a *wow*?" I leaned in and bonked his shoulder with mine.

He chuckled. "It's just that you two seem kind of like a mismatch."

I wrinkled my nose. "I hate to admit it, but we did go out a couple times. That was of course before I found out what a creeper he is."

Blake looked off into the distance. "Well, we all make mistakes. We take people for who they show themselves to be . . . who they pretend to be. But sooner or later the truth comes out and you find out who they really are."

"Sounds like you're speaking from experience."

"Yeah," he nodded.

"We have that in common then," I smiled.

"So . . . did you guys go out, as in boyfriend and girlfriend?

"Jason was *never* my boyfriend," I shivered. "I meant that we went out on a couple dates, as in dinner and a movie."

There was a hint of a smile on his lips.

I wanted to see where this conversation might lead, but knew I couldn't stay any longer. "I better get going, I have an appointment, and I promised my mom I wouldn't be late."

Blake stood up with me and followed me the few steps over to my Jeep. "Becca, you were about to pass out, not even five minutes ago. Are you sure you're okay to drive?"

"I'm fine," I half smiled. I really didn't know if that was true, but I had to go.

"Look. I feel like this is one of those moments where a gentleman might have to insist on chivalry."

"I can't ask you to do that. It's kind of far."

"You don't seem to understand. I'm asking you to do this for me. I'd never forgive myself if something happened while you were driving."

"I'll be okay. Really." I shut my door. Blake took a few steps back and stood there with his hands in the pockets of his West Johnston High sweatshirt, a worried look on his face.

I put my key into the ignition and turned it, but nothing happened. I tried a few more times and pumped the gas. But still nothing. Not a sound.

The government had strict penalties for procedure patients who missed their counseling appointments -- automatic admittance to one of their psychiatric hospitals. I preferred to keep my freedom, so I never missed an appointment.

Blake opened my door. He looked almost happy that my car wouldn't start. "Pop the hood. I'll take a look."

He walked to the front of my Jeep. I pulled the stubborn hood release, then got out and came around to stand next to him.

"I see the problem," he said.

"I'm glad you do, because I don't have any idea what I'm looking at."

He shook his head, then pointed. "Your battery is missing."

"How could that . . ." I felt my eyes well up with tears. They began rolling down my cheeks as I stared at the spot Blake had pointed to. Disconnected wires dangled in the vacant hole where the battery should have been. It looked so obvious now that he pointed it out.

Blake shut the hood of my car and put his arm around my shoulders. I couldn't stop the tears. He pulled me in, wrapping me in his warm embrace. "I'm sorry this is happening to you," he said.

His shirt felt soft against my cheek. I had longed to be in his arms, but not this way. If only he was holding me because he wanted to be close to me, not just to comfort me.

My emotions were out of control. I didn't want to cry, but too much had happened today. I had arrived at school afraid my friends knew my secret, then ended the day afraid that I was about to be abducted. But in between, I had been full of excitement, unexpectedly seeing Blake in class and getting that note from him.

Now standing here, learning that my Jeep was sabotaged, but simultaneously being wrapped in Blake's arms -- the series of extremes were more than I could believe. Oddly, I felt a calm come over me. His shirt was wet against my face from my tears. I pulled back.

He let go, looking down into my eyes. "Becca, may I take you to your appointment?"

"Yes. Thanks." I started walking toward the driver's side door of my Jeep, wiping my face with my hands. "I need to get my stuff."

"I'll get it," he said walking past me.

I turned around and headed to his car, grateful that he was here, and glad that our time together hadn't ended yet. I was about to reach for the door handle, but he beat me to it. I stepped inside, sliding down into the leather seat.

He bent forward, handed me my things, started to back away, then stopped. As I turned my head toward him, he inhaled. I thought he was about to say something, but then there was a change in his expression. He exhaled slightly, then stood up and shut my door.

What was he going to say?

My eyes followed him as he walked around the car and got in. His wide shoulders filled his seat, crowding toward me. There was a cell phone charger in his car. I pulled out my phone from my backpack, then plugged it in.

I watched his movements as he started up the car. Being with him felt like a dream, and I didn't want to wake up. It was hard to believe that I was sitting next to him in his Mustang. Just the two of us.

He turned off the radio, adjusted the air, then reached his arm behind my seat as he looked over his shoulder, backing up. He drove around to the parking lot exit, came to a stop, then looked at me. I sat there silently, waiting for my fantasy to play out, still hoping he would say what he had held back earlier.

"Just tell me how to get there," he said.

"Oh." I looked out at the road in front of us, about to tell him which way to go, but stopped. My fantasy quickly crumbled, falling to the ground in a million pieces, as I realized where he would be taking me. He was going to find out that I had an appointment with a shrink. I was already late, and I couldn't miss this, so I had no other choice. But what would he think of me when he found out?

"Turn left," I said. My voice cracked. I cleared my throat. What if he thinks I'm some emotional wreck, a drama queen, ready to break down at any moment? What if he thinks that I'm lying about everything and that I'm some paranoid delusional?

I held down the button on my phone. After a couple seconds, it finally powered back on. I typed out a text message, 'This is Becca's Number,' and sent it to him. A moment later, Blake's phone beeped.

"Don't look at it while you're driving," I said, wishing I could already take that message back and write a better one.

He chuckled. "Okay. I promise I won't look."

I set my phone down on the center console. "I just sent you my number is all."

"So when I look at your message, there won't be some kind of amazing secret reveal or big confession?"

"You'd have to earn something like that," I said. "I don't give away my secrets that easily."

"I see." He moved his right hand from the steering wheel, adjusted the temperature, then rested it on top of the brake, inches away from my legs. I remembered feeling the touch of his fingers this morning, when he dropped that note onto my desk. . . . I wanted to feel it again.

"What test were you making up?" he asked.

"Math."

"You were in there for a long time."

That was because I couldn't stop thinking about you. "Yeah, it was kind of a hard test to take. Turn left at the stop sign . . . I thought you waited for me, because you needed to talk to me about something. I mean, with your note telling me to text you and all."

He glanced over at me with his clear blue eyes. "What did you think I wanted to talk about?"

"I don't know."

"No guesses?"

I shrugged. "I don't know . . . the weather."

He chuckled. "If I ever waste time talking to you about the weather, do us both a favor and kick me in the shins."

"I'll make sure I'm wearing pointy shoes first," I smiled.

Blake laughed, then glanced over at me. "I'll remember to watch what I say around you." He adjusted his hand. I watched out of the corner of my eye, hoping he'd keep moving it closer to me. He did, but not close enough.

"Do you need me to give you a ride home?"

My eyes sprung away from his hand. A ride home? That was the last thing I wanted him to do. I could just imagine him sitting in that waiting room, then peppering me with questions all the way home. "My mom can come and get me." I picked up my phone and looked at the time.

"Are we late?"

"I'm still within the 15 minute grace period."

Blake reached up and palmed his hand through his unruly, begging to be touched, blond hair. Then he rested his hand close to me again. "I can't believe someone stole the battery out of your car."

"I know." I couldn't believe it either, and I couldn't believe that he was about to see what kind of appointment I was going to. I needed to let him know that I wasn't a drama queen. "I feel really embarrassed, crying on you like that. Has your sweatshirt dried, yet?"

"I didn't even notice." He pulled his sweatshirt away from his chest. I could see remnants of my black mascara on it.

"Oh my gosh." I cringed. "Some of my makeup got on your sweatshirt."

"It's not like I'm afraid of getting a little dirty," he smirked. "It's fine."

"Take a right here," I said urgently, as we almost passed the turn.

"You kept yourself together pretty well," he said. "I didn't know anything was wrong until you collapsed onto my car."

I did not want to keep talking about this. I changed the subject and asked him about the ranch and the horses. He didn't seem to mind talking about those things. I could tell he loved what he did there.

"So what were you staying after for?" I asked. "Test make up, like me?"

"I helped the librarian move some boxes. When I came out and noticed your car was still in the parking lot, I figured I would wait for you."

"How long were you waiting?"

He chuckled.

"What?"

"Yeah. I had to wait awhile," he said, with a big grin on his face.

"Is there something funny about that?"

"It was just a long time to wait. Moving boxes only took like fifteen minutes. Waiting for you . . . easy forty-five."

Was he serious? "Well, I'm so glad you waited for me, although I'm sorry it took so long."

"It was worth it."

"Turn here." My stomach started to churn, realizing our location.

Now was the moment of truth. We had turned onto

a road full of beautiful, old Victorian homes that had been renovated into law offices and medical practices, one of which was my dreaded psychiatrist's office.

"You can pull up to the curb," I said pointing to the right side of the road.

Blake stopped the car, then leaned in toward me, his face only inches from mine. He looked out my window. "This is a cool old house."

I grabbed hold of the door handle and pushed the door open, trying to hurry, in part because I was late, but also because I didn't want him to see the sign on the front lawn that read, 'Dr. Stella Howard, M.D., P.L.L.C.'

"Thanks. You were a lifesaver today," I said as I got out of the car, forgetting that my phone was still tethered to the charger. It jerked out of my hand and fell onto the seat.

Blake unplugged it, reached out and handed it to me.

"Thanks," I said, as I quickly backed away from the car. I was about to shut the door, but he leaned across the seat to make eye contact with me.

"You know, I can head back to school and put a new battery in your car. It's real easy to do."

I shook my head. "You don't need to do that. I'm sure my dad can take care of it. I gotta go."

I stepped away, onto the sidewalk. As I shut the door, I stole one last look at his gorgeous face and alluring blue eyes, then hurried into the building, hoping I hadn't just ruined my chances with him.

CHAPTER 27

Becca

I climbed the steps to the covered porch and opened the heavy oak door. The modern aesthetic of the converted lobby contrasted sharply with the Victorian colors and gables outside.

Since I was late, and I didn't see the receptionist, I walked straight ahead, knocked on Dr. Stella's door and pushed it open a crack. It sounded like she was on the phone. I was about to turn away and go take a seat, but stopped when I heard her say my name. I leaned in close, with my ear to the crack of the door.

Someone cleared their throat behind me. I quickly spun around, feeling like a kid caught with their hand in the cookie jar. The receptionist was staring at me from behind the counter, her narrowed eyes glaring.

I smiled at her as I approached the counter. "Hi, I'm Becca Tanner. I'm running a little late for my appointment."

She shot a disapproving look at me from behind her thick glasses. "I know who you are, Miss Tanner." Her tone struck that special kind of politeness that borders on condescension. "Dr. Stella will be with you in a moment."

"I'll just sit here and wait," I said as I walked toward the row of chairs lined up against the wall.

I never could tell if the person waiting for the next appointment was a procedure patient, or someone who randomly wound up here by picking from a list of therapists on the Internet. But I was the only one in the waiting room today, aside from the Moray eel, hiding in the fish tank across from me.

Most of the time, the long, green eel hid inside an artificial hollowed out log. It would poke its head out and watch me with its sneaky, dark eyes and pointy teeth. I read that these eels will join forces with other species of fish to hunt for food. The eel's ability to squeeze into narrow crevices helps them flush out prey, which is why other fish depend on them to hunt.

I pulled out my phone. There wasn't much battery life remaining, but I sent Mom a lengthy text explaining that my Jeep wouldn't start, and I needed her to come get me. When I looked up, Dr. Stella was standing outside her door staring at me.

"I'm ready for you now," she said, then turned and headed back into her office. Her long ponytail darted from side to side with each step she took.

I followed her, looking around the room to see if anything was different from the last time I was here. This was my own version of an I spy game. It usually helped the time go by faster.

The room always felt a little cold to me. I mentioned that to Dr. Stella once, and I could swear that the next time I came for my appointment, it was even colder. That was just one of the many times she made it clear to me that she really didn't care about my feelings or comfort. She knew I was stuck with her as my therapist, because she was the only one authorized to see procedure patients in this area.

I headed toward the big flower patterned chair. I remember the first time I saw it, how it looked so inviting and soft with its red and green velvety fabric. I plopped myself down onto it, expecting to be taken in by soft cushiony comfort, but instead my body slammed down in a crash against a hard, rigid seat. It must have been made of steel, with only the thinnest of material hiding the unyielding frame beneath the surface. I had never complained about the uncomfortableness of the chair, for fear that she might bring out something even worse the next time -- perhaps something covered in sandpaper.

Dr. Stella apparently liked abstract art. Small sculptures were scattered throughout the room. I found some of the pieces interesting, but I didn't quite understand her particular taste. There was one piece she had on her desk that was eye catching, in a disturbing kind of way. It sort of looked like a bunny with a dagger stabbed through its heart. Makes me feel all warm and fuzzy inside to see that . . . said no one ever.

She sat down and crossed her legs in a real lady-like manner, pristine and proper. Her appearance was always one of perfection -- no hair out of place, no excess shine to her face, no run in her stockings.

She reached over and turned on a small, handheld audio recorder. "You look like you have been crying."

Oh great. I started rubbing my fingers under my eyes.

"Are you upset about something?" she asked as she picked up her pad of paper and pen.

I told her about my battery being stolen and left out the part where I had been chased.

She sat there listening with her collagen injected lips pursed together, and her emerald green eyes fixed on mine. Actually, that was an overly generous way of describing her eyes, because they only resembled emeralds in color, not shine.

"Do you frequently cry over things like this?" Her tone was strictly clinical, utterly lacking in compassion. Normally, I would call that being insensitive, but I had gotten used to her callousness.

Here we go. These were exactly the kinds of questions that made me loathe my appointments with Dr. Stella. "I had just finished a very hard test that I wasn't prepared for," I explained.

She scribbled something on to her pad. "Why do you think someone would want to steal the battery out of your car?"

I shrugged my shoulders. "Maybe they needed one."

More scribbling. "Are you having any trouble at school?"

"Nothing out of the ordinary for a typical teenage girl, I guess."

"But you're really not typical, Becca."

"I'm living a normal everyday life, just like any other girl my age."

Dr. Stella raised her eyebrows as if to signal a very scientific 'I see.' This time, she shook her head as she wrote. Whenever she jotted things down on paper, it came across like she was turning and whispering in somebody's ear.

"Tell me about your relationship with your friend Nora."

Where was this question coming from? "Um, we're good friends?" I replied searchingly.

"Have you confided in her about your medical history?"

"Nora has no reason to know about that, and I don't feel the need to tell her."

"So you would tell her if you needed to?"

"I'm not saying that. What I'm saying is that I choose not to tell her, because I find no reason to do so."

"And if you found a reason, then you would tell her?"

Why did she always have to twist my words? On top of the day I'd already had, this was beyond irritating. "Well, I thought I was clear with my first answer. Maybe I should have answered you differently. What I meant was, I will never tell her until the day I die." I hoped that was emphatic enough that she'd drop it.

She raised one eyebrow. "Interesting choice of words. Would you like to talk more about your feelings on death?"

I wanted to smack myself in the forehead. "No. I'm good. Really."

Dr. Stella didn't respond.

"I'm alive, and I love my life," I said. "There's really nothing I need to talk about."

"Don't you feel lonely, not being able to talk to any of your friends about your "secret," as you like to call it? It is such a big part of your life."

I shook my head. "Nope, I can't say that I do."

"It must wear on you to have to carry this secret around day after day. Do you think that confiding in a close friend could help relieve some of that stress?"

"Who says I'm stressed? I'm not stressed."

"What about your reaction to your stolen car battery?"

"I think my reaction was normal. It's not like I was sobbing uncontrollably. It was just a couple of tears."

She started writing again. "Sometimes people cry easily when they have built up stress and anxiety," she said, not looking up from her pad of paper and not skipping a beat with her writing.

I was trying desperately to outrun this avalanche of

questions but felt like I had already been crushed . . . and all because of a few streaks of mascara on my face. If only I had looked in a mirror before I came in here. Thank goodness she didn't notice the dried blood on my sleeve.

Dr. Stella put her pen and paper down on her lap again and crossed her hands over the top. "How are you sleeping at night?"

"Fine. Perfectly fine."

"Have you experienced any nightmares or insomnia?"

"No." No nightmares. Not even a single dream.

"And what about your medication . . . "

It was impossible for her to know that I had stopped taking my pills, but I was dreadfully worried that she'd figure it out somehow. She had a way of picking apart every word and finding meaning in the subtlest body language.

I tried to remind myself to stay focused and calm, but on this day, after all I had been through, calm was a resource in short supply. Her ridiculous questions were pulling me dangerously close to my tipping point.

"Let's see." She opened up a notebook and flipped through some pages. "You've been on the same dosages for these past six months. Does that still seem to be working well for you?"

I looked away. "I believe so." But really, how was I supposed to know? I didn't understand why I was taking those pills in the first place. I had never been given a straight up explanation as to their purpose -- not by Dad, by Dr. Brimley or by Dr. Stella. All those pills did for me was make me tired and weak and keep me from dreaming.

"Have you experienced any increased irritability, or excessive nervousness?"

What a weird question. Was that a common side effect from the medication? I shook my head. "No." But the truth was, every time I stepped foot in this office, my irritability shot through the roof. I bet she didn't want to hear that.

"Have you experienced any depression, thoughts of hopelessness or feelings of despair?"

She had never asked me these kinds of questions before. What were those pills anyway? "No."

"Has there been anything else you've experienced that you might consider to be unusual or out of the ordinary?"

"Like what?"

There was a flicker in her eyes, as if I had opened a whole other door into her mind. "I mean out of the ordinary, as in going against all logic." Her eyes zeroed in on mine. "Have you experienced any hallucinations -- seeing or hearing things that really aren't there?"

"No," I said firmly. It seemed like she was the one who was living in some kind of parallel universe, not me. Next she was probably going to ask if I had seen any UFOs or been abducted by little people with green skin and large heads.

Dr. Stella sat motionless and unblinking, scanning my face. I fidgeted. Her eyes surveyed my entire body, from head to toe. If she was deliberately trying to make me feel uncomfortable, she was succeeding.

"Is there anything else you would like to talk about?"

She's gotta be joking. I shook my head. "I can't think of anything."

"There's one more thing I want to talk about. Some procedure patients have a hard time adjusting to the changes in their lives," she said. "They worry that others will discover their secrets. Some even start becoming a little paranoid, believing that they're being followed, or that someone is spying on them." Her face became serious. "Have you experienced feelings like these, like you were being followed, or stalked?"

"No, I'm not a paranoid person." I forced a calm countenance, but inside my fears were churning. How did she know? Did Dad tell her about the other night?

"I didn't say that you were."

No, she didn't say it, but her implication couldn't have been more obvious. Was I supposed to believe that her question was just a freakish coincidence, because it sure felt like she was talking about a certain truck on a certain rainy night. It must have been Dad who told her about the truck. She couldn't possibly know about whoever chased me through the hallways at school this afternoon, could she? It happened like an hour ago, and I hadn't told anyone but Blake.

No matter what she knew, or how she had come to know it, I wasn't about to give her the satisfaction of admitting anything. "Maybe you should give those people you are talking about the benefit of the doubt," I said. "What if it turns out that there really was somebody following or stalking them? Wouldn't that be terrible?"

"Hmm. Interesting."

I could tell by the tightness of her lips that she didn't really want to hear my opinion.

"I had a meeting at the main facility this morning and ran into your dad. He looks like he is doing well."

She waited for my response. I didn't give her one.

"And how's your mom?"

I didn't think Dr. Stella really wanted to hear about Mom. I think she wanted me to worry about what Dad might have said to her, and I was all but certain that he had told her about me being followed. "My mom is doing great," I forced a smile.

Dr. Stella uncrossed her legs. "We got started late, so we had better move on to the psychoneural analysis."

She stood up and motioned for me to go over to the couch. I laid down on my side and moved my hair out of the way, so that she could attach the DNI to the back of my neck. The feel of her cold fingers on my skin sent shivers up my spine.

"Okay, you're hooked up," she said.

I rolled onto my back. Dr. Stella unlocked a rolling cabinet filled with equipment, and connected the cable from the DNI.

"There has been a change to this procedure," she said as she rummaged through the cabinet. "We've replaced the oral sedative."

Thank goodness. I hated how I felt after drinking that stuff, and the disgusting cherry medicine flavor always made me want to gag.

"From now on, you will be put under with this." She produced a syringe with an imposing needle.

I jerked my arm away from her.

"Becca," she said sternly. "Are we going to have a problem?"

"What's in that?"

"Would it make a difference if I told you? This will relax you. It works more quickly than the oral delivery. Everything will be fine."

I didn't move.

"Are you afraid of needles?" she asked condescendingly.

"Does my dad know that you are doing this?"

"Of course he does," her tone sounded almost nurturing, but I doubted her sincerity. "This entire program was his idea even before its implementation." She held her hand out. "Your arm please."

Why wasn't I allowed to be in control of my own body? This was mine now. It didn't belong to them.

I gave her my arm and looked away. "Ouch!" I turned back to see the needle inserted in my arm . . . then things started to go black.

CHAPTER 28

Becca

Dr. Stella pulled the needle out. "See that wasn't so bad," she said soothingly, taping a small cotton ball to my arm. Her touch was gentle. For a moment, she seemed almost nurturing.

Her back turned to me as she discarded the needle. Almost instantly, my eyes began to shut. I strained to keep them open. Everything was going dark. I tried to lift my arm, but it wouldn't move. My limbs and even my chest began to feel heavy, as if someone were stacking a pile of bricks on top of me. My body was shutting down, no matter how hard I fought against it.

The hum of the nearby electronics faded into absolute silence. I tried to speak, but my tongue felt like it was disconnected from my mouth. My last remaining physical sensation was the rising and falling of my chest with each labored breath I took.

This was new for me. The oral sedation Dr. Stella had given me previously just made me fall asleep, but this new injection left me wide awake, trapped inside a body that I could not control, and one that I was helpless to defend. I wondered if this was what a coma felt like. I was terrified at the thought that I might never wake up.

Time became abstract, foreign, meaningless. Logic informed me that seconds and perhaps even minutes were ticking by, but I had lost all ability to measure them.

Then, even more quickly than the heaviness had overcome me, I felt as though the weight was lifted, and I could move again.

I opened my eyes. At first, all I could see was black, but then the darkness began to dissipate like a heavy fog giving way to warm sunlight. Blurry images started to appear. I blinked my eyes, then reached up and rubbed them. When I opened them again, the images started to come into focus.

I heard cars driving by, horns honking, engines roaring. There were birds chirping. I could see it all now -- the busy street, the trees, the office buildings. This place wasn't familiar to me. I had never been on this street before. How did I get here? Was I dreaming?

A police car pulled up to the curb directly in front of me. The window rolled down.

"Are you Becca Tanner?" the officer inside asked. He was wearing a police uniform, but for some reason, I couldn't see his face. The interior of the vehicle was still blurry and shadowed.

This had to be a dream.

"Yes, I'm Becca, but how do you know my name?"

"There has been a situation at your father's work, ma'am. He's in trouble. I need to take you to him right away." The officer reached over and opened the passenger side door. "We need to hurry."

The next thing I knew, I was buckled in, and we were speeding toward Dad's work. Time skipped forward, bypassing the long drive, placing us near the facility.

I looked over at the officer. His face was still darkened and blurry. "What's happened to my father?"

"I can't say exactly," he responded, "but you'll find out

soon."

The only thing putting me at ease was seeing that we were pulling up to the security checkpoint right outside Dad's work. As I looked closer, I noticed that no guards were on duty and the gate was open. The officer suddenly veered to the right and drove off the road.

"Where are we going? This is the wrong way!"

"There is a secret entrance. It bypasses all of the security."

What security? There wasn't anybody manning the checkpoint. "Where are all of the military police? I didn't see anybody at the gate."

He didn't respond. His attention remained forward. We traveled down a long and bumpy dirt road, weaving between trees until I finally saw the familiar chain link fence that surrounded the facility.

The officer reached into his shirt pocket and pulled out a thin metal device that looked like a tiny calculator. He pressed a few buttons, then slid it back into his pocket. Up ahead, a portion of the fence swung open.

We continued through campus, passing right by Dad's building.

"You missed it. It was back there," I said, pointing out the window.

"Your father is in a different building." The officer's head remained forward, his voice level and monotone.

We turned off the paved road without slowing down. The car bounced where the asphalt met the gravel. Flying rocks pelted against the metal underneath the vehicle. The sun was descending gradually and soon would be completely hidden. I looked over at the faceless officer. Fading rays of sunlight bent around the outline of his head.

My eyes traveled downward from the blur where his face should have been, following the line that was drawn by the retreating sunlight, outlining his neck and arms. I noticed his hands firmly gripping the steering wheel, his knuckles white, and his fingers red. His wrists were exposed. Lines and swirls of dark ink spilled out from under his sleeves. Both arms appeared to be painted in tattoos, but his long sleeves hid their significance. Then I realized I had seen those tattoos before . . . on the officer outside my house, on the night I was followed by that black truck. This was the same cop!

My eyes traveled back upward. His collar was buttoned up tight around the large, round trunk of a neck that supported his head. I didn't notice any markings on the side of his neck, but I still stared at it, as if something might magically appear.

His head turned abruptly to face me. There were no eyes for me to see, but I could feel the heaviness of his stare. I jumped ever so slightly, hoping he didn't recognize my fear. I was growing more nervous and apprehensive by the moment.

"Are we almost there?" I asked, my voice slightly shaky, my eyes searching out the window.

One more turn and out popped a gigantic mound of a hill. We were headed straight for it, with no reduction in speed. I sat up straight, my feet pressed onto the floor searching for a brake pedal that wasn't there.

"Aren't you going to . . ." Just as I was about to scream for him to stop, the side of the hill slid open. It was a door -- big enough for a semi truck. The squad car easily slipped through.

Inside, there was darkness all around, except for the rows of lights that formed a path for the car to follow.

"What is this place?" I asked, my eyes glued to the lighted

path in front of us.

"You've been here before."

That broke my stare. "What?" I whipped my head toward him.

"You will recognize the room."

What was he talking about? I'd never seen this place before. I tried to exude a calm demeanor, but inside I feared that he was not taking me to see Dad.

My body jolted forward and slammed against the seat belt as he skidded to a stop. Pain surged through me from the force. I reached back and grasped hold of my neck. I stared at him with my mouth open, my breathing quickened from the burst of adrenaline rushing through me.

"We're here. Get out," he said, in his flat, robotic tone.

I had no idea if it would be safer in the car or outside it, but since those were the only two options, I chose to get out. There was an elevator door a few feet in front of us. He pressed the button, and it opened instantly.

"Get in," he said, stepping to the side.

"Are you coming, too?" I asked hesitantly, trying to give myself extra time to think. I didn't know if I wanted to get in there with him. This might be my last chance to make a run for it.

The elevator doors started to shut. He slammed his foot down in front of them, sending the doors flying back.

Seeing how the doors ricocheted off his leg, instantly got me moving toward the elevator. It was obvious that he was much stronger than I was, and if I tried to make a run for it my chances for escape would not be good.

He stepped inside after me and pressed the button for the fourth floor. When the elevator jolted, I lost my balance and almost fell. I was expecting it to surge upward, but we were going down.

Inside, it looked like most any other elevator. There were no windows. The walls were shiny and silver. It had a panel with buttons, but there was no emergency phone to call for help.

I stood there, my back up against the handrail. The cold metal sending shivers through me. The officer stood in front of me facing the doors. His black, curly hair matted against the back of his head with only a few unshaven renegade hairs extending down his neck and stopping just above his collar.

There it was. The black ink on his skin, just like on his arms. As I stared at his tattoos, trying to make out the pattern, the dark lines started to move, reaching up from his shirt, climbing out, bending and turning. I jumped back in shock. The tattoo was traveling across his skin and covering his whole neck, like it was alive. I moved to the far corner of the elevator, pressing myself against the wall.

The lights flickered, and then the elevator started falling like a rock. Had the cable snapped? I grabbed onto the handrail, both arms wrapped around it, holding on for dear life. My hair flew up. I screamed.

After several seconds, I knew that we were approaching terminal velocity. I closed my eyes tightly, certain that we were going to splatter against the ground.

"Please no. Stop!"

I was hovering in the air. I expected impact at any moment, but we kept falling. Then without warning, the elevator jolted to a stop. I slammed down to the floor, but not as hard as I should have given our rate of descent.

I laid there in a heap, gasping for air, looking all around in shock. We hadn't crashed. Everything was intact.

Remarkably, the officer was still standing. He hadn't even moved from his original spot. I looked at the back of his neck and noticed that his tattoos were gone.

Slowly, I stood up, pressing against the wall of the elevator, trying to steady myself. The doors began to part, and a beam of light wedged through the crack between them, growing brighter as they separated.

The officer was blocking my view. I leaned to the side and raised onto my toes, but he was too big for me to see around him. He stepped out of the elevator, and I quickly followed his footsteps, eager to be on solid ground.

His back was still to me. "Here we are."

What did he mean? I didn't see Dad anywhere. In fact, I didn't see anybody here.

My eyes scanned the room. There were computers lined up in rows on tables. There must have been fifty of them. Several large screens were on the wall directly in front of me. The furniture in the room was all positioned to face the screens, but there wasn't anything to see.

Nothing here seemed familiar to me, except for the strange pungent smell that hung in the air. The stale odor was so strong that I could almost taste it in my mouth. There were no windows and the ceiling was low. I already knew we were underground, but this room made me feel like we were in some futuristic tomb.

Large double doors were on each side of the room. I immediately turned to the doors on the left and started walking toward them. There were small, round windows on them, but all I could see was darkness on the other side.

I turned to look back at the officer, but he was gone. I hadn't heard the elevator open again. He must have slipped through the other set of doors.

I wanted to return to the surface, but there was no way I was getting back on that elevator, and I wasn't about to wait around for that creepy faceless tattoo guy to return. There had to be another way out.

I continued walking toward the doors on the left and was about to push one open, when it startled me by opening on its own, as if inviting me to enter.

Darkness filled the entire door frame. Only a couple steps inside, the floor tiles disappeared into mists of black, impenetrable by the light coming from the room behind me.

I swallowed hard. "Is anyone here?"

Nobody answered. I was surrounded by an uneasy, solitary calm.

My feet stepped carefully and cautiously inside, trying not to disturb the nearly tangible darkness. In spite of my best efforts to be stealthy, I noisily fumbled my way along the wall, hearing every step and movement reverberating above the surrounding silence.

The pungent odor was stronger here and a dampness hung in the air. I had no idea where I was, or what was around me, causing me to rethink the hastiness of my actions. I retreated back toward the door, until I found the point where I could begin to discern a trace of light spilling in from the room outside. From there, I headed back inside, just a few more steps into the darkness.

I stood there, thinking through my situation. For the moment, at least, I was hidden. That gave me only a sliver of comfort.

After several minutes, it became clear that my eyes were not adjusting to this darkness. The light from the previous room, which had once seemed so bright, was completely erased beyond the threshold. If I continued on, I would have to rely on other senses to guide me.

I stretched my hands out and began to feel my way along the cold wall. My hands pressed and glided across it as I walked. My fingers searched high and low for a lightswitch. I walked slowly, turning to follow the corners, making sure not to miss anything.

Though I could no longer see it, I still didn't want to venture too far from the door, for fear that it would disappear just as the officer had, and I would be trapped alone in darkness, with no way out.

The longer I searched for a source of light, the greater the sense of desperation that swelled inside me. I should just leave. I should go back to the light. In fact, I should run.

My fear was teetering on panic when a violent metallic crash sliced through the silence. I gasped, my body slamming against the wall. Silence returned briefly, followed by the unmistakable sound of a switch being flicked.

Hope arose in my chest, as light once again triumphed over darkness. I reached up to shade my eyes from the sting of the blinding lights. I squinted, standing frozen against the wall.

Before my eyes could adjust, my ears confirmed the sound of a familiar voice that said, "You're just in time."

"Dr. Stella?" I never thought I'd be relieved to see her, but even so, I still didn't trust her.

"Yes, Becca. I see you have found your way here." She smiled.

"What do you mean? What is this place?" And where is my dad?"

Her eyebrows narrowed, head tilted to the side. "Well, he went to save you of course."

What kind of thing was that to say? Should I be scared? Was I in danger? My eyes widened. "Why does he need to save me?"

"See for yourself." Dr. Stella turned and walked toward two tables draped in white sheets.

My legs suddenly became heavy. I didn't think I could take another step. I knew where I was . . . this was the procedure room. And those white sheets must be covering dead bodies.

"Who's under there?" I asked, barely above a whisper.

Dr. Stella's noisy heels struck the floor with each step she took. I glanced down at her shoes, then noticed she had a run in her stockings that started from her heel and traveled up the back of her leg.

She didn't respond. She walked directly toward the tables, as if she hadn't heard me at all.

What's going on? "Dr. Stella," I called out.

She stopped and turned around. Her plastic smile remained unchanged, like she was in her own little world, unaware of my growing desperation. She looked down at the table to her right and reached for the sheet. I wanted to look away. I knew I should, but couldn't help myself. My eyes stared at the sheet in her hands, waiting for the unveiling of the body.

She paused and looked straight at me, then looked back down at the sheet and pulled it slightly upward, folding it back gently. She stepped aside as if to make sure my view wasn't blocked.

A dead girl lay on the table. I didn't recognize her. "Who is she?" Her silky blonde hair billowed around her frozen lifeless face. Closed eyes and thin lips were the only contrast against her sallow complexion.

Dr. Stella turned to the other table. My eyes followed her. She bent over, grabbed hold of the sheet and lifted it up, this time holding it in place. It was too high for me to see over. I raised up on my toes, to no avail. Why was she holding the sheet up like that?

"What's wrong?" I asked.

Dr. Stella stared at the body under the sheet. "I don't think I'll have to tell you who this is."

I ran over to the table, grabbed the sheet from her hands and pulled it down.

The next thing I knew, I was lying on my back staring up at the ceiling. The light was so bright, that I could barely see anything. There were two people standing over me. At first, I could only make out their silhouettes. I squinted and lifted my hand to shade my eyes from the intense light, struggling to see.

Slowly, colors and definition began to come into focus. First, I recognized Dr. Stella's coat and her dark pony tail dangling in front of her shoulder. She stood on my left. On the other side, I noticed curly brown hair. Then, the yellow of a worn shirt came into view, with a silver heart necklace hanging down.

A dreadful chill crept over me. That was my necklace. And that was my shirt! The person standing there was . . . me! I screamed, but it didn't escape my lips. Instead, it just echoed inside of me until I composed myself enough to speak.

"What's happening to me?" I grabbed hold of Dr. Stella's arm. "How am I lying here on this table, and standing next to it at the same time? Am I dead?"

It didn't make any sense, but there I was, standing across from Dr. Stella, looking down at myself. How could I be in two places at once? "I'm not dead!" I screamed.

Dr. Stella nodded her head. Her emerald eyes gazed into

mine. "Time to wake up. Becca, do you hear my voice? It's time to wake up," she smiled.

I opened my eyes and sat straight up with a jolt, looking around the room. My breathing was quick. I jumped up from the couch. "What's going on?" I demanded, barely able to speak.

Had I been dreaming? Hallucinating? Was I really awake now? Everything had felt so real, it was difficult to tell the difference. What was clear was that I was in my therapist's office again. Dr. Stella sat in her black leather chair, with a pad of paper in hand, just as she had for all of my previous counseling sessions.

I reached my hand to my chest, feeling for my silver heart necklace. It was there, right where it was supposed to be. Underneath, I could feel the softness of my comfortable yellow shirt. I grabbed my hair and pulled it in front of my eyes -- long, brown and curly.

"What time is it?"

"Becca, are you alright?"

I looked over at the clock. It was just before six. My purse sat on the floor next to me. I grabbed it and pulled out my phone, swiping it to see the date.

Everything started to make sense -- sort of. I still wasn't sure what to call that experience. Nothing quite like that had ever happened to me before, but then again, I had never had a dream in this new body. Maybe dreams felt like this for some people.

Or it could have seemed so real, because it had been so many months since my last dream. Maybe I had just forgotten what it was like to dream. Anyway, if I had been dreaming, at least I knew I was wide awake now.

"Becca, is everything alright?" Dr. Stella's voice was slow and deliberate, her demeanor cautious and controlled.

I sat there a few feet away from her, still reeling from what had just happened. Why had she been in my dream?

I looked up at the clock and wrapped my arm through the strap of my purse. "I'm fine. I just felt a little disoriented. Maybe I tried to get up too fast." Or maybe it was that new injection you stuck me with.

I started walking toward the door. "My mom's probably waiting for me."

Dr. Stella swiveled her chair in my direction. "Do you need something to calm your nerves? I can give you something before you go." She reached into a drawer and produced a small number of pills wrapped in plastic with a foil backing. "You should probably take these tonight before you go to bed."

That was the last thing I planned on doing. I didn't want one more pill, or a shot, or anything else she had to give me.

She looked me up and down. "You seemed quite shaken when you woke up. This will help you to be able to rest peacefully tonight."

I didn't want to stay one more second longer than I had to. I just wanted to get out of there, without giving her any more cause for suspicion. I reached out my hand to accept the pills and acted like I was grateful. She'd never know if I actually took them.

"Here you go." Dr. Stella smiled. "Take two at bedtime. There's enough in there for the week."

I dropped them into my purse, then walked to the door. I had barely opened it when she called to me again.

"Becca." She cleared her throat. "I would like to see you in two weeks, instead of our usual three week interval."

I forced a smile and turned to look at her. "Okay." I watched her face to see if I had convinced her of my indifference.

She turned away too quickly for me to get a good look straight on, but I caught a glimpse of her reflection from the mirror above her cabinet.

Her eyes looked hard. Her lips were pursed together so tightly, I was surprised they didn't bleed. I had never noticed any wrinkles on her face before, but there were visible lines around her mouth, and creases in her forehead. She looked angry. Her face seemed colder than ice. Was that what lied beneath her superficial beauty?

I was about to wheel back around and leave when my eye caught one more little detail. There, on the back of her leg, was a run in her stockings, just like in my dream!

CHAPTER 29

Darla

Dr. Stella used to be in the same building as Becca's father. Their offices were even located on the same floor, but hers was way down at the opposite end of the hall. The day she learned that she would be relocating from the facility in Faison and moving closer to Raleigh, she seemed really upset about it.

I remember exactly how she looked that day, standing there, watching in silence. Surprisingly, when the movers came to pack up her things, she didn't bark any orders at them, even when they touched her fragile sculptures. There might have been a slight hint of sadness in her eyes, but mostly it looked like she was seething with anger.

Some of the secretaries were gossiping about Dr. Stella's unexpected exile, and the abruptness of it all. One of them worked for Becca's father and sat right outside his office. She was older, with glasses and a short haircut. She also had on this distinctive bright red lipstick. The other lady worked one floor below. She was much younger and new to the job.

I saw the new girl walk into the lobby of the fifteenth floor, weaving her way through the men who were moving Dr. Stella's boxes and carrying her sculptures into the elevator. She stopped at the desk of the older secretary with the bright red lips. They exchanged some whispers and gawked at the chaotic spectacle in the lobby.

A few minutes later, when Becca's father left his office and disappeared around the corner, the two ladies began speaking loud enough for me to hear.

The new girl pulled up a chair. "So, did she get fired?"

"Not so lucky. Odds are we'll see her face around here again. She's just being relocated."

"But why?"

The lady with the red lips had a gleam in her eye, as if she was about to reveal something juicy. She pulled her glasses down and peered over the top of the frame. "From what I hear, Old Stella Cruella isn't going by choice. She's being forced to leave Faison."

"Really? But this place is huge. There are tons of buildings here."

"Exactly. In this very building half of tenth and almost all of eleventh is still vacant. It's not like anybody is running out of space around here."

"Weird. There has got to be more to the story."

"I couldn't say," the lady with the red lips shrugged, all the while giving her younger companion a knowing look and a Cheshire grin.

The newer girl leaned in and smiled. "So what else do you know?"

The lady with the red lips appeared to hesitate in her reply, but at the same time, she didn't seem to be bothered in the least by the question. Her eyes narrowed. "You can't repeat this to anyone, but Dr. Tanner and Dr. Stella were arguing. I heard them myself."

"Get outta here. Dr. Tanner got her kicked out of Faison? Go Dr. T!"

"Let me stress this. You can't tell anyone that you heard this from me, okay?"

"Who am I going to tell? I don't know anybody else here. You're the only other person I talk to."

The lady with the red lips considered her friend's response briefly, then continued. "So, this is what happened. Yesterday, they were in there arguing. I couldn't hear them behind the glass, but it was obvious they were yelling. As Dr. Stella walked out of Dr. Tanner's office, I heard their last little exchange."

The new girl hung on every word, eyes dancing with intrigue. "What did you hear?"

"Well, Dr. Tanner told her that what she did was a fireable offense."

"Wow. And what did she say?"

"Dr. Stella told him that he didn't have the authority to fire her." The lady with red lips smirked. "But then Dr. Tanner told her that she was about to find out what he had authority to do."

"Oh my."

The lady with the red lips nodded. "And apparently, as we see now, Dr. Tanner had the authority to get her kicked out of here. He may not have been able to fire her, but she's going bye bye."

I desperately wanted to know what had happened. The secretary was the only person talking, and unfortunately she didn't have anything more substantive to reveal.

I wanted to know *why* didn't Dr. Stella get fired?

CHAPTER 30

Becca

Another restless night. I went back and forth between laying on my stomach with hands tucked under my pillow, then switching to lay on my side, bent in the middle with knees pulled up. Once in a while I even tried laying on my back with one leg dangling off the edge of the bed. It was all useless.

At one point, I got up and did some homework, hoping that something boring might send me into a deep blissful coma, but not even that helped. No matter how I tried to get past them, the thoughts of that dream I had in Dr. Stella's office kept racing through my mind, preventing me from getting any meaningful sleep.

How freaky was that dream? I mean, who dreams of being dead, looking up at themselves, staring back down at their own dead body? It was just bizarre. And who in the heck was that blonde girl on the other table? I couldn't stop replaying the moment Dr. Stella pulled the sheet back, revealing that dead girl's face.

Every detail, down to the position of the procedure tables, the sound of the sheets sliding, and the disgusting pungent odor of the place, lingered in the forefront of my mind like unwelcome guests at a funeral.

On my drive to school, my mind was still in a haze. Gradually, as morning gave way to afternoon, I felt like I was settling down and getting control of my thoughts. The final bell of the day rang. I had made it through the entire school day on a couple hours of sleep. That was no small feat.

I was standing in front of my locker, emptying it of old

papers and other random trash, waiting for Nora. My phone buzzed. It was a new text message.

Unknown Number: Becca, this is Jason. It's really important that I talk to you. Please respond as soon as possible.

Ugh! This guy again. Would it have been too much to ask, to get just one full day without having to hear from him? Normally, I could have just ignored him, taking it in stride without getting all worked up. But today, it felt like the straw that broke the camel's back. Not that I was comparing myself to a camel -- it was just the expression that fit.

With the lack of sleep and everything else I was dealing with, his text message felt like he was intentionally piling on. It was as if he knew that I was near my breaking point, and by pestering me constantly, he hoped I would somehow eventually give up, surrender and submit to his will.

I deleted the text, then made sure that all of the other messages from him were erased as well.

There were a lot of old texts stored on my phone. Since I was already in a cleaning mood, I scrolled through the list, deleting several more messages. Most were from my friends, even a few that Sierra sent me from Mom's phone. The further down I scrolled, the more disappointed I felt. What I had really been hoping for today was a text message from Blake.

I put my phone away and finished cleaning out my locker, then turned to watch for Nora. As my eyes scanned across the hall, I caught sight of Blake, but it wasn't a good thing. He was with none other than little miss perfect, Valarie, at his side.

His tall, strong body made her petite frame look even tinier. She had curled her hair today. Loose, flowing waves of blonde spirals caught the breeze as she walked, like a model on a runway. Straight or curled, up or down, her hair looked good no matter how she fixed it.

My head went limp on top of my neck, drooping from my shoulders. Who was I to think that I could compete with her? It was easy to see that she and Blake looked absolutely perfect together. They had to be the best looking couple at school. Why would he ever choose me, when he could have her?

I pulled my phone out again and looked down at it, trying to appear occupied and unaware as the two of them headed toward me. After several seconds I glanced up, risking a peek. They were still headed in my direction. Blake was talking about something, and Valarie was obviously going out of her way to seem interested in whatever he was saying. They hadn't noticed me yet.

As they were about to pass me by, Blake slowed down. We caught sight of each other. No words were spoken, but our eyes locked for a brief moment, almost captured in time, playing in slow motion.

Whatever the reason, it sure felt like there was something between us. I think Valarie noticed as well.

"Blake," she said, tugging his arm, demanding his attention. "We better get out to the parking lot before we get stuck behind that never ending line of buses."

I looked back down at my phone feeling utterly confused and frustrated. It sounded like they had plans to go somewhere, together. She obviously already had his time and attention. She could have at least let him stop to say hi. What did she have to worry about anyway?

"Becca." The unexpected sound of Blake's smooth, deep voice surprised me. I turned and looked up. He was standing right in front of me. I wanted to bury myself into his chest and feel his arms around me. I was so glad that he had stopped.

He stared at me, the same way he did yesterday, when he watched me get into my Jeep. He looked worried. "Why weren't you in class this morning?"

Valarie stepped in close, arms folded, obviously irritated.

I ignored her and looked up at Blake again. The warmth

of his searching eyes immediately melted away the frost from Valarie's ice cold stare. "I accidentally slept in," I said.

Valarie rolled her eyes.

"So no more car trouble?"

"No. Thank goodness. I just didn't sleep very well last night. I was up so late that when I finally did doze off, I slept right through my alarm."

The expression on Blake's face conveyed that he understood there was more to my answer than what I had just explained. He probably thought that I couldn't sleep because of being chased yesterday and because of my stolen car battery. Those things had little to do with my restless night, but in fairness, when I got to school this morning, I remembered all too well how terrified I had been, walking down the hallways and right past the room where I had almost been caught.

"You didn't miss much in class," he said. "We just watched a movie."

"What class is this?" Valarie jumped in.

"English," Blake replied.

"I didn't know you two had any classes together."

"I just transferred in." Blake turned his gaze back to me. "I sit two seats behind Becca."

"How . . . nice." The expression on Valarie's face went from bothered to alarmed.

"I could start giving you wake up calls in the morning, if your alarm doesn't seem to be doing the trick?" A mischievous smile spread across Blake's face.

I couldn't believe he just said that, and in front of Valarie. "Hmm," I smiled back at him. "I may have to take you up on that offer."

"Blake." Valarie tugged on his arm, harder this time. "I don't mean to be rude, but your aunt is going to be wondering where you are."

"Yeah, I better get going . . . I'll see you Monday."

Monday? Why can't I see you tonight, or tomorrow, or Sunday? All you have to do is ask me out. I'll say yes. My heart felt achy. I was already missing him. "See ya," I said, trying to hide the disappointment that was crushing me on the inside.

They headed off toward the exit. I stood there and watched him, thinking about how wonderful it would be to wake up to his dreamy voice every morning, but I'd never in a million years ask him to do that.

When the two of them reached the door at the end of the hallway, Blake opened it for Valarie and stepped to the side. I knew this was an opportunity for him to look back at me. I wasn't sure if he would, but I didn't want him to think that I was some kind of desperate charity case, or hopeless stalker, so I turned away and started messing with my locker.

When would Valarie ever get out of the picture? And when would Blake stop opening doors for her? Ugh! This was so infuriating! Was I just setting myself up for a broken heart, waiting for the day that he finally asked me out? What if that day never comes?

My phone buzzed again. I didn't bother to check it this time. It was probably Jason sending me another *urgent* text message.

"Becca," a high pitched voice called from behind me.

I turned. It was Fiona Phillips.

"Oh, hey," I said.

"Here are your notes back," she held out the papers. "Sorry it took so long for me to return them to you."

"No problem." I stuffed the papers into my notebook.

Fiona's long, silky dark hair hung down in front of her shoulder in a loose braid. I envisioned in my mind the girl with long dark hair getting out of that black truck, trying to compare it to hers. If hair length and color were enough for a jigsaw puzzle, I'd snap this piece in place right now, but to be sure I'd still need to connect her to that truck.

"Let me know if I can ever return the favor," she said.

"Sure."

"You know . . . I couldn't help but notice." Fiona paused and bit her lip.

"Notice what?"

"Well. I saw the way you were staring at Blake a minute ago."

Was I being that obvious, or was she suddenly paying way too much attention?

"I don't blame you for looking." Fiona smiled mischievously. "He is the hottest guy at school."

I shook my head. "I think you got the wrong impression. Blake and I are just friends."

"Becca, don't worry." She placed her hand across her chest. "Your secret's safe with me."

I shrugged. "I don't have any secrets. There's no secret about Blake. We're seriously just friends."

Her smile became a smirk. "Everybody's got secrets." Fiona's bright green eyes locked onto mine in a knowing stare. "And I bet you have some *real big* secrets."

That statement rocked me back on my heels. Was she talking about what I think she was talking about? Did she know my secret?

I tried my best to act confused, in an effort to conceal my utter panic. "Huh?"

Fiona's phone rang. She reached for her pocket, pulled it out, then turned her back on me as she walked away. There was no wave goodbye, no nod of the head, nothing. She acted as if I no longer existed.

I had no idea what she meant by that bombshell of a comment about secrets. Was she just being presumptuous regarding Blake, or was she deliberately dropping major clues?

A small group of boys passed by in front of me, obscuring my view of her as she headed down the hallway.

Nora finally showed up.

"Sorry it took me so long." She looked freshly put together and smelled like citrusy perfume. "I'm ready to go now. Jeff's going to meet us there."

"Do you know that girl?" I pointed to Fiona. She was halfway down the hall, getting books out of her locker, still on the phone.

"Love her shoes. I need to get me some of those." Suddenly, Nora's face lit up. "Oh wait. That's the girl Jeff used to have a crush on." She nodded. "Yep. That's totally her. He thought she was the hottest girl at school. . . . Why do you ask?"

"Jeff had a crush on her?"

"Oh yeah. Big time. I think she's gorgeous, but there's something about her weird eyes that bothers me."

"What do you mean, *weird eyes*?"

"It's the color. At first, I thought she was wearing green contacts, but she's not. Eyes only look that way in pictures. You know . . . they have been photoshopped.

"I guess."

"Yeah. Anyway, why do you want to know about her?"

Nora, if only I could tell you. I sighed. "No reason. I was just curious."

We sat at our usual spots on the second floor of the public library -- Jeff to my right and Nora straight across from me.

Nora twisted her platinum blonde hair up into a bun, stuck a pencil through it, then cracked opened a novel to read. Her dark eyeshadow was plastered on thick. She said she was going for a smokey look, hoping it would make her seem more grown up.

Jeff pulled out his thick biology book, dropped it onto the table and mindlessly flipped through the pages. He stuck his bottom lip out and exhaled. The breeze blew up through his red hair that dangled over his forehead.

I had been waiting for the opportunity to tell them about being chased in the hallways after school yesterday. I didn't want to do it in front of Stephanie, not after her big mouth blabbed to the entire world when I told her about the truck following me. And since school property had been damaged, I definitely didn't want this story flying around campus.

I told Jeff and Nora everything, except for the Blake stuff. I was saving that for a time when Jeff wasn't around. Each of them reacted more or less the way I expected they would.

Nora was in freak out mode, probably afraid that something bad would happen again at any moment. She didn't say much. She mostly stared at me with her mouth agape.

Jeff was angry. He wanted to protect me, but obviously had no way to do so. He suspected Jason right away. No other culprit even landed on his radar, but I didn't think it was Jason, and I told Jeff that, hoping it would help calm him down.

I explained that the person who had chased me seemed more agile and much faster than Jason. He countered that I was underestimating Jason's football conditioning and athleticism. But I knew that I had other enemies out there, and since Jeff wasn't aware of that, he couldn't imagine anybody else ever wanting to hurt me.

Nora stared at me some more. Her mouth was still agape.

Honestly, I didn't know who it was. I had to admit there was abundant circumstantial evidence pointing to Jason, but there were also some big holes in that theory. He may have been athletic in certain ways, but he was truly awkward in others -- heavy-footed and slow beyond more than a short burst. He played lineman, not running back. I couldn't imagine that it was him who had chased me all that distance through those dark hallways. Jason had also never smelled like cigarettes before, as far as I was aware. I couldn't convict him without hard evidence, and it just didn't exist.

It turned out that Jeff had science class in the same classroom where the window got shattered. He said that the glass shards had all been cleaned up, but the window hadn't been replaced yet, so kids in the hallway kept sticking their hands and even their heads through the hole, much to the delight of the students inside, and to the consternation of the teacher.

My phone buzzed, practically vibrating the whole table. I

ignored it.

"Aren't you going to check that?" Jeff asked.

"I'll look at it later." I had a pretty good idea who it was, and didn't care what he had to say to me.

A couple seconds later, like clockwork, it buzzed again.

"At least turn it off." Jeff picked my phone up. He fumbled for the power button, but then stopped and just stared at the screen.

"I thought you were going to turn it off," I said.

He looked up with a bewildered expression on his face, then handed me the phone. "I think you'll want to see this now, instead of later."

"What is it?" Nora asked.

I enlarged the screen. "It's a picture."
"Of what?"

"Of the three of us, outside the library, right before we came in here." I turned the phone toward her so she could see.

"Who sent that?" Nora gasped.

"I don't know. The number is unavailable," I said.

Jeff got up from his chair.

"Where do you think you're going?" Nora snorted.

"I'm gonna take a look outside. I'll be right back." He raced toward the stairs.

"Now this," Nora pointed to my phone, "this is getting completely out of hand." She walked around the table, then sat next to me, examining the picture again.

Jeff returned several minutes later. I could tell he was still agitated. I was just relieved that he was back and that he was okay.

"I didn't see Jason, or his car," he said.

"Good. Then he's gone and hopefully won't be coming back." Nora pulled the pencil out of her bun and shook her head, letting her hair fall onto her shoulders. "I've gotta go to the bathroom. Jeff, don't let her out of your sight until I get back."

Jeff turned to me. "Do you think it was Jason who sent

that?"

"He has been texting me today, claiming that he has to talk to me about something important."

"And," Jeff said intently.

"And what?"

"Did you respond to his texts?"

"No."

"What do you think he needs to talk to you about?"

"Who knows. And I don't care."

Jeff began a rant about how terrible Jason was. I sat there, watching his face progressively turn darker shades of red the more impassioned and angry he became. I knew that somebody was after me and that it might not be Jason. It might not even be any one person -- could be five, ten, even more. But as I sat there listening to Jeff berate Jason, I allowed myself to deposit all of my fears, and frustrations in one place. For now, I let myself blame Jason.

"He is *not* going to get away with treating you like this anymore . . ." Jeff continued speaking, but his voice faded away into the background as I noticed Nora rushing toward us from across the room.

"You're not going to believe this," she said, catching her breath.

"What's wrong?" I asked.

"Jason. I saw him by the bathrooms, then I followed him to his hiding place over there." She pointed to a row of bookshelves about forty feet away. "He quietly and carefully moved a couple of books out of the way, then aimed his phone at you. I think he took more pictures, or maybe even a video."

I scooted my chair out and was about to storm over there to confront him, but Nora grabbed hold of my wrist. "Becca. He's not there anymore."

"Are you sure?"

"I waited until he left before I came back to tell y'all."

"I can't believe this." Jeff slammed his book shut, then took off, without saying another word.

"Where are you going?" I called after him. He didn't respond. I shot up out of my chair, turning to Nora. "We have to find Jason, right now!"

"Don't worry. I saw him leave. Jeff won't find him. He's gone." The certainty in her eyes convinced me.

I sighed in relief. "While you were gone, all Jeff did was rant and rave about Jason. He is really worked up right now. If the two of them run into each other it's gonna be bad."

Nora snickered. "I wish I would have been here to hear that. You know how I love a good Jason bashing session."

"I don't think I've ever seen Jeff so angry."

Nora started rummaging through her purse. "He'll calm down soon enough. By the time school rolls around on Monday, he'll have forgotten all about Jason." She pulled out a pen and clicked it.

"Not if those pictures keep showing up on my phone, or online, or whatever he is doing with them."

She paused her writing. "Yeah, you've got a point there. What is up with Jason taking pictures of us?"

"Your guess is as good as mine." I turned my phone off, then stuffed it inside my backpack.

Several minutes went by and still no Jeff.

Nora crossed her legs and started bouncing her foot rapidly, while her eyes scanned the room. I knew she was looking for Jeff, and so was I. He should have been back by now.

"Maybe we better--" Before I could finish my sentence, I was interrupted by the sound of loud voices arguing off in the distance.

CHAPTER 31

Becca

The sound of arguing grew in intensity. I stood at the railing that overlooked the first floor of the library, scanning in the direction of the voices. There were several people converging on the scuffle, but Jeff's red hair wasn't hard to spot, right in the middle. "He's downstairs," I called back to Nora, before taking off for the fray.

I had no idea what I'd do once I got there, but hoped I would arrive in time to stop them somehow. I darted down the stairs and across the first floor, weaving around tables, chairs, shelves and people.

There they were, Jason and Jeff each with their fists clenched, grabbing one another by the shirt and shoving back and forth. Jeff shouted at Jason, that no one wanted him around, and he had better leave me alone. Jason fired right back that Jeff had better mind his own business.

A few of the library patrons had gathered, and someone had gone to tell the librarians what was happening after the two boys ignored demands to quiet down. This was already way out of hand.

"Knock it off. Both of you!" I yelled. "Jason, let go of him!"

They started pushing each other more violently as I approached. I tried to jump in and grab hold of Jason's arm, but had to duck out of the way. Jeff had knocked him off balance, and his huge body was falling backward, straight for me. I barely made it out of his path before he crashed into a bookshelf, causing it to fall over, scattering books everywhere.

I watched, frozen and speechless as Jason gathered his footing, then lunged toward Jeff in a fury of untamable rage. I felt pathetically hopeless. I was too late -- I couldn't stop them.

Jeff's face looked almost as red as his hair. Veins bulged out on the side of his neck. Jason's eyes belonged on a giant beetle -- bloodshot, darting around wildly. His wiry goatee stretched and contoured around his gritted teeth. The two of them were similar in height, but Jason had a definite size advantage. He was at least twice as wide as Jeff, and tackling people in football games was what he did best.

"Leave him alone Jason!" Nora squealed running up from behind me.

Jason exhaled, letting out a loud grunt, then swung his arms forward with all the force of his massive body weight behind him, slamming both hands into Jeff's chest. The impact sent Jeff flying backward, crashing into a cluster of wooden chairs before tumbling to the floor.

Maybe that would be it. Maybe the fight was over.

"Now you boys stop it!" someone yelled.

I ran toward Jeff, to try and help him up. "Jeff, are you okay?"

"Becca, get out of the way." Jeff scolded. It seemed the only thing that had been hurt was his pride. With a mixture of humiliation and determination he scrambled back to his feet, then charged at Jason once more.

No Jeff! Don't do this.

Jason grabbed hold of Jeff's shirt and flung him around, sending him straight into the wall with a booming thud. I buried my face in my hands as he made impact, then slowly looked again to see if he was alright.

"Someone help!" Nora screamed.

An older, frail looking woman arrived, demanding that the fight stop, but the boys were oblivious to her demands. They continued to grapple and struggle.

A small crowd of spectators had formed, made up mostly of teenagers. Anyone who was big and strong enough to intervene appeared more entertained than upset.

I continued to scan the room, then in desperation reached for the bookshelf next to me. I picked up a heavy, hardback book with pointy edges. This will have to do. I turned towards Jason, brought my arm back, then stepped into my throw with all of my power aimed straight at him.

The book went flying into the air. . . . Time seemed to slow down. It felt as though I was holding my breath, watching the book sail toward its target. I hoped my aim was true, but wouldn't know until the final moment. Further and further the book floated toward him. Jason, don't move, I pleaded in my mind.

A perfect hit! Jason grimaced, then whipped his head toward me, anger permeating from his face. He gave Jeff a hard push to break away and immediately started toward me.

My eyes got big. I stood there motionless, watching him come at me. What's he going to do?

Jeff ran up from behind and tripped him, knocking him to the ground. There was hope . . . but it only lasted for a moment.

As soon as Jeff had him down, Jason spun over on top, out muscling him once more. Jeff couldn't budge. He was pinned on his back and Jason was too heavy for him to push off. Jason kept Jeff's arms pinned down, then started laughing, wickedly. He slapped Jeff on the side of his head with his open hand, laughing harder. Then the evil smile on his face suddenly disappeared.

Jason looked at me with menacing eyes. "Tell your boyfriend here, to mind his own business." He looked back at Jeff, shaking his head. "So pathetic."

To add insult to injury, he leaned down and whispered something in Jeff's ear, then slugged him before he got up. Jason walked towards the exit, glaring at me, nostrils flaring. The automatic doors opened, then closed behind him.

Jeff scrambled back onto his feet, about to take off after Jason. I ran over to get between him and the door. "Don't! Just let him go!"

"Jeffrey Alma Anderson, you knock it off now!" Nora hollered.

"He's not worth it," I said. "Listen to me, Jeff."

Jeff stood still. Before anything else could be said, the librarians arrived threatening to call the police.

"I'll go get our stuff," I told Nora. "Take him outside. I'll meet you there."

They headed out the door. I hurried up the stairs to our table, stuffed everything into my backpack, then rushed back down toward the exit.

The doors slid open. Cool air swept across my face, and I shivered. The sun had nearly disappeared, and the sky was darkening. I scanned the parking lot until I spotted them. They were sitting on a bench not far from the door.

Jeff's head hung low as he sat there, bent forward, staring at the ground. Nora heard the doors close and turned to look. I walked toward them. Nora mouthed something to me, but I couldn't figure out what she was saying.

Jeff looked beat up, and this kind of beat up was on the inside. How was I going to console him? I didn't think there was anything I could do to make him feel better.

I sat down next to him. His hair was tousled and his shirt was torn, exposing his bare chest.

I was afraid to even ask this. . . . "Are you okay?"

Jeff started chuckling but didn't sound happy. His head remained low, eyes still staring at the ground. He took a deep breath and shook his head. "Man, I didn't expect all of that to happen."

Nora and I looked at each other, amazed that Jeff had calmed down so quickly.

He sat up and placed his arms over our shoulders. "I'm sorry you guys had to witness that train wreck. I didn't want that to happen. I'm really sorry."

"You don't need to apologize. If it wasn't for me, you wouldn't--"

"Becca," Jeff said softly. He took another deep breath, then gently placed his fingers on my shoulder. "Don't say it, okay? I chose to confront him. You didn't ask me to do it."

Nora pulled his arm off her shoulder. She began retrieving her things from my backpack, then started giggling.

"What's so funny?" I asked.

She smiled at me. "The librarian picked up that book you threw. She was waving it around while she was yelling at us to get out." Nora exploded into laughter. "Did you even notice which book you picked to hurl at Jason?"

"What?"

Nora's smile grew wider. She giggled again, then took a deep breath to gain her composure. "Okay, okay," she chuckled, reenacting an exaggerated wind up, throw, and impact on Jason's head. "It was none other than *The Life of Gandhi*."

We all laughed out loud -- even Jeff.

"I can't believe you noticed the title. Oh my gosh. Of all the things . . ." I said.

Nora continued her reenactment. "Well, that short librarian with the weird glasses was waving it at us like she was about to throw it again, just like you did. Honestly, I didn't know if I should duck or run. She was massively ticked off."

"Of course she was," I said.

"Did you see Jason's face?" Nora laughed. "He was absolutely stunned that you clobbered him like that . . . with a library book no less."

"He didn't look stunned to me," I said. "He looked like he was going to kill me."

Nora smirked. "Not while Jeff was there to protect you." She looked at Jeff's arm on my shoulder, then zipped her backpack shut. "Jeff, I meant to ask you," she said, in a serious tone. A decidedly devious gleam flashed across her narrowing eyes. "Was that the first time you had ever been sat on?" She snorted, then cleared her throat, struggling to hold her composure. "No, seriously. Could you even breathe?" After a few seconds, it was too much. She tried to keep a straight face, but her wry grin could no longer be contained.

I was stunned. Why in the world was she making fun of Jeff? I glared at her.

"You know, Nora," said Jeff, patting his lap. "Why don't you come sit on me so I can remember what it felt like. You and Jason have about the same sized thighs."

Nora smacked him on the shoulder. "You're a jerk! You can just forget about going to the movies with me. I'm leaving."

"Come on, I was just kidding," Jeff sighed.

"Forget it. Go ahead and spend the rest of your Friday

night sulking on that bench like a loser."

"Have a good night," Jeff waved, faking a smile.

Nora spun around and stormed off to her car.

"What's her problem . . ." Jeff started in. I sat there and let him ramble for a while. He had earned the right to let it all out. Nora was way out of line.

As soon as he was calm enough, I brought up the thing I had been waiting to ask him. "Hey Jeff. What did Jason whisper in your ear?"

"Nothing."

"You're not going to tell me?"

"He said nothing."

"Jeff, you don't have to protect me."

"Yeah, well that's fortunate, because I just proved how incredibly bad I am at that."

I knew Jason had said something to him about me, but there was no way I could continue to press him any further -- not after what he had been through and especially not after that comment.

"You might want to cover up," I said, as I pointed to the rip in his shirt. His whole pocket was lying flopped forward, showing his bare chest underneath.

"You don't think this makes me look irresistible?"

I got up. As I headed toward the parking lot, I spun back around. "Oh, but that's the exact reason why you should cover up."

"I knew you only wanted me for my body," he called out.

CHAPTER 32

Becca

After I got home and ate dinner, I watched some movies, staying up later than everyone else. When I finally went to bed, I laid there looking through my phone in the dark. The door knob squeaked, and I lowered my phone. Slowly, the door inched open. I sat up, greeted by a bright light shining directly in my face.

"Becca," Sierra's soft voice whispered.

"What are you still doing up?"

She lowered her flashlight and stood there with messy hair and a sad look on her face. "I can't sleep . . . can I come sleep with you?" She pointed the light back in my face.

I tossed a pillow at her. "Stop doing that."

She quickly lowered the light. "Please?"

"Only for a little while--"

I hadn't even finished my sentence before she bounded over and started climbing into bed beside me. She set her flashlight on the nightstand, facing up. A bright white circle glowed on the ceiling of my dark bedroom.

"How come you're still awake?" she asked.

"I was just about to go to sleep, until you came in here." I set my phone down on the nightstand, then pulled the covers over her.

"Who were you texting? A boy?" she giggled. "Was it

your boyfriend?"

"I don't have a boyfriend." I fluffed up my pillow and laid down. "I was texting Nora."

"Oh," she sounded disappointed. "I thought it was Jeff." Sierra rolled onto her side. "I like Jeff. He's funny. Can you scratch my back?"

"Alright. But only for a few minutes, then you need to go to sleep."

"Okay. I promise. I'll go to sleep."

As I scratched her back, I started thinking about the fight between Jason and Jeff again, realizing that it really was a good thing their fight happened at the library and not at school. Jeff would have been humiliated and probably teased for the rest of the year if the kids at school saw, not to mention the fight would have been posted on the Internet for the whole world to see. The worst part of it all, was the way Jason smacked him with an open hand . . . so humiliating. I didn't think that I could hate Jason any more than I already did, but my disdain for him had risen to a whole new level.

"Becca."

"Yeah?"

"You don't scratch backs like you used to."

"What are you talking about?"

"I mean like you used to . . . before you changed."

"You're being silly. I still scratch your back the same."

"No. Before you scratched with your other hand. Now you do it with the wrong one."

"But I still do it the same as before."

Sierra rolled over to face me. "It's not the same. Can't you use your other hand?"

"Fine," I agreed. "I'll try."

It was awkward using my right hand, but I figured I better go ahead and let her find out for herself that it's no better this way. Surprisingly, she didn't complain. After a few minutes, her breathing slowed. I reached over and turned her flashlight off, then stuffed a pillow between us, just in case she kicked during the night.

After laying there for a while, still not able to fall asleep, I decided to get up and go downstairs. Maybe it was time for a piece of that chocolate cake Mom made yesterday.

I carefully climbed out of bed, feeling my way through the dark. As I headed downstairs and into the kitchen, I didn't feel hungry anymore, so I went into the den and laid down on the couch, staring out the window.

The night sky was bright. There was a full moon out, and I could see the dark clouds slowly drifting by. I tried counting the stars as I laid there under the window, listening to the clock tick.

Hours passed by. I finally gave up on trying to fall asleep after I heard the clock chime three times.

When I got back to my room, I climbed in bed, pulled the covers up and reached over to adjust the pillow between Sierra and I, but she wasn't there anymore. Good. She must have gotten up and gone to her own room. Maybe I'll finally get some sleep now. I sprawled out over the entire bed, lying on my stomach, my cheek pressing into the soft mattress.

In the morning, Sierra woke me from a dream, singing in the hallway near my room. I had been dreaming of that same girl again, lying on the table under the sheet in the procedure room. This time, Dr. Stella pulled the sheet off of her face and said, "Her name is--" But right when she said the name, her voice became muffled and distorted. I couldn't hear it.

When I dreamed of the dead girl I didn't feel scared. I looked at her face, and her body lying there stiff and motionless. She seemed so familiar, as if we had once been close friends. The bond I felt for her transcended death. I didn't understand how I could feel that way about someone I had never met before.

Chocolate cake for breakfast sounded really good. I never did eat any last night, and was craving a piece. I walked out of my room and ran into Mom heading up the stairs with an empty laundry basket in her arms.

"That was nice of you to let Sierra sleep with you last night. You two were lying there so peacefully." Mom shook her head. "She's almost too big for me to carry. I'm surprised I didn't wake you when I picked her up. It took me a couple tries to lift her."

I squinted my eyes. "Huh?"

"I thought for sure I was gonna wake you, but you slept right through it."

What was she talking about? "I wasn't in bed when you came and got her. I was downstairs trying to fall asleep on the couch."

"No, you were sound asleep in your bed. I saw you."

I stared at Mom, trying to figure out if she was being serious, or if she was trying out some ill-conceived parent humor on me. It made sense that she had come and gotten Sierra, but I definitely wasn't there when she did it. I was downstairs.

Mom was sticking with her story. Whatever. Maybe she thought the pillow was me. I did have it wedged under the covers pretty good. I guess it could have looked like a body.

"Becca, are you having a hard time falling asleep?"

Uh oh, here we go. "No, I just didn't want Sierra to wake me up in the middle of the night. She tosses and turns a lot."

Mom's expression was all business. "But if you are having trouble sleeping, then we should talk to Dr. Stella about adjusting your meds. It's important that you get all the rest your body needs at night."

"I don't have a problem falling asleep, Mom. I'm good. Everything's fine with my medication."

Mom's eyes searched my face. Finally she took a deep breath. "Okay. Just please let your dad or I know if you ever do have trouble sleeping. Dr. Stella said that she would have to adjust your dosage if that started happening."

"I will. I'll let you know." There was no way I was going to keep that promise.

Mom brushed her hair away from her eyes. "I'm going to go take a shower. Make sure that Sierra gets something to eat for breakfast."

"Okay."

She turned and walked down the hall.

I heard my phone ring and went back into my room. I saw that in addition to Jason's countless voice messages and texts, Jeff had also texted me, asking me to call him before noon. I was a little late, but called anyway.

He told me that Nora sent him a text apologizing for how she treated him after his fight with Jason. Then he sent a text back, apologizing for calling her thighs fat. I felt certain this was a good move on his part.

Making fun of Nora's weight was the highest offense Jeff could have committed -- a fact that he was well aware of, and yet he did it anyway. This signaled to me that Nora had touched a nerve with him -- one that he may have tried harder than Nora to keep hidden, but it was equally as sensitive.

Jeff had to go somewhere, so our conversation ended much quicker than usual, but my thoughts lingered with him. I was surprised and relieved that he had resolved things so quickly with Nora. I didn't want to be caught in the middle. Plus, Jeff had plenty to deal with, without one of his closest friends mad at him. He was going to need our support.

It was impossible to predict the extent of the rumors that would be flying around school, but there was little doubt that the fight at the library would be big news. It was also a safe bet that Jason would take full advantage of the opportunity to soak up some extra attention in order to boost his already over-inflated ego.

I had never experienced two guys fighting over me. It was strange. Before it happened, I used to think how romantic it would be. I imagined how it would feel to be swept off my feet by the heroic victor. I suppose that was all part of the fantasy. In reality, there was nothing heroic or romantic about it. The good guy didn't win.

My phone started to ring. I cringed, not wanting to look. Thankfully, it was Nora and not Jason.

"Hey."

"You need to do something for me," she replied.

"What?"

"You have to ask Blake about going to the ranch again. I have absolutely got to see Hunter."

"I'm not going to ask Blake again, and I don't want you to ask him about it either."

"Are you kidding me? What's gotten into you? I'm talking about Blake Pierce . . . the guy you've been drooling over. Are you gonna tell me that you are suddenly no longer interested?"

"No. I'm obviously . . . interested. But there's such a thing as coming on too strong. I don't want him to think that I'm obsessed."

"Becca," Nora groaned. "Come on. You have to strike while the iron is hot."

"Sorry, but I don't plan on doing any striking with any irons, hot or otherwise. Blake said we can come, but we don't need to rush over there. I want to wait a little bit."

"Well, I've been waiting long enough," she grumbled. "What if he's already forgotten?"

"Nora, promise me you won't bug him about this."

"But what if--" she started in again, until I interrupted her.

"Interested. Not obsessed," I reminded her.

"But you get to see Blake at school every day. I almost never get to see Hunter."

"I want to go back to the ranch just as bad as you do. Trust me."

"I hope Hunter isn't one of those guys who only likes cheerleaders or anorexic supermodels. I wish you would've been here last school year, so that we could have tried out for cheerleading together. I would have totally tried out if you had done it with me."

"What makes you think that I would ever want to be on the cheerleading squad? You want us to spend even more time around Valarie?"

"Oh. Yeah. I didn't think of that." She continued lamenting over her missed opportunities and her hopes for a relationship with Hunter. I half listened, but my mind was busy unpacking something she had said. Cheerleading tryouts happened near the end of the previous school year. I hadn't put that timing together before.

Fact: My mystery girl attended West Johnston High School. The note she left in the computer lab made this much clear.

Fact: She had to have started school here at around the same time as me. Actually, this was more of an assumption, but it was a really strong assumption. Our body transplant procedures must have been performed very close together, if not on the same day, so she must have started school within the last six months.

I had known for a long time that Valarie was new to the school, just like me. This detail had helped to propel her to the top of my suspect list, but now I had new evidence to consider -- timing.

There was only one possible conclusion. Since Valarie was on the cheerleading squad, that meant that she wasn't as new to this school as I was. She had to have arrived here months before I did, in time for cheerleading tryouts. She couldn't be the mystery girl. The timing didn't work.

My suspect list was getting smaller, for the first time. Now, the strongest remaining contender was Fiona Phillips. She isn't on the cheerleading squad, but she is beautiful, stuck up about her looks, and way too interested in my business.

"Nora, do you know when Fiona started going to West Johnston?"

"Uh. I have no idea. Why?"

"I was wondering if this was her first year at this school."

"Who knows. I never talk to her. Like I said, weird eyes. Creeps me out."

"Seriously, you don't remember if she was in school last

year?"

"Becca, this is like the second time you've asked me about that chick. What's going on?"

Think of something to say. Quick. "I heard that she likes Blake." I hadn't actually heard that, but it was the only thing I could think of to say. And in actuality, she probably did like him. Everybody liked him.

"Becca, I wouldn't want to be you."

"And why is that?"

"Do you realize how many girls there are lined up just waiting for a chance to catch Blake's attention?" she asked. "If you're gonna get jealous over every girl that bats her eyes at your man, you've picked the wrong guy. Maybe you should consider liking someone else."

"Well, I definitely don't want to turn into a Valarie. That's for sure."

"Don't you realize how many other guys already like you."

"Like who?"

"Do I seriously need to list them for you?"

"No. It doesn't matter. My heart is set on Blake. I can't even begin to explain it. I've never felt like this before. It's like I'm drawn to him. Does that even make sense?"

"Totally," Nora said, wistfully. "You know what? Scratch what I said before about considering someone else. Go get your man."

I liked hearing her say that, even though I felt certain she was still angling for a trip to the ranch so she could see Hunter.

"I've got to go get my sister some breakfast. I'll talk to you later," I said.

"Alright, bye."

I began to feel an enormous sense of relief from the knowledge that Valarie was not the mystery girl. Although she was gorgeous, and her hatred toward me was fierce, two qualities which placed her at the top of the contenders list in the first place, it turned out that she didn't hate me for the reasons I had most feared.

However, the more I thought about her, the less relieved I became. If anything, I liked her even less. It was a clarifying moment to discover that I had no more confusion in my mind about my own distrust and dislike for her. It was quite simple. She was a mean, nasty girl, with her hands all over the boy I was falling in love with.

I decided that I would ask Blake how he felt about Valarie. I was nervous to say anything about her to him, fearful of the kind of answer he might give. But what was motivating me to overcome that fear, was how I felt when I saw them together. It was like my heart was being crushed, a little bit more each time. The pain I felt was devastatingly real and torturous.

I promised myself that I would be bold. I would ask on Monday, before class.

CHAPTER 33

Darla

Security guards kept the Tanner family home and the neighborhood under surveillance. They also followed Dr. Tanner back and forth from work. Usually, they tried to remain unseen, except when suspicious activity cropped up.

This morning at the facility, Becca's father spoke to one of the guards who protected his home last night. The guard reported that he had seen a van drive onto the Tanner's street and park a couple houses down on the right. Apparently the man in the vehicle never exited. He turned his lights off and sat there for several minutes. The guard described the vehicle as an older cargo van, gray, with no back windows.

The guard pulled out his notepad before giving more details. "I approached the driver, a caucasian male, approximately six feet tall, two-hundred, fifty-five pounds, brown hair, brown eyes, goatee, possibly early twenties. The driver indicated that he was lost and had pulled over to look at his phone for directions to a friend's house."

"Sounds harmless. Do you think there's something to be worried about?" Becca's father asked.

"I encouraged him to move along. He didn't hesitate to comply, but then I ran his plates."

"And what did you find?"

The guard looked away. "The license plate was from North Carolina, but the van had recently been reported stolen."

"Did you detain the driver?"

The guard swallowed hard. "I didn't run the plate until after he was gone.

Becca's father became visibly agitated at that response. He leaned back in his chair, folding his arms across his chest, eyes narrowed. I half expected him to start yelling at the guy, but he didn't. He kept his lips pressed together in a hard line.

"Sir, the driver didn't present any initial cause for suspicion. He had a football on the front passenger seat and a stack of textbooks. His story seemed legit. I thought he was just some college or high school kid looking for a party."

That was the end of the report to Becca's father. I wished I would have gone on patrol with that guard last night and seen the driver of the van for myself. I wondered if it was someone who went to school with Becca -- perhaps someone I might have recognized.

CHAPTER 34

Becca

Arriving at class a little earlier than usual, I hung my bookbag on the back of my seat, pausing to stare at the empty desk behind me -- the one Blake would soon occupy. It wasn't hard to imagine how his six foot, two inch frame would fill it up. I had logged plenty of hours with that very scene prominently featured in my daydream playlist.

"Becca," a smooth, deep voice came floating to my ears. It was Blake. He was early. This was perfect.

My head turned as if on a swivel, watching every broad confident step as he passed by. "Hey," I replied.

It never failed. No matter how bold or determined I felt ahead of time, as soon as Blake arrived, those things all melted away, replaced by an overpowering desire to simply be near him.

He spilled his books onto his desk and slid into his seat, all in one fluid movement. My gaze traced the hard line of his square jaw, lingered briefly on his soft lips, then settled upon the endless depths of his alluring blue eyes.

Time stood still briefly, until a nagging, irritating inner voice shouted at me from beyond center stage of my thoughts, snapping me back to awareness. I should just get this over with, and ask him about Valarie right now. Don't be nervous, I told myself.

"You made it to class today," he said, interrupting me before I could begin speaking.

I had rehearsed this conversation in my mind countless times. I knew exactly what I wanted to say, but at the last minute had hesitated, second guessing myself. Now, I was completely thrown off. It took me a moment to refocus. "Yep, I made it. And before you."

Some kid walked in and headed for his seat on the other side of the room. In another two minutes, every desk would be filled. Time was running out, and I had promised myself that today was the day. All I had to do was spit out the words that I had been planning all night.

He leaned toward me, resting on his elbows, as if to share a secret. "Your alarm clock must have worked this morning."

I thought he had just been joking last Friday when he offered to give me a wake up call. But maybe he was being serious. "I hope I'm not giving you the wrong impression by being early this morning."

"How would that give me the wrong impression? Are punctual people bad where you come from? Is that one of those California things?" he smiled.

Apparently my comment had amused him, even though that wasn't my intention. I giggled, mostly out of embarrassment, wishing that I would have said something witty and clever. "No. It's just that you offered to give me a wake up call, so I wouldn't oversleep. And since I'm here early . . . I didn't want you to think that I'm trying to avoid you . . . or a phone call."

Blake raised one eyebrow and grinned playfully. "So you *do* want me to call you?"

I absolutely wanted him to call me. Was he just teasing me, or was he really offering? This topic warranted immediate and thorough exploration. The topic of Valarie would have to wait.

I smiled, intentionally flashing a mischievous expression of my own. "I don't need another alarm, but there's lots of other reasons for you to call me, you know."

"Really?" he asked, in a hushed tone. Blake sat up. "What kind of reasons?"

"Well," I replied, twisting my hair. "For example, you

might call me if you had a real hard decision to make."

"Hmm. Hard decisions," he echoed, nodding his head contemplatively.

"Yeah, decisions like what kind of outfit to wear to school the next day," I said teasingly.

"I see." He brought his hand to his chin. "And should I expect to get similar phone calls from you? You know, about difficult outfit decisions?"

I smiled, shrugging my shoulders. "Possibly."

"I may as well warn you right up front." He cocked his head to the side. "I'm afraid you'd find my wardrobe advice a bit lacking in variety."

"Oh really?"

"There is really only one look I'd ever suggest for you."

"Just one? I'm dying to hear this."

He laughed for a moment, then straightened his smile into a more serious expression. "Well, I'd advise you to wear some camo."

"As in army camouflage?"

"Not exactly. Not army. The look I see you in involves hunting camo. That'd look way hot."

I laughed. "With combat boots?"

"Once again, California. You're close, but not quite. Regular boots."

"I hate to disappoint you. I'm afraid that I don't own any camo."

"We can fix that."

I wasn't sure exactly where this was going, but it was spectacularly good fun to play along. "I had no idea I was so . . . hideous. I mean, all this time, with no camo of any kind."

Blake immediately waved his hands as if to stop me. "Now, don't get me wrong. You've got a perfect record for looking . . ." He paused, leaned out from his desk to take in my full ensemble. "You're just stellar."

I was wearing jeans and a striped shirt. It wasn't that fantastic. "Stellar? Wow. I haven't heard that word since I left

California and usually only from surfers, not hunters."

"What can I say? I'm a well-rounded, cultured guy."

"Yeah, the redneck culture. Camo? Seriously?"

"Hold up," he laughed. "Did you just call me a redneck?"

"Well, your uncle's name is Cletus and you do work on a ranch."

"That's true, but there are no cars up on cinder blocks in my front yard, and I still have all my teeth, in case you're counting."

I smiled and leaned in a little closer. "I actually have noticed your teeth. You have a very nice smile." I couldn't help but notice how enticing his lips looked, opening slightly, then closing, with each word he uttered. Even though other people had steadily been entering the classroom, it felt as if we were in our own private universe.

"So a nice smile is all the evidence you need?" he asked.

"I don't know. I'll probably need to see your house at some point, so I can count the cars and cinder blocks in your yard. That's the only way to be certain."

"Becca, there is a difference between redneck and country."

"Oh really. Which one are you?"

He held a finger up while looking at the ground with eyes closed. "Since you're new around here, I won't hold that last comment against you."

I could tell he was smiling on the inside, while trying to appear serious on the outside.

"What I am, is country. Not redneck," he paused. "Country."

"So when I called you a redneck, that was an insult?" I asked.

"I'm not sayin' that. There's not a resident in Johnston County that doesn't have at least a little redneck in 'em."

"Well, my guess is that redneck means hunting, agriculture, and something to do with racing. I was wondering how NASCAR figured into all of this."

Blake shook his head without saying a word.

"What about hunting and fishing?" I asked. "I thought those were like the main pillars of redneckery." He seemed to be enjoying this conversation, so I decided to really lay it on thick.

"Oh, we most definitely bait our own hooks and skin our own deer."

"So other than the absence of cinder blocks and the addition of oral hygiene, what makes you country? What's the difference?"

"Country is more of an attitude. There's nothing wrong with having some redneck skills. In fact, it's a very good thing. But if you combine those skills with the ability to act like a gentleman, that's what makes you country."

I liked that explanation. Guys like Jason and J.D. were redneck. Guys like Blake and Jeff were country. I guess I had a thing for country boys all along.

"So do all country guys like a girl in camo?"

"That depends. It has to be the right girl."

"Am I the right girl?"

"You drive a Jeep."

"Yeah," I looked at him with playful suspicion.

"And I've seen you in a pair of boots. You obviously like horses."

I was now looking at him like he was talking crazy, just for the fun of it.

"And you look amazing in a hat."

That comment made me smile. "You're going to make me blush," I teased.

"Trust me. The importance of the hat can not be overstated."

"It sounds like I might be the right girl."

"You're definitely the *right* girl."

That last sentence lingered in the air like distant thunder. There was a sense of intensity in his words and depth of meaning in his eyes. I was speechless, certain that for once

I had heard him speaking directly from his heart. I stared into his eyes hoping he'd see that I felt the same way about him.

The bell rang, breaking our almost hypnotic trance. I turned and faced the front of the room, but soon snuck a peek to catch him flipping through the pages of his textbook. He looked up and smiled when he noticed me staring back at him. I smiled, then turned around to face the front of the classroom once more.

Instead of getting started on the assignment posted on the board, I began an in-depth reevaluation of my plan to ask him about Valarie. I knew I still needed to get this resolved, but all I wanted to do right now was enjoy this amazing high I was on.

The class period couldn't end soon enough. My excitement was growing with anticipation of what might happen when we got up and walked out into the hallway. I wondered what else he might say.

The teacher got up from his desk and headed to the front of the room, announcing our next assignment, which sounded like a big one. He said it would account for a large portion of our final grade. I was starting to dread it already when he said something that piqued my interest. This was to be a group project.

"Each group will be assigned a specific individual of historical significance," the teacher explained. "Your research paper will focus on how this individual helped to influence the American Revolution."

The guy everyone called Spider raised his hand. "Do we get to choose our own groups?"

I looked intently at the teacher. Oh my gosh. Please say yes.

The teacher shook his head. "Groups will be determined by random drawing." He held up his light blue, University of North Carolina ball cap. It was full of tiny pieces of folded up paper with names scribbled on each one.

This gesture was met with catcalls and boos, most of

which were coming from a sizable contingent of faithful North Carolina State fans. At West Johnston, it was a foregone conclusion that every student was either a UNC Tarheel or an NC State Wolfpack supporter, as if those were the only two universities on the planet.

A few of the rowdier boys did their best to whip this friendly rivalry into unfettered classroom chaos. Spider was among the most rambunctious of them all. He was probably the one who started it.

The teacher walked up and down each aisle, ensuring every student drew a slip of paper. Mine had the name Edmund Burke written on it. I wondered what name Blake would pick. I turned around in my chair and watched him pull a slip from the hat.

He read it, then looked up at me. "Who did you get?" he asked.

"Edmund Burke. Who did you get?"

He shook his head. "Some other guy."

Of course we didn't end up in the same group. That would have been too lucky, too perfect. I started scanning the room, categorizing who I did, and who I did not want to be stuck with for this assignment.

"Alright class," the teacher said. "You have ten minutes to find your group and discuss your project together. All of the requirements are listed on the rubric that I just handed out, and remember, keep the noise level down."

Students immediately bustled around the room. No one was being quiet. Blake headed to the far end of the classroom. I was about to get up, but Spider appeared at my side, hovering over my desk. His collar was flipped up on his pink Polo shirt. Draped around his neck was a pair of Costa sunglasses and a set of earbuds, one still in his ear.

Spider was in two of my classes this semester, which was two, too many. Each time I saw him, I was reminded of what he had said about full body transplant patients in our other class. He called us zombies. That comment was one of the meanest and most hurtful things I had heard, yet.

He pulled out his earbud. "Edmund Burke?"

Oh great. "Yep," I held up my slip of paper, waving it like it was a white flag of surrender.

"Cool," he grinned, then pulled a desk over, wedging it tightly, beside mine. "Edmund Burke over here people," he called out. "Come join our web if you dare." He straddled his desk in a super hero pose, pretending to shoot invisible webs from his wrists.

I rolled my eyes, and made the mistake of looking down, catching a glimpse of his feet. He was wearing flip flops, like usual. His toes were almost as long as his fingers and just as skinny. Curly, long black hairs crawled out from the knuckles on each toe.

"This is going to be an awesome group," he said.

I wasn't so sure. I sat there, remembering the other thing he had said about full body transplant recipients, when he proclaimed that we should all be "rounded up and shipped off to a deserted island." It was intolerance and ignorance like his, that made it impossible for people like me to ever be accepted by society.

"Hey," he called out as he tipped his desk back, balancing on its two back legs. "We're missing two more people." He dropped his desk back down, then started drumming with his pencils.

Someone pulled up a desk on the other side of mine. My eyes broke away from Spider's amateur pencil drumming, to the sight of Blake's heavenly smile. My shoulders relaxed.

I shot him a confused expression. "Are you in this group?"

Spider gave Blake a head nod.

"It took some trading, but I managed to get the right ticket." Blake laid out his slip of paper next to mine, then leaned in close to whisper in my ear. "You looked a little uneasy over here. I thought I better join you in case you don't like spiders."

I turned to Blake and smiled. Thank you, thank you, to whoever traded with him. "I am so glad you're in this group."

Spider stopped drumming. "Ah! Our final group member has come to join our web."

I turned my gaze to see who it was. What were the odds? It was Fiona Phillips -- Miss top five on Jeff's list and my possible mystery girl. She had arrived with a stack of books in her arms and a smile like the cover of a magazine.

"I guess I'm with y'all." Fiona quickly turned and dropped her books onto an empty desk, then pulled it over, directly across from Blake.

Spider perked up as he inspected Fiona from head to toe. She was tall, thin, poised, perfect in every way, but there was something off about the way she interacted with me. I wasn't sure if that was because she didn't like my note taking skills, or if it was because I was in her old body, or if she hated me for some other reason. One minute she seemed warm and inviting, then the next, she was cold and distant. I hadn't spoken to her since she made that strange comment about me having secrets, and I still wasn't sure what she meant by that.

Spider and Blake were talking to each other about baseball, discussing which teams might make it to the World Series this year. Spider was getting a little overly animated, almost shouting, flailing his arms around in excitement. He was easily the loudest one in the class, like usual.

I turned my attention back to Fiona. "Welcome to the group," I said, trying to squeeze my words in between Spider's baseball rantings.

"Thanks."

As soon as she sat down, her eyes settled onto mine. Nora said that Fiona's eyes looked weird, but I thought they looked amazing. They were bright green throughout, even to the edges. Her dark pupils seemed to get swallowed up in a wondrous sea of tranquil green.

"Well isn't this an interesting group," she smiled knowingly, signaling to me with her eyes -- looking over at

Blake, then back to me again.

I tried not to react to her comment. I didn't want her thinking that we were sharing some kind of secret together about Blake.

"I was wondering," I asked her. "Are you new to West Johnston, like me? It seems like most everybody else at this school has been going here since the ninth grade."

She stared at me, straight faced. "You started here at the beginning of the school year, right? I transferred in a couple months after you."

"Oh." She knew exactly when I had enrolled. I hadn't told her that. All I said was that I was new. I looked down at my folder and started fumbling through the pages inside, trying to look busy.

Everything was starting to add up. Fiona was beautiful. Her hair matched the girl who I had seen getting out of that black truck. She was in my technology class. She made that comment about me having secrets. And until recently, she never even existed at this school.

It had to be her, but how could I be certain? I couldn't come right out and ask her if she was a full body transplant patient. If I did that she'd probably just lie to me anyway. And if she hated me as much as the computer document said, then I needed to be extremely careful. Most of all, I couldn't let her know that I was on to her.

The mystery girl had no idea that I read that document on the computer. And that fact was all that was saving me right now. After all, I could just as well expose the mystery girl's secret, too. The mystery girl believed that I was unaware of her existence, and I needed her to keep thinking that.

But before I made any move with Fiona, I had to be absolutely positive that she was the girl. She could still just be some random girl with a mean streak, who knew nothing about full body transplant procedures, or about me.

Fiona straightened her pile of books, brushing her long, satin black hair out of the way. That caught Spider's attention.

"Now this is an all star group," Spider said. "I know we're gonna get an A. And I am one-hundred percent dedicated and committed to putting as much time into this as humanly possible."

"Are you a human, or an insect?" Fiona giggled. "Spider, I'm sure you're not the only one who's committed to the group." She looked to Blake, then to me.

Blake nodded his head. "Good to know Spider. And since you're so dedicated, I'm sure you'll even get your share of the work done ahead of time, right?"

"Oh, you know it, bro. I'm also available for private study sessions, if any of you need help." Spider's eyes darted back and forth between Fiona and me as he wrote down his phone number, then slid each of us a copy. "I am available day or night. Don't hesitate to call me any time."

Fiona smirked. "I'm not sure that all of us are quite as *available* as you are." Fiona signaled to Blake with her eyes, then stared at me again. "Some of us have girlfriends or boyfriends that we spend most of our time with."

When was she going to stop with the innuendos?

Spider cleared his throat. "Well, I happen to be single and available." He turned in his chair to face me. "Becca, what's your number?"

"You don't need my phone number."

"Why not?" Spider asked.

"Because." I handed the piece of paper with his phone number back to him.

Spider pushed it right back onto my desk. "You keep this, baby. You might need it when you get lonely."

"I'm not sure you have a complete grasp of the assignment here, Spider," Blake interrupted. "This is a group project, not a group date."

"Dude." Spider threw his arms up. "Why do you gotta kill my roll like that."

"Oh, is your roll dead now?"

"Yeah," Spider scoffed. "Thanks to you."

"Good." Blake said. "Keep it that way, 'cause if it comes back to life, then your contribution to this group might start to look like an independent study type of situation." Blake's words were calm, yet the look on his face was serious.

Spider sat there, contemplating Blake's warning. He didn't look upset, only deterred. "Ah, alright. I apologize ladies. Sometimes I do come on a little strong." Spider flashed Fiona and me a smile and then a wink when Blake wasn't looking. So much for the apology.

The conversation continued, and before long, Fiona began flirting with Blake. I had no idea if she really liked him, or if she was just doing it to spite me. At one point, she reached over and felt all up and down his arm, under the guise of admiring his watch.

What I wanted to know was why in the world Jeff had put her on his top five list? If Valarie didn't deserve to be on his list, for reasons of lack of character and substance, then neither did Fiona.

"So when can everybody get together?" Fiona asked cheerfully.

Spider leaned forward. "My time is your time. Just say the word, and I'll be there."

"Let's exchange our school emails," I said, as I scribbled out Spider's phone number on the sheet of paper. "That way, we can check our calendars before we make any commitments."

I wrote my email down, then passed it to Fiona. Spider was the last one to write his. I was about to put the sheet of paper in my folder, when Fiona suddenly reached out and snatched it from my fingers, causing a loud ripping sound, but somehow the paper remained intact.

"I'll take it," she blurted out.

I looked down at my fingers, amazed that she hadn't left me with a monster of a papercut.

"Dang woman," said Spider. "You snatched that paper out of her hand like it was Willy Wonka's last golden ticket."

"I did?" Fiona acted innocent, but I wasn't fooled. She

held the paper out. "Here, you can have it back."

"No, you keep it. That's okay," I said.

"Are you sure?"

Quit with the act already. "Yeah, I'm sure."

Spider held out his hand. "I'll take it."

Fiona shook her head, but Spider kept on asking for it.

Blake leaned in close, reaching his arm around the back of my chair. "I guess an email is just as big a prize as a phone number," he whispered.

I giggled slightly. Blake was still leaning in close. I could feel his arm against the back of my shoulders.

"I hope you didn't mind me butting in earlier, with Spider. I assumed that you weren't interested in him. But who am I to judge. You might find his long toes adorable."

"Ha! Oh yes, they're my favorite," I shivered. "No, you just saved me from having to embarrass him."

"I think I would like to have seen that."

"Who knows," I said. "Before this project is done, you may get another chance."

"Uh, excuse me," Spider said loudly.

Blake pulled away and turned his attention to Spider. My reaction was more delayed.

"Didn't you guys hear? It's time to put our desks back."

I hadn't even noticed the commotion going on around the room. I was busy feeling mesmerized by Blake's touch and the soothing sound of his voice.

"Blake," called Fiona. "Can you move my desk for me?"

He got up out of his chair. "Sure."

"Thank you. I've got so much stuff to carry . . ." Fiona continued to talk with Blake, sticking to him like glue. She was not about to give up. She was trying to stake her territory, and her sights seemed to be firmly set.

Class was almost over. I turned to reach for my backpack. My hair fell across my face, as I caught sight of Blake. He was slouched back in his chair, arms folded, desk cleared off. It seemed like the entire time he was listening to Fiona ramble, his eyes were on me. After class, he somehow managed to give her the slip, and we headed out the door together.

"There's a work day at the ranch coming up and we need volunteers to help do some upkeep for the therapeutic riding program. Would you and Nora be interested in helping? After we're done, maybe we could go riding together."

"Yeah. That sounds great. I'll tell Nora."

"I'm not sure about the exact date, but I'll let you know. Other people from school might be there, too."

"Is Valarie going to be there?"

"She'll be there, along with some of her friends."

"Does Valarie help with the therapeutic riding? I don't think I remember seeing her there."

"We board a couple of her horses. She comes to the ranch all the time to work them out."

"What kind of riding does she do?

"English style. Her horses are jumpers. She's actually pretty good . . . travels up and down the East Coast doing competitions."

I nodded my understanding. At least that explained why they were always hanging out together. My earlier excitement was replaced by frustration as I realized I might never be free of Valarie. She had made herself a permanent fixture at the ranch. Between Valarie and Fiona and every other girl trying to flirt with Blake, I wondered if he had any room left for me. Blake said I was the "right girl," but he hadn't said I was the only girl. Once again, I had let my heart go faster than my head.

Blake glanced over at a group of his friends. "I better get going. I'll see you later."

"Bye."

I turned and headed down the hallway to my locker, trying to figure out what to do about Fiona. One by one, I pulled the books from my backpack and wedged them into my tiny locker.

"Becca," a husky voice called, sending shivers up my spine. It was Jason. He stuck his face right next mine. "Hey,

I'm talking to you. . . . Why did you send your boyfriend over to threaten me at the library? Huh? That sissy little carrot top, Jeffry." Jason tossed his head back, causing his patchy goatee to protrude from his chin. "What a wimp."

I slammed my locker shut and turned to walk away, but he stepped in front of me. "You know it's rude to ignore people." Jason's blood-shot eyes were now glaring with anger.

"What do you want?"

"Why don't you ever return my calls or text messages?" He stepped in closer.

I backed up. There was a loud crash from the back of my shoe banging into the metal lockers.

Jason feigned concern. "Are you scared of me?" he cooed. "You know," his tone quickly became devilish. "It doesn't have to be this way." He reached out and leaned onto the lockers with his tall body towering over me, his hand right above my head. I quickly ducked under his arm and hurried away, not looking back.

"Hey!" he called out.

I kept walking.

"Hey!" he yelled louder. "Next time, I won't go easy on your sissy boyfriend. You tell him that."

I kept my pace quick. I hadn't gotten far, when I heard a huge bang. I spun around.

Jason pointed to a fresh dent in my locker. "That'll be his face next time."

At the far end of the hall, I noticed Blake, staring at Jason. I didn't want to be the cause of another fight. I turned around and kept walking.

CHAPTER 35

Becca

Jason had been running his mouth to everyone at school, bragging how he beat Jeff up. I knew he would do that, but I still fumed with anger when I heard the story he was spreading. It wasn't enough for him to have bested Jeff physically in front of a few people at the library. Now, he wanted to humiliate Jeff in front of the entire school.

Fortunately, since Jeff didn't have any visible marks on his face, and no one was corroborating Jason's story, it didn't gain much traction. The rumors mostly subsided by lunch time.

Even though the worst of things seemed to be over for Jeff, that wasn't the case for me. I still had plenty to worry about with Jason. I had seen what happened at the library, and knew exactly what Jason was capable of. I just didn't know what I was going to do about it. Jason's harassment had steadily gotten worse. Now, he was turning violent, and no longer seemed to care if people were around to see.

After the punching of my locker incident, I tried to stay clear of Jason's usual hangout spots. That meant I had to take the long route after two of my classes and didn't have enough time to go to the bathroom or back to my locker again.

After school I went straight home. I tried to make progress on some assignments that were due the next day, but it was a struggle. My head was aching really bad. I couldn't let my parents see me like this. If they found out a headache was causing me this much pain, they'd probably rush me in for a CAT scan or something.

Right after dinner, I told Mom that I was going to bed early and headed up to my room.

There was a light knock on my door.

"Becca." It was Sierra's voice.

"Yeah?"

"I brought you your pills. You forgot to take them."

Dang it! I flung the covers off me, jumped out of bed and ran to the door, hoping to quickly confiscate the pills before Mom or Dad came poking their head in my room.

Sierra was wearing one of Dad's T-shirts as her nightgown. The hole of the neck was so big, it hung off one shoulder. She held her little hand out, displaying the two pills, then handed me a glass of water.

"Thanks," I said, as I took them from her.

There was a sweet smile on her face. I could tell she took some satisfaction in having helped her big sister. "You're welcome," she said in a sing-song voice. She turned and skipped down the hall. The curlers in her hair bounced as if waving goodbye, before she disappeared into her room.

I shut my door, threw the pills into the trash can, then took a sip of water and set the glass down on the desk next to me. I climbed into bed once more, hoping to escape the pounding pain in my head by falling asleep quickly.

If I took those pills, I'd fall asleep within a half hour. That idea was only tempting for a split second. I would gladly endure the headache rather than be controlled by whatever Dr. Stella was prescribing. In the garbage they stayed.

I closed my eyes, pulled one pillow behind me, the other in front of me, then wrapped my feet up in the blankets as tight as I could, like I was in my own little cocoon. Thankfully, it didn't take long before I felt myself start to doze off.

It was one of those hard sleeps. Hours later, I awoke without any sense of how much time had passed. I forced my eyes open and strained to make out the glowing, red numbers of my alarm clock in the otherwise pitch black room. It was early morning, just barely after two. I closed my eyes and tried to go back to sleep again, but my body wouldn't cooperate. The more I tried to force the issue, the more futile it became.

Frustrated, I spun to the edge of the bed, sat up and planted my feet on the floor. At least I wasn't in pain anymore. My eyes adjusted to the darkness easily. Since I was wide awake, I decided to go downstairs and find something to watch on TV.

Silently, I tiptoed my way down the dark hall, then the stairs, being careful not to wake anyone else. As I reached the bottom step, I caught sight of something in my peripheral vision, moving across the other end of the room. I jumped back, expecting my heart to start pounding wildly in my chest, but it was strangely silent.

Whatever I had seen, it vanished as quickly as it had appeared. I froze in place, instinctively trying to blend into the wall to keep out of sight. My focus remained fixed on the area where I had just seen the strange movement.

I reached my hand out, carefully feeling along the smooth wall for the light switch. My fingers made contact, and I flicked the light on, unsure of what I might discover, or what I would do next.

Fortunately, I was the only person to witness the folly of this plan. Instead of casting light on some unseen intruder of the night, all I had managed to do was to illuminate myself and everything immediately surrounding me, like a grand beacon.

I tiptoed slowly through the living room toward the distant hallway, trying not to make any unnecessary sound.

I could have sworn that what I had seen moments ago was a person. It looked as if someone had passed from the den into the family room. But since it happened so quickly, I wasn't quite sure what I had seen, or if I had truly seen anything at all. It could have just been the headlights of a car driving by, flashing through the window, or maybe the clouds had momentarily uncovered the moon's light. Those explanations seemed plausible, but they didn't feel right. I wasn't satisfied with plausibility. A gnawing feeling deep down inside told me that what I had seen was something much worse. Someone else was downstairs in this house with me.

I slowly crept toward the distant hallway, trying to convince myself to be brave, but the thick darkness wasn't helping. Every curtain, obscured corner, piece of furniture -- they all looked like perfect hiding places.

I quickly took the last couple of steps, then flicked on the next light switch. The shadows in the hallway disappeared. The gray walls looked almost black as my eyes adjusted to the brightness of the lights. Even though the hall was large, the dark walls and floor closed in and surrounded me.

At the end of the hall sat a small antique table. The base was made of hand carved wood, with a cherry stained finish. The tabletop was ceramic and shiny, with swirls of gray. A large, curvy red vase took up most of the space on the table. Just above the vase, hung a painting of a tree with a long, knotted trunk and branches devoid of leaves, surrounded by a tangle of vines almost completely covering an old, disheveled stone wall. I had never noticed how spooky that painting was, until now.

I stepped closer, absorbing every eerie detail of the painting before breaking free to shift my attention toward the family room. In doing so, I had the realization that my visual acuity had become heightened somehow. I could detect tiny flaws in the plumbness of the walls, and imperfections in the ceiling. I could see everything, yet I wasn't sure I wanted to see what might be waiting for me around the corner.

Mustering up all the courage I had, I stepped toward the open door to the family room, my face pressed against the wall, hands holding on tight to the chair rail. I slowly leaned in toward the opening.

As my eye broke the plane of the door frame, my line of sight swept slowly from left to right. Inching my head slightly to the left, the visible space expanded, as if taking in an ever increasing slice of pie. Having barely exposed myself beyond the edge of the wall, I stopped to look around the room as best

I could.

No one was there -- at least not in the places I could see, but the room still had blind spots. The light from the hall behind me didn't penetrate to the far side of the family room. It was harder for me to recognize the familiar shapes I expected to see there.

Directly across from the TV sat our big leather sectional, with its back to me. Next to the couch, was an end table with a lamp and a couple books stacked on top. I wasn't able to see much further than that, but what concerned me even more than the darkness was the obscured space right in front of the couch. I couldn't see over it. Someone could easily be crouched down there, waiting for the right moment to lunge out at close range.

I leaned back, slowly separating myself from the door. Should I dare go in there without something to defend myself with, like a baseball bat, or maybe a big knife?

A muffled noise came from behind me. I wanted to scream. I had seen something, and now I had heard something. On top of that, I had one of those odd feelings, like my life was about to flash before my eyes.

The sound had come from the other end of the hall, near the kitchen. I snapped my head around in that direction, but saw nothing. Then, the sound returned, like something heavy was being pushed across the floor.

I backed away from the family room a couple more steps, unsure of where to go. Either I could head toward the ominous sounds, or go into the eerie family room. Both options were freaking me out. I wished I had gone right back upstairs from the start.

I heard a soft tap from the kitchen, like the sound of the cupboard door shutting. There was definitely someone in there . . . but how did they break into the house without setting off the alarm? Mom always activated it before she went to bed. Had she forgotten, or was my imagination just out of control?

I tiptoed down the hall toward the kitchen. The closer

I got, the more frequent the rustling noises came. Why was there so much noise?

I eased the kitchen door open a crack, slowly and gently. The door let out a loud creak like a sick bullfrog. If I had been trying to frighten an intruder away by alerting them of my presence, that would have been impressive.

Seconds later, the hallway light behind me flicked off. I didn't turn around. I was too petrified to go either forward or back. Yet there was something very strange in this feeling. It wasn't how I usually reacted. Why wasn't I trembling or shaking? Why wasn't I gasping for air? I felt completely terrified, yet my body remained steady, almost calm.

I pushed the kitchen door open a little wider. Through the crack, I could see a light turn on, then off, then back on again. I pushed the opening wider. There was a glass of milk sitting on the counter. The refrigerator door was open. A small hand appeared, reaching toward the handle, then the refrigerator door slammed shut. It was Sierra! She turned toward her glass of milk, picked it up and took a drink.

Her hair was set in pink sponge curlers. It still looked neat and orderly, all except for one ringlet, which hung lower than the rest, barely clinging on to a few strands of hair. Her eyes appeared sleepy, barely open. I looked around, but didn't see anyone else. She had done a good job pouring the milk -- no spills.

Her slippered feet shuffled back and forth across the tile floor. That was the noise I had heard from the other end of the hallway. Sierra took another drink, then set the glass back down, the upper part of her lip now white.

I flung the door all the way open and walked toward her. "Sierra, what are you doing up? Don't you know how late it is?"

She scratched her head, curlers jiggling, then picked up her glass and headed toward the stairs without answering me.

"Sierra?" I paused waiting for her reply. "Sierra?" I said again, my voice a little louder.

She kept walking, never glancing back, no response at

all, just sipping her milk like I wasn't even there.

"Hey," I called to her from the bottom of the staircase. But still she didn't respond. Moments later I heard her bedroom door creak open, then close again.

She must have been sleepwalking. I had never seen a person sleepwalk before, and had no idea that Sierra did that. How strange. I had heard her talk in her sleep a couple times before, but that was nothing like this.

I turned off the light downstairs, then headed up to my room, stopping to look in on her before I went to bed. Her glass of milk sat on the dresser, still mostly full. She had already climbed into bed, covers pulled up tight under her chin. Her room was bright from the glow of four night lights -- one on each wall. I stared at her sweet little face for a moment, then quietly headed to my own room.

I pulled the door shut behind me and felt my way back to bed through the darkness, careful not to stub my toe on the corner of the bedpost, like I had done so many times before. My hands grabbed hold of the soft comforter, and I tugged it toward my head, finally feeling relaxed and ready to fall asleep. It was funny how I could so easily become terrified over the unknown, then feel such relief when it turned out to be nothing after all.

I sat up one more time, thinking I heard Sierra outside my door. I waited, listening, but the house remained still. I really needed to quit being so jumpy.

I peeked at the clock once more, prepared to calculate the maximum possible sleep time remaining, but noticed my door open out of the corner of my eye.

"Sierra," I sighed. "Go to bed."

I turned my head and looked toward the door, but it was shut. That's freaky, I thought. I could have sworn my door had just opened. I looked back at the time again, then buried my head in the pillow. I closed my eyes and covered my ears, hoping that nothing else would distract me from the precious few hours of sleep remaining. But one troublesome thought lingered. If Sierra was in the kitchen, then who had turned off the light in the hallway behind me downstairs?

CHAPTER 36

Darla

I didn't think anything else would ever surprise me. I had seen it all. But this . . . it was truly astonishing. It was absolutely miraculous.

Best of all, I now knew that there was a way for me to talk to Becca, face to face, and no one would ever know.

For so long I had been frustrated by my inability to reach her. I never thought I'd be able to tell her my story . . . what had happened to me. I worried that I wouldn't be able to warn her about what might happen to her, or to others. I knew that if I could just communicate with her, she would understand.

The only thing I had to do now was wait until the miraculous thing happened again. Hopefully it would be soon, maybe tonight.

CHAPTER 37

Becca

I straightened my top and positioned my bag just right on my shoulder as I approached the classroom door, anxiously anticipating seeing Blake's mesmerizing face. I stepped through the doorway.

Inside, I found only disappointment. Blake didn't make it to class until the last possible second, so we didn't get a chance to talk. Then after class, a couple other guys monopolized his attention, showing him something on their phones. I went ahead and left.

The next hour, instead of going to the pep rally, I stayed behind to help my art teacher with some cleaning. It wasn't exactly my idea of fun, but it was better than the alternative. I didn't want to have to watch Valarie up in front of the crowd doing her cheers.

I finished up with the cleaning early, so my teacher let me leave for lunch before the bell rang. I went to the cafeteria and sat at our usual lunch table. The place was a ghost town. The pep rally was held clear on the other side of campus, and it wouldn't be over for another five or ten minutes. I'd probably be done eating by the time everybody got here.

I set my lunch down on the table and pulled out my sandwich. I was about to take a bite, when somebody tapped me on the shoulder. I turned to see who it was. I felt the blood drain from my face. Jason was standing inches away from me. I had to tilt my head way back to see him. There was a devious grin on his face. I had become all too familiar with this look.

When he saw my reaction, he stuck out his lower lip. "Aww. What's the matter? I thought you'd be happy to see me," he sneered sarcastically.

"You've got to be kidding me."

He started laughing. His mouth looked huge, despite being surrounded by a scraggly goatee that crept over his lips. I could practically see all the way to his tonsils, as he belted out his wicked laughter. There was no joy or mercy in any part of him -- only selfishness and vengeful cruelty. I quickly became worried.

As I stood up, Jason reached out, grabbing hold of my arm. His laughing stopped. His face became hard. "You're not leaving. You're going to talk to me." His thick, dark eyebrows scrunched so hard toward each other, that a deep indentation appeared, running halfway up his forehead. "Don't you want to find out who followed you in your car that night?"

I yanked my arm out of his grasp.

"You think that I did it." He leaned in, bent forward. "You do, don't you."

"No. I don't think you did it."

"Good. Because I didn't," he paused, "but I know who did."

I searched his face, skeptical of anything he might say, but hungry for the answer to this question. "Why should I believe you?"

"Because, I'm telling you the truth. And because I'm certain you want to know who did it. And most of all, because it's somebody close to you, and I can't wait to see your expression when you find out who it is."

"Sorry to disappoint you." I turned to walk away, but Jason sidestepped to block my path. I stepped back, then tried to walk around him again. This time, he deliberately bumped into me, and I stumbled against the bench, falling and hitting my back on the edge of the table. He seemed amused at my pain.

"I'm just trying to help you." He smirked.

I stood up. "I don't want your help!" I reached out and pushed him as hard as I could, but his big body didn't budge.

Jason grabbed both of my arms and pulled me in toward his chest. "Listen you little--"

"Let go of me!" I struggled to free myself from his grasp, but his hands only squeezed harder. "You're hurting me!"

"Stop struggling, Becca." His smirk was growing into a devious smile. "See, this is the problem with you."

I looked around, but only a few people had arrived in the lunchroom, and they were just standing there, watching.

Jason started pulling me with him. I had no idea where he was taking me, but the thought of whatever he had planned was absolutely horrifying. I planted my feet, pulling in the opposite direction. Somehow, he still managed to drag me along, my feet sliding across the floor. I tried to sit down, but my arms were still in his vise-like grip. He snorted mockingly before turning and dragging me.

A small group of people were gathering around. "Hey," someone said. "That's not cool dude. Let her go."

Jason turned. "You want a piece of me?"

I had to do something while he was distracted. Still on the ground, I spun my body to face him, cocked one foot back, then my leg exploded into an upward kick. I aimed for his knee, but just as I extended my leg he moved, and I missed my target, only scraping the side of his leg.

An expression of anger tore across his round face. He yanked me up to my feet, pinning my arms into his chest. "Is that how it's gonna be then?"

I looked over his shoulder and nodded, as if communicating with someone nearby. "Now you're in trouble."

As soon as he turned his head to see who I was looking at, I stomped down onto his foot as hard as I could, digging in with my heel. He yelled out in pain. I tried to pull away, but his grip was even tighter than before.

The voices around us erupted. The size of the crowd was growing.

"Get your hands off of her," came a booming voice, parting the crowd.

Without loosening his grip, Jason turned to see who it was. "Speak of the devil."

I leaned to the side, so that I could see past Jason's wide torso. It was Blake.

Jason pulled me back toward him, his face inches from mine. "Blake is the one who followed you in your car that night, almost running you off the road," he whispered in my ear. "Don't trust him."

I winced, cinching my shoulder up to my ear. Jason's hot breath made me shiver in disgust. I couldn't believe that he was blaming Blake for that night.

Blake closed the gap between us quickly. He looked down at my arms where Jason had hold of me. "Get your hands off of her, or I'll take them off for you." There was no mistaking the seriousness of his words.

Jason let go of one of my arms and turned to face him. He was a couple inches shorter, but easily outweighed Blake by forty pounds or more. They both looked equally ready to fight. Nobody in their right mind would get in the middle of the two of them.

Jason finally released my other arm, then puffed his chest out. He paced back and forth with an exaggerated swagger. "I'll take you down right now!" he taunted, keeping his eyes focused on Blake.

The crowd amplified the energy of the two, with a sense of inevitability. Dozens of phones were out and recording. The crowd's chanting started to grow louder, "Fight, fight, fight." The sound of enthusiastic voices filled the air, probably exceeding the pep rally they had just come from. More people rushed in, expanding the throng, trying to see what all the commotion was about.

All I could think about was what happened between Jason and Jeff. I feared that this would be another victory for Jason. Blake looked more confident than Jason, but I wasn't sure if he could fight, and I already knew Jason could.

The circle of bodies pushed in closer. I had once been in the center near Blake and Jason, but now I was part of the crowd of onlookers.

Blake stood in place, eyes focused, without saying a word while Jason kept strutting around. "So what's it gonna be? You want some of this or not?" He pounded his chest with his fist. The crowd erupted in excitement.

Jason moved closer to Blake, with his arms raised and extended to either side. He stuck his head out in preparation for delivering another insulting taunt, but never got the chance. Blake stepped forward as quick as lightning, grabbing Jason's shirt with one hand, and swinging his fist right at his big mouth, stopping just a whisker away from impact. Jason flinched. The crowd cheered.

Still holding his fist next to Jason's jaw, Blake looked him in the eye. "Don't think I won't do it, because I will."

"Hit him!" someone yelled.

Blake stared Jason down for several seconds. Jason no longer looked angry and ferocious. He looked to the side -- whether due to fear or shame -- he was unable to look at Blake.

"If you ever lay a hand on Becca, or even look at her wrong again . . . I'll finish this. You got it?" Jason didn't respond. "Got it," Blake demanded, jerking Jason by the shirt.

Jason nodded slightly. Blake pushed him back and let go. A wrinkled ball of cloth lines extended across Jason's shirt where Blake had released control. Jason finally spoke, still looking away, "Hey man. I didn't mean anything. I won't bother her anymore." He turned away.

Blake immediately searched the crowd. I started to step forward.

A flurry of movement exploded behind Blake. Jason had spun back around, fist shooting straight toward Blake's head. He connected a solid blow, knocking Blake forward. Jason grinned, ready to begin a victory celebration, but to his astonishment, Blake didn't go down. Instead, he turned to face Jason, fists raised.

Jason charged, throwing another head shot. Blake reacted instantly, deflecting the punch with his arm and slipping to the side with a counter to Jason's gut.

The crowd went wild. "Fight, fight, fight!"

Jason buckled over and lunged at Blake, head forward, jamming his shoulder into Blake's chest. He wrapped his arms around Blake, pushing him backward. Blake sliced the point of his elbow down into Jason's back, then grabbed him by the hair, slamming Jason's face into his knee. The jabs and punches continued . . .

The whole thing looked like a choreographed fight scene, straight out of a movie. Blake's movements were quick and fluid, maneuvering smoothly from one thing to the next, without taking a second to think. It was as if he had done this many times before.

Jason's punches looked devastatingly powerful, but only a few landed. In frustration, he lowered his head once more and drove his legs, pushing Blake as if he were a tackling dummy. It appeared he finally had the upper hand, but after being pushed back several feet, Blake slipped to the side using Jason's momentum against him, flinging him into the crowd.

Jason stepped toward Blake again, but a couple guys held him back. He didn't try very hard to break away, as evidenced by the lack of strain his friends exerted as they held onto him. But Jason was a good actor. Feeling protected by his friends, he suddenly found renewed courage, or at least new boldness. "This isn't over!" his voice thundered, as his friends pulled him away in the opposite direction. "You're dead!" he yelled from over his shoulder. Then Jason broke away from his friends, turned around and faced Blake, narrowed eyes glaring with a venomous stare. "Pierce. You're the one who's lying to Becca. Stealing her car battery, following her, trying to scare her."

Something inside of Blake flipped on at that moment. Everyone could sense it. It was like something dangerous had just been let loose. Only moments before, he would have allowed Jason to walk away, but now, Jason has crossed a line with his lies.

I was scared. I just wanted this to end. The chances of something going terribly wrong were increasing by the second.

A couple of Jason's friends moved around the crowd, closing in on Blake from behind. They looked like they were getting ready to jump him. I stood there helpless, just as I had done when Jeff and Jason fought. Guilt pummeled me like someone was hurling bricks, and I couldn't get out of the way. If Blake got hurt, I'd never forgive myself.

The crowd went wild in eager anticipation of round two. Their cheers only made me feel worse. I wanted to throw in the white towel, to end it right now, before things got any more out of control. Where were the teachers? Where were the security guards? I looked around, but no one in authority was coming to stop this.

Jason yelled out something else, but I couldn't hear what he said -- the crowd was too loud. Then Blake took off, charging toward Jason, and everybody scattered out of the way, like cockroaches under a sudden light.

Jason's friends ran at Blake from behind. Jason swung. Blake dodged and countered with an uppercut, landing square on Jason's jaw. It stunned him. He stumbled on his feet, looking disoriented. The two guys from behind were closing rapidly.

"Look out!" I yelled.

Blake saw them and moved out of the way at the last second. They both flew past him. Jason charged again, swinging. Blake got him in a headlock. Jason struggled to get away, but Blake held him there, squeezing tight. Jason's two friends looked on in shock, as he went down to his knees.

Blake squeezed harder. Jason gasped, red faced, trying to pry himself free from Blake's arms.

A girl next to me started freaking out. "He's going to kill him! He's choking him."

"No he's not. Shut up," one of her friends said.

"He's going to murder him!" she replied.

"Security is coming," somebody else shouted.

Blake finally let go, and Jason fell to the ground. He wasn't dead, but he was gasping for air. Blake turned toward me. Our eyes met. Everything stood still for that moment. I wanted to go to him, but found myself engulfed in a sea of scurrying students, now in full retreat.

I lost him in the crowd, swept along by the bodies all pressing toward the exit. When I finally caught sight of him again, he was much further away and walking in the opposite direction.

CHAPTER 38

Becca

As soon as school got out, everybody congregated around their phones, watching the video of Blake and Jason's fight. I heard someone say there were already more than three-hundred views on the video that Spider took. They said Spider had a knack for capturing the best angles and close-up shots.

Apparently my altercation with Jason had ended before the video footage began, because nobody was hounding me about the fight. Thank you Spider, for getting to the lunchroom late.

After school, I tried to catch up with Blake. I purposely skipped stopping at my locker and headed straight to the parking lot, but his car was already gone. I guess he wasn't ready to deal with his instant celebrity status.

The rest of the day felt different somehow. It took me a while to realize what it was. Then it hit me. My troubles with Jason had likely just come to an end. I finally felt the weight of it all being lifted from me. My very soul seemed weightless and free.

Later that night

I had expected a good night's sleep, now that Jason had been dealt with, but morning arrived with a slap of harsh reality. I found myself lying flat on my back. Directly above me, a spinning ceiling fan sent a cool breeze through my hair, which was drenched with sweat.

I sat up and scanned the room. The off-white curtains, hanging at the edges of the large bay windows, were bunched together, swaying softly in the gentle breeze. Next to the windows stood a full-length three-way mirror. I could see my reflection in it from my position on the bed. I leaned over to the nightstand and fumbled around for the correct button to turn off the alarm.

This was my room. I was in my bed, surrounded by all my things. Everything was exactly where it was supposed to be, including me. But for some odd reason, I felt like a visitor, waking up in an unfamiliar place.

It would have been convenient to dismiss the sensation as nothing more than the after effects of a dream, but the disorientation was overly pronounced, and lingered much too long. I felt like I had just been ripped from someplace far away and deposited here in this bed only moments before.

I leaned back against the tall headboard and looked down at my body. My legs were covered by the silky bedspread. I had on the same pajamas that I put on the night before -- button up shirt, long sleeve, black with white polka-dots.

The sensation eventually faded. I rolled over, burying my head underneath an oversize pillow to keep the light from insisting I wake up. I began to relax, sinking into the softness of my welcoming bed. It must have been a dream after all. That was the only plausible explanation. I was simply disoriented, like anyone would be after waking up from a vivid dream. This was normal, I told myself.

I tried to focus on what I had dreamed about. The first thought that came to my mind was of a horse. . . . I had dreamt of riding a horse. It was a tall, pure white, muscular horse. It was well trained, obeying my every command, like it was connected to my mind; whatever I willed the horse to do, it complied.

I jumped the horse over fences, bushes, streams, and anything else that presented itself. The wind rushed over me as we cut through the thick air, like a knife, galloping at incredible speed. My hair whipped back and flew behind me as we raced down a wooded, dirt trail that seemed to go on for miles; climbing up and down small hills, ducking under low lying branches, carefully maneuvering through rocky soil. It seemed so real -- the coarseness of the horse's mane, the grunts it made, the exhilaration I felt. It was as though I had ridden thousands of times before. I could do everything a professional rider could do, with grace and style.

This pleasant memory soon vanished from my mind like a raindrop sliding down a slippery window. Other memories crowded my mind. One of these was the thing that troubled me, the reason I was so disoriented when I woke up. I had seen her in the procedure room again.

I didn't dream about the faceless cop with tattoos or Dr. Stella. I dreamt about the other lifeless body I had seen lying on the procedure table. In my dream, when I saw the white sheet draped over the table, I reached out and pulled it back again exposing her face. Everything looked the same -- soft, billowing hair, pale skin, eyes closed, purple lips.

How could I make up all of that in a dream? There was so much detail. I could see the strands of hair on her eyebrows, a few light brown freckles on her cheeks. Her ears were pierced, but she wore no earrings. Her eyelashes were the same blonde color as her long hair. But that wasn't the part of my dream that was troubling.

That sensation I had when I woke up was because of what had happened when I was standing over the dead girl's body, looking down at her lifeless face. I remembered how a chill ran through me. I shivered and wrapped my arms around my shoulders. There were hushed whispers. I felt a tap on my back and spun around, arms up, not knowing whether to fight or run. It turned out that I didn't do either.

In my dream, she was standing right in front of me. The ghost of the dead girl. For a split second I wanted to jump back, until I saw the color and sparkle in her eyes. Her lips were pink, her skin vibrant. There was a glow about her. Without words she spoke peace to my fears. My breathing calmed.

She said to me, "Don't let this happen to anyone else."

I had a million questions for her. She seemed to sense this, but before any could be asked or answered, the calm surrounding us evaporated. Fear swept over her face as she focused on something behind me. I turned and looked. Five black shadows were running straight toward me. I didn't know who or what they were, but I knew I needed to flee for my life. She wanted me to follow her, but I couldn't move. Then the dream ended. That was the last thing I could remember before my alarm woke me.

I reached down and flung the covers off my legs, then jumped out of bed. I didn't want to think about ghosts or shadows anymore. I headed to the bathroom and started up the hot water in the shower. I needed to hurry so that I could catch Dad before he left for work.

I had just finished blow drying my hair, when the aroma of fresh bacon came wafting up the stairs. I slid my feet into my shoes and hurried down to the kitchen.

The full brightness of a North Carolina morning hit me like a burst of warm air. The drapes were open, and sunshine was pouring in. Smoke swelled up from the stove, the sound of sizzling and popping promising something delicious on the way.

Mom turned from the stove, still wearing her robe, spatula in hand. "I hope you're hungry."

Dad was sitting at the table, cutting his pancakes. His black and gray hair still wet from his shower, but carefully combed into place. He glanced up, raising a fork to his mouth, but his hand stopped when he caught sight of me. "Hey sweetheart. Glad you made it down for breakfast. How did you sleep last night?"

If he only knew. "Fine." I sat down across from him and started piling pancakes onto my plate. "How about you?"

"Oh, never better."

Sierra was spreading butter onto her pancakes, going for what looked like her third or fourth helping, when Dad reached over and took the knife out of her hand. "Woah. Way too much, honey." Sierra sighed in disappointment. "But it's better that way."

"Of course it is," he replied. "And it's also bad for your health. Just because it tastes good, doesn't mean it's good for you."

"Dad," I said. "I've been meaning to ask you about something. At my counseling appointment, Dr. Stella gave me an injection to put me under for the psychoneural analysis. I was wondering about that."

"Wondering? Wondering what exactly?"

"Well," I scrunched my nose. Did he honestly not anticipate this question? He knew how much I hated needles. "I was wondering why it had to be a shot. Why doesn't she have me drink that fruity liquid stuff anymore?"

"The injection provides more accurate results in the analysis. It helps the patients to be more relaxed. When the body is in a relaxed state, then our computer program can analyze the data and not have skewed results . . . you know, from a fluctuating heart rate or breathing . . . things that can occur when a patient is in a more alert state."

"What if the injection doesn't relax the patient more than the liquid?" I was nowhere near relaxed. That dream I had with that cop and Dr. Stella probably skewed my data big time.

He looked at me contemplatively. "There could still be some tweaks needed in the formula." He took a bite of pancake. "But we'll have to use this long enough to reach any conclusions. Just bear with it. We should know within a few months how well this new method works, and if it works for some and not others, we'll adjust it." He took another bite, then set his fork down. "Did you feel more relaxed?"

I swirled my bacon in a puddle of syrup on my plate, remembering my dream again. "I don't know, but if I was given the choice between some nasty tasting drink or a painful shot in the arm. I'd choose the nasty drink every time."

"I never want to get a shot," Sierra, shook her head. "Shots hurt!"

Dad nodded, got up from his chair and took his plate to the sink. "Alright, I've got to go girls," he called from the kitchen. "Have a good day at school." Mom walked with him out to the garage.

As soon as I heard the door shut, I turned to Sierra. "Four scoops of butter? Next time, keep it at three."

She pulled the cup away from her mouth and smiled, exposing the fresh milk mustache on her upper lip.

"You know what? I think you really like milk, too."

Sierra grinned. "Yep."

"The other night, I saw you sleep walking. You came downstairs and poured yourself a big glass."

Sierra's brows furrowed. "Huh?"

I nodded. "You were sleepwalking."

"Really? When?" she asked.

"Not last night. Maybe it was the night before."

Her little eyebrows scrunched together. "When someone sleepwalks, do they remember doing it?" she asked.

"I'm pretty sure most people don't remember sleepwalking, but I'm not a hundred percent positive."

"Well, I remember getting up to get a drink of milk. I wasn't asleep."

"You do?"

"Yes," she nodded emphatically.

"I'm pretty sure you were asleep."

"Nope. I wasn't sleeping," she protested. "I was awake."

"Then why didn't you answer me when I talked to you in the kitchen?" I asked.

"You weren't in the kitchen."

"Yes, I was. And I called your name several times, loudly."

Sierra shook her head. "No you didn't."

"Yes, I did."

"Quit teasing me!"

"Sierra, I'm not trying to tease you."

"Yes you are, and if you don't stop, I'm gonna tell Mom."

"Don't get upset. I wasn't trying to be mean. I promise. This was just a misunderstanding. Okay?"

She let out a big huff. "Well I don't like misunderstandings."

"Me either." How in the world could she not have seen me in the kitchen? This made no sense.

At school

The first bell was still ringing as I slipped through the door. Not a second to spare, I thought. I had never been the type to rack up tardies, or in school suspensions, but unless I pulled myself together, and quick, that's where I was headed.

As I hurried toward my desk, I noticed Blake glance up at me. There was a softness in his eyes, and an inviting warmth in his smile. I hadn't talked to him since the incident with Jason at lunch yesterday. I wanted to express a dozen feelings and emotions all at once, but before I could even exchange a smile, his focus returned to his paper. Words raced from his pen like a stampede. Our conversation was going to have to wait.

I sat down and pulled out my notebook. An assignment was posted on the board. 'In class writing: 1,000 word essay on yesterday's assigned reading. Proper Thesis and Conclusion.' Beneath the instructions, underlined and scrawled in giant capital letters, was the word 'SILENTLY.'

As class came to an end, I leaned forward onto my backpack, resting my chin on my hands. I should have called him yesterday. Why didn't I do that? It would have been so much easier then. Now the moment had passed. I worried that whatever I said to him was going to seem awkward and lame compared to the way he appeared out of nowhere, like my own personal superhero.

Blake could have been seriously hurt, suspended or even expelled for fighting, but none of that caused him even one moment of hesitation. He risked all that to defend me. And so far, I hadn't even uttered so much as a thank you.

Finally, the bell rang. I didn't know how the next sixty seconds were going to play out, but I sensed that this was going to be one of those pivotal moments either celebrated or agonized over. It would be replayed, reanalyzed, and remembered for a long time.

Before my heart, head and lips could all agree on exactly what to say, the rest of my body had already gotten up, turned, and closed the short distance between us.

I stood beside his desk, fingers clasped together, nervously rubbing the palm of my hand. The flood of emotions washing over my heart collided with the swirling thoughts in my mind. Still, the right words didn't come. I stared into his hypnotic eyes, as if standing on Carolina beach, surveying the endless blue ocean. Neither of us spoke. After a few moments I sensed that Blake had his own questions. He seemed to peer into my soul, probing for answers. Could he see from my stare what I wanted to say? Did he see in my eyes how grateful I was for what he did?

He stood up. "How are you doing?"

Say something. "Blake . . . I . . ."

"Are you okay?"

I nodded. "I don't know what to say to express how deeply grateful I am for what you did yesterday. You stepped in when nobody else would. People stood there watching, but you didn't. Somehow, you knew exactly what to do. I'm sorry that I didn't call you last night to thank you. I shouldn't have waited this long, but I wanted to say it in person. Thank you."

He shook his head. "I wasn't about to stand by and let him do that to you."

An overwhelming feeling came over me from head to toe -- a flash of warmth, and at the same time, chills. The sensation hit me hard, and I let it take over, like a magnet pulling me in. Next thing I knew, I was hugging him. The whole world came to a halt around us, or at least it seemed, until we were interrupted.

"Get to class," the teacher said, peering at us from across the room.

We let go of each other and gathered our things.

He turned to me as we stepped through the doorway. "Jason hasn't bothered you any more, has he?"

"I haven't seen him, or heard from him."

"Good. What was going on anyway?"

I shrugged my shoulders. "I really don't know. All of a sudden, out of nowhere, he just came up to me, and he wouldn't let me leave."

"Did he hurt you?"

"He grabbed my arms, but I'm fine now."

"Somebody said that he knocked you down."

"Uh, yeah, but just onto the bench. I didn't fall on the

ground or anything."

Blake's eyes narrowed as he stared off.

"I think you took care of him though. Not only did you bruise his face, you also managed to pulverize his over-inflated ego."

Blake relaxed and looked at me with concerned eyes.

I smiled, trying to reassure him. "The way he flinched when you swung at him that first time . . . now that was priceless."

"He deserved worse."

"People eventually get what is coming to them," I said. "Call it Karma, the law of the universe, or whatever. What goes around, comes around. As far as I'm concerned, I'm just glad that it's over. Thank you so much."

We walked to my next class together, still talking about the fight. But by the time we got there, the hallways were just about empty.

"You're gonna be late," I said smiling.

"Yeah, I better get going." He started down the hall, then turned to face me, walking backward. "I meant to tell you yesterday, but I got distracted. Can you come over tomorrow? That's when we're doing work at the ranch."

"What time?"

"Nine," he called out just before disappearing around the corner.

CHAPTER 39

Becca

I saw Nora walking toward the barn, the sunlight reflecting off her bright hair.

"Nora," I called.

She stopped and waited for me to catch up to her. Punctuality was never her strong suit, but apparently she had the right motivation today.

I rested my boot on the bottom rung of the fence. "How long ago did you get here?" I asked, adjusting the way my jeans tucked inside.

"A while. I was beginning to wonder if you were coming."

I turned my head to look at her and we both smiled. "As if anything could keep me from coming today."

"I know, right?" Nora turned toward me and pointed so only I could see.

Over by the stables, Hunter was pulling hay bales off a truck. He was wearing leather gloves, boots and jeans, but no shirt. The weight of the bales was making his muscles bulge. His skin was damp with sweat.

She took a deep breath. "Now that's quite a sight."

There were several other volunteers helping with the hay bales, but my eyes didn't linger there long. I continued to scan the field. "Have you seen--"

"Lover boy?" Nora interrupted, grinning mischievously. "Follow me."

On the other side of the barn, a group of girls were congregated around Blake. He was doing way more talking than working.

Nora whispered to me. "*She's* also here."

I knew she was referring to Valarie. "Oh joy," I replied.

"Some of her minions were hovering around Hunter earlier." Nora sneered. "But I really can't blame them. He is pretty irresistible. But he'll soon realize that I'm irresistible. Check out my jeans," she spun around. "These were made to accentuate the positive and eliminate the negative. My tummy looks so flat in these."

I slowly nodded. "Nice," then paused. How in the world had she gotten those things on?

"What?"

"Are you sure you can straddle a horse wearing those?"

"Of course."

I raised my eyebrows in disbelief, but Nora ignored my stare and flipped her hair with a flourish. "Come on, let's go help Hunter."

Hunter was still unloading the truck. I took on the task of breaking apart the bales that he had piled in the stalls, spreading them out. Fortunately, I got the better half of the stalls. They were mostly clean, although I still wished I had a nose plug.

Nora was doing more flirting than working. Hunter didn't seem to mind. Maybe her jeans were doing their job after all, because I caught him checking her out when she wasn't looking.

Eventually, people began putting away the rakes and shovels and heading toward the parking area. We'd been busy helping with the upkeep of this place for a couple hours. I hadn't really spent any of that time with Nora. She was sticking to Hunter like glue.

I wandered around until I found Blake. He was finally alone, next to the barn, fastening a saddle onto a horse.

He heard my footsteps and turned to me. "I haven't seen you all morning," he said.

"You looked like you were busy, so I went and helped out

at the stables."

"I'm glad you didn't leave yet. I promised you that we'd take a ride."

I tried to keep it together, but had the realization that my smile was growing way bigger than I wanted it to be, and I couldn't do anything about it.

He looked around. "Did Nora want to come?"

"Uh, I think she's with your brother."

"Gotcha. You mind if we go ahead and get started without her?" Blake patted the horse he had just saddled. "This is your horse here. He's a good one to start off with."

Everything at that moment was pure excitement. I had to restrain myself from bouncing up and down, or looking ridiculous in front of him.

"Place your outside foot in the stirrup, then swing your inside leg over."

I approached the horse and tried to put my foot in the stirrup, but it kept moving. Blake grabbed the stirrup and held it still for me. "Grab hold up here at the top of the saddle and climb on."

I tried to pull myself up, but the horse kept moving, with my foot stuck to it. "Blake," I giggled.

He steadied the horse, then grabbed hold of my waist. "Ready . . . now up." He lifted and I tried to jump, but he had already pulled me up off the ground before I was ready.

"Oh, sorry," I said. I was sure I could have timed my jump better, but I lost focus on the task when I felt his hands wrap around my waist. I pretty much became jello.

"That's okay." He walked around, grabbed my other foot and placed it in the stirrup, then rested his arm on the horse, and looked up at me. "How does that feel?"

"Really good," I smiled.

"Just hang out for a second. I'll be right back." He turned and walked away. "Now don't go anywhere," he called back to me.

I was so high up. I looked down at the horse's black mane

and started stroking it. "You are going to go easy on me today, right fella?"

"What do you think you're doing on that horse?" Valarie's shrill voice called out.

I turned to face the approaching girls. Valarie almost always traveled in a pack, but she only had two henchmen with her today. At least the odds were a little better than usual.

"What?" I replied.

One of the girls who had her hair in braids, stepped forward. "Who gave you permission to get on my horse?"

"Blake said I could ride this horse."

"Well, I don't see Blake anywhere," snapped the other friend.

"He's coming right back."

The insults had just begun to fly when Valarie lifted her hand slightly, signalling them to stop. She had a devious look in her eye. "Blake picked out a very good horse for you."

"He said this is a good one to start with," I nodded.

The shorter girl flipped her long hair and smirked. "Have you ever ridden before?"

"A couple times."

"So you really don't know what you're doing, do you?" asked the girl with braids.

I tilted my head to the side and smiled. "That's why Blake is helping me."

Valarie folded her arms. "Are you paying for a lesson or something?"

I reached out and stroked the horse's neck without giving the girls eye contact. "Nope." I gave the horse a couple more strokes, then looked over at them.

The girl with braids mouthed something to Valarie, then turned to me, a fake smile plastered on her face.

"So pathetic," the other girl said, rolling her eyes.

Valarie headed toward me. She reached out and started petting the horse just behind the saddle. I turned around as best as I could to see what she was doing.

She didn't look at me. "You know, I think the best way to learn something is to dive right in. You either sink or swim."

"You've either got it, or you don't," her friends echoed in unison.

"What are you talking about?"

"I'm going to do you a favor, Becca."

"No thanks. I'll pass."

She chuckled. "Oh come on. It'll be lots of fun."

My internal alarm bells were going off. This wasn't good. Not at all. I looked around desperately, hoping to see Blake, but he wasn't coming.

"This is a very gentle horse. But even the best of horses can have a fault. You know about faults, right Becca?" Valarie paused as she glided her finger across the back side of the horse. "This horse happens to have one specific spot . . . sort of an Achilles heel."

My eyes got wide. "No," I pleaded. "Valarie, don't."

"Sh--sh--sh. But I'm doing you a favor." She smirked. "Lesson number one. Coming right up." She cocked her arm back, then swung it forward, smacking the horse with full force.

The horse jerked. I grabbed tight onto the reins, as it reared up onto its hind legs. A loud shriek escaped from my mouth. I leaned forward, clutching onto the saddle, trying not to fall off the back. Valarie's friends roared in laughter.

"Enjoy the ride," Valarie called out.

As soon as the horse dropped back down onto all four legs, it bolted forward, racing us off toward the woods. I was losing my balance and felt like I would fly off the saddle at any moment. The horse continued to pick up speed. I was at its mercy. My entire body tensed up in anticipation of the hard crash into a tree or the ground, which would inevitably come.

The wind whipped across my face, tearing through my hair. My eyes watered, vision blurred. I gasped for air, having forgotten to breathe. Each bounding stride of the horse surged through me, its hooves striking the ground with unstoppable force. I reached for the reins that had slipped from my hands shortly after take off. I tried to pull back and coax the horse to slow down, but it wouldn't obey.

Panic set in . . . I screamed, but the sound had barely escaped my lips when the horse jerked forward even faster. I almost lost hold of the reins again.

The horse kept going, not showing any sign of slowing down. It tore through brush and skirted low hanging branches, forcing me to lean and duck. I felt certain we had traveled miles away from the ranch. The horse grunted, breathing heavily now. We were headed deeper and deeper, into a sea of tall trees, on a trail so narrow, branches and vines seemed to reach out constantly, whipping across us as the horse wedged its way through.

The trail was barely noticeable. Weeds had overtaken it, almost completely covering up the dirt path. Even though the sun was up and the sky clear, it felt like dusk. The thickness of the woods on every side blocked out the light.

I thought about Valarie and could almost hear the echoing sound of that smack she gave the horse, ringing through my ears again. A sinking pit in my stomach grew, as I realized that only Valarie and her friends knew where I was.

I thought about trying to jump off the horse before getting so deep and twisted up in the woods, that I would never find my way back. I glanced down and saw the power and quickness of the horse's legs striking the ground over and over. I was up too high. I would surely get mangled up under its legs, stomped on and slammed against the rocky ground. If I got hurt, I wouldn't be doing any walking, and I'd be stuck out here . . . alone.

I leaned forward, almost hugging the horse's neck. My fingers still held onto the reins, but loose enough to press the palm of my hands against the horse's warm body. I closed my eyes, keeping my head low, right beside the horse. I felt the hard muscles under its skin, the softness of its hair. I listened to the rhythm of its gallop and breath. I felt the movements of its large, powerful body. Instead of fighting against it, I decided to let myself go; let myself match the horse's movements, like a boat floating on the ocean.

The tenseness I had been holding eased and I began to relax. I opened my eyes again. It seemed as though my heart began to beat in sync with the horse's pace. My breathing started to slow. The intense pounding of my heart began to lighten. The grip of my fingers relaxed. I concentrated on what I heard. The galloping horse sang to me with its feet.

I no longer felt at odds with this magnificent creature. Instead, exhilaration washed over me, like the rush of a cool shower on a hot day. My eyes widened. I knew what to do . . . I had known it all along. It was there in my memory, just like in my dream. I didn't hesitate another moment. My body took control. I had been trying to command the horse to stop by using the reins, and he refused. Now, I shifted my weight, used my legs, and the horse obeyed. I couldn't believe it. Just like in my dream, I was riding as if I had done this thousands of times before.

When I wanted the horse to veer right or left, I steered it instinctively. I made it slow down, then speed up again with ease. Everything I wanted to do came to my mind and body, as naturally as breathing.

Amazingly, I had this knowledge, this experience, inside of me this whole time; it had never left this body. I remembered Dad calling this kind of phenomenon "shadow copy." He said that sometimes abilities and skills remained in donor bodies. He described it as a rare gift that only a small percentage of transplant patients experienced. A shadow copy would allow for me to know how to do things without having to spend the time learning first. Whoever used to inhabit this body must have ridden horses a lot. She was an expert -- maybe even professional. And now, I was a professional too!

I didn't want the horse to stop. I wanted to keep this ride going for as long as either of us had the endurance to keep moving. The overwhelming excitement was impossible to suppress. I felt free, and nothing could hold me back. It was just me and this horse; this magnificent horse.

We continued on, the horse cutting through the thick forest, with ease and grace . . . then I remembered. Nobody knew where I was. I had to go back.

I leaned back and gently tugged on the reins. The horse stopped. I patted him on the neck and whispered, "Are you ready?"

We turned and took off again like a lightning bolt, racing down the trail, through the thick, green trees and over the thin layer of patchy grass. Now, the wind danced across my skin and played in my hair as we sped toward the ranch.

All around, the forest awoke from its quiet slumber as we approached. The leaves stood still, until the moment of our arrival. Then they awoke, dancing and cheering, finally seeming to wave goodbye as they slipped from view.

I saw some deer grazing in a clearing not far ahead. At first, there were two. Soon I noticed another, and another. There were five all together. They stopped suddenly, turning their heads to watch as we approached. In an instant, the biggest one bolted for the safety of deeper woods. The others followed, disappearing into the endless covering of trees.

Soon we approached a small hill. The trail widened, and the trees weren't as thick anymore. Yellow, purple and white wild flowers, sprung up across the grassy spaces where the sunlight penetrated through the trees.

At the bottom of the hill, there were large rocks scattered all over. Some looked as tall as me. The bottom half of the rocks were covered with a light dusting of an orange color that came from the clay dirt they sat upon.

A fast moving stream ran parallel to the path, not far away. I could hear water rushing over and around rocks, crashing and splashing its way through the woods. In places, the sun reflected off the water so brightly, it looked like a million sparkling diamonds glistening beneath its surface.

I slowed the horse to a walk, then hopped off. This place

was too beautiful to pass by. I laid down in a bed of soft clover and felt the sunlight on my eyelids. I had only planned on staying for a couple minutes, but the horse got a mind of his own and he took off running in the direction of the ranch, leaving me behind.

Even though I was stranded, the serenity of this place was too amazing to accommodate worry. I watched the horse disappear in the distance and laid my head back down, still marveling at the ride I had just experienced. The exhilaration I had felt still made me tingle.

After a few minutes I got up and sat on a rock next to the stream, watching the little fish swim by. Soon, I heard the sound of horse hooves approaching. I stood up scanning in the direction of the sound, expecting to see my horse again, but it wasn't him.

It was Blake, riding a big black horse. He quickly closed the distance between us.

"Are you okay?" he asked, as he jumped off his horse to meet me.

"I'm fine."

His worried eyes were still on alert. "Are you sure? I saw your horse, without you on it. Did you fall?"

I knew I couldn't tell Blake that he had nothing to worry about and that it turned out I was an excellent rider. "No, I didn't fall. The horse finally slowed down, and I managed to get off."

"What happened?"

"Well, after you left, my horse got spooked and took off. I just tried to hold on." I smiled. "I promise, I didn't mean to go anywhere without you."

Blake let out a breath of relief. I knew he was glad to see that I wasn't hurt or upset.

I pointed behind me. "Isn't this beautiful? I got off the horse so that I could get a closer look at the stream, and I guess he decided that he didn't want to wait for me, because he suddenly just took off."

Blake's eyes scanned the landscape. "He might have seen a snake."

"What?" I gasped, now feeling on edge. I absolutely hate snakes. They creep me out. I spun around, eyes searching the grass. Then stopped and faced Blake. "Okay, this place doesn't seem quite so beautiful anymore."

He chuckled. "Don't worry. I think we're fine."

I wasn't so sure about that. I kept watch, looking for anything slithering or moving.

We sat down on some rocks next to the water. His horse started gnawing on some nearby grass.

"What if your horse takes off and leaves us out here, too?"

"This one's pretty good about staying close."

I knew he was the expert and that I should take him at his word. Still, the idea of being stuck outside, in a place teeming with snakes, gave me pause. It might have created considerable misgiving in my mind, if not for Blake's thoroughly disarming smile.

Thankfully, the more time that passed, the more relaxed I became. Soon I had forgotten all about snakes and found myself lost in the moment with Blake.

A long knotted log stretched out across the stream creating a convenient bridge to the other side. Blake held my hand as we carefully stepped along its narrow surface. When we got to the other side, we found a grassy spot to sit down. I started picking at the clovers surrounding us, searching for one with four leaves. Blake was leaning back onto his elbows, his hat cocked forward slightly, shading his eyes. I reached up and snuck peeks at his perfect face between breaks from searching for a perfect clover.

He plucked one from the ground. "I think I found one."

I asked to see it, but he wouldn't let me. Then a struggle ensued as I tried to retrieve it from his hand. He laughed as he watched me try to pry open his fingers. It was impossible to move them. The touch of his skin seemed to make me feel a lot less powerful. Something about him made me feel weak and sent butterflies swirling in my stomach. Finally, he let me open his hand.

"This isn't a four leaf clover."

A big smile spread across his face. I realized that I had practically tackled him, trying to retrieve the clover and quickly pulled back away from him.

He sat up, still smiling. And I was, too. I couldn't believe that I was here, with him. There weren't any distractions, no Valarie, no Jason, or anyone else to get in the way. It was just the two of us.

Everything seemed so perfect. The conversation was light, flowing freely like the stream. I felt like I could stay in that exact spot forever, and never tire of it. If anything, I couldn't get enough. The only thing that wasn't perfect was the knowledge that we would eventually have to leave.

CHAPTER 40

Becca

We talked and laughed as effortlessly as a summer breeze. Being with Blake felt comfortable, like a favorite T-shirt or a faded old pair of blue jeans is comfortable. Everything fit perfectly between us.

Blake's voice trailed off into the background as I became lost in my own thoughts. It had already been an amazing day, and now here I was, in this beautiful spot, all alone with the guy of my dreams. If there were ever a perfect place for a first kiss, this little patch of grass, next to this little stream, would be hard to beat. Had he picked this spot on purpose?

I gave myself permission to wonder, just briefly, what it would feel like at the moment our lips first touched. Usually, I tried not to dwell on that sort of thing, but today my normally harmless private thoughts were swiftly becoming a fully involved five alarm daydream.

I could practically see the two of us, lying there on the grass, as if watching actors on a stage. Palpable anticipation flowed from somewhere, deep inside, as I saw how our eyes would meet, and our bodies would lean in toward one another.

Only with concentrated effort was I able to push those actors off the stage of my mind and snap back to reality.

I vaguely understood that Blake had been recounting past outings in the surrounding woods, possibly describing the various animal life he had seen, and perhaps the beautiful places he looked forward to sharing with me on future adventures together.

Right about there is where he stopped talking and stared

at me, seemingly waiting for a signal.

I hesitated.

Blake filled the void before it could become awkward. "So, tell me about your family."

"My family?"

He shrugged and raised his eyebrows slightly, inviting me to respond.

If any sliver of my mind were still daydreaming, it had just come to a screeching halt. I went into total alert mode, watching all of our previously carefree, comfortable conversations vanish like dust in the wind. "I don't know where I'd even start," I said, stalling. "Is there something in particular you'd like to know?"

"Nothing in particular," he smiled, "Start from the beginning if you want."

He had no idea what a frightening prospect that would be for me. I marvelled at how only moments before I had felt completely at ease and unguarded. How quickly the crushing burden of my secrets had returned.

"The beginning . . ." I stammered, groping for a reasonable reply. What would Blake think of me if he knew the truth? Would he accept me for who I have always been on the inside, or would he think me a monster for occupying another person's body? I wanted more than anything to tell him the truth and be free of the weight of my secrets. But did I trust him enough to tell? It would either be the best choice or the worst mistake ever. Once I started, there could be no middle ground, and no going back.

"The thing is," I began, eyes low, "I sort of had a new beginning when my family moved here." I paused and glanced up at Blake, hoping for some sign of encouragement.

"What brought you here anyway?" he interrupted. "Did your dad move y'all out here to North Carolina because of a job transfer or something?"

I felt a cold shiver run down my spine and instantly, I knew that telling him the truth about me was a terrible idea.

The worst ever. How could I even consider it? He wasn't my boyfriend, and I certainly wasn't his girlfriend.

I did *not* want to talk about Dad or what he did for a living, but if I didn't answer his question it would probably only create more interest.

I pulled my knees toward my chest, pretending to inspect the dust on my boots, trying to look casual so he wouldn't pick up on any weird anxiety vibes. "Yeah, my dad got transferred here. It was an easy decision to move here, since my brother Brandon is going to Duke, but I don't see him that often. I have a little sister, too. Her name is Sierra . . . she's seven. A real sweetheart." I shifted my attention from my boots back to Blake, hoping that what I said was enough. I leaned over and nudged him with my elbow. "What about your family?"

"Hmm . . . only one brother, who you've already met, and he's around a lot, so I always get to see him. And you can be sure I would never call him a sweetheart, so I guess there are a few things right there we don't have in common," he said with a playful grin.

His reaction helped to ease my mind. Maybe I wouldn't have to talk about Dad.

I sat up taller, crossed my legs and started running the palm of my hand across the pointed tips of grass. "Nora sure is into Hunter."

"She's not the only one," Blake added under his breath.

I pulled my hand away from the grass and shot him a sideways glance. "Is Hunter not interested in her? Does he already have a girlfriend?"

"Not exactly. Hunter goes out with a lot of different girls. He's not really a steady boyfriend kind of guy."

"Should Nora stay away from him?"

Blake shook his head. "Look. I don't like to run my mouth, so I'm only gonna say this -- Hunter is way too busy thinking about himself to focus on anyone else for more than a minute. That's just the truth."

"Well, do you think that maybe he just hasn't met the right girl yet."

"Maybe," Blake shrugged.

"Does he spend all his time at the ranch, or does he have another job? Or does he go to college?"

Blake smirked. "Just so I get this straight, are you supposed to be finding all this stuff out for Nora, or do *you* like Hunter?"

"No." I rolled my eyes. "I don't like him. Nora does."

Blake laid back with a grin on his face. "Okay." He held his hands up. "I just wanted to make sure, because I could probably get Hunter to come out here for you, if you'd prefer that."

I ripped a handful of grass from the ground and threw it at him. "Yeah, right," I scoffed. His amusement was now in full force with laughter, so I threw a couple more handfuls of grass at him until he teasingly apologized. Then I switched the topic of conversation again by asking him about the ranch, hoping the subject of family would be forgotten, but I wasn't so lucky. He brought it right back up.

It shouldn't have been a big deal. After all, I had already told the cover story about Dad more times than I could count. After we arrived in North Carolina, Dad had drilled us for weeks on end, and even made us do role play at the dinner table to ensure we would be able to keep all the details straight. Still, in one very important way, this was a new experience. It bothered me to have to lie to Blake.

I made him tell me about his parents first. That bought me a few minutes to rehearse in my mind what I was going to include and what to avoid. It was my turn now. Keep it simple Becca -- Just keep it simple.

"My mom is a stay at home mom, and my dad works in RTP at some pharmaceutical company."

Blake's face lit up with curiosity. Much to my relief, he wasn't interested in Dad at all. Instead, he wanted to know what it was like having a mom around all the time. Both of his parents had worked outside the home since he was little, so he felt like he had missed out on something.

I almost started in on how little I saw Dad, but caught myself just in time. "So, you talked about all the girls Hunter sees earlier . . ."

Blake tossed his head back and chuckled. "Hunter discussion time again?"

"Well, no," I said. "I'm actually more interested in talking about you. I counted at least a dozen girls hanging around you today."

"Are you talking about the moms and the over forty crowd? You think I should watch out for them?" He smiled, feigning innocence.

"You know exactly what I'm talking about. And I didn't see any moms in there."

"I wasn't really paying attention to any of them."

"How could you not? They wouldn't leave you alone."

"Is that why I didn't see you until after the work was done? Was it because of those girls?"

I winced, trying to be playful, but with some truth under the surface. "Yeah, well, I never was much of a groupie."

"Next time, don't stay away. And just so you know, I would never treat you like a groupie."

Blake reached over and brushed a few strands of my hair behind my shoulder. The butterflies in my stomach went wild. Then he took a deep breath, shaking his head. "It's now or never."

Now or never? What was that supposed to mean? I held my breath, hanging on whatever he was about to do next.

Blake looked into my eyes. "I hate to do this, but if we don't get back soon, Aunt Sue will be worrying over us. As far as she knows, I'm out here looking for you and still haven't found you."

My mouth fell open. "You didn't have to hang out here with me, you know. You should have said something. Now everybody's probably out looking for me." As soon as the words escaped my lips I realized I had said them with more frustration than was deserved. Our perfect opportunity had slipped away without a perfect ending, and that bothered me more than I wanted to let on.

"Don't worry. If we leave now, we'll be back before they send the cavalry out." He picked up his hat, set it on his head, then stood up. I was about to get up, but he reached out for my hand, and in one swift motion, he pulled me up and I went flying into his chest. "Sorry," he said, grabbing hold of me to help me balance. "I didn't mean to pull so hard."

I laughed nervously as my heart fluttered from his touch. "That's okay."

He slid his fingers down my arms until they reached my hands, holding them firmly while taking a half step back. "I don't want to leave yet."

My heart started to race. I didn't want to leave either. Not ever.

He looked down into my eyes. "There's something different about you Becca Tanner . . . you're not like the other girls."

"I'm not?"

"No. You're kind of . . . mysterious."

"Is that a good thing or a bad thing?"

Blake smiled. "It's a good thing."

The butterflies in my stomach started churning. I didn't like the idea of him thinking that I was mysterious. Why did he say that? Had someone said something to him about me?

Blake's penetrating blue eyes sparkled intensely. As I stared up at him, my doubts were quickly swept away. He once again closed the distance between us and whispered softly, "I've wanted to do this for a very long time." I looked up, watching as his gaze traveled slowly from my eyes down to my lips. My breathing stopped in anticipation of what I hoped was about to happen. This was the moment I had dreamed of. He reached up to remove his hat, then gently brushed the tips of his fingers across my cheek. With part instinct and part anticipation, I closed my eyes as Blake's lips pressed against mine. When I pulled away, our eyes met once again. Except for the pounding of our hearts, we both stood in perfect, amazing silence.

A loud neighing interrupted the moment. Blake glanced back at his horse. "It looks like one of us is ready to head home."

We made our way over the stream. Blake lifted me up and helped me into the saddle before climbing up to sit behind me. He reached his arms around and grabbed hold of the reins.

As we rode back toward the ranch, he explained how a rider uses their legs to communicate with their horse, to change the horse's gait from a walk to a trot and up to a gallup. He told me to take hold of the reins, and showed me how to gently use them to signal the horse to turn or to stop. He complimented me on how I sat up tall in the saddle, telling me I looked like a natural. Blake had no way of knowing, but I had already discovered each of these things for myself on the way out here. It didn't matter. I liked hearing his velvety smooth voice whispering in my ear.

Further down the trail, another hill approached. The stream alongside veered off in the opposite direction, until it was completely out of sight. When we reached the top of the hill, I could see the ranch in the distance -- the red barn, white fences, the stables. As welcoming a site as that was, I was disappointed that our time alone together was almost over.

I wanted to go slow, but our horse insisted on picking up the pace to a trot as we approached the barn. Blake's uncle appeared, leading a big brown and black horse, followed by Nora and Hunter, who rode around the corner and stopped immediately. Nora's horse called out as if welcoming home a long lost friend. Our horse called back, clearly happy to be home. Nora pointed toward us, as Sue Ellen stepped out of the barn to see for herself. We closed the distance quickly enough.

Sue Ellen tipped her hat back. "It's about time you two got home."

Blake hopped off our horse, then reached up to help me

down. I held onto his broad shoulders as he lowered me.

"Becca wasn't that far. Just over the hill."

Sue Ellen nodded, then looked at me. "Valarie said that she thought your horse got spooked and took off. Is that what happened?"

I just shrugged, not wanting to rehearse the details. "I don't know."

"Well, I'm glad you're alright, hun."

Everyone chimed in, expressing their relief.

The conversation didn't last much longer, before Blake's aunt and uncle headed off, leaving the boys to take care of the horses.

Hunter jumped down and led his horse toward the barn. Somehow, Nora achieved the most awkward dismount imaginable. Her impossibly tight pants wouldn't allow her to bend in all of the places that needed to be bendable. I had no idea how she managed to get up on that horse in the first place.

Hunter came back for her, due in no small part to Blake getting his attention and giving him a sly brother signal. He grabbed the reins of our horse and Nora's. "I'm going to take them to the stables," he said, flashing his crooked grin.

Once Hunter was gone, Nora approached us. "I saw what happened, Becca." Nora continued before I could respond, all too eager to share the story. "Blake, you should have seen it. Valarie walked right up to Becca's horse and gave it a huge smack on the butt. I've never seen a horse rear up like that. Not in real life anyway."

Blake's eyebrows drew down. He looked over at me as if he expected me to call Nora a liar. I watched the expression of disbelief on his face, not wanting to give him the slightest indication her story had been exaggerated in any way.

Nora gestured toward the stables. "I was standing right over there, and I saw the whole thing. Oh, and your brother saw too." She folded her arms. "It's a wonder that Becca stayed on the horse. She could easily have wound up flat on her back, wind knocked out of her, even trampled, needing CPR."

Blake looked surprised. I couldn't understand why. Didn't he know that Valarie was a vengeful witch?

He studied Nora's expression. "Why would Valarie do that?"

Nora stared right at me, as if pointing out the reason.

Blake looked at her, then at me. "Never mind. I get it." He reached for my arm. "I'm sorry."

"You don't need to apologize," I said.

"Yes, I do. For one thing, I shouldn't have left you on that horse alone."

"But it's okay. Nothing bad happened. I'm fine. I didn't fall."

Nora mumbled something, then glared at me. "No, you didn't fall. But that was blind luck, Becca. You went for a crash course in riding a scared horse, and amazingly, didn't break any bones. Congratulations. But just in case you're wondering if it was an accident, you better believe Valarie and her friends were laughing. They all thought it was hilarious."

Blake looked mortified. The hard line of his jaw flexed.

Nora pointed her finger at him. "Valarie does not want you near Becca."

Blake turned to me. "I can't believe she did that to you."

"Believe it!" Nora scolded, but her attention was quickly pulled from the conversation when Hunter walked by. She huffed one last time before following him to the barn.

Blake drew in a deep breath. "I should have known better. I should have seen it coming."

From the corner of my eye I noticed movement across the open pasture, in a large fenced off area. Someone was jumping their horse over obstacles. A long, blonde ponytail protruded from beneath the rider's helmet, bouncing and flailing in rhythm with the horse's tail.

"Who's that?" I asked, motioning with my eyes.

Blake shook his head. "Valarie."

I watched as horse and rider easily jumped over fences, across ditches and water obstacles. They moved together, as one, with power and grace.

"How long have you known Valarie?" I asked.

"I don't know. Maybe six months."

"Six months. Are you sure?"

Blake nodded. "Since school started."

That couldn't possibly be true. Valarie had lived here much longer than me, hadn't she? My mind began to race, questioning all of the facts and evidence about Valarie I thought I knew to be true.

"You didn't know her before this year?"

"No. I never met her until she showed up on the first day of school. Her family moved here from somewhere out West."

"Out West?" I repeated.

"Nevada, I think. I don't know. She always says she doesn't like to talk about the past, so I quit asking."

My head was spinning. "You're saying she moved to North Carolina about the same time I did?"

"I guess so."

"How did she make the cheerleading squad when tryouts were last spring? She had to have been here at least nine or ten months ago."

"I don't know about the cheerleading thing, but she definitely didn't go to West Johnston last year."

The world seemed to be closing in on me from all sides. Even the sky and the trees were making me feel trapped.

"Are you okay?" he asked. "You look kind of pale all of a sudden."

I headed over to a nearby stump and sat down. "I'm fine. I'm just thirsty. Can you get me a drink of water?"

"Sure. I'll be right back."

I sat there horrified, watching Valarie ride her horse on the other side of the pasture. We both liked horses. We both knew how to ride, only I had never taken lessons. The only explanation was that I had picked that skill up through the shadow copy effect.

Valarie hated me -- that was for sure, and she loved

Blake. So did I. I had never completely understood how that figured in, but I had always known there was something much deeper than jealousy.

We were both in the same technology class, and she was definitely prettier than me, just like the mystery girl's note had said. The only thing that had thrown me off of considering her as my prime suspect was the presumed alibi that she had lived here much longer than me. Now, it seemed, the facts told a different story. She actually had moved here at the same time. Everything pointed to her. The realization of who she was hit me like a train. It was her. It had to be her. Valarie was the mystery girl! She wrote that note, and she knew my secret!

Blake came back with a bottle of water. I wasn't all that thirsty. I just needed some time to think, but I drank some of the water anyway.

He scrutinized my face. "Is there anything else I can do for you?"

"No I'm good, thanks."

I could tell that Blake didn't want me to leave, but I didn't dare stay. My mind was flying all over the place. I couldn't focus at all. I could hardly even breathe.

"I better take off," I said.

Blake's serene eyes met mine, but I had to look away, for fear he might see how shook up I really was. He walked me to my Jeep and opened the door for me. I was about to get inside, when his hands wrapped around my waist and he pulled me into his chest for a goodbye hug.

From over his shoulder I could see Valarie, still riding. I felt like I was about to be sick. I didn't want anything to do with her, but I no longer had a choice. The fact was, I had become forever connected to her.

Blake pressed his lips to my ear, his warm breath caressing my skin, ripping my attention from her. "Next time, plan on staying longer," he whispered, holding me tight one last time.

I hesitated, lingering in his grasp, trying to recover from

the spell of his touch, then finally managed to turn and get into my Jeep. Blake watched as I backed up, then drove away.

When I got home, I collapsed onto the couch in front of the TV. Every thought was of Valarie and the clues that had been in front of me all along.

She had chosen a new body -- one which she thought was better. Yet Blake didn't want her. He wanted me. It had to be driving her crazy to know that Blake was attracted to the girl inside her old body.

What Valarie didn't seem to understand was that Blake had been attracted to her, at least until he got to know who she really was, I suspect.

I wondered how long it would take before she would find out how Blake felt about me. What lengths would she be willing to go to, once she learned about our kiss? Would she tell him my secret?

Was that amazing first kiss with him also my last? Then I realized something most unexpected. Valarie had a secret too, and now, I knew it. This little bit of information seemed very likely to be of great importance in my future.

CHAPTER 41

Becca

There was nothing particularly remarkable about the alarm clock next to my bed. Normally, I wouldn't have taken notice of it at all, but tonight I found the brightness of its display blindingly infuriating.

Unable to sleep, I stared at the clock until the searing red numbers of the display burnt themselves onto the back of my eyeballs. It was both a curious and an irksome thing how each passing minute felt like a hundred. The clock's dreadfully slow advance from one digit to the next seemed to intentionally taunt me. It was as if all of space and time were held bound by an unseen and unchangeable slow motion setting.

When a full hour had passed, I watched all of the digits flip at once. It was an empty victory at a dear price. In just four more hours, it would be time for school. Ugh. Four more hours. I hadn't been able to sleep a wink, yet I knew that I needed sleep badly. My body was begging for it, but my mind was spinning much too recklessly for any sort of calm to be present.

How had my life become such an endless twisted minefield? That was exactly what it felt like -- a minefield. It had become impossible for me to predict or avoid the consequences of my own steps, no matter how carefully I made them. I was afraid to move forward, and just as terrified to go back, yet I dared not stop and be overtaken.

With more fear than resolve, I convinced myself to keep moving, one step at a time, from one spot to the next, almost taking solace in the certainty that only one of two outcomes were possible in my personal minefield: either an explosion would take place, or it would not. The bombs buried all around me were my fears. Some had been placed there by others. Some, I had created myself.

I feared that Valarie would expose my secret to the whole school and that I would be an outcast -- that people would think me a monster for having taken the body of a dead girl.

I feared that my closest friends would turn their backs on me when they discovered the secret I had kept from them for so long. How could they ever trust me again? Why should they?

Blake would probably hate me for lying to him about my past. It wasn't fair of me to let him fall for someone who wasn't real. He only liked the girl I pretended to be, not some freak in a second hand body. I couldn't stand the thought of watching the affection in his eyes turn cold and dead when he learned the truth about me.

I also worried that Mom and Dad would find out any day now that someone had been stalking me. I didn't want them to make us move to Faison. But my worst fear of all was that they were right to worry. What if someone really was after me?

I rolled over onto my back, eyes wide open, unable to see anything. In spite of the fiery red display of the alarm clock, the bedroom remained mostly pitch black.

I craned my neck to look at the clock again. After waiting a small eternity to watch another number flip, I decided to give up on sleeping altogether. It simply wasn't going to happen. I exhaled deeply, then sat up.

I had no particular plan. I just couldn't stand lying in bed any longer. But once my feet hit the carpet, my well-rehearsed middle of the night instinct kicked in, and I moved like a zombie down the stairs, headed for the kitchen, hunting for food.

Once through the doorway, my hand found the light switch. I squinted, adjusting to the flood of light in an otherwise dark house. My second order of business was to pay a visit to a faithful old friend -- Mr. Cookie Jar. He was overflowing with my favorite homemade cookies, semi-soft, and loaded with chocolate chips and M&Ms. I reached out to open the lid, but my hand froze in place, inches away.

In the reflection of the cookie jar's shiny surface, I caught a glimpse of something moving behind me. I instinctively froze.

The reflection in the jar was blurred and distorted, yet this much was unmistakable. I wasn't alone. A person was standing behind me.

It couldn't have been Mom or Dad. They would have said something to me by now. And it wasn't Sierra. She was way too small. Whoever this was had to be at least my size or bigger.

My entire body remained still, except for my eyes. They darted back and forth, searching for anything within reach that could be used as a weapon. The block of kitchen knives was only a few feet away. With one quick step I might be able to snatch the big one on the end and pivot around in a single motion.

I eyed the reflection, hoping to get a better look, but whoever was behind me wasn't moving a muscle. I hadn't even heard them breathe.

Summoning all the courage I had, I lunged toward the counter, grabbed a knife, planted my foot and spun, hoping against hope that none of this was real -- praying that I was actually safely asleep in my bed and this was all just a bad dream.

Before that thought had even run its course, the much more likely reality of my grim situation started to sink in. I panicked. In a fraction of a second, the scenario played out, and I found myself backed up against the counter, holding a bread knife with a broken tip instead of the carving knife I meant to grab. Fear must have been written all over my face -- hardly the formidable image I had hoped to project.

Our eyes met. I made a sound that can only be produced when one gasps and screams simultaneously. The broken knife slipped through my fingers and fell to the floor with a thud, barely missing my toes.

The intruder stood directly in front of me, only five or six feet away. I recognized her instantly. It was the girl from my dreams, just as I remembered her -- smooth and flowing blonde hair, flawless skin, dark eyes, white dress.

In my scariest voice I yelled, "Come any closer and I'll cut you!"

The girl looked down to the floor where the knife lay, then back up at me.

I felt like an idiot for saying that, but I was terrified and couldn't think straight. We both stood there, silently acknowledging that I had no knife with which to cut anyone. I quickly twirled around and grabbed another knife from the butcher block, pointing it at her wildly. "Don't think I won't do it!"

The girl didn't even flinch. She remained motionless, studying my face, as if assessing what my next move might be.

"You better get out of here! My dad's going to come in here any second, with his gun!" I motioned with my knife toward the doorway.

She looked at the door, then back at me. "Becca," her head shook, "I'm not going to hurt you." Her expression was one of frustration. No hint of fear.

She had to be crazy -- showing up here dressed like that, in my kitchen, in the middle of the night! Why else would she be here, if not to cause harm to someone, in some way. "Oh yeah," I snarled. "Well, I'm going to hurt you!" My eyes widened. "I said, get out of here!" I shifted to a lunging stance, wielding the knife in the most menacing way I could think of. I hoped my bluff would be enough to frighten her away. I was the one with the weapon, after all.

The girl's arms remained at her sides, but she wasn't backing up. And that only worried me more.

"Don't be afraid," she said calmly. The expression on her

face wasn't reassuring. She looked annoyed, like my dad does when he gets tired of being pestered.

It took a moment for me to register what she had just said. I felt thrown off by the girl's strange, chastising, parent-like demeanor. Did she just tell me not to be afraid? The psycho girl who I had never seen before, except for in my scary dreams? Oh, I wasn't afraid. I was terrified.

She tilted her head, placing her hand on her chest. "My name is Darla."

She said that like I should have known who she was. I only knew she was nuts. I had never met a Darla before. Ever! And dreams don't count.

I started inching my way closer toward the door, lengthening the distance between us, still wielding the knife to deter any advance. I had outrun a pursuer before, and if I had to do that again, I wanted the biggest head start I could get.

She placed one hand on her hip as she spoke. "I'm a friend. I promise you, I mean you no harm."

Like I would believe a psycho. What was she wearing anyway? A wedding dress? Why hadn't Dad come in here, yet? He had to have heard me yelling.

The girl, Darla, remained in place, motionless. Her eyes were fixed and unblinking. Then she shook her head, biting her lip, as if she was debating with herself. "Listen, Becca, I truly am sorry I scared you. I just want to talk."

"Talk! You want to talk to me! Are you kidding? Listen crazy girl. You can't just go around, breaking into other people's houses, in the middle of the night, so that you can *talk*!"

That was when it happened. An unexpected sensation of calm began to fill the room. It seemed as though the entire universe had decided in that instant that all was well. Every single thing in the room -- the countertops, the cabinets, even the floor tiles knew that I would be okay. It was inexplicable, but before long, I also knew it. I had never felt anything quite like it before.

Darla continued to speak about how she was not a threat, and how important it was for us to talk. I could hear her voice, but had stopped listening.

As my eyes adjusted better to the light, I began to notice things, like Darla's pure white dress. It was long and flowing. Her flawless skin glowed. She looked spectacularly radiant. In my dreams, she had always been pale and lifeless, lying on a cold operating table.

"I've been trying to help you for months," Darla said. "I know what you've been going through. I know about your transplant procedure. I know everything. Your dad, his job, the facility in Faison . . . and I know that you're lying to everyone. You're in someone else's body."

"How . . . how--"

Her expression softened. If anything, she looked like she felt sorry for me. There was pity on her face. "Becca, I know this is hard to believe, but you need to trust me. Just watch." Light emanated from Darla. She held up her hands and they seemed to become translucent.

I blinked in disbelief, staring at her now shimmering body. Then the room dimmed again and she appeared solid, like before, like me. "Are you . . . dead?" I couldn't think of an appropriate way to ask such an unimaginable question, so I just blurted it out, already certain of the answer, but determined to hear it from her own lips.

"I've been dead for over six months now."

I stared at her wide-eyed, full of questions, realizing that there was far more being revealed to me than I could possibly process at that moment. "Why are you dressed in white like that? Are you an angel?"

She raised her eyebrows and bounced her head from side to side a couple times. "I like the sound of that, but spirit is probably a more accurate way to say it."

Images and sounds streamed through my head at warp speed. Had my dreams actually been glimpses of reality?

"Listen," she said, "I know this is a lot to take in, but I

promise you, everything's going to be okay."

I didn't know if I should cheer or scream, not because I was afraid, fear had left me, but because of what it meant. Not only did this make me a freak, living in someone else's body -- now I was also a freak who talks to dead people. I had never considered that my life could actually get weirder than it already was.

Darla didn't seem to find any of this weird. Her movements, words, and expression all conveyed an urgency, like there was a lack of time for her to tell me what she came here to say.

"How do you know my name?" I asked, my voice cracking. "Am I supposed to know who you are?" I searched her face for a reaction. "I mean, I've seen you before, in my dreams, but we've never met, right?"

Darla nodded. "You are correct. We've never formally met before, but . . ." Her thought lingered, incomplete, unresolved, hesitant.

"But what?"

She looked me in the eye. "Well, things are just complicated."

I had a million questions, but like an insensitive jerk, I started with probably the most rude thing one could ask of a spirit. "How did you die?"

Strangely, Darla seemed to almost welcome the question. "My life was taken from me . . . stolen."

"Stolen? What do you mean?" I got a sinking feeling in the pit of my stomach.

Her dark eyes stared intently into mine. "I was murdered."

"What! Oh no. I'm so sorry." My compassion for her was genuine, but it was cut short by a horrifying thought. Someone had been after me, too. Could it be that this same person was Darla's killer? Was this why she was here? Did she have answers for me? I had to ask. "Do you know who killed you?"

She nodded. "Some very bad men."

"Do you know why they killed you?"

Again she nodded. "Do you remember how I was lying on that operating table, in your dreams?"

"Yeah."

"Those weren't just dreams. All of that stuff actually happened. I was part of the full body transplant program, only I wasn't like you. I wasn't sick."

"I don't understand."

"No one was trying to save me, Becca. I was killed, so that my body could be given to someone else."

I didn't want to believe her, but I had always known deep down that something very wrong was going on at Dad's work. I hadn't been able to figure out what, but I was certain that Dr. Stella and Dr. Brimley were part of it. Finally, the pieces were starting to make sense, and it was more horrible than I could have imagined.

"Becca, I want you to know that I thought long and hard before deciding to share this with you, but I felt it was necessary. You deserve to know."

"Okay, but why me? Why not tell someone who could do something about it?" Was it because of my dad? Was she going to ask me to do something to hurt him, or make him stop his work? "I guess the part I don't understand is, why *me*?"

Darla sighed, then leaned forward as if telling a secret. "There are things . . . things that involve you." She paused, as if summoning strength from an unseen reservoir. "My body was supposed to be given to you."

What! "That can't be true."

"Trust me. There is no reason for me to lie about it. Look at me. I'm already dead, and there is no way back."

I was speechless. What was I supposed to say? When you bump into someone you say excuse me. When you damage their property you apologize and replace it. I had no idea what the proper response should be for having someone killed so that you could take their body.

Darla must have sensed my discomfort. "It's not your fault," she said, "I don't blame you for what happened."

It was only slightly comforting to hear that the dead girl standing in front of me didn't blame me for her death. My mind was a swirl of guilt, clues, dreams, and memories of the past six months. I felt her words pierce me to my heart, and I knew she was telling the truth, but the pieces were still unsettled, and I at least needed everything to fit. "I don't understand this. How did I end up in Valarie's old body if I was supposed to be given yours?"

Darla began to tell me the story. The look in her eyes suggested to me that she had been wanting to tell this for a long time. "After I died, I found myself in a strange place, there in the procedure room. At first, I didn't understand what was going on. I guessed maybe there had been an accident. I thought I might be able to will myself back to life, but it was all so confusing. I was standing only a couple of feet away when they tried to transfer your spirit into my body . . ." she shook her head. "I could tell what was happening then. I had been killed so that my body could be used by someone else. Even though I couldn't bring myself back to life, I didn't want anyone else to take my body, so I stopped you.

"I don't remember anything about this, Darla. I wouldn't have . . ."

"I know," she interrupted. "I didn't really know what I was doing either, but I understand it now. You weren't fully transitioned yet. That was why I was able to stop you."

Every word she uttered hit me with both anguish and gratitude. I had been so selfish in my desire to live that I had unknowingly been the cause of a stranger's death. Yet she was almost apologetic in her explanation of what happened that night.

"Did my father know that you were killed for me?"

"I don't think he knew. I saw my chart. It said I died from carbon monoxide poisoning and that I was a foster child, abandoned by my parents at an early age." She shook her head.

"It was all a lie."

"I'm so sorry."

Darla reached out and placed her hand on my shoulder. It surprised me that I could feel the warmth and pressure of her touch. "I-I didn't know I would be able to feel you."

"Don't be frightened. This is just how it works."

She explained more about what it was like to be a spirit. I listened intently, but it was hard to comprehend everything she described. I asked about her body. She explained that she had lost track of it long ago, but supposed it had been buried, or perhaps cremated. It didn't matter to her anymore.

"You have to understand, Becca, you're not like most people. Not anymore. Since you technically died during your procedure, and your spirit was moved from your original body, you are no longer subject to the normal limitations of a mortal body."

"What kind of *limitations* are you talking about?"

"The bond that your original body had on your spirit was broken." She paused.

"And?"

"Well, you're not confined to a physical body anymore, unless you choose to be."

"What exactly does that mean?" I wished she would just tell me what was going on in a way that I could understand.

"When you free yourself of physical constraints, you can comprehend the non-physical world. That is what you've done tonight, thus allowing you to see me."

My eyes started scanning the room. "So . . . can I see other spirits, too?"

"Yes. You will be able to see other spirits, but only when they are near you."

"Why is it that I have only seen you? Aren't there billions and billions of other spirits around?"

"Remember how I said that you weren't confined to your body anymore?"

"Yes."

"Well, something has to take place before you can see the other spirits." Darla gestured to the door. "I want you to follow me." She turned, walked out of the kitchen and headed up the stairs, stopping just outside my bedroom. "I need to impress upon your mind a couple things," she said. "First, everything is fine. There is nothing wrong. You are perfectly healthy, safe and alive."

Why was she saying these things to me, and why was she telling me that I was alive? This made no sense. Of course I was alive. I was standing right there talking to her.

Darla reached out and placed her hand on my arm. "I'm going to show you something in your room."

The seriousness of her tone started to worry me.

"Now remember," she said, "everything is fine. *You* are fine. Okay?" She stared at me, waiting for an affirmative confirmation.

I forced a half smile and nodded, wary of whatever she was preparing me for.

Darla reached for the doorknob and pushed open the door, then gently took me by the hand and led me inside. My eyes searched for something out of place, anything strange, but there was nothing unusual. At first glance, my bedroom looked just as it always had.

She led me over next to my bed. It was piled high with blankets and pillows. Then she folded the covers down.

I opened my mouth, but no words came out. I grabbed hold of the covers and yanked them down further, in disbelief of what I was seeing.

"No!" I finally managed to say under my breath. "I'm dead!"

"You're not dead," Darla insisted. "I told you. You are very much alive."

"But I'm standing right here and . . . " I pointed to the bed, ". . . my body is there."

Darla sat down at the foot of the bed. I didn't look at her. I couldn't. My eyes were fixed on my body, lying there, wearing my fluffy pink pajamas, hair tousled all over the place, arm draped over the pillow, eyes shut. "If I'm not dead, then what? Do I suddenly have a twin?"

"Well, yes and no."

I winced at her response. "Tell me what's going on!"

Darla got up and stood next to me, turning to the bed. "There's only one body," she said, almost impatiently.

I broke my stare and turned to her, flailing my arms in the air, head shaking. "But you just said--"

Her lip twitched, like she was holding back a chastening lecture, just itching to let it come spewing out of her mouth. She stepped in front of me, blocking my view. "Okay. Let me explain. I promise I will answer all your questions."

I felt like I had just walked into a real life nightmare. I had no idea what to think. How could Darla possibly explain this? I quickly moved around her, now closer to the bed. All the proof I needed was right in front of me -- I was looking at my stiff, lifeless body.

She leaned over, sticking her face in front of my view. "Becca? Are you listening to me?"

I nodded.

"The reason your body is lying there without you, is because your spirit is no longer confined by your body. Your spirit can leave whenever you want it to. And, you can also go back into your body whenever you want to, like nothing ever happened."

"So, somehow," I pointed to the bed, "I just magically stepped outside my body and left it there?"

"Yes."

"And you're sure I'm not dead?"

"You are alive."

I moved even closer to inspect my body. I didn't know how this was possible, but it appeared as though my body was lying there in a deep sleep. It didn't look pale, nor did it seem to be showing any signs of distress. I could see my chest rise and fall. Somehow, my body was breathing.

My hands and feet looked smaller than I realized. The dimple in my chin seemed more pronounced. The shape of my face was almost like a heart, just like my lips. I was surprised to see how beautiful I was.

The only way it made sense for my body to stay alive, without me in it, was for it not to be asleep, but rather to be in a coma-type state. I knew that people could stay in a coma for months, even years.

The longer I stood there looking at my body, the more anxious I felt. I didn't want to be like one of those coma patients who *never* wakes up.

That overwhelming fear was building inside me, like a volcano about to erupt. I had to re-enter my body and make sure that everything was okay -- that I would be able to wake up. I couldn't stand the thought of leaving it there like that any longer.

"Darla, how do I get back into my body?" I asked urgently, hands shaking.

"It's okay, Becca."

"No. No it's not okay. I can't leave it there like that."

"Alright," she sighed. "I understand. Listen, everything's going to be fine," she echoed, trying to convince me. "Becca, you are in control. Your spirit does what you will it to do."

"What does that mean?"

She tapped her index finger to the side of her head. "It means that if you think it, then your spirit will obey."

"Are you sure? And that's all I have to do?"

"It just takes concentration. Okay? Focus. Visualize what you want to happen."

I sat down on the bed, then paused and looked at Darla. "Will I still be able to see you when I go back into my body?"

"You'll only be able to see me while outside of your body . . . and when I am around."

"But if I go back into my body, I'll be able to come back out whenever I want?"

"Yes."

"So, I can tell my spirit to leave my body, and it will just leave? It's that simple?"

"That's right."

I closed my eyes and was about to do as she had instructed, but realized I needed to ask her something. "Darla! I'm going to come back in a couple minutes, after I make sure everything's alright. Will you wait for me?"

She smirked, as if that was the dumbest thing I had said yet. "Yes, I'll be here."

I closed my eyes and concentrated, blocking out everything else from my thoughts. *Go back to your body*, I told myself, repeating the phrase in earnest.

I didn't feel anything happen. There were no lights, sounds or sensations. Had it worked the way she said it would? I waited a few extra seconds before opening my eyes, just in case.

The first thing I saw was the familiar, dusty ceiling fan spinning directly above me. I jolted up to a seated position, looked down at my legs and feet for a split second, then jumped out of bed, spinning around to look; I had to make sure that my body wasn't still lying there without me.

The bed was empty.

I ran over to the wall switch, flipped on the light, then went right back to the bed. I pulled every last pillow and blanket off of it. I even rummaged through the pile of blankets on the floor to make sure my body wasn't somehow lying under the big heap of fabric. Nothing. There was no body.

Had it really worked? I held my hands up in front of my face, examining both sides, followed by my arms. I reached up and touched my face, my neck. I ran my fingers through my hair. Everything seemed normal.

I stepped in front of the full length mirror, jumped up and down, twirled around, hopped on one foot, then the other. There were no obvious negative side effects. Apparently, leaving my body didn't cause poor balance or delays in movement. I seemed to be doing fine.

I walked over to the window, pulled it open another few inches and shivered as the cold air hit me. I took in the first full breath since uniting with my body again.

I was alive, and I was fine. The world felt right again. Realizing that any potential crisis had been averted, I looked out the window at the pink and blue sky. It was beautiful. The stars may have hidden their faces, and the moon no longer hung within the window frame, but the sun was on its way. I knew it was there somewhere because of the soft colors painted across the sky. I pushed the window shut, turned and sat back against the windowsill, enjoying a couple more purposeful deep breaths.

Darla was right. My body was fine. She was also correct that I wouldn't be able to see her. She had vanished from my view the moment I rejoined spirit with body.

Now, for the last test. In order to know for sure that I was truly in control, I had to do as she had described and leave my body once more.

I leaped to my bed, laid down and closed my eyes as if sleeping. But this was nothing like sleep. It was pure excitement. I concentrated on leaving my body. The desire to separate spirit from body pushed all else to the side. This time, I noticed the tiniest sensation of change. When I opened my eyes again, I was sitting up in my bed, next to my body.

"Darla!" I quickly jumped up and hugged her. She let me hold on to her and didn't pull away, but I could sense that she was uncomfortable. And why wouldn't she be? She was stuck on the other side, a prisoner to an invisible existence, continually watching an unjust world and unable to do anything about it.

Darla laced her fingers together and pressed her hands up to her mouth, like she did the last time she dropped a bombshell on me, which made me nervous. "Now, Becca . . ." She began speaking as she lowered her hands back down. "The real reason I came here was to tell you something else, and to ask you a favor."

I wasn't sure if I was ready to hear what else she had to tell me. Based on my track record with weirdness, the odds of it being something good didn't seem to be likely. I'd prefer to just do the favor. "Do you need me to give someone a message or something?"

"It's more complicated than that I'm afraid."

"What is it?"

"I bet you've probably already guessed this . . . but I'm not the only one who was murdered for their body."

"I wondered that," I admitted.

"The problem is only getting worse." Darla's dark eyes filled with compassion. She must have known others who had shared her same fate. "What I also came here to tell you, was that I think that the same people who were involved in my murder are the ones who are after you."

That was the last thing I wanted to hear. Now, I was officially terrified.

"But it's not for the same reason. They only want you so they can punish your dad."

I turned and looked at my body lying on the bed. "They're going to kill me!"

"They're going to try. But there is a good chance we can stop them, if we work together."

I turned back toward Darla. Seeing her standing there in her long white dress, I could only wonder if I was looking at the reflection of my own soon-to-be fate.

Darla held out her hand, inviting me to take it. "We have a lot to do, Becca. Come on, let's go."

(To be continued...)

AFTERWORD

To the reader:

Thank you for reading this book! We hope you enjoyed it and would love for you to leave a rating/review on Amazon! *Shadow Copy: ENTER LIGHT* is available on Amazon. Follow the Michele Leathers author page on Amazon to find more of our books and keep up with the latest new releases!

BOOKS IN THIS SERIES
THE SHADOW COPY SERIES

Shadow Copy: Enter Light (The Shadow Copy Series Book 2)

ACKNOWLEDGEMENT

Many thanks to Denise for her endless encouragement and support along the way.

We are grateful to Carole, who inspired us to start this journey.

And thanks to the local writing groups, *Southern Scribblers* and *Johnston County Writers Group*, for your critiques and the encouragement to publish this work.

ABOUT THE AUTHOR

Michele & Ryan Leathers

Ryan and Michele have five children and a large extended family. They reside in North Carolina, but both originally grew up on the west coast. Ryan is a United States Army Veteran who now works in the computer science field. He has traveled the world and is fluent in Japanese and Persian Farsi. Michele earned a degree in Philosophy and worked in the health and fitness industry for over a decade before discovering her true passion for writing. She loves getting lost in the fictional worlds she creates. When she is not with family or writing, she is somewhere in the community volunteering and serving others. Their unique life experiences, educational backgrounds, and passions bring depth and creativity to their writing. THE SHADOW COPY SERIES was a shared labor of love.

-- www.MicheleLeathers.com

Printed in Great Britain
by Amazon

34187262R00212